At the
Broken Dreams

Love and War in the Middle Ages

Laurence Baillie Brown

First paperback edition 2022

ISBNs:
Paperback: 978-1-80227-702-9
ebook: 978-1-80227-703-6

Extracts from contemporary reviews of "Addictions":

1. Laurence Brown's intriguing novel "Addictions" is both an exercise in form and a hearty look at the conventions of literature-especially gay literature…..With wit, insight and precision, Brown manages to dismantle these cliches before our eyes….In the end it turns out that all these characters have been inhabiting a farce – and a Shakespearian one at that. Delightful." Sebastian Beaumont in Gay Times, April 2001.

2. We suggest you get stuck into 'Addictions', the new novel by Laurence Brown. This witty portrait of gay life in Margaret Thatcher's Britain is told through the (often bitchy) correspondence of two highly-sexed gays, Francis and Jeremy, which, as you can imagine, had us in stitches (perhaps some of it hit home…?)
BOYZ, 19.12.00

3. I loved it, it's full of good things; full of notes and chords which chime and resonate. I am particularly fond of Baillie and his "Sketches"- like a brief history of our past. And Francis and Jeremy – complex and brave, bitchy and true. (A picture of a friendship, beautifully handled.)….O God, has there been an Anthony in all our lives? Many congratulations. I hope the book sells well, I'm sure it will…Delicious and sad, sexy and civilized." William Corlett to the author,
16.12.00, author of "Now and then" etc.

4. "...an hilarious, but poignant comedy of errors, which brings all the main characters and their diverse backgrounds together in a delightful, well-written meaty novel. Deserves to be read. G-Scene, Brighton.

5. ...Baillie was lovely. I know nothing of Jewish life...But so much of the rest of his experience – the North, London, and 70s and 80s gay London – was my own and I found it very well done...I even had the odd moistening of the eye. Dr. David Starkey to the author.

6. Just the thing to take on holiday. www. Rainbownetwork.com

7. ...really enjoyed it. Very ambitious and rich. Professor Jeffrey Weeks author of "Sexuality and its Discontents", to the author.

Acknowledgements

At the risk of this reading like the infamous Oscars' speech,

I want, and need, to thank quite a lot of people who have brought me to this point in my career.

First, it must be the wonderful organization with whom I live and to whom I have dedicated this book: Jewish Care. Over the last 3 years that I've been living here, they've brought me back from the brink. When I arrived, I wasn't eating or drinking or reading, let alone writing. Gradually, with their help, I recovered – and went back to writing this book which I had started about six years before, inspired largely by the discovery of Richard III's bones beneath a Leicester car-park.

Secondly, I must thank for their inspiration, my favourite authors of historical novels, whom I read from childhood: Robert Graves (I, Claudius), Gore Vidal (Burr and 1876) and the great though sadly forgotten, Mary Renault (The King Must Die, The Alexander Trilogy).

Then, I want to thank my first reader, Jane Spiro, professor in Education at Oxford Brookes Uni, my friend since we were both about 20, whose praise of this book gave me the confidence to go forward with publication.

Next, I must thank my ex-partner, George, who lived with me for 11 years and, despite that, remains a very close friend, who said to me "publishers are old technology, the way forward is self-publishing", which pointed me in the right direction.

That takes me on to my partner in crime, Publishing Push, headed by the human dynamo Patrick Walsh, and my project manager Scott Nathan who are not publishers but who brilliantly facilitate self-publication by writers like me who need guidance – and a lot of it. I must also express my gratitude to two wonderful women who have worked hard on this book: my two translators, Jessica Rostro Benigno, my translator into Italian, who works in Soriano Nel Cimino, in Italy; and Maria Valentina Diaz Herrera, my translator into Spanish, who works in Mexico. My thanks to them both. I also want to thank my close friend and photographer, Judy Morgenstern, for the photo of me on the back cover. She bears no responsibility for my personal appearance or costume.

(Not many more to go!) Just to say that my next collaboration with P.P. will be a second edition of my first novel Addictions, first published by Gay Men's Press, whose heart was in the right place but who understood nothing about marketing, back in 2,000. There's only one thing I'm going to change in the new edition; and that takes me on to the people who actually taught me everything and gave me the Jewish foundation which eventually brought me here: of course my late parents. My Dad who would have had his centenary in 2011, and my Mum who would have had hers this very year. The original dedication read: "For my parents, who would never have understood." That's going to change subtly to: "For my parents who would never have understood......unless my books make a great deal of money."

For the carers, nurses and managers of Jewish Care.

In a real historical *Game of Thrones*, a disgruntled younger son, Eddie De-la-Pole, sardonic and bisexual, dominated by his Beloved Mother, nurtures a bromance with the brother of the Yorkist queen. But the vain queen separates them. How will Eddie choose between his beloved friend and the rising, sinister star of the dynastic firmament, Richard, Duke of Gloucester? And who is the mysterious Catalan rabbi, who hangs around the English court, and eventually has a powerful influence over Eddie's life? Read and enjoy *At the Court of Broken Dreams* — a tale of love and war in the Middle Ages — to learn the answers to these and other fascinating questions.

Preface

As a researcher in Judaica, I discovered the manuscript of the following book in the *genizah* (which is a kind of synagogal book depository) of a long-abandoned synagogue in Barcelona, that most beautiful and referential European city (with apologies to Paris, Amsterdam, Rome etc.). After all, Barca still has its medieval warren of streets and inhabits them.

It was when I was researching for my PhD in Jewish-Islamic relations in the fifteenth century, that I stumbled upon this repository of decaying manuscripts, mostly Hebrew, amongst the ruins of a Catalan synagogue (which may also have been used in the course of its life as a church and a mosque at various periods). So, imagine how surprised I was to come upon a scribbled manuscript in late Middle English. I can only imagine the mysterious Rabbi Abraham di Mayorca, who is a figure playing a major role in this palimpsest (for such it is, like many another medieval text), may have survived his aristocratic friend and student, Edward De-la-Pole and returned, at some point, to his natal city, Barcelona, in the early sixteenth century. After all, his master King Ferran lived a long life until January 1516, several years after his friend's story ends.

How said manuscript — written in quite elegant script, clearly by a skilled scribe — came to end up in the otherwise almost wholly Hebrew collection (there are a few pieces in

Moorish Arabic) of old and battered texts is a mystery. But then so was the career of this somewhat incredible rabbi and his relationship with the English aristocrat. But I hope you will agree with me that this curious apologia was worthy of rescue and, subsequently, of publication. Only you, dear reader, can decide.

– Gordon Bar-Lev, PhD.

Post Scriptum: Along with this manuscript — which I present to the public unabridged – I have taken the liberty to construct, and reproduce on the following pages – a series of genealogical trees of the great families who dominated the late fifteenth century in England, and whose off-spring play a major role in the text. I hope these charts elucidate the intricacies of the history. And now, as they say, I submit this text to the judgment of the general public who alone can decide whether it was worth the rescue. Enjoy!

YORK AND LANCASTER 1327–1485

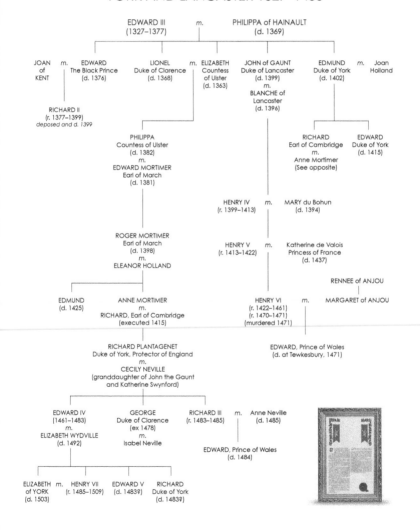

EDWARD III   _m._   PHILIPPA of HAINAULT
(1327–1377)   (d. 1369)

JOAN _m._ EDWARD   LIONEL _m._ ELIZABETH   JOHN of GAUNT   EDMUND _m._ Joan
of   The Black Prince   Duke of Clarence   Countess   Duke of Lancaster   Duke of York   Holland
KENT   (d. 1376)   (d. 1368)   of Ulster   (d. 1399)   (d. 1402)
   (d. 1363)   _m._
   BLANCHE of
   Lancaster
   (d. 1396)

RICHARD II
(r. 1377–1399)
deposed and d. 1399

PHILIPPA   RICHARD   EDWARD
Countess of Ulster   Earl of Cambridge   Duke of York
(d. 1382)   _m._   (d. 1415)
_m._   Anne Mortimer
EDWARD MORTIMER   (See opposite)
Earl of March
(d. 1381)

HENRY IV   _m._   MARY du Bohun
(r. 1399–1413)   (d. 1394)

ROGER MORTIMER
Earl of March   HENRY V   _m._   Katherine de Valois
(d. 1398)   (r. 1413–1422)   Princess of France
_m._   (d. 1437)
ELEANOR HOLLAND

   RENNEE of ANJOU

EDMUND   ANNE MORTIMER   HENRY VI   _m._   MARGARET of ANJOU
(d. 1425)   _m._   (r. 1422–1461)
RICHARD, Earl of Cambridge   (r. 1470–1471)
(executed 1415)   (murdered 1471)

RICHARD PLANTAGENET   EDWARD, Prince of Wales
Duke of York, Protector of England   (d. at Tewkesbury, 1471)
_m._
CECILY NEVILLE
(granddaughter of John the Gaunt
and Katherine Swynford)

EDWARD IV   GEORGE   RICHARD III   _m._   Anne Neville
(1461–1483)   Duke of Clarence   (r. 1483–1485)   (d. 1485)
_m._   (ex 1478)
ELIZABETH WYDVILLE   _m._
(d. 1492)   Isabel Neville   EDWARD, Prince of Wales
   (d. 1484)

ELIZABETH _m._ HENRY VII   EDWARD V   RICHARD
of YORK   (r. 1485–1509)   (d. 1483?)   Duke of York
(d. 1503)   (d. 1483?)

THE DE-LA POLES

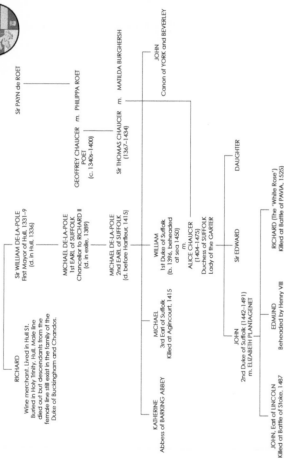

WILLIAM DE-LA-POLE
Merchant of Ravenserod. Early 14th century

Sir PAYN de ROET

RICHARD
Wine merchant. Lived in Hull St.
Buried in Holy Trinity, Hull. Male line
died out but descendants from the
female line still exist in the family of the
Duke of Buckingham and Chandos.

Sir WILLIAM DE-LA-POLE
First Mayor of Hull, 1331-9
(d. in Hull, 1336)

GEOFFREY CHAUCER m. PHILIPPA ROET
POET
(c. 1340s–1400)

MICHAEL DE-LA-POLE
1st EARL of SUFFOLK
Chancellor to RICHARD II
(d. in exile, 1389)

Sir THOMAS CHAUCER m. MATILDA BURGHERSH
(1367–1434)

JOHN
Canon of YORK and BEVERLEY

MICHAEL DE-LA-POLE
2nd EARL of SUFFOLK
(d. before Harfleur, 1415)

KATHERINE
Abbess of BARKING ABBEY

MICHAEL
3rd Earl of Suffolk
Killed at Agincourt, 1415

WILLIAM
1st Duke of Suffolk
(b. 1396, beheaded
at sea 1450)
m.
ALICE CHAUCER
(1404–1475)
Duchess of SUFFOLK
Lady of the GARTER

Sir EDWARD

DAUGHTER

JOHN
2nd Duke of Suffolk (1442–1491)
m. ELIZABETH PLANTAGENET

JOHN, Earl of LINCOLN
Killed at Battle of Stoke, 1487

EDMUND
Beheaded by Henry VIII

RICHARD (The 'White Rose')
Killed at Battle of PAVIA, 1525

LINE COMES TO AN END

THE WYDEVILLES

RICHARD WYDEVILLE
1st Earl Rivers K.G
(1405–1469)

m.
1437

JACQUETTA of LUXEMBOURG
widowed DUCHESS of BEDFORD
(1415–1472)

ELIZABETH WYDEVILLE
Queen Consort of England
(1437–1492)
m.
EDWARD IV

ANTHONY WYDEVILLE
2nd Earl Rivers
(1442–1483)
m.
ELIZABETH SCALES
Also entered into a pact of Blood Brotherhood
with
EDWARD DE-LA-POLE

12 OTHER CHILDREN

CHAUCERS and BEAUFORTS

Sir PAYN de ROET (lived in HAINAUT in the HOLY ROMAN EMPIRE)

GEOFFREY CHAUCER   m.   PHILIPPA ROET
POET   (1346–1387)
(c. 1340s–1400)

ISABEL
Canoness of Saint
Waltrude Collegiate
Church, Mons

WALTER

KATHERINE   (2) m. (3)   JOHN of GAUNT
SWYNFORD   DUKE of LANCASTER

Sir THOMAS CHAUCER   m.   MATILDA BURGHERSH
(1367–1434)

ALICE CHAUCER   m.   WILLIAM
(1404–1475)   Duke of Suffolk
Duchess of SUFFOLK
Lady of the GARTER

JOHN BEAUFORT
1st Earl of Somerset

HENRY
CARDINAL BEAUFORT

LADY MARGARET BEAUFORT

HENRY VII

THOMAS BEAUFORT
DUKE OF EXETER

JOAN BEAUFORT
COUNTESS of
WESTMORELAND

Book I: Winter

א (aleph)

Last night, I dreamed of Richard II.

Not that I ever met him, of course. He died — was murdered — in conditions not fit for a serf, let alone a king, fifty years before I was born. At least — unlike his great-grandfather Edward II — he wasn't killed by the thrust of a white-hot poker up his anus. More likely, Richard died of starvation which, for a man of his exquisite sensuality, may have been almost as appalling. But, though I never knew him, like other noblemen I have seen the great diptych altarpiece painted for Richard; the only great work of painting that England has to compare with the masterpieces of Netherlandish art in its great cities of Brussels and Bruges. Cities I have come to know all too well in my grey hairs.

In the picture, he kneels, clothed in majesty, with his favourite virginal male saints giving benediction; but in my dream, he sat enthroned in his great Chair of Estate, and there, with his sweet beardless childlike face and his golden locks, his head, his whole being, was numinous with a shimmering nimbus. His face glowered and his eyes shot sparks of righteous anger.

"Those who have dethroned and done to death their lawful king have transgressed grievously."

His voice was, actually, surprisingly strong and clear, if a bit reedy. Of course, he must have been speaking in French. All people of quality did in those days.

"At last, the true Plantagenet, like the root of Jesse, arose to restore the line of the Lord's anointed, but — like verminous curs — his issue fought and devoured their own. And with only York's granddaughters left, who then shall reign in England?"

With this, his voice had risen to a piercing scream. "A bastard, by our Lady, Welshman." His strength subsided. "God forgive you, England, for I never shall."

He turned, suddenly gay, to his child bride. "Will my lady take wine with me?" Then turning back to face me, trembling before his bright blue eyes, he said, "And as for you, De-la-Pole, one of your great-grandfathers was my chancellor — a bright boy, though the son of merchants — and the other was my bard. And what are *you*?" His face was now terrifyingly close to mine. "An exile, an outcast, little better than a churl!"

Then suddenly, confusingly, his face was that of the other Richard, the one I did know only too well. He of the hog, shorter, his body twisted, bending forwards, not as handsome as his elder brother, with his sonorous, pedantic voice saying, "Your pretty nephews will succeed me, De-la-Pole, God having seen fit to take my beloved only son; protect them…" His sensitive face contorted. "Make them kings, or that fucking Tydr takes everything!"

Then he was transfigured into a screeching winged demon — which perhaps he was — and dissolved in air. I woke up dretched, sweating and screaming. Thank the Lord, Rabbi Abraham, my beloved friend, was there to comfort me. For no one else would.

***

I dreamed again last night.

I am stuck here, like a white and dainty mouse in a trap, wounded, captive, creeping towards death, whilst waiting to beg, ay *beg*, for the good lordship of Philip of Burgundy and his mad wife Queen Joanna. Yes, I, a Plantagenet prince — by marriage — having to beg charity from a pair of foreign sovereigns, a half-Flemish Habsburg and a crazed Castilian at that. I am now used to waiting, accustomed these long days to attending on the still powerful, and being disappointed. And so, I am also used to dreaming.

This time, I dreamt not of Richard II, III or even I. No, last night I dreamt of Anthony, my beloved Antonio. He did not reproach me. He should have done; God knows he should have done. But his beautiful hazel eyes were smiling at me, the eyes of his frigid sister, Elizabeth Wydville, the eyes of his ambitious niece, now Queen of England as wife of that usurping Celtic turd…

But I forget myself and the principles of soulfulness and loving kindness with which Rabbi Abraham inspires me… My heart was filled as in the earliest days of our friendship with overflowing love of Anthony and — God forgive me — I overflowed onto my cambric sheet before I awoke. Only a little, mind you, as age has now weakened what was once a torrent. I don't remember what he spoke… I am a liar. I do remember. He said (in a strange reverse echo of the last Plantagenet king) in that rich warm voice of his, "Protect my sweet nephews, Eddie. Protect the young princes from the teeth of the boar."

No commentary is needful. Another trust betrayed; another Camelot destroyed.

***

You may ask why, with a Jew as my closest companion — and a rabbi at that: a scholarly, mystical, Catalonian rabbi — I am living, *we* are living, out our days and dreams in the fine and canalised city of Bruges, the Netherlandish Venice. The answer to that will emerge from the story in this manuscript. You may also wonder why at this moment, in the year of their Lord 1506, we have dragged our weary bodies several hundreds of country miles to here: the Castilian capital of Toledo. Which feels distinctly less comfortable.

But, of course, we are now once again in the lands and territories of the co-sovereigns of this realm, the fair Philip, Duke of Burgundy and his adoring, intermittently mad wife, Joanna, daughter of my companion's former master, King Ferran. Well, there are several answers to that question, none of them particularly true. For one thing, you can get bored with Bruges. The Flemish are very nice but a bit, well, stolid. And the weather: even worse than in England. Moreover, you should be mindful that as a prince of the House of York, the true blood royal of England, I reside here with my household under the protection of the Archduke Philip. One day, he calculates, I may be of some use to him. I say a household. I *wish*. It is a group of four Englishmen: Quidnunc, my ancient chamberlain, of course, of whom more later; my lieutenant and friend Malcolm, now a man of middle age with grown children;

my old codger, Phineas, the grumbly Yorkshireman, who takes care of my few remaining falcons and hounds; and my "Master of the Horse", who once had the charge of a stud farm and extensive stables, and now looks after a couple of old nags: Abraham and me. No, I jest; we still have a few old mares. And His Highness graciously gifted me a fine peregrine falcon just the other day, which brought back old times, old memories...

Abraham counts as an honorary Englishman and both of us have a form of heraldic immunity. Without which all diplomacy, all international treaty-making would, of course, be impossible. In any case, despite the official expulsion of the unredeemed Hebrew race from all the realms of their Catholic Majesties, the Catalan lands are, surreptitiously, less poisonous towards Jews, and Moslems for that matter, than their Castilian neighbours, providing they are discreet. And, far more pertinently, Rabbi Abraham has done the state some service; some service indeed. Therefore, he also counts as an honorary bishop in the Holy Church. And none outside our little cabal need know that I too have become a secret Jew and, like him, a Kabbalist.

So here we wait, and wait, in the hot dusty landlocked city of Toledo, outward Christians but secret Jews in a city now Christian but once both Moslem and Jewish, waiting for a call that will never come from an unconcerned Austrian-Flemish king and his hysterical, passionate Spanish queen, dreaming of a land that has changed beyond recognition, dreaming of battles fought in a distant realm, in a century gone by...

ב (beis)

I was sixteen. The weather was atrocious, with snow, sleet and every other kind of freezing shit being thrown at us. It was my first battle. And, in fact, the first really big fight of the Cousins' Wars. It was spring, though it didn't feel like it, Palm Sunday, 29th March in the year of grace, 1461. We were in the English Midlands, where the two opposing parties were bound to rub up and clash. Because, although people talk of Lancaster and York, it was more truly the north that, very broadly, supported Lancaster, while London and the south gave its backing to York. Inevitably, the midlands of England were our main battle ground. Funny how, in war, and by extension in politics, the country so neatly divides in two. So, here we were, not far south of York, the great northern capital, out in the middle of the rolling English countryside, between two little villages, Saxton and Towton, as I recollect (strange, isn't it, as we grow older, we remember every detail from many years ago, yet have no memory of what we ate for this morning's breakfast).

Like everyone else in our army, from nobleman down to churl, and all the camp followers — those whores get to know everything — I knew two unavoidable facts: first, the Lancastrians ("Henry's rabble" we called them with the usual bravado) had already got comfortably ensconced on the higher ground and were sitting there awaiting us; second, their army, containing the affinities and households of most of the nobility of England, was patently larger than ours, maybe by as much as half. And there they sat, the smug bastards, up on their slope, the chivalry of England, dukes, earls, knights on their magnificently caparisoned steeds, and well behind them (never in front, you'll notice), their womanish king and mannish queen. They looked impressive, solid, immovable.

But, you know, we weren't nervous or frightened. We were serious, we were concerned, we knew we had business to do; but we had faith and belief in our destiny. The wheel of fortune would turn for us. Just as, sixty years before, it had turned against King Richard. And why such belief? Several reasons: we had right on our side; for surely and in Heaven's name, our leader, Edward of York, former Earl of March and newly proclaimed King Edward IV, was the heir-general, in succession to his illustrious father, the Duke of York, of the foully murdered Richard II, done to death by the traitorous hand of Henry IV, grandfather of our opponent, the mawkish Henry VI. More practically, we were led by the strong alliance of King Edward and his noble cousin, Richard Neville, Earl of Warwick and Salisbury, the greatest landowner in England and a magnificent military and political leader, far beyond any the party of Lancaster could produce. I don't know what effect Warwick had, at that stage, on the enemy but, by Christ, he terrified us! We were the party of David: small, lithe, youthful and godly, opposing the bloated and over-confident bulk of Goliath: the fat old giant.

Two weeks earlier, the call to arms had come to Ewelme in Oxfordshire, where I was staying with my Beloved Mother in her favourite manor, the house she had inherited from her father, Sir

Thomas Chaucer, the brilliant diplomat, who had represented his (Lancastrian) king on many occasions abroad, and received good and honest treasure and manors for his labours.

When the letter arrived, sealed with the brand new, very handsome signet of His Grace, the young King Edward, I had asked my mother's blessing to join the Yorkist army and win my knightly spurs, renewing the honour of the De-la-Pole name. She had, of course, wept and begged me not to depart, honouring my brother for his wiser counsel in sitting out this particular, unpredictable affray.

I wish I could say that, but I cannot. It would be a lie.

My "Beloved Mother" looked me over coolly and said, "Yes, I want you to go. Try to keep out of too much mayhem but if it is God's will that you perish — and make sure it's honourably — then at least your brother will remain alive, here with me. And, if necessary, we can make our obeisance to Henry, if he triumphs, and thus save the family estates."

"But Mother—" my older brother, the second Duke of Suffolk, began, but he was cut off pretty damn quickly.

"You have the mind of a boy, John, and you are not *yet* married to Elizabeth Plantagenet. Betrothed, yes, but there's still time to draw back should your intended brother-in-law be hacked to pieces in this campaign. We can always find you another wife. You *are* a duke — though it's hard to believe, looking at you."

B.M. was often harsh but always accurate. And she was, since Father's death, the undisputed head of our family. My brother pursed his lips and looked away, but he did as he was told. I blanched with nervous anticipation, a touch of fear and a heap of excitement. I was going to win my spurs.

Mother, who looked after our family finances well, had not stinted on my accoutrements. In my armour, which I was very proud of — made to measure, black, gilded and heavy, with the De-la-Pole crest of deep azure and three leopards' heads in gold upon my helm — I was weighed down, breathless and sweating like a hog. But how else can a knight, nay a lord, go into battle?

As the son of a duke, I was entitled to the honour of serving in the vanguard but as a mere kid (thanks be to God), I was placed in the third rank, which seemed close enough. In front of me, therefore, were two massed ranks of mounted men-at-arms, glittering in such rays of the early morning sun as managed to pierce the curtain of snow, and you could smell the horses — and a certain heady aroma of noble sweat and male aggression. Quite arousing really and incredible exciting for a teenage boy. Oh, and, of course, you could smell the archers massed to our right — they always stink of sweat and shit — they're all mere villeins after all. Useful soldiers as they are.

We could see the Lancastrian forces — just, through the sheets of sleet — and they looked a hell of a lot more numerous than we were. We had passed the night in prayer and fasting — as good Christian soldiers should — and battling with our fears and demons, sent to us by Satan himself. Now it was morning, and despite the absence of our ally the Duke of Norfolk, whose forces, said rumour, had been delayed by the slow duke's indisposition at Pontefract — the very castle where the late King Richard II had been murdered — we knew the battle could not be long delayed.

As the snow and rain and hail came vertically down, our leader, the newly proclaimed King Edward, appeared before us on his white stallion; his standard-bearer, almost as impressive, mounted by his side with the sun-in-splendour badge of York flapping and throbbing in the wind and snow. There was massive cheering from all our ranks. I had not seen our new king in recent years and now I had the chance to feast my eyes.

To describe Edward of York as beautiful could be likened unto calling the Almighty *quite* strong. He was… magnificent, resplendent, gorgeous. Even married men who were unattracted by the male body looked upon him in awe, mouths gaping in admiration. We were all ready to be his minions. He was very tall, well over six feet, golden blond and manly like a Greek hero. I fell in love. Here was a king to worship, a leader worth dying for.

He reined in his equally handsome horse before us, raised his hand for silence, and said in a powerful, deep voice, "My friends, we are here to avenge my revered father, Richard Plantagenet, Duke of York, Protector of the Kingdom and heir to England. We are here to avenge, at last, the cruel murder of the late King Richard, the last rightful, Plantagenet King of England. And we are here to remove the usurper, the idiot, useless, redeless usurper, Henry of Lancaster, and replace him with me, your rightful king. Are you with me?"

I nearly fell off my horse with excitement. Was I *with* him? I was virtually *in* him.

"God for Edward, Plantagenet and York!" I yelled, along with several thousand others.

My night-terrors had vanished. Edward replaced his helm and rode off to lead the vanguard. He must have signalled to the commander of our longbowmen, for at that moment, they let off a thick, overarching hail of arrows. My companion — Sir Gerald Dispenser, an old De-la-Pole retainer appointed by

B.M. to keep me out of harm's way — took hold of my harness to lead me off to the side.

"Let us watch the battle, my lord."

"Let us, fuck," I replied, imitating soldier's talk. "I'm following my king."

And, by God, I did. Which is to say, I neither withdrew nor advanced but stood my ground, there in the third rank, with the other men-at-arms, awaiting the call to charge.

I learnt that day that it's not all charging and killing, you know; there's a lot of waiting around on battlefields, a lot of boredom and, if you're not watching out, you can easily miss the sudden flurries of violent action. I even saw some poor buggers miss their own deaths it came so unexpectedly.

"What happens now?" I turned and asked Sir Gerald.

"Keep your visor closed, sir," he replied sternly — but wisely.

"Expect the arrow shower coming back!" shouted someone behind me.

I looked up — foolishly — then looked around but fortunately no arrows were reaching us.

"The wind's against them. God's with us!" said another voice from behind.

I turned in my saddle to squint through my visor at a roughly good-looking yeoman on his feet behind me, whom I vaguely recognised as one of our affinity; we'd brought about three hundred in our following. Not bad for a scratch squad. He smiled up at me, and, as he did so, a stray arrow — probably one of our own blown back — hit him full in the eye. He just stood there, still smiling, blood drizzling down his cheek. I thought of King Harold and, selfishly, rejoiced in the protection of my armour. Then he simply keeled over and was dragged away by a couple of squires — *helpful chaps*, I thought — when I heard the cry: "They're coming. Hold the line."

Hold what fucking line?

Fortunately, our vanguard held, but the impact of the enemy's attack was like a battering ram on our massed ranks. My horse reared up and here my excellent knightly training came into play; as did that of Sir Gerald, who helped me control the poor frightened nag, who hadn't been in a real fight before any more than I had.

The melee seemed to go for hours and hours, which it actually did, though from our position it was more pushing and shoving and sweating than anything else. But gradually — and this was deeply worrying — their greater numbers were pushing us back further down the long meadow and there wasn't much we could do about it. At one point, I saw the king, with just a handful of his household knights, charging up in front of us, brandishing his sword in a sort of ecstasy and cutting through a whole swathe of the enemy. I felt a similar ecstasy as I watched from within my hot sweaty tin box. But I was also worried for him and aware we were slowing, ineluctably losing ground, which meant losing the battle.

At that moment, a huge Lancastrian man-at-arms fought his way through the first two ranks right in front of me. I unsheathed my sword for the first time that day and raised it. I felt anger, determination and passion for my king. He raised an axe in his right hand, and somebody shouted, "The duke's here. Norfolk's men are coming."

There was a huge cheer from our ranks. My massive opponent was distracted, and Sir Gerald smoothly cleft his head in two. It was not a pleasant sight, but it was a welcome one. As welcome, in fact, as the arrival of our friends. *Interesting*, I thought — already a bit of a philosopher — *how the arrival of fresh reserves can change the whole course of a fight.*

Almost at once, that stale smell of defeat — the sweat of tired and dispirited men — was replaced by a sweet scent of optimism and renewed strength.

"Beat the bastards. Kill the traitors, kill the traitors," went the chant, like a crowd at a bear-baiting match (those things are so cruel, you know, though fun) and we went at it like loyal liegemen of the House of York.

It's nice to know you're winning. But remember: even if you're winning, you can still get killed. Desperate men can be pretty lethal. But at last, we were moving, and in the right direction, pushing forwards, enjoying the thrill of the chase. Only it wasn't beasts we were hunting, it was men. Now we were at a gallop, chasing those frightened bastards towards the River Cock — truly, that's what they call it — and although I didn't kill anybody with my own hands, I must have trampled quite a few to death under my horse's hooves. Well, they asked for it. They were on the other side and they were churls, mostly. And they had lost.

When we rode up to the riverbank, we could hardly see water; just bodies, thousands of them piled up to form a kind of human bridge. A bridge of carnage that our men were clambering over, as they caught and killed and looted the dead and dying. Not lovely or chivalric or very courageous really. I began to feel slightly sick.

Sir Gerald, still honourably in attendance, lifted his visor. "Had enough, sir? I think it's time we returned to camp."

"Do we have to?" I kept up the bravado.

"I think it's wise, my lord. Your Lady Mother would never forgive me if something happened to you when the day was already ours."

His faith in the B.M.'s devotion was stronger than mine, but I yielded and we returned, feeling hugely satisfied, to our camp.

A couple of hours later, it was dark and, warmed up with mead and hippocras and bread and meat, I was summoned to the royal tent.

His Dazzling Grace was standing amongst a group of the best and brightest lords, including his darkly handsome brother George — not much older than me — and the overwhelming, bulky presence of Richard Neville, my Lord of Warwick.

Noticing me — a squire must have muttered my name into the royal ear — the king, his golden hair tousled and his luminous face bloodied, turned on me his utterly seductive, regal charm; what the Greeks call: charisma.

"Eddie De-la-Pole, they tell me you were the youngest on the field. Come here, young man, and receive my thanks."

I approached and the knights around the king politely applauded.

"Give me my sword," he said to one of his knights.

I knew what to do, having been instructed in the ancient ritual years before as a little boy by my late, kindly father as we had play-acted this scene, though imagining then the king would be the monkish and defeated opponent of our new liege lord.

I knelt and His Magnificent Grace tapped me on both shoulders.

"Arise, Sir Edward."

"Your liegeman in life and limb forever, my Lord King."

"I do believe the boy's in love," said George Plantagenet, in a casually supercilious tone.

"Ignore him," said King Edward to me, "*I* usually do."

All the knights around laughed uproariously at that one, as His Grace tousled my hair affectionately, and, Sir Gerald, quietly in attendance as ever, fitted on my new silver spurs.

"With God's grace, we shall be brothers-in-law soon as well as brothers-in-arms, when our sister Elizabeth marries your brother, the duke."

"It will be to our honour, Your Grace."

The king smiled; the sun in splendour. I was floating on a magic carpet of teenage adoration.

"Even if that brother sent excuses for not being here himself today," bawled Warwick, big, gruff and never shy to speak his mind.

"There will be other days for him to prove that he is as loyal and manly as his younger brother," said the king.

I bowed. There wasn't anything I could say.

As I was guided back to my tent by a squire, I realised I had, that day, learnt even more about politics than I had about war.

***

The next morning, we learnt that thirty thousand men were killed in that battle, named by our king as the Battle of Towton, the most ferocious and murderous ever to be fought on English land; a battle that changed the course of English history, knocking Henry of Lancaster effectively off his tottering throne and replacing him with my heartthrob, the gallant Edward IV. And I was a part of it.

We moved on that morning — the massive, bloodied but triumphant army including this newly-dubbed knight — and descended on the northern capital, the fair and ancient city of York, whose great towering minster was still in the throes of being built. I wonder if they've finished it now. I know I shall never see it. That was my first sight of York; my first sight, I am embarrassed to say, of Yorkshire, even though it is the homeland of our House (I mean the House of De-la-Pole, of course). The good burghers of the city must have been waiting with baited breath to hear the result of the scrap, especially as Their dis-Graces the Lancastrian king and queen were ensconced with their substantial household in the huge castle which broods over the prosperous town. We laughed, as you can imagine, when the townsfolk told us of the haste in which the ex-monarchs jumped on their horses, screamed at their grooms to make haste with as much luggage and treasure as they could grab and galloped north for their lives! With them was their little boy, the so-called Prince of Wales, Edward of Lancaster, and the two Lancastrian Dukes of Somerset and Exeter. They rode for the border with Scotland, our ancient foe, allies of the Lancastrians' other friends, the bloody French, always ready to make trouble for England.

Meanwhile, the town of York put on a splendid show for us; I wonder why? They welcomed us with open arms. You would never guess they had done the same for the other party just a few days before. But King Edward, gracious as ever, was pleased to accept the submission of his northern capital. And submission it was, as the lord mayor and aldermen, with all the prosperous burghers, came to greet him outside the city gates crawling on their knees. The old mayor, in a rich padded gown, practically touched the earth in front of the king's horse with his forehead in the sort of obeisance only Turks would usually make to their sovereign. But the king — I saw it for I was close behind him — alighted from his horse (at which we in the king's immediate party did the same), went forwards and raised the shivering old bugger from his knees and kissed him on the forehead. I was jealous.

"Arise, my good Lord Mayor. As my honoured father was the duke of this fair county… I am happy to accept the homage of this old and noble city of York, as a loyal servant to the royal house of York and its king… *now*."

The lord mayor immediately fell on his knees again; the rest of them stayed down there quaking. But the king gave a great, manly belly laugh — some belly, some laugh — and, lifting him once again by the shoulders, said, "Come, my good Lord Mayor, and all your fellow burghers. We are friends, you are my subjects and you have my love."

At which all the assembled citizens of York — and there were several thousand thereabouts — threw their hats up in the air. The lord mayor stood and kissed the king's hands, and all of us shouted, "God save King Edward, God save the king."

Edward had defeated an army; he had also captured the hearts of the north by his charm. The armed fist in the richly velvet glove: it always works.

We processed to the castle with wild rejoicing. I heard later from my chamberlain, Quidnunc — to whom you will be introduced — that the household servants at the castle, those who had not ridden off at the gallop with Henry and Margaret, were working with feverish speed to sweep away every last vestige of Lancastrian presence and prepare the state apartments with fine fresh linen, bowls of fruit and wafers, scrubbed close-stools, and every modern convenience for the comfort and happiness of the new royal party. Certainly, when we got to the castle, all was in remarkably good order and I was conducted to a pleasant chamber just a few doors from the king's, as befitted my rank.

After resting a little, we were summoned to the Great Hall, where His Grace was seated on a grand Chair of Estate, with his brother George, tall, pretty and sour-faced as usual, to his right, and the Earl of Warwick to his left. The old Duke of Norfolk, last of the Mowbrays, whose arrival on the field had been pretty well decisive, stood behind.

King Edward, just eighteen, and until recently a lad in the shadow of his father, the late Duke of York, had slipped — or grown — with astonishing ease into the role of our leader and king. He knew precisely what to say and do, how to walk and look in regal manner; truly his bearing proved he was the man born to be our king. Every glorious inch of him.

The heralds called for order. In the silence, the king spoke.

"I thank ye all, my trusty and well-beloved liegemen and true. And, some special thanks. When we are back in our capital — our *southern* capital — of London, we shall be pleased to honour our closest followers and lords — my Lord Duke of Norfolk, my cousin of Warwick, my Lord Fauconberg, Sir Edward De-la-Pole (remember I was soon to become His Grace's brother-in-law) and others — with gold chains of suns and roses in memory of my late honoured father, Richard Plantagenet, Duke of York, so traitorously done to death by

19

my adversaries, the soi-disant Henry VI and that foul she-devil, Margaret of Anjou."

Much applause and bows from the nobles aforementioned, including myself now blushing with joyful adolescent pride.

"And let it be known that it is our will to invest our good brother the Lord George with the royal title of Duke of Clarence, and our youngest brother, the Lord Richard, too young to be on the field of battle, but he is, I hear, eager for the fray, with the dukedom of Gloucester, as they are, while I remain in the unmarried state, the heirs to my crown."

More polite applause, as George, soon-to-be Clarence, now smiling triumphantly, took a bow.

I heard someone mutter behind me, "I didn't see *him* doing much in the field."

Another whispered, "I hear young Richard's a scrapper though and the image of his late father."

"Not beautiful like King Edward then…" And they both guffawed.

"Thank you, gentlemen," finished the king, "And, of course, those few ladies whom we have the honour and delight to have here amongst us."

A frisson went through the gallery above, where a small number of ladies were standing, trying to look demure.

"Spend this night in joy and pleasure all, for ye have earnt it!"

A scratch band of minstrels started to play and sing gay songs as we began to mingle sociably. Sir Gerald whispered in my ear that the king wished to speak with me. I moved forwards eagerly, but gracefully as a knight and a gentleman should, and placed myself near to the king with eyes downcast as etiquette demanded.

"Ah, young Eddie." Oh, the excitement when he used that pet name. "Give our love to your noble mother, Duchess Alice and to your brother, Duke... the duke, and we shall have a reward for you, my friend. We shall be writing to your Lady Mother to express our thanks."

His lips came near to my ear and I almost fainted as I could feel and smell his breath.

"And find yourself a sweet damsel to fuck with those strong young loins, eh?" And he slapped me powerfully on the back.

There was dancing that evening to timbrel, harp and pipe (I could have played the harp better myself, but that would never do, of course, for a duke's son. Though I was itching to show the pretty lad who was making such a mess of the Flemish tunes they spoilt), and there were many handsome young people cutting a dash in the Great Hall. It wasn't long before I found a pubescent girl, a little older than me I think, pouting and making eyes at me, as many people, men and women, did in those days. I was often told I was a very handsome lad with my mother's green eyes and my noble father's height and bearing.

Following the damsel's lead and finding a side chamber strewn with plenty of rushes for just such an occasion, I did what comes so naturally to the young. The sound of other young studs prodding their damsels with greater gusto than I felt inclined to manage was highly encouraging. And, in truth, the smell of young male flesh in the near vicinity, pouring their hot molten spunk into a welcoming quim spurred me on to do the same. Anyway, the girl seemed satisfied. And I felt confirmed in my newfound manhood. To fight your first battle and cover your first mare in two days seemed pretty fine going to me.

21

ג (gimmel)

Sitting here — an old man, almost — in my private chamber in this pretty but alien house in the unbearable heat of Toledo, waiting, always waiting, to hear a word from those who now have power, my memory ranges back much further, before the Battle of Towton, before I came of age, before I even started my schooling, to the time of Eden, when all the world is young and we are tiny children knowing nothing of the harshness of the world. My earliest memories are of sitting on my father's knee — not my mother's — and feeling his soft, loving breath on my neck as he whispered tales to me of his life at court.

And this is the first picture my dear father, Duke William, painted for me when I was that little bairn, telling me of our good king and queen, whom he served so closely and so loyally, as Lord Great Chamberlain of the Realm, and how one day I should be presented to them at court and serve them, and their posterity in my turn, as it was our family's duty ever to do. He painted a picture of them, like eager children, and indeed they were young and innocent then: Henry and Margaret, sitting up in the huge royal bed on New Year's Day, as he stood by, as they received their gifts from the great persons of the court and delighted in examining each one. And now that picture seems to me, across the long sad years, like an illustration in a book of hours — *Les Tres Riches Heures du William, Duc de Suffolk*

— when all things were good in the world and I was a happy, loved child and there were no wars or divisions in England...

Those were the years, the late 40s and early 50s, when my noble father was chief minister of the realm and saintly, soft King Henry's right-hand man. And who, think you, slept in the king's chamber — for the king must never be unattended — when His Grace slept, even when he occasionally shared the royal bed with his pretty young French queen, the haughty Margaret of Anjou? Two courters: an ambitious young baron, James Fiennes, Lord Saye and Sele, Chamberlain of the King's Household, (they have always been great climbers and actors, that family) and, attending his principal, the Lord Great Chamberlain of England, my father, William De-la-Pole, first Duke and fourth Earl of Suffolk.

So, my father must have been present in the royal bedchamber when, after many years of false starts and misplacements of the royal sceptre — and who knows how many tutorials and exhortations from him — *finally* from within the hot confines of the heavily-curtained regal bed of estate came grunts of satisfaction and shrieks of delight from the royal pair as, after years of trying, the regal cock finally penetrated — and *ejaculated* — into the royal quim. But where, at that precise moment, was my handsome, loyal, ducal daddy? Was he, as we assumed, egging on the less-than-virile king with manly whoops of encouragement, "Get it in there, Your Grace. Your Highness can do it. Give Her Grace a good thrust", that sort of thing? Or, was he, as some have whispered, on top of the young and wide-open Margaret, who was gagging to be royally impregnated, entering the regal quinny with his own manly and, I vividly remember, well-proportioned De-la-Pole dick, with the dear dithering but impotent king giving then both a grateful and helping hand?

***

Memories are like waves smashing on the shore, or ridges of earth and soil. You look behind one and then behind another, and find yourself deeper, further back in the recesses of your childish mind.

We were at Ewelme in the county of Oxford. The manor house there is one my Beloved Mother inherited as heiress to my grandfather, Sir Thomas Chaucer, son of the renowned poet and himself a worshipful royal man of state, fluent in many languages and, above all, in the subtil language of diplomacy. The apple blossom was thick on the trees, I recollect, and it was a heavenly spring morning, or so it seems in my pale blue haze of recollection. "Heavenly" the day was to turn out to be in other modes too. The house — which remained in our family until the Battle of Stoke took so much from us in '87 — was not, I guess, large, but to me, as a child, it was vast and filled with enormous halls; yet comforting too and grand and wise like our Beloved Mother. Ewelme was not a castle but a fine, part-fortified manor house, built in the modern style in a time when England was a land at peace, and who better than Duchess Alice to be the lady of the manor? But my memories of that handsome home with its gorgeous Flemish tapestries and the great carved oak beds with their hangings delicately embroidered by the B.M.'s own hands and her gentlewomen's have been forever sombred by the sorrow of that day.

Just a few weeks before this, my father had fallen from power, forced out — with an irony unforeseen at the time — by the very Duke of York, soon to be Protector of the Kingdom, whose daughter became, some years later, my sister-in-law (and thus the cause of all my House's glory and sorrow). My noble father had made a long and masterful speech to Parliament — much reported at the time and recorded by the clerks for posterity — in which he had sought to turn the hearts of the burghers and lords to remember the many years of good service he had given and how no one could have prevented the great loss of Normandy, except perhaps my Lord of York who had led our armies. But as York, now gagging to be Protector, had most members in his pocket, and they were grimly determined on finding a scapegoat, my dear father it had to be. This news had come to my mother the duchess' hands in a letter written in the duke's own, so she knew of its truth. Though, of course, she had said nothing of it to us children. But, shortly after, he had written again to assure her — whom he loved deeply, for they had married for love as much as for duty and advancement — that he, my father, still had the favour of the king — or of the wide-eyed fool they called king at that time — and that the lords of the council had advised His Grace that my father's "punishment" on his trumped up charge should be no worse than a period of civilised banishment, without confiscation of any of his lands or titles. Exile from England would be bitter indeed for my father, and, much bitterer, separation from my adored mother and their much-loved children, for he was a father who cherished and loved, perhaps overmuch and uncritically, his three little ones.

The duke was given some weeks by the weak, if kindly, king to order his affairs and spent those weeks, away from us, with his beloved duchess at their new home at Wingfield. Duchess Alice, always his rock and his wiser half, advised him to be of good heart, to travel to the pleasant, rich lands of Burgundy where there were noble friends to reforge affinities with and, from there, to make pilgrimage to Rome or Compostela. She would supply him with funds from her own estates and his in the counties of Oxford, Suffolk and Norfolk, lands which she would nurture and nourish as well as their cherished children. He knew his livelihood and his babes were in the strongest and safest hands. She knew — and now told us, on her return to Ewelme — that Father would have to depart almost at once on a long journey, all part of his service to our good lord, the king, and that he would not have time first to come and see us, but that we would certainly be foremost in his thoughts. Mother even told us we might look forward — at some time in the future — to a sea voyage over the English Channel to visit our father in the fair city of Bruges: a city I was to come to know well, also in times of exile. But that must wait till due time in my narrative.

So, on that spring morning, I was playing a game of boules with my elder sister Margaret, having completed my lessons in Latin — Greek was to start later — with my tutor the Reverend Doctor Haskyns. Our elder, dullard brother, John, was pursuing his training as a future duke in the house of another great lord as befits the heir to a great estate.

I knew we would not see my father for a long time to come, for Mother had promised us he was safe and well and was going on a long journey at the king's command. So, we were content with that. Nevertheless, we were aware, as children so often instinctively are, that something was amiss, and that my father's long absence foreboded something ill. It was in the B.M.'s slightly sad smile, in the way she gently touched our heads and even in the restrained way in which the servants did their tasks around the house.

So, Margaret and I were playing with our toys and prattling on about what we would do when we were grown up. I remember distinctly her saying, "I shall marry the son of a king and become the queen of a beautiful country," when of a sudden, a great wailing and ululation broke out from the B.M.'s women who were in her chamber above ours. I remember the cold fingers of fear that grabbed my heart and, as I began to cry, my sister, being older and stronger like Mother, looked sternly at me and said, "Come, Edward, stop your crying. We shall go up to Mother. Stop it!"

I stopped weeping as she ordered and followed her quickly up the curving stone stairway to the duchess' withdrawing chamber above. There stood my Beloved Mother, silent like a stone statue, like the cold effigy of her that lies now in Ewelme Church, staring straight ahead in her fine turquoise blue robe — the last time I ever saw her in any colour but black — a letter crumpled in her right hand, her left hanging limp beside her, and all around, her women, five or six of them, crying and lamenting inconsolably; but not one tear was on her face.

We stood in awe before this; my first fearful sight of grief, struck dumb with amazement. After perhaps a minute that lasted hours, our mother — not duchess-like but queenly, more queenly than any of the reigning queens I have known and served since — smiled bravely at us and said, "Come hither,

27

children. Women, be silent and go from us. I must speak to my babes of our doleful news."

When her women had left us — all except one, her favourite, a poor northern cousin who stayed with her always — she held us on her knee and said, "My darlings, your noble father has been taken up to Heaven and is with our sweet Lord Jesus. He has died in the service of the king. Never forget he was a great man, a very noble and worshipful man, a great nobleman and a good Christian. You must be proud of him and live nobly to serve his memory."

After that, I remember only bewilderment and tears, and being consoled by her and by our kinswoman.

It was months — maybe years — later when my siblings and I learnt the full story of our father's death. How he had taken a ship into exile, been kidnapped from that ship to another called, ominously, *The Nicholas of the Tower*, whose captain and crew, in the pay of his enemies, had held him captive and cut off his head. To add insult and disgrace to murder, they had cast his body on the sands of the Dover coast.

Mother, that remarkable lady, would not and did not allow herself to be undermined by this terrible death, despite her overwhelming grief. It was as if the outer walls of her estates had been thrown down but the portcullis to her moat and bailey remained intact and, within it, all that remained to her: her children, her noble status, her wider family, her dignity and wealth. Not for nothing was she a Chaucer and a De-la-Pole, a duchess and now — as the lawmen of the temple term a widow — a *femme sole*. Within two or three days, she had written an accomplished letter to the king, a missive worthy of our national poet's granddaughter, couched thus:

Most Gracious and Dread Sovereign Lord,

Your Grace has, by now, been apprised, I wist, of the doleful and murderous end of my most honoured lord and husband, Duke William. My Dread Lord, to speak to Your Grace of my late lord's allegiance and loyalty to Your Grace and Your Grace's House — the most royal and noble House of Lancaster — and of his long years of devoted service to Your Grace, would be to recount those things which any good servant of Your Highness would do or have done. But done it is, and — like all the deeds, both good and bad, of men — written on water, whispered on the wind, for all flesh is grass and the doings of men are but the seeds of grass, scattered on the breeze.

But, if it please Your Highness to patronise his humble servant and Abigail — Dame Alice Chaucer, relict of the first Duke of Suffolk — with my lord so foully done to death without process of law or rites of absolution, ighness to patronize his I humbly beg Your Grace to have pity on her and her little chicks, fatherless now in this harsh world, and to grant this grieving widow the right to reclaim his body, as Achilles the Greek hero was given leave to bathe and tend to the body of his beloved companion Patroclus.

And your humble petitioner begs Your Grace to remember his loyal liegeman, John De-la-Pole, now, with Your Highness' leave, second Duke of Suffolk, a child, betrothed by Your Grace's loving kindness, to Your Grace's royal cousin, the Lady Margaret Beaufort, daughter to the late and noble Duke of Somerset, and so a kinswoman to Your Grace, as I look forward with happy anticipation to that union of the noble Houses of Beaufort and De-la-Pole.

Begging the king to accept the honest and true petition of his loyal liege-woman, Dame Alice, now woefully Dowager Duchess of Suffolk, and ever at His Highness' command.

***

In my darker moments, I see life as a series of griefs and losses, of continual abandonments, each eased a little by being a mite less unexpected than the last, as, one by one, we are divested of our hopes and expectations. And that was the first of all my griefs. But not the last. Far from the last.

***

The 1450s — the decade following the murder of my father and the collapse of King Henry's government, and his sanity — were a very confusing time, when the realm of England sought a strong man to roll back our humiliating losses in France and prevent the ever-deepening chaos in England, where knights and barons were settling ancient feuds and taking the king's law into their own hands, not waiting for the arrival of the Royal Justices on assize. My ducal family no longer had a strong man at its helm but, thanks be to God, a strong woman, who protected our interests, especially the estates of my brother John, older than me but still underage (and woefully inadequate).

My Beloved Mother was much hardened by the death of my father. Up to then, she had been a young aristocratic wife, an excellent manager of a ducal familia, consisting of several households, many domestic serfs and a circle of women, whom she headed competently; she was always rightly proud of her own fine descent and breeding. But now she matured, in a matter of weeks, into a woman of power, the head of both her own dower estates and her son's inheritance, fierce protector of children and, when necessary, leader of men. Later, she even became a gaoler of state prisoners. If only my brother — the heir to our noble House — had inherited her strength, her diplomacy, her knowledge of men's minds; instead, he had our father's kindly vacillation and the bookishness of the Chaucers without their acumen. Exactly the wrong things for a time of civil wars, in fact.

But now, dear reader of a later century or millennium, imagine, if you will, King Henry, the sixth of that name, symbol of majesty, King of England, France and Ireland; son and heir to the valiant hero, Henry V victor of Agincourt and conqueror of France; Suzerain Lord of Britain, Sovereign of the Most Noble Order of the Garter; Duke of Normandy, direct descendant and heir of the Conqueror; grandson of Bolingbroke, founder of the Lancastrian dynasty, and great-grandson of the warrior-statesman John of Gaunt, Duke of Lancaster and King of Castile; our liege lord and king. Do you see him in your mind's eye? Do you see him blinding in his dazzling majesty? Do you? Be assured: you don't. Imagine a meek man, tall, quite slender, with a bland, almost blank oval face (a pale copy of his warrior-father, like a fading manuscript), and kindly, slightly watery eyes, sitting in a heavy gilded chair that seemed too big for him and wearing a plain grey woollen robe with food stains down the front. And I think I saw a yellow gobbet of egg on his receding, hairless chin.

It wasn't an awe-inspiring sight. Although I did notice a burgundy red ruby the size of the Isle of Thanet sitting on a fat gold band on the third finger of his left hand, so he clearly wasn't — as I had suspected — an itinerant friar who had wandered in and sat in the king's chair by mistake.

I bowed low — I must have been about twelve — and, carried away by my own imagination, kissed the hem of his robe. It was musty.

He patted me kindly on the head. "Greetings, my son, and my blessing."

Did he have a delusion that he was pope?

"How fare's your good brother, my loyal servant, the duke?"

Well, he either had a far better memory than I would have given him credit for or he had been accurately briefed by the obsequious chamberlain, Lord Saye and Sele, more likely (my father's former deputy and now despised replacement), hovering behind his chair. His voice — the king's that is — was quite melodious, if high. He could have sung a good "Agnus Dei". In fact, he probably did.

He was already of mature age, and looked to me, to be an old man. His gaze was so gentle I suspected he was charmed, even seduced, by my pubescent good looks — I was a ravishing youth (whereas now I can't even find one, no, I jest) — but I later discovered he looked at everyone like that, out of a species of vapid saintliness.

What did I reply? What does one ever reply to royalties? Do they even listen? Something as bland as his royal features, such as, "My respected brother, the duke, lives only to serve Your Grace, as do I, Sire," or some such persiflage. Which is why it must have been such a traumatic shock when eventually the cotton wool of royalty was removed from around him and His dis-Grace fell into the pit of oblivion from which no monarch ever returns — except that, strangely enough, he briefly did. But I anticipate my story.

"Pray, tell your dear brother he has our full and joyous consent to his marriage with the Lady Elizabeth, daughter of my well-beloved cousin of York." He smiled benignly.

I wondered if I had permission to leave the royal presence. The chamberlain whispered in the royal ear.

"You may further tell him, sweet boy…" Was he leering, the old devil? "How it has troubled our conscience that his betrothal to the Lady Margaret Beaufort, my *most* dearly beloved cousin, was sadly annulled. It was with rejoicing that we consented to the Lady Margaret's nuptials with our honoured and well trusty brother, the Lord Edmund, Earl of Richmond." And at this, a tear like a creamy pearl, dropped from his left eye. "Now recalled unto Our Lord." There was a pause, without a pregnancy, and again I twitched to depart. But apparently there *was* a pregnancy in the case.

"But the Lord, having taken the lady's husband was pleased to grant her a healthy son, my nephew the Lord Henry Tudor, an infant for whom I foresee a great destiny."

I swear those were his words, the sly old fortune teller. Another pause; another twitch.

"Your Grace—" I fluted — I had a heavenly voice as a youth, both in speech and song — but the chamberlain placed his second finger tightly upon his lips.

"It is now to my great joy and liking that your trusty brother is betrothed to a most suitable bride of ducal rank. And let us pray their sacred union too shall be blessed with healthy fruit to continue a noble line for whom we have great love and affection."

Another pause, and twitch and whisper and…

"If the queen and I are not able to attend their happy nuptials this is merely because Her Grace and I have been lent… a castle…" The royal voice trailed off, then the chamberlain whispered vociferously.

"That is to say, because of the coming of Lent and my forthcoming retreat… to a house of religion… for a short season."

The next pause was very long, as the king stared vacantly into the middle (or was it the far?) distance. At this point, I recollected my aunt, Dame Katherine, the Abbess of Barking, telling me of His Grace's strange bout of madness — a trance-like state of abstraction — some years previously. Perhaps he was due another? Perhaps it had already started? I grimaced quizzically at the chamberlain. He mouthed something.

It could have been Mandarin Chinese or Farsi for all I understood. He whispered — same result. The king continued to gawp, as his mouth fell open.

"Please leave," hissed the chamberlain, so I did.

The king was clearly mad, but he wasn't stupid. That much was clear.

It was the only occasion on which I met the mad old bat. It didn't inspire loyalty, just contempt.

‫ד‬ (daled)

It was when I was about eight that my brother's marriage to Margaret Beaufort had been annulled on the orders of the king. That man could be a bitch when he felt like it. And I well recall the B.M.'s reaction when she received a letter under the signet announcing this, from that same chamberlain, Lord Saye and Sele. I was playing my little harp — I know the harp is now a girl's instrument but I was only eight, and it was once the medium of the troubadour — and Mother was seated with her ladies and my elder brother when the letter was brought in. This time she did not look shocked. She was angry.

"So, the king, in his gracious wisdom, has determined that the Lady Margaret, descendant of Duke John of Gaunt and mighty heiress that she is, should not marry *you*, John, but instead a young man called Edmund Tydr."

"Who, Mother?" asked my rather confused brother.

"The king's uterine half-brother whom he has just created Earl of Richmond. The honour of Richmond being a royal perquisite. Not that the new earl is royal, of course, *half*-royal at most." She sniffed. "He is apparently now the premier Earl of England. But still, of course, behind you in precedence, my ducal son."

"Well, I hope they'll be very happy together, Mother."

"Oh, don't be such a dullard, boy. This is a dynastic match, don't you see that?"

"What does that mean, Mother?" I asked, always more curious than my brother.

"It means His Grace may have something very serious and important in his plans for that happy couple. But we may not speculate on that." She gave me a very hard look.

"Who's John going to marry now, Mother?"

"You ask exactly the right question, my son. Someone who will cause His Highness to take notice, I promise you, boys... Perhaps my Lord of York has a daughter we might bid for. Eh, boys?"

"I don't like my Lord of York, Mother," said Johnnie, "He's a fat, ugly man."

My mother suddenly lashed out at Johnnie, knocking him off his chair. He looked at her in shock then began to bawl.

"You are going to have to grow up very quickly if you are to live to be a man, let alone a great duke like your father, John. Eddie, why do *you* think a daughter of York would be a good match for your brother?"

The answer was on the tip of my tongue. "Because Duke Richard *is* a great duke like my father?"

The B.M. looked at me quizzically. "If only you were the older boy, Eddie. Not only is York a great duke indeed, but he is also a cousin of His Grace. Indeed, some people even say that he..." Her voice trailed off.

"Yes, Mother?" I knew from my mother's reticence that this had to be an essential and exciting piece of information.

"That he should be the king...?" shouted my brother triumphantly. "*I* heard that—"

But before Johnnie could tell us what he had heard, he had received a whack compared with which the first one had been, well, child's play.

"If you *ever* repeat what you have just said, I will see to it that you are disinherited of your title even if I have to declare myself an adulteress to do so!"

And poor Johnnie began to cry all over again.

***

Perhaps, at this point, I should say something to introduce that obnoxious — but increasingly important — family: the Tudors. Let's start at the beginning because that upstart, varlet family don't go back very far, I promise you.

How can I describe Jasper Tudor? Or rather Jasper ap something ap something ap Tydr as I am told he should properly be called. There's only one word to describe him: Welsh. And the English, God bless us (and He usually does), don't *like* the Welsh because we don't *understand* the Welsh. We conquered the Welsh, therefore we resent *them* even more than they resent *us*. Because they are a constant reminder that — far from the saintly Christian nation we take ourselves to be — we are evidently Anglo-Norman oppressors of the British nations, now scattered into the corners of Cornwall, Scotland and Wales. Now, of course, those bloody Welsh have the last laugh (or think they do) with their "unknown Welshman" on the throne of England. So, the last English king of England called him. But that was, of course, a bit of "spin", a touch of patronising propaganda delivered from on high by His late

Plantagenet Grace. For Henry's uncle, Jasper, was, of course, well-known to all of us — and by "us", I mean the extended royal family of Lancaster, York, Beaufort and De-la-Pole. And enmity and bloodletting are always more savage within families than without them.

Jasper, with his French-Welsh face and his graceful swan-like neck — rather feminine actually — inherited usefully from his mama Queen Katherine de Valois — whose presence in the genealogy gives her descendants greater proximity to the throne of France than to that of England — was *clever* as well as Welsh. You have to concede that. Those centuries his ancestors had spent as advisers and middlemen in the Welsh hills and valleys mediating between Celtic princes — they call themselves princes but they're hardly as powerful as English earls really — and English Crown officials, developed their sharp negotiating skills to the utmost. You could see him thinking in three languages, weighing up the advantages of this course and of that, and always guarding his own back, and his nephew's. One can only marvel at this extraordinary fusion — this miscegenation as most of my class saw it — of ancient Celtic blood with the sacred blood of the House of Valois, and obliquely with the blood of Plantagenet. How did that old Welsh wizard — Owain Tydr — magic that about? I imagine it happened something like this...

Long, long ago — nearly a hundred years ago, in fact — a victorious King of England, Henry, the fifth of that name, captured the heart (certainly the body anyway) of the mad King Charles of France's youngest and most beautiful daughter, Katherine de Valois. Their marriage, in 1420 in Troyes (it's somewhere in France, will that be good enough?) symbolised the happy union of France and England, a union in which the English Lion was the ravisher and La Belle France, the ravished. Kate probably quite enjoyed it; I am told on good authority (a page who helped dress His late Grace) that Hal was hung like a rampant Arab stallion. And we all know that Kate's mother — Isabeau of Bavaria, Queen of France — was the biggest tart in Christendom. Some say it was her utter insatiability — coupled with countless infidelities — which drove her poor husband insane (in Seine? Probably). Her oldest sister — named after their mother-whore — was, you may remember, the second child bride of our late and sadly murdered King Richard II, and was then sent politely packing back to France in high Valois dudgeon. She then married her cousin Charles, Duc d'Orleans, whose enmity to their other cousin, the powerful Duke of Burgundy, caused the fissure through which the English tore into France — but that's another, barely relevant story.

But back to Kate, enjoying her new-found status of Queen of England, laughing all the way to the font with her baby Henry, knowing he would soon replace her dreary brother the so-called dolphin (or, if you prefer, dauphin) as King of France as well as England. But far sooner than any had anticipated, that toddler was monarch of both realms and Kate was a lovely young dowager, very comfortably dowered but far less comfortably hemmed-in by her late husband's brothers, uncles and courtiers who formed the Regency Council on which (as a young and foreign woman) she was not accorded a seat. So picture the scene: the young and nubile queen-dowager with her pretty French accent, bored and frustrated (remember who her mother was) being waited on, amongst many others, by a strong-limbed chamberlain, Owain, who had formerly been in the household of her late husband's steward. She noticed two things about Owain (and who wouldn't?): his odd accent — clearly not French — and the fact that he was built like a stone shithouse. She couldn't decide which turned her on more. Women are like that: whores. But then again, so are men.

Her ladies whispered in her eager ears that her menfolk — including Welsh-boy — were off that afternoon to go skinny-dipping in the burbling local stream (probably a minor tributary of the Thames at Windsor, if truth be told). So, Katy, blushing not at all, took a few of her favourite girlfriends-in-waiting down to the woods by the stream, very quietly, to hide and watch the proceedings. And, lo and behold, there were the handsome boys and — couldn't you guess it? — Owain's todger was even bigger than that of His late Grace, Kate's first husband. For all at once, she had chosen her second.

When, how or where the marriage took place, nobody knows and there are some of us who doubt if it ever happened at all in a canonical sense. Let us assume some priest and a couple of complaisant witnesses were dragooned into officiating at a quick, secret ceremony to ensure that, technically at least, the three or four children who were extruded from the happy woman's womb in the early 1430s would not be subject to bastardy or, worse, the penal statutes against the Welsh — though Owain himself would be subject to severe penalties under the statutes of 1428 concerning the queen's putative remarriage. And so, it befell the Tudor when his wife and protectress sadly left this world in the year of our (I should say their) Lord 1437 after a long and grievous malady, nursed by the kindly sisters in the royal apartments of Bermondsey Abbey.

Owain, urgently summoned by the council, sought immediate sanctuary in Westminster Abbey, until eventually his silver Welsh tongue convinced the councillors of his marriage and love for the late queen and his lack of any personal ambition whatsoever. But who do you think took pity on the poor wretches: his three young sons, Edmund, Jasper and Owen, penniless, untitled children with an unpronounceable surname and no obvious prospects? Come on, guess, who would have been kind (or possibly far-sighted) enough to do such an uncalled-for act of charity? My aunt, of course, Katherine De-la-Pole, the Lady Abbess of Barking Abbey who was ready as always to step into the breach, clear up the mess and give those boys a bloody good education. If Jasper Tudor, Earl of sodding Pembroke, did damn well for himself later in life (forgive my swearing but this really does infuriate me) and managed to put his presumptuous usurping nephew on the high throne of our ancestors — well, my sister-in-law's ancestors — then it is largely due to the love, care and excellent training my dear Aunt Katherine lavished on him and his siblings as homeless, and virtually hopeless, striplings in the late 30s and early 40s of the last century. She shouldn't have bothered. She got no thanks. And nor did we.

In about '43 or '44, the feather-brained young king suddenly remembered, in a flurry of goodwill, that he had a trio of Welsh half-brothers over in Barking whom he might deign to take an interest in. He became their patron and took control of their education; it was one of the very few things he actually had the capacity to control. And then, in the early 50s, it was decided that the House of Lancaster, flimsy and fragile as it was, needed to be bolstered up and by whom other than the two strapping young Welshmen half-brothers (the third became a monk), whom it was decided Henry VI would acknowledge and ennoble as, frankly, he had no one else of his blood whom he could look to. And at that point, there seemed no prospect of an heir to his affectionate but hitherto totally flaccid marriage to that cunning she-devil Queen Margaret, or more correctly *Marguerite,* of Anjou.

***

My brother's wedding, as you would expect, was splendid, and was celebrated in St. Paul's Cathedral (Westminster Abbey wouldn't have been big enough, and, anyway, the king had only recently held his coronation there and didn't want it associated with any other connotations). There they stood before the altar to exchange their vows (of course, betrothed couples only make their vows at the lych-gate of country churches, not in great cathedrals): brother John looking every inch the royal duke, tall and saturninely handsome, appearing as he ought to have been in character, regal and dominant; and his bride, the Lady Elizabeth Plantagenet, sadly without the fine looks of her brothers or of her sisters Anne and Margaret, a little plain and dumpy (rather like her father, the old duke) but with a fine and haughty air about her that became a king's sister.

The Bishop of London officiated, while above in the royal gallery His Grace King Edward smiled down, radiating gracious benevolence and manly charm, flanked by his brothers, the handsome, vapid George, Duke of Clarence, wearing the latest slit doublet from France in the most gorgeous of silks (even more gorgeous than the king's I noticed quizzically) and his youngest brother Richard, several years younger than me, just a boy really, with one shoulder slightly higher than the other and a keen look on a face just as expressive, if a mite less handsome than his brothers. It was a strong expression; intelligent, and very self-assured for one so young. I dismissed it, but could not forget it. Also sitting by them was their regal mother, Duchess Cecily, proud and haughty, she who later styled herself as "queen by right"; embittered because, by her husband's death in a skirmish on the orders of her great rival Marguerite of Anjou, she had been denied the chance ever to be queen.

I, still a very young man, was almost moved to tears, when my ducal brother said those lovely old Anglo-Saxon words: "Till that the death depart us tweyne," even though I was fully aware that this marriage was a dynastic union, a wedding of two great and powerful families, not a sentimental love-match between two burghers or peasants' children. And I wondered if I should ever say those words, or ever mean them. For whilst I was aware of female sexuality and, in a coarse way, felt its allure, I doubted if I could ever feel the kind of courtly love, the depth of passion expressed so feelingly in French poetry by le Duc d'Orleans, or Monsieur Villon, both of whom were still living at that time. But, as I was musing, day-dreaming as I was wont to do as a lad, my Beloved Mother, by whose side I was standing, very near the newly wedded pair, always, despite her ancestry, so much less poetic and more practical than I, nudged me and said in a stage whisper, "She's looking down at us, the Rose of Raby as we used to call her. You can see the resemblance to her brother's son though, when they stand together."

She was referring to Duchess Cecily, by whose side stood foursquare and monumental, her nephew, the great bear of a

43

man most people assumed, with some reason, was the real ruler of England, Richard Neville, Earl of Warwick and Salisbury, the greatest nobleman in the realm. Not as tall as the king but much broader, with magnificent shoulders and ample girth, even in the royal gallery it was uncertain who had the greater presence: Warwick or the king. Not for nothing was Warwick's symbol the famous bear and ragged staff; the staff stood for his phallic masculine power and the bear, well, you just had to look at him. He treated the king, his younger cousin, as a benevolent uncle should, but an uncle who intended always to keep hold of the pretty boy's reins.

***

"The king has granted you the lordship of Holderness, Edward," said my mother.

"Has he?" I said in astonishment.

"Didn't you tell him, John?" said my mother exasperatedly to my brother.

"Well, I... I thought he should be told... by the court," he muttered.

"Am I to have a title of my own at last?"

"Of course, dear," said the duchess. "You have a knighthood."

That was not what I meant.

"Myton and Holderness," said my ducal brother. "They were the original manors granted to our great-great-grandfather, Sir William, Lord Mayor of Kingston upon Hull, who founded our House, and I take it rather badly that they should be alienated from the dukedom..."

"Oh, don't be a fool, Suffolk. It's an honour to the family to have your brother recognised like this, and thank the Lord one of you has some wit… and it isn't you."

"Can't I be a viscount, Mother? I'd much like to be a viscount. Viscount Holderness sounds courtly… and right for the brother of a great duke." I smiled at John; it was always wise to keep him sweet.

"Viscounts and marquesses have been discredited since the days of Richard II, my son."

"Easy for you to say, Mother, as a duchess."

My Beloved Mother sighed, and stared hard at my brother. "Tell him where he is to go, and why."

"Well… you realise, Eddie… because…"

"Christ's wounds, boy, act like the head of the family! The fact is, my son, we have interests to protect in the north. Now, as you know, my side of the family, the Chaucers and Barons de Burghersh, have never been associated with the wild north country—"

My brother interrupted. "Oh really, Mother, your snobbery about the north country… Your ancestors were merchants just the same as Father's…"

"Merchants?" she sniffed. "My grandfather was this kingdom's greatest poet and the Burghersh line of my mother has been landed and gentle since at least the Conquest… Howsomever, it is to protect and preserve the interests of your royal brother-in-law, His Grace…"

"God preserve him," said the duke and I.

"God preserve him," said my mother, "As well as those of our family that you are going to… what is that odd place called? Kingston upon Hull." She spoke the name as if she was eating bat droppings.

"There is a Suffolk Palace there for you to stay in…" John put in, encouragingly.

"Oh yes," said my mother suddenly amicable. "They say it's… habitable. You'll have a lovely time there… And a splendid family church nearby. You like family history…"

"And a *very* pretty river…"

"The River Hull, of course."

"No, Mother, the River Humber, from which our family wealth originally derives…"

"Not *my* wealth or *this* House, I assure you, my sons. And you will have a good opportunity to visit the manors which the king has been generous enough to endow you with. Holdy—"

"Myton and Holderness, Mother, the manors which should never have been alienated…"

"Yes, yes, yes, John. We have taken your point—"

"And spat it out, Johnnie."

"Now don't be disrespectful to your brother, Edward. A fool and a jester he may be…"

"Now really, Mother…"

"I repeat, a fool and a jester he may be, Eddie, but he is nonetheless the head of our House and brother-in-law to the king, and you should always treat him with respect. In public, anyway."

"Yes, Mother."

"Now, you had better go and prepare for your trip to the north. Is your tutor going with you? I think he should."

"My tutor? *Mother*, I am now a knight, dubbed by the hand of our king *himself*. Oh, you should see His Grace, Mother, so fine a man…"

"Hero-worship ill becomes you, Edward, now you are indeed a knight. Maybe you should meet some *women*." My brother's tone was mordant, not brotherly.

"At least I have seen battle, and been bloodied by His Grace's side, while others have lain in ladies' soft beds…"

We glared at each other and John stood. He was now tall, five foot ten inches I should think, and, I couldn't help noticing, quite good-looking, despite the angry lines in his brow. I thought he was about to strike out at me.

"That is enough," said Mother sharply.

John subsided. He always listened to Mother. And, like me, he was essentially a courtly lover, not a fighter.

"Boys, one day, you will be totally alone in this world and brothers-in-law to the king. How will you survive? You must support each other. If you fight, you will be destroyed. Remember your noble father's fate." Her voice cracked momentarily.

"*Mea culpa*, Mother," said John. "We shall always be friends and loving brothers."

His voice as he said it was sincere, but his eyes, as usual, were dull. He was passive, which was one of the few states my brother's comely features could register. He had inherited all my noble father's weakness, little of his charm, and none of his skills.

A short whistled tune came from the doorway.

"*What* is that?" said the B.M.

"Oh… just a message for me, Mother," said my brother, "May I take it?"

The B.M. looked at him hard. "A duke who asks his mother's permission to take a message in his own house is a sorry thing, Edward."

This was a bit harsh as the house definitely belonged to her.

However, John whistled back sheepishly, and his page, a long-haired youth who had been hiding just beyond the doorway pretending not to overhear us, glided over and whispered the message.

"The horse doctor has arrived, Mother, and presents his compliments to Your Ladyship, and I particularly wish to see him about the gelding I am giving to Elizabeth."

One thing John really knew about was horses. His wife — his Plantagenet wife — was quite another thing.

"And how doth the Lady Elizabeth?" asked Mother, searchingly.

"Oh, well, Mother, very well… She is with Duchess Cecily."

Duchess Cecily was, you will remember, the king's formidable mother. She and the B.M. had a healthy respect for each other.

"I trust there is a good reason why she is with the duchess?"

"There *is*, Mother…" My brother almost leered. I was bewildered.

Mother looked flushed. "Because she is…"

"With child, Mother," he said triumphantly.

"Praise be to God, my boy! Why didn't you tell me before?" She kissed John more passionately than I had ever seen her do before. I felt jealous, left out. "Now go and play with your horses. At last, you are doing your duty!"

Brother Duke gave me a self-satisfied look of disdain and sauntered out with his page in tow.

Mother looked at me, was about to speak, bethought herself, then said quietly, "Don't look so surprised, dear boy. While the king remains unmarried, your brother's sons may yet be his heirs; as well as heirs to our House. But let that remain between us."

I was mollified that the B.M.'s political instincts had not been blunted by the prospect of grandchildren.

"Of course, Mother. You know I understand discretion and high politics better than my brother. So, why must I be sent into exile in Hull?"

"My son…" The B.M.'s look was menacing, "While your brother performs his procreative duty, there is no need for *you* to marry… *yet*. But understand these are interesting times. Remember what happened to your noble father? I do." Her voice wavered. "Every day, almost every hour of every day. We must protect the family inheritance. And now we are linked indissolubly with the House of York, we must do everything in our power to keep them on the throne. The northern counties are conservative and many of the gentry have a residual loyalty to the House of Lancaster. We must show them that *our* interest — and *their* interest as our people — lies with York, the dynasty of future days. Henry of Lancaster is not a bad man, Edward, though his treatment of your father was weak and unworthy, but he was a bad king. Which is why we have another. Who is your brother-in-law. And whom you worship."

I opened my mouth, blushing.

"Which is a good thing, Edward. And His Grace *is* very worshipful. Your task in Hull and East Riding is to hold it — firmly — for York… and for De-la-Pole."

I accepted that I had to do my duty. So did my brother John. He and the Lady Elizabeth did theirs nine times. At any rate, it took the pressure off me.

***

Perhaps now it is time, dear readers of the future, for me to formally introduce myself. I am Edward De-la-Pole (or de-la-Pole, it matters not). My House emerged into national prominence from Kingston upon Hull, that important port in the East Riding of Yorkshire, in the latter part of the century before last — that is to say, the fourteenth century of the Common Era. They were vintners and merchants in the city and county of that name who had come from… who knows where. Some say they had originated locally in Wyke or in a village called Ravenserodd. Others — perhaps inspired by the wealth of our family as it grew into the knightly class — said we were descended from the ancient princes of Wales; a most unlikely scenario. Undoubtedly there was a family connection with one John Rottenherring of Ravenserodd — no doubt a fish merchant — whose grandfather, it has been rumoured, gloried in the name of Levi Rottenherring. To me this seems evidence that, in spite of King Edward I's expulsion of the Jews from his kingdom in 1290, some vestige of the Hebrews remained in the north of England to add that tincture of the ancient and noble race which has resurrected itself in me.

***

It was a cool, breezy autumn day and the brownish leaves crackled and scudded along the half-baked mud of Lowgate. Suffolk Palace, hardly palatial by London standards but resplendent with its gatehouse and gardens running down to the Humber amongst the solid but much smaller merchants' houses of the business quarter, matched only by the lovely Gothic tower and tracery of St. Mary's, stood handsome and imposing if a little seedy due to recent decades of neglect. So named after the earldom — then dukedom — bestowed on the upwardly (and southernly) mobile De-la-Poles, it was quite old-fashioned and a little rundown in comparison with the family's grand London residence, a ducal, quasi-royal mansion fronting that even greater arterial waterway, the Thames. But — as the family, deep in their Yorkshire bones never forgot — Humberside, not Suffolk, enshrined their roots.

Edward didn't like coming up to Hull — who the hell ever has? — but as a politician playing for the highest stakes, he knew it was an occasional necessity. As younger brother to the second Duke of Suffolk — *and why Suffolk, for Jesu's sake?* he thought, bingeing on dried apricocks and cashew nuts which he feared would cause him to lose that slim build that had made him so appealing a figure to both men and women — Edward, as Lord of Holderness and various other surrounding manors, knew perfectly well, though now empurpled by the golden threads of Plantagenista — out of the marshy sludge of Humber they had emerged and if, by some quirk of history, they should happen to be attainted by some future Parliament and written out of history, then to it they could yet return. Something almost as catastrophic had befallen his great-grandfather — chancellor to King Richard II before his headlong fall — and should it happen again, the family, the dynasty, would need desperately to have strong roots up here from which to draw renewed strength…

No. Though I have always, like a troubadour or chronicler, observed my own historic life, I cannot write of it as an observer. I have been a prince, a player in the drama, a minor one, it's true, but with intimations of greatness; so that now, with the turning of fortune's wheel, to be a mere observer of these powerful histories is not for me. I must resume my own voice, tired of it as I have become…

Suffolk Palace was large and habitable but lacking in comforts and growing threadbare; no member of the family had there resided for ten years or more. For a while, my noble father was the king's chief minister, why should he care to inspect the outer fringes of his great estates? Nor did the family much wish to be reminded of its humble origins in Kingston upon Hull.

But there I was, and would walk from the palace down to the wharfs by the side of the River Humber and watch the sturdy local husbandmen loading vast bales of wool onto the great barges, and unloading spices sent here across the kingdoms and cities of Europe from the silk road far off in the east, and purple wines from the vineyards of Gascony. We might have lost those southern lands of Aquitaine to the French king — and that was well before my noble father came to power — but trade between our merchants must still go on. And many of those casks of wine were bound for Suffolk Palace; even if they had not been, I made sure they were. For I was flattered to discover that, in this part of England, my word — as the brother of *the* De-la-Pole — was law. For there, they still remembered my ancestor Sir Michael, the famed Lord Mayor of Hull who made his fortune locally and then bank-rolled the Scottish campaigns of the great King Edward III. Why do they always think it is the Jews whose so-called usury provides the funds for such campaigns? A usury, of course, to which they have no alternative, denied as they are every other role in society. Unless, of course, there was the blood of our saviour (as I used to call him) in the veins of those shrewd merchants whose forebears were once called Rottenherring?

My rabbi companion laughs and tells me I have a Jewish nose, to which I respond it is a Norman nose borrowed from our Plantagenet cousins!

And from the wharfs came fabrics too and cloaks and tapestries. Oh yes, the north is not quite such a wilderness as you southerners may imagine. And these I also appropriated to my house, beginning to make it a palace once again, and imitate and surpass the beauties of my Beloved Mother's house at Ewelme too. I also did my duty. As lord of these manors, I enforced the laws of regal, young King Edward, my adored monarch; or rather, I provided some muscle for the local Justices of the Peace, officers who had embodied the king's law since the reign of the late lamented King Richard II. Truth to tell, I had more fun sending Quidnunc — a mere stripling then of three and twenty, who had been my personal varlet almost since my birth — out to the nearby towns and villages, to Beverley and Myton and to the little hamlets that pepper the vale of Holderness to seek out the handsome products of local crafts and trades to adorn the palace and myself.

There was one occasion when Q whispered to me — in his almost obscenely intimate way — that a large, plain coffer had arrived in the port of Hull apparently consigned by a rich but less than worshipful York merchant, which, rumour whispered, contained a large and very remarkable piece of craftsmanship intended for a great Italian prince. This called for immediate action by the local lord: me. Calling for two of my grooms — sturdy Yorkshire lads both — I immediately rode down to the wharf (it was only a short walk, but arriving on horseback always gives added authority) and rode up just as the coffer was about to be loaded onto the rather handsome carack which was waiting patiently by the wharf.

"Whose is this?" I demanded.

Three local sailors and two rancid-looking foreigners looked at each other and stammered.

"Well? Duties are owed to our Lord King on all works of craftsmanship leaving the kingdom. So, whose is it?"

They looked at each other again and the senior mariner said, with sour reluctance, "It is *yours*, my lord."

The lads lugged it back to the old palace and, opening the deceptively plain box, we found a most extraordinary object. There stood a huge urn almost as high as a man, with three large funnels sweeping upwards from a broad base all in white richly glazed maiolica with wondrous and complicated figured patterns most delicately painted all over it. It was magnificent and, as far as I then knew, unique. A letter of consignment also in the coffer did indeed state that this *objet d'art* was crafted to the order of Cosimo de' Medici, at that time the richest man in Christendom and de facto ruler of Florence, that fabled jewel of Italian culture.

At that moment, I conceived an overwhelming ambition to visit Florence and all the great Italian cities — Rome, Milan, even Naples — and realised, for the first time in my life, that being the younger son of a great duke could be to my advantage. Unlike my dull elder brother, I had no need to stay tethered like a bullock to my lands and houses, and produce heirs. I could travel instead like my grandfather, Sir Thomas Chaucer, who amassed great honour and wealth as a herald and ambassador, going abroad to charm, negotiate, and sometimes lie, on behalf of his monarch. So, of course, did my noble father, but with less success, I fear. How I longed to visit the fabled Italian city of Florentia and deliver this lovely masterpiece into the hands of the great merchant prince (not unlike my own De-la-Pole ancestors). But what precisely was its provenance? I had no idea. Until, that is, thirty and more years later when first I arrived in the kingdom of Aragon and kicking my bruised heels, an impatient petitioner at the court of King Ferran — yet another court, for me, of broken dreams — there, in the courtyard of the palace of the King-Counts of Barcelona, I saw two such wonderful urns fashioned exactly as mine had been in white ceramic and similarly decorated with abstract and lovely patterns. These were clearly not works of our own Gothic Christian craftsmanship but created in the style of the very finest Mussulman artistry, by those Saracens who had once ruled so great a part of the kingdoms of Iberia.

But to return to my story: my dream was personally to present this beautiful piece of art to Duke Cosimo, its rightful owner. But as that clearly would not be possible in the near future, I decided… to keep it. Come now, wouldn't you? And there it stood in the solar of my home. First in Hull, then later in my London house: The Holderness on Upper Thames Street, conveniently near to St. Paul's and almost next door to Baynard's Castle where our late King Richard often visited his mother, the crabbed old Dowager Duchess of York — a delight for all whom I invited there to see and enjoy. And thus, piece by piece and month by month, was my empty and old-fashioned manor house transformed into the elegant and well-furnished princely palace it was meant to be.

But I longed for company, preferably noble, preferably male, but as neither was on hand, on occasion I would send Q out to scour the waterfront and send me a local strumpet to satisfy a young man's needs and give my large and lonely bed some human warmth. And there were times when Q returned alone — perhaps intentionally — and I would order him to share my big bed of estate — he being then a comely youth if a little effeminate. And if some things happened and fluids spilt, well, who could complain or even know of it? To a young lord, full of spunk, the need for human warmth is all, and one carnal orifice is very much like another.

Another frustration was that there was little chance for me to improve upon my soldierly skills — so recently first tested on the field of Towton — so I would summon up the local lads — both serfs from the villages and sons of the local franklin class — and marshal them on the flat dreary vale of Holderness to fight mock battles, while I rode up and down on the best horse I could muster, playing at being a general, while at least maintaining my knightly skills. I would even set up a tilting yard where I would tilt at the ring while gawped at (admiringly? jeeringly?) by the local lads and wenches. But as there was no one of my rank to tilt against, this was little more than exercise without the necessary pricks of rivalry and competition so necessary to the stripling knight.

There was, of course, the occasional courtesy visit paid on me by the few Yorkshire knights and esquires of our affinity who farmed their small estates on the flat wold of East Riding — fattening up the sheep who generously donated their wool to be transported from the port of Hull to the great Staple of Calais; now already the last stronghold of our once great Angevin empire in France.

In Hull, they speak a local dialect, of course, which is not even the same as that spoken by the peasantry of the East Riding villages which lie close to it. Hull is *peculiar*, because stuck out on a limb, not very far from Spurn Point, is that excrescence of land on which Henry Bolingbroke landed returning from his exile in France in 1399, ostensibly claiming only his dukedom of Lancaster, but then having gathered massive support from the nobility, grabbed the crown from the vain head of Richard II. Yes, we Hull and East Riding folk have been at the forefront of English history for a century or more. Yet Hull feels cut off, being better linked by seaways to other north European ports — Bruges, Gothenberg, Muscovy even — than by roadways to the other towns of England. Evidently, the townsfolk — whether franklin or varlet or whatever falls between — don't speak the half-Frenchified, Latinised English which people of quality have spoken since my great-grandsire delighted the court of Richard II with his lays of the Canterbury pilgrims or of Troylus and the fair Cryseyde. It was the bard who placed the seal of his usage on south-eastern Anglo-Saxon, seasoned and refined with Latin and French, as the language of court and government, though for reasons of policy it had already begun to be adopted under the third Edward — the one whose fecundity in fathering seven sons caused all this damned dynastic trouble. What they speak in Hull is a harsher, more Viking-influenced Anglo-Saxon harking back, I guess, to the ancient days of the Danelaw. They call their children "bains" (as, I am told, do the Scots, but without adding the rolled Scots' "r" in the middle); they call stinking fish — which oftentimes distempered the wharfside — "manky"; and, correctly, speak the name of their city, without an aspirate, to rhyme with "bull", rather than with "cull" or "dull". They also interject "like" at the ends of sentences for no apparent reason ("Will you walk this way, my lord, like?").

In spite of this, I was pleased when resident there to patronise the local grammar school, where bright young scholars were schooled in the rudiments of Latin, the catechism and arithmetic; some of whom later came into the service of my family or of the king. Of course, the local grammar school is less famous than its much older sister at Beverley, the nearest country town, about ten miles from the walls of Hull, which is home to an educational foundation dating from the seventh century of the Christian era. The north of England is far from being the unlettered desert that most southerners would have you believe.

In those years of my distant youth, I was often filled with melancholia, feeling that my days were wasted in Hull, when I could be doing knightly service for my adored king. On some days, I dreamt of jumping into a carack standing in the harbour and taking ship to the Low Countries or the Nordic lands or Prussia, where, a hundred years before, Henry Bolingbroke had gone on Crusade. I knew my noble father, before his terrible demise, had negotiated the famous marriage treaty with King Charles of France and the illustrious King René of Naples and Jerusalem (not that he ever ruled either), which brought the beautiful, headstrong fifteen-year-old girl called Marguerite of Anjou to her fateful, finally tragic marriage to the luckless Henry. I knew I was born to be a diplomatist and not to maunder my days away in the dreary northlands of England. And yet, as I look back now, thirty years on, I have nostalgic dreams of Hull and Humberside where at least I was respected, comfortable, and learnt so much about governance and men. And about my family's roots.

I learnt a lot about all of these things from a young man whom Q had found scavenging amongst the heaped-up coffers, bales and barrels on the wharves late one night. True, he looked a low varlet, but Q, with his remarkable eye for detail, even in pitch darkness with just a flaming torch to guide him, had noted his handsome face and sturdy figure and dragged him, resentful, to my solar late one night.

The lad was about seventeen, not much younger than I, with long unkempt red hair and the beginnings of a reddish beard. He had strong, manly features which I took to be Nordic, presuming him a descendant of the Vikings who had occupied this country long before the Conquest. He was wearing little more than rags and his tattered peasant tunic revealed a superbly muscled upper chest and shoulders. Q knew me only too well. The boy's handsome face was marred only by that resentful, angry sneer that teenagers so often hide behind.

"What's your name, lad?"

"Malcolm."

"Malcolm, *what*?" hissed Q, prodding the lad with a horsewhip. He always carries the right equipment.

"Malcolm, *my lord*," the boy blurted with heavy sarcasm.

"Quidnunc, leave us."

"But, my lord, the boy may be feral."

"Go!"

He withdrew, deprived of his vicarious excitement.

"How does a young man in Hull get a name like Molco?"

"*Malcolm,* my lord. My mother was Scots."

I had heard of various Macbeths and Malcolms up there in the wild northern kingdom.

"By Jesu, Malcolm, you're a good-looking lad but are you strong? I need strong young men to serve me, and King Edward."

"Aye, my lord."

"How strong?"

He flexed the upper arm muscles in his right arm. I could smell his rank armpits. I was not complaining.

There was a heavy, a very heavy, sword hanging on the wall behind him, which was a family heirloom. It was the sword my uncle Michael, the third Earl of Suffolk, had wielded at Agincourt, where he had perished, to the great honour of the family, in the service of the renowned Harry V. The blade was still encrusted with the blood of Frenchmen and — possibly — of Uncle Michael. The hilt was encrusted with rubies. I had never been able to lift it.

"If you can lift that sword behind you — a sword used by my uncle to kill damned Frenchmen in battle — I will take you into my service. And train you to become a man-at-arms in the service of our king."

It was a high-risk stratagem: he might have used the damn thing to kill me and rob the house. But the look that came into his brilliant blue eyes was one of wonder and healthy excitement.

He turned round, steadied himself and coolly lifted the sword off the wall and, like a courtier, held it firmly, blade upward, in front of his face. Then he laid it respectfully at my feet and looked me steadily in the eyes.

"If it please you, my lord, I would like to serve the king…
and you," he added suddenly bashful.

I took his hands in mine.

"You are a good boy, Malcolm, as I thought, and you will
be a good liegeman of King Edward and of mine."

And he was.

***

Some months later — as Malcolm continued to grow in my
confidence and alongside Quidnunc's jealousy — the young
man said to me one morning as he was holding my shirt, having
warmed it in the usual way by wearing it for a few minutes
(well, a nobleman does it for the king, so why not a trusted
servant for me?), "I met an old townsman who fought with your
uncle at Agincourt, my lord, who says he knows a lot about the
history of your family. Shall I bring him to you?"

I was sceptical.

"How old is this greybeard? That's nearly fifty years ago,
Mal."

"Well, sir, he *thinks* he's about eighty-five but his great-
grandson — he's a pal of mine, sir — thinks he's even older
than that."

"What? A likely tale, Mal."

The lad's face, as he put on my shoes, looked disappointed.

"Bring him to see me anyway. Not today. After hunting,
I'll be far too tired and you can pour me a nice scented bath.
Bring him tomorrow, after breakfast."

"Aye, sir."

I liked to see the lad happy. His smile lit up the day.

The next morning, he brought the old retainer to me. He looked like Methuselah, with his wispy white hair, a stick and a very small lad to lean on.

"God be with you, old fellow. Prithee take a seat."

"If Your Lordship please, I never sat before Earl Michael and I won't sit before Your Lordship, so please you."

"So, you were at Agincourt with my uncle Michael, were you? Tell me about the battle."

"Nay, my lord, I wasn't at Agincourt. I was never out of England. Always serving Your Lordship's house."

I was getting bored with this and began rereading a letter on my reading stand from the B.M. where she told me about the birth of John and Elizabeth's second son who, with the king's permission, was to be christened Edmund. My presence at the ceremony would not be required...

"He was a good lord to his people was your uncle, my lord, and very straight and true... Different like from his father, the first Earl Michael, the one that was chancellor to the late lamented King Richard. God rest his soul..."

My grandfather, the first Earl of Suffolk, had died in 1389.

"You remember my *grandfather*?"

"Oh aye, may it please Your Lordship. I was taken into his service as a very young lad... I was a pretty lad and he was very fond of me was Earl Michael..." He looked directly at me. It was impudent, but I got the message.

"How nice. Did you leave the city?"

"Oh yes, my lord, he... found me here on one of his visits to the palace and took a fancy to me and took me as his... page, you see, sir. and he took me down to London, sir, in the mid-eighties when he was chancellor to good King Richard, sir… I saw King Richard, sir, and, saving your presence, sir, he was a bit mad, sir, at times, sir. And your grandfather took the blow, sir, when things went badly wrong… He was a fine-looking man your granddaddy, sir, not unlike yourself, sir, if you'll pardon me. And so was your other granddaddy Master Chaucer, the poet, my lord…"

This was becoming rather more than real; sir-real, you might call it.

"You remember Geoffrey Chaucer, my great-grandfather, old man?"

"Oh yes, sir, he was a great man at King Richard's court. With such presence, sir, such nobility. More nobility than the nobility you might say, sir, if you'll forgive me."

"Bring this old man some hippocras! This is remarkable and I insist you sit on that stool. Bring it nearer, boy."

"As you wish, my lord. I really loved your grandfather, sir, though he wasn't always kind, my lord. He was like the wind. When he blue cold, you got out of his way. But when he blew hot… he was a wonderful, worshipful lord, sir."

There were tears in his eyes.

"He died in exile in Paris, sir… I wanted to go with him, sir, but he sent me back to 'ull, my lord, on a whim. He was blowing cold that day, you see…"

He went into a reverie, which I didn't like to disturb. And he had sent me into one of my own.

Then he said, "And there was a ring, my lord, a ring he gave me in trust for his sons. But I never gave it to them, my lord, and my conscience is playing me up in my great age so here, my lord…" He produced from a rather festering leather pouch, an ethereally beautiful gold ring with an enormous ruby clasped in place by a golden hand. "It belongs to you, my lord. It had come from his father, Sir William, who founded the De-la-Pole fortunes, my lord, and didn't he have his troubles with old King Edward…"

"I thank you, good old man." I searched around the solar. "Take this bag of crowns and I will see to it that you and your family never go hungry. This is beautiful…"

And it truly was.

"One other thing, my friend. Did you ever know where or whom Sir William got the ring from originally?"

He smiled; he still had quite a few teeth. He sipped the hippocras contentedly. I only served the best.

"Well… if Your Lordship's grandfather is to be believed — and he wasn't always — Sir Michael had been given it by *his* grandmother. She was an old Jewlady…"

"What?" This was not welcome news.

"She was an old Jewlady called Rifka Rottenherring — they were in the fish business, you see, from Hamburg or Gothenberg or someplace overseas — and she told him this was an old family heirloom that one day would belong to a king. Earl Michael — the one who was chancellor, you remember? — told me he had thought about giving it to King Richard, but then thought better of it. He was right, don't you think, my lord? Seeing how kings have treated your noble family…"

He sighed a great sigh, so did I, not believing — or wishing to believe — the latter part of his story. There have been no Jews in England — at least, legally — since the time of King Edward I who expelled them. I had never met one and considered them to be unreliable, even devilish, alien heretics. To be told I might be descended from one of them was an unpleasant shock. But it also inspired a frisson of excitement.

I looked down at the ring. It looked bigger and darker. I quickly put it into the inner pocket of my doublet.

"Thank you, my friend." I called for Malcolm. "Malcolm. See to it that this good old man and his family get food and coals and whatever they need every month from my cellars. He has done me and our family good service."

When the old man had left, I turned to Malcolm. "An interesting old fellow. But you never told me his name."

"Rottenherring, my lord. Alfred Rottenherring."

***

It was around this time — or was it on a later visit to that wonderful metropolis of Kingston upon Dull? I seemed to spend the first half of the 1460s sitting up there waiting for a call to serve my king — that a messenger rode through the rather handsome gates of Hull, at the end of Whitefriargate, not very far from my increasingly well-adorned palace, wearing the tabard of a king's messenger and announcing loudly that he had brought a letter for me. Howsomever, I soon discovered the letter was not from the king or his council at Westminster, not from either of the king's royal brothers, nor even from the royal deputy in York. No, it had come from the far north of the kingdom, almost on the dangerous borderlands with Scotland. For reasons you will later understand, I have preserved this letter and indeed have it before me on its crushed and crumpled vellum, written in a florid, fine Italian hand, which I came to know so well. Here it is:

To His Grace's trusty and well-beloved knight, Sir Edward De-la-Pole, Lord of Myton and Holderness and brother to my Lord Duke of Suffolk, greetings.

I am commanded by our liege lord King Edward, the fourth of that name, to order you, sir, to join me and His Grace's army in the county of Northumberland with all your following and affinity that can be summarily mustered in East Riding of the county of York and to make post-haste to the environs of Bamburgh Castle there to give aid and sustenance to His Grace's loyal forces in the siege of said castle and by all means to capture, disempower and extirpate the vile usurper Henry of Lancaster, formerly styling himself Henry VI, now being protected by the traitorous forces in command of said castle and wickedly and treacherously refusing to submit to the king's loyal liegemen and I hereby summon you in the king's name to answer to his command on your life honour and fealty given in haste in the third regnal year of King Henry (sic) near Bamburgh in the county of Northumberland under my seal as the king's deputy in the northern counties.

Anthony Lord Scales.

My immediate reaction to this turgid, importunate and alarming missive was unhappy and distrustful. Who is this Lord Scales? I snorted. And how dare he presume to send *me* orders?

I shouted for Quidnunc who even then made it his business to know everything worth knowing about everyone worth knowing, so that I did not need to.

"Who is this Anthony Lord Scales who has the audacity, like Ajax at Troy, to send me orders in the king's name?"

"Scales, Scales…" He pretended he needed time to ponder this. "Well, my lord, there was a wedding some time ago between the heiress of Lord Scales and this Anthony. He is a Woodville, sir, or Wydville as some men prefer to say it and perhaps more properly because—"

"Woodville, Wydville… Fuck me, or rather fuck you, Quidnunc, these Wydville are, by our lady, Lancastrians, the varlets. Which might explain his tell-tale error in his last paragraph where he speaks of King *Henry's* regnal year. This is a trick, Q, to lure me up to Northumberland of all the Godless places and leave the port of Hull unmanned and unprotected for them to grab. They might even bring that bitch Margaret of Anjou back into this kingdom by ship with her little whelp. We're not falling prey to that calamity. I shall write forthwith to my Lord of Warwick to know the mind of the council in this matter… and to my Lady Mother for her guidance…"

"Ah, Your Lordship's Blessed Mother. There is no one in Christendom who can proffer wiser counsel to my lord…" And Quidnunc reverently bowed his head.

I am never sure when Q is being sarcastic, but, in my haste, I let it pass and the urgent letters were soon despatched. Meanwhile, I waited anxiously, but determined not to fall into this Lancastrian trap. I did not wish to lose my head while not yet twenty years of age. I *did* wish to impress His Grace, my beloved, golden king, with his loyal knight's intelligence and strength.

I felt very complacent in the ensuing few days, at not having fallen into this treasonous trap; though there were several times when, as he was serving my hippocras and sweetmeats or preparing my perfumed evening bath, I detected a strangely sardonic expression on Quidnunc's face as his eyes avoided mine. But a young lord does not care to understand what's in the cunning mind of his varlet, even — or especially — one as preening and precious as Q.

Within days, my B.M.'s magnificent messenger service, riding post-haste and exhausting several poor nags, had brought me a characteristically strong response, which I read first eagerly then with increasing nervousness.

My son Holderness (it read — the B.M. did not do Christian names in letters),

Is Kingston upon Hull so many hundred leagues from Westminster that news has not yet penetrated the ears and head of our son — or of his household — that our Lord King is wed? The marriage remains secret and, if you value your life and mine, shall remain so until it pleases His Grace to make it otherwise. It is bruited about that the lords of the council, even the greatest earl in the realm, were not consulted and have been taken unawares. That earl, as you ought but it may hap do not know, has been in Paris treating with the French king of high policy for a mooted marriage treaty between the two Crowns (a development which your late noble father would have much to say upon) but which now are, I wean, in… well, you may see what they are in, and what may come of it. See, but do not say.

More to your question: the earl himself has now gone north with his own retainers and other loyal forces to reinforce the siege of Bamburgh Castle in which the idiot Harry of Lancaster may be closeted. So, be ready and quick to serve your king by hastening to add the full muster of our followers in the north country to join my good Lord of Warwick forthwith.

And one more piece of news. The lady, with whom it is said His Grace has been joined in holy wedlock, is a lovely and most worshipful widow, by name Dame Elizabeth Grey, nee Wydville, and her worshipful and noble brother is Anthony Wydville, Lord Scales. That was no trap, you prattling boy; the letter was a royal command, sent through His Grace's (as yet unacknowledged) beau-frère, Sir Anthony Wydville. Answer his summons as fast as you may or you will be a poltroon as big as your ducal brother. Long live King Edward.

Your *Mother*,

Dame Alice Chaucer, Duchess of Suffolk.

I glared at Quidnunc who had brought me the letter to gauge his reaction but his face was a picture of respectful subservience.

"You knew of this, Quidnunc?"

"Of what, my lord?"

"Of what my honoured mother speaketh?"

"Of what is that, my lord?"

"Of the king's marriage, of course, you lordswike!"

"The king's marriage, my lord? This is good news. Who is our new queen, my lord?"

I glared at him. I knew he was lying but his expression was a picture of cunning innocence.

"Bugger off!"

"My lord."

I called him back. "We must prepare to depart Hull as soon as possible. And we need to send out letters to all our nearest neighbours, Sir Eric, Dame Jane and her sons, the Prior of Beverley, all our local affinity. And—"

"Yes, my lord. The letters are prepared, just awaiting my lord's command."

"Oh… good. Send them out post-haste, Quidnunc."

"At your command, sir. And will my lord be requiring my presence at his side?"

"No, I think not, Q. I don't see you as a man-at-arms. Do you?" I smiled mischievously.

"As Your Lordship pleases."

"Send Malcolm to me. He will be my squire. We need to talk weapons."

"My lord…" Q was outraged. As I intended. His outrage always amused me. Still does. "The boy is not even a gentleman. Sir, as the brother of a duke, the brother-in-law of the *king*…"

"Don't teach me my knightly duty, varlet… If I do it, it must be right…"

His eyes shot jealousy, but he withdrew.

Almost at once, Malcolm ran in. "Forgive me, my lord…"

"Forgiven, as you were sent for."

His handsome, innocent face registered surprise. "No, I wasn't. I just got a message. The king's arriving in three hours. He's coming 'ere to restock and meet his ships and then we're all off to the siege, my lord. Awesome, isn't it, my lord?"

Malcolm was the only one of my servants I would allow to speak to me like that. Except that I was so shocked I hardly noticed.

"The king? Here? Oh, sweet Jesus!"

"Worry ye not, sir. I'll speak to Q and the chef de… you know, and we'll have everything ship-shape before the ship arrives. Can I come with you to meet the king, sir? Is he as tall and beautiful as they say, sir?"

"As beautiful as Helios, the Greek god of the sun, my boy! Get everything moving. Speak to Q and the chef, and yes, you can be at my side when we meet His Grace."

By sundown on that day — with Quidnunc, Malcolm and the rest of my small household working like slaves — I had assembled the cream of our local affinity, with their retainers: about thirty men-at-arms with fifty assorted foot soldiers, mostly archers. Most of the former were in our family livery of blue and gold. I was painfully aware it wasn't an army, but it was a contribution to one, and I expected a similar number to join us in Hull over the next two or three days. I had them drawn up in ranks just outside the heavy wooden Myton Gate of the town — named for my own manor, to which it led. Thank be to Heaven it was night time. Under the flaming torches Q had strategically positioned, our little force looked almost impressive. At least the horses were healthy. I knew old Sir Gerald, my mentor at Towton, would be in the king's train, approaching Hull, with more retainers to strengthen our little force. I also knew that the B.M. would, of course, have assembled a stronger force from the family lands in East Anglia and around her own demesne at Ewelme in the county of Oxford, but that my brother Duke John would bestir himself from siring issue on the king's sister I would not wager a groat.

I was nervous, and very excited, to be receiving the king on my home territory having seen him received with pomp and great humility by the burghers of York the day after Towton — a reception prepared in even greater haste. The worshipful Lord Mayor of Hull was fussing about in his furred mayoral robe. I was in chainmail, helped into it by Malcolm, of course, with a tailored tunic in bright vermilion. I looked sharp.

As custodian of the city, I took precedence over the lord mayor, not to mention, though I often did, being His Grace's brother-in-law. But the mayor of Kingston upon Hull was also Admiral of the Humber and he was scared almost witless that some mishap would befall the king's ship, as it made its way up the Humber estuary to meet us.

"We should 'ave barges available for the royal party and we don't have nothing suitable. If on'y we'd 'ad more notice, Lord Edward. I 'ope you'll point out to His Grace how cunningly we've maintained the walls. Give us some credit for that, my lord."

"We can share the credit for that, Lord Mayor, after all—"

Then suddenly, there were horses' hooves and two outriders almost upon us, shouting, "The king approacheth."

"God save King Edward," I shouted.

The lads took up the shout. Soon we were all hoarse and almost out of breath. The royal party was further off than I had realised.

Then, a few minutes later, there he was: the sun in splendour, Edward of York, King of England, tall and unmistakable, on his great white war horse. On his right rode his pretty, over-dressed brother George Clarence, and on his right a solid, very respectable lord I didn't recognise.

Q, materialising out of nowhere and reading my thoughts, whispered, "That's Lord Hastings. An intimate chamberlain to His Grace."

A tight group of lords and knights were in close attendance, one of them holding the royal banner, which fluttered above him in the evening breeze. It was October after all. How I longed to enter that charmed circle. This could be my chance.

There were men-at-arms and foot soldiers behind, but not more than ten score. The rest of the royal forces had clearly gone ahead — with the unknown man who had written to me: Anthony Wydville, Lord Scales — and were already laying siege to Bamburgh.

As they rode up, I noticed Hastings whispering in the king's ear. He was, it seems, His Grace's Q.

"De-la-Pole, forgive us for arriving at such short notice. We have need of our big siege guns stored here. I shall take them by ship."

"Your Grace." I was kneeling, bemused and panicking. What siege engines? I grasped at a nearby straw. "The lord mayor here is my murenger. He does a praiseworthy job on the walls, sire, and on the… siege engines."

I looked to the lord mayor, also kneeling, to my right, imploringly. He shot me a withering glance.

"Your Grace's city of Kingston upon Hull with its walls and three great bombards are ever at Your Grace's command."

I exhaled — having almost expired. Well, you can't think of everything.

"I thank you for your travail, gentlemen." He paused a moment, not yet urging us to rise. "You have had missives, De-la-Pole, from my good brother Scales, already in the field?"

"I have, Your Grace," I replied, trying not to sound sour.

"And from the Earl of Warwick?" His voices hardened slightly as he said this.

"No, Your Grace."

Again, he missed a beat. "I know you are liegemen of the House of York." The voice became very hard. "But are you liegemen for *me*?"

"Sire, we offer our bodies and souls for *you*," I replied and soon all around had taken up my words. I felt distressed by His Grace's doubt of us. But looking up, I saw his usual sunny demeanour had returned.

"Of course, you are. Arise, my trusty friends, arise."

"Your Grace will dine and honour our little house with his presence tonight?" I asked trying not to sound callow.

The king's broad, flat handsome face put us all at our ease. "If you will forgive us for our hasty arrival, yes. I will lodge with you, De-la-Pole, along with Hastings. My brother Clarence with you, Lord Mayor."

The lord mayor looked flattered, Clarence disdainful.

Greatly excited, I guided His Grace, with Hastings and three or four of his closest household knights, as we processed through the city, down Whitefriargate, past the house of the eponymous monks — all seven of whom were kneeling and chanting blessings as we passed along — up to our beautiful St. Mary's, the parish church with our family crest and livery in its painted windows, at the corner of Lowgate, opposite my much embellished Suffolk Palace; a home I recreated, since stolen by the Tudor usurpers. How glad I was then to have had the chance and time to make our manor house suitable to host a king.

But what were we to offer our glorious king for supper?

Trumpets were sounded as we entered the Great Chamber. Quidnunc appeared and handed me a bowl of water, and Hastings a fine linen napkin. We both knelt and presented them to the king, who laved his hands, and invited us to join him at the High Table. One of His Grace's ushers acted as his trencherman, cutting up the fine white bread for him to eat his meal on. Meanwhile, Q had rustled up at least twelve dishes — I rarely dined on more than six — to offer His Highness. One magnificent meaty concoction was placed immediately before him.

His Grace looked serious. "Ah... I was hoping for a healthy dish of your famous Hull cod, De-la-Pole. But I see your steward puts before me alows of beef..."

There was a moment of awed silence. Q had hoisted us on his own petard. I felt sick.

Then the king winked at Hastings and both roared with laughter.

"Your face, Eddie... Alows are my favourite dish..."

He was served a generous portion and tasted a surprisingly delicate mouthful. "And a splendid stuffing. Bloody good marrow... And just the right soupcon of ginger. You have excellent cooks, De-la-Pole. Hull is civilised by your presence."

Q had triumphed. I would not forget this. Nor would he.

I bowed low as His Grace served me a portion from his own trencher. Eating from the king's plate: paradise. Now, at last, I felt like a royal brother-in-law.

"And what is this... greenery?"

"That, sire, is broccoli. A vegetable from Italy. I pray it please Your Grace?"

The king glared at me with mock solemnity as he picked up a handful, but was pre-empted by his usher, who made to taste it.

Hastings said, "For your safety, sire," but the king brushed him away.

"We fear no danger in the home of our kinsman... And it tastes... interesting."

We laughed at His Grace's curious expression as it dissolved into a look of bliss. King Edward enjoyed his food.

We ended the meal with a course of five diverse English cheeses, which are, of course, the best in the world.

Hastings and I then led the king ceremonially back to the "state bedchamber" as it became for the night — my own chamber, of course, into which some of the finest pieces of my collection of curiosities had been moved for His Grace to enjoy. My spacious bathtub had been prepared with lovely Turkey carpets adorning the sides. Q and I bowed low as Hastings helped the king remove his garments revealing manly shoulders, small brown nipples set on exquisite pectoral muscles, a broad almost hairless chest and a flat stomach. Hanging below was a magnificent set of male equipment, with a truly royal cock, the size of a splendidly ripe English pear. His Grace could certainly satisfy the many damsels he was famed for bedding.

I also noticed — it was a large birthmark — a big, black mole on the king's right thigh, surrounded by several smaller ones. It was the one ugly thing on an otherwise superbly beautiful body. At the time, it held no other significance for me.

He stood before us proudly. The king, I mean, as his cock was mainly flaccid, though a little pert at our clear admiration.

Both Hastings and Q lunged for the two huge ewers of steaming water standing by the tub.

Hastings growled to Q, "*I* pour the king's bath."

Q made a pouty mouth, as he stepped aside and handed me a ceramic bowl filled with fine spices; the scent of cloves was especially rich.

"Come, Eddie, are you going to share those delicious herbs or eat them?" the king laughed.

I scattered them in the bath as His Grace stepped in; Hastings poured more warm water over his shapely back.

"This will be my last bath before the campaign starts in earnest, gentlemen, so I give ye thanks."

When His Grace had sufficiently enjoyed the bath, Q presented a large mantle to me, and I to Hastings to wrap around the king as he rose from the water.

Q whispered something to me.

"Perhaps before Your Grace is ready to withdraw, my servant might tempt you with a little local entertainment..."

Q beckoned to a fine, buxom girl of about sixteen or seventeen years standing at the door with a knowing look. He had been keeping this one up his sleeve.

"Ah, gentlemen, would you tempt me from my betrothed with this lovely devil? But then, my lady is not here and, as Hastings knows well, if I pass one day without carnal congress, my head aches terribly the next. So, how could I say no?"

Q and I bowed out as the king carried the girl bodily within the heavy bed curtains. Hastings would be sleeping, as he often did, on a fairly comfortable pallet we had placed for him at the foot of the bed. And, as I withdrew, I had a sudden image of my honoured father sleeping at the foot of the fallen king, Henry of Lancaster, as he repeatedly failed to impregnate his young French wife. *Sic transit gloria mundi.*

The next morning, we prepared for the king's departure. We were all lined up on the quayside ready to follow His Grace onto the royal ship when he turned to me and said,

"De-la-Pole — Eddie — we shall depart with the armoury. Take the land route with your men. Meet us at Bamburgh. If you arrive before us, give ear to Anthony Wydville. He is leading the siege, with my Lord of Warwick, of course."

Why did he always hark back to Wydville? Had he really married the man's sister? Was he the new favourite?

"And, Sir Edward, you have our thanks a thousandfold for your loyal and hearty hospitality." He smiled and the royal charisma flowed over me.

The royal demi-god turned to go… and then, as if casually, turned back towards me. He spoke more intimately, just for my ears.

"Eddie…" He paused, conspiratorially. "I have heard there was a ring, a rare and lovely ring, a great balas ruby set in gold, given to your great-grandfather Sir Michael De-la-Pole, by my own great forefather, King Edward III. They tell me it is to be returned one day to the true king, and as I am he, do you have the ring?"

It was one of those moments when you have to make a fateful decision in the flash of a blade.

"I regret no, sire. The king is the owner of all my gems." And I showed His Grace a magnificent deep green emerald ring which I removed from my right middle finger and, kneeling, presented to him. I had recently purchased it on that very wharf from a Netherlandish trader who had bought it, so he said, in Venice whence it had been carried from the Indies.

"Ah, no, De-la-Pole, that is not the ring. Have back your emerald. No matter. Be at Bamburgh within three days." His eyes flashed a sudden menace. Did he disbelieve my disavowal of the balas ruby?

But a voice had told me it was not for him.

ה (hey)

So, in spite of the king's unexpected visit to Hull, ostensibly to collect a couple of hoary old siege engines, and his departure with them by barge, I and my affinity found ourselves following on as we would have done anyway, by land, hot-footing it up into the wilds of the north country to the great craggy fortress of Bamburgh. Why a line of huge but isolated castles, standing like monstrous monuments up there near the borderland with our rough northern neighbour, should have reverted to their old, out-dated allegiance to the clapped-out House of Lancaster with its cardboard king and paper-tigress queen, I could not understand. The momentum of the future was clearly with the House of York and by now King Edward was firmly established on the throne with the strongest clans of the nobility — Warwick, Hastings, Norfolk, De-la-Pole — united around him. To imagine the possibility of a Lancastrian revival was risible.

But the Percys — great marcher lords up near the borders — had been rivals of the Nevilles — Warwick's family — for generations and this was one factor in their revolt against the king. Another was, of course, the Scots — those northern barbarians — intriguing with the French Margaret of Anjou, who had promised them the city of Berwick-on-Tweed, that city palatine that stands between England and Scotland, claimed by both. She was always happy to give anything away for help to invade England, especially something she didn't actually have.

We galloped up to Bamburgh in two and a half days of what they call "forced marches"; always hard on the poor horses, and probably even harder on the poor bloody serfs with their huge bows and quivers, but they're used to hard physical work. We arrived in sight of the castle, and of the royal encampment outside it, at evening and I was keen to present myself and forces to the king at once, to show I had achieved his deadline.

I threaded my way between the many multicoloured pavilions, making such a fair sight that the place looked more like a pleasure ground than a siege. I asked for the king's tent and was told His Grace was sleeping — or perhaps otherwise engaged — and I should report to his deputy, Lord Scales. I was already bristling towards Wydville or Woodville or Scales or whatever his name was, for putting me in an embarrassing position in relation to the king, and this instruction exacerbated my resentment.

I found the king's tent, with the royal standard flying proudly above it. It was, as you would expect, a splendid pavilion, and as I lifted the flap and entered the outer chamber, I saw two lords conversing: a younger man, presumably Wydville, and a bigger, much older man who was laughing raucously.

My first impression of Anthony Wydville was a shock. He was deeply handsome and immaculate in a fur-lined crimson gown. I felt both angry and envious of his fine features and light auburn beard. He was quite trim but his friend, with a saturnine face, a greying beard and a paradoxically huge laugh, was tall and strongly built. If a knight, he looked a wild one, the rough foil to Wydville's smoothness.

"My Lord Scales?" I asked with great formality.

"Yes, sir, God be with you, and prithee, sir, who are you?"

"De-la-Pole, sir, Edward De-la-Pole. You were not expecting me and my men?" I was being deliberately brusque.

"The boy looks angry, Ant. And we wouldn't want to anger the great House of Suffolk, would we?" The wild knight bared his teeth and looked first at me then at Wydville.

The latter laughed, but then seeing the anger in my eyes, spoke seriously in a mellifluous tenor. "You must forgive my friend Tom for his rough humour, Sir Edward. On my honour, he means no disrespect. Welcome to the king's camp. Would you care to wash and take refreshment?"

I knew I was being childish but I couldn't help myself.

"First, I wish to present myself to His Grace."

"His Grace is resting. But allow me to present my good and noble friend, Sir Thomas Malory of Newbold Revel in the county of Warwick."

Malory was indeed a large man and he appeared even larger due to a massive spirit matched by a deeply resonant voice. He was not a handsome man — though who would appear handsome next to the angelic Wydville? — yet he had a manly warmth about him and a deep sense of chivalric honour that made him hard to dislike for long. I was to discover he was part of the old courtly world of Lancastrian chivalry that my father had moved in, before the new world of steel and money and gunpowder had come to pass.

"De-la-Pole... You're not one of the Poles of Devon, are you?"

I glanced at him, goaded again; he was clearly toying with me. Wydville looked amused.

"No…? You are Suffolk's brother! Suffolk… You don't see him around much, do you, Anthony? Especially not on campaign, eh…?"

"The king has spoken often of Sir Edward's bravery at Towton, in his first battle, Thomas."

"Ah, well, that puts a different gargoyle on the buttress, I wean." Malory was full of fanciful phrases, though he rarely spoke as he wrote — few writers of romances do, in my experience. "By God, I knew your honoured father, Duke William, may Jesu guard his soul. He was a goodly counsellor, in the days when we were all subjects of King Henry's grace, before the Cousins' Wars began…"

"My honoured father was certainly a worshipful counsellor of the sometime king, but got no thanks for it."

"You have every right to feel woeful on that score, De-la-Pole," said Wydville. "Henry was far too weak to protect his best officers."

"Ah, kings care only for their state," said Malory, "The rest, even the best, are little more than flies to them, to be swatted by the Olympian gods."

Wydville and I looked at each other, a little uneasy at Malory's lèse-majesté.

"Boy," called Wydville, "Bring hippocras and wafers for our guest." He turned to Malory. "And, of course, you must know this gentleman's esteemed mother, Duchess Alice. She is held in the highest regard by His Grace."

"Ah, Duchess Alice, a dame of high renown."

I glanced sharply at Sir Thomas to detect any sign of ridicule but his eyes betrayed only respect.

"And thereby, sir," he continued, "You are the great-grandson of our greatest storyteller, the poet who made English our national tongue."

I bowed.

"No, sir, it is I who must bow to you." And he did with a flourish. "One day, poets will again be honoured as were the troubadours in the days of King Henry II and fair Queen Alienor, or Homer, the great bard of Hellas."

"The great bards and troubadours!" said Wydville, raising his glass.

We drank heartily to that toast.

Somewhat grudgingly, I was losing my resentment.

"Sir Thomas is also a teller of tales and legends, Sir Edward."

The brash Malory suddenly became quite bashful, as embarrassed as a stripling.

"When he isn't raping ladies and ambushing royal dukes…"

"All false allegations put about by the damned lawyers with their bloody pleadings and rebuttals. Why can't we do trial by battle as our fathers did?"

"Ah, the good old days, Malory… Like Sir Lancelot freeing Queen Guinevere and defending her honour, eh?"

"The Knights of the Round Table… They were goodly men and true," I said. For as a child, in addition to the lays of ancient Greece, my father and my tutor had told me tales of King Arthur and his glorious brotherhood of knights.

"By Jesu, fine hippocras, Anthony," said Malory.

"Excellent good i'faith, Anthony," I agreed, then realised I had called my rival/friend by his Christian name, something a gentleman should do only *after* a knightly brotherhood has been established. And I was aware both Wydville and Malory were recent converts to the cause of York. For all I knew, they may both have fought — valiantly, no doubt — on the Lancastrian side. Could I, should I, broach that subject?

It had grown dark outside the royal pavilion, and the grooms were lighting torches.

"How goes the siege, gentlemen?" I asked, belatedly.

"Like all sieges, and I've seen plenty. S-l-o-w-l-y."

"But we'll smoke 'em out," said Wydville.

"Is old Henry in the castle?" I asked, trying to smoke *them* out.

"Oh, he's in there all right," said Malory. "Poor old fool. But living or dead, he's not of much consequence to us. It's Margaret and her whelp who threaten us for the future. And they're over the border."

"They say the old battle-axe has already promised Berwick to James of Scotland in return for an army."

"She's a strong woman, Margaret. Hard as nails. And having possession of the Prince of Wales gives her a major piece on the board of chess."

"The sometime Prince of Wales, Thomas," corrected Anthony, with a smile.

"The king's heir is Clarence," I said, stating the obvious.

Malory growled. Even then, nobody trusted Clarence.

"But not for much longer, with such a virile king," said Anthony.

"Is His Grace to marry?" I asked, innocently.

Wydville said, "Malory is a poet, as I said, like your grandfather."

"*Great*-grandfather," I corrected. Why do people keep getting that wrong?

"Not a poet, just a teller of tales."

"A romaniste," said Wydville.

"Like Christine de Pisan?" I said.

"More like Chrétien de Troyes, I'd say," said Wydville, "But I drink to you as a fellow scholar."

"A true gentleman," said Malory.

We all drank.

"And what tales do you tell, Sir Thomas?"

"The tales of King Arthur and his brotherhood of the Knights of the Round Table, the romance of King Uther Pendragon and Merlin the Wizard, and the tragic history of Sir Lancelot du Lac and the fair but false Queen Guinevere."

There was a hush, as if Malory, with his deeply growling voice, had cast a spell, like Merlin himself.

The inner tent flap opened and the king walked in, handsome, magnificent and tousled from sleep. We knelt.

"No, no, be seated, my good friends. And welcome, De-la-Pole. Did someone mention my hero King Arthur?"

A groom, following the king, handed him a goblet of wine, and we took up our own.

"Malory is composing a romance of the tales of King Arthur, sire," said Wydville.

"I know. That is why I pardoned Malory his wicked crimes…"

Malory bowed his head.

"Because Anthony here vouches you tell a bloody good tale. He'd better be right, for all our sakes…" The king laughed like a great wild bear. And so, of course, did we.

I (VOV)

Of course, we took Bamburgh Castle — what else would you expect with our side led by such a sun in splendour and our opponents by a redeless monk? And we took another two or three castles up there in the far north which had relapsed back into their stale, old allegiance. For the time being, old Henry eluded us. All that remained of him in the handsome solar at Bamburgh, tumbled on the chamber floor as some groom had packed up in haste, was Henry's battle helm encircled by a golden coronet. How were the mighty fallen. This man who, as a child, had been crowned King of England, and then King of France at Paris, had had to flee so fast that he'd left behind his last vestige of kingship. Our Sovereign Lord adopted it as his own.

Around this time, my Beloved Mother was having some trouble with the Duke of Norfolk; or should I rather say that the truculent old duke (the last of the Mowbrays to bear that title) was having trouble, that he fully deserved, from the B.M. Like many nobles, he schemed to take advantage of the continuing disorder in the realm — as pockets of Lancastrian supporters fought on — by harassing tenants-in-chief of neighbouring estates who appeared vulnerable, especially when those tenants were women — even if ostensibly on the same side. As my readers will have gathered by now, anyone foolish enough to fancy Duchess Alice as vulnerable was in for a rude shock. As Norfolk, with his large and rowdy affinity, was launching raids on several of the B.M.'s own manors in East Anglia which abutted his own, she took stern action, sent my decorative brother to join his vain wife at court and called me home as her battle-hardened deputy.

I was, as ever, content to be of use to her in the vital task of preserving the family estate but, as an ambitious young commander and courtier, I was peeved that it prevented me from being present at the Battle of Hexham where a Lancastrian force led by Henry's cousin the Duke of Somerset — head of the Beaufort clan — was roundly smashed and the sometime King of France and England again had to make a mad dash for safety. Margaret of Anjou, however, having failed to marry off her little boy to a daughter of the Scottish king (not actually having Berwick to offer in return), sailed off to France with the lad to one of the castles of her long-suffering father, that pattern of chivalry, King René of Anjou — and of Jerusalem, oh and Naples; in name only however. They were an ill-starred family.

My brother, Duke John, whom we could at least use to send us vital intelligence from the Yorkist court, was reporting in his simple, literal way, that the king was rumoured to be secretly betrothed to Dame Elizabeth Grey, a very handsome widow, and was evidently showing favour to the lady's father, Earl Rivers, a notorious Lancastrian who had years ago married the old Duchess of Bedford (King Henry's aunt, of course), and to her brother, my new acquaintance, Anthony Wydville. *Quelle surprise.* Brother John had also had the wit to notice that my Lord of Warwick, who was anxious to outflank Queen Margaret by an alliance with King Louis of France and to bring this to fruition with a grand French marriage for the king, was mooching around the court in high dudgeon, like a bear with a very sore head.

As the B.M. wisely commented to me, this was still not proof positive, as the virile King Edward in the course of scattering the Plantagenet seed, had already been reported as being betrothed to several well-favoured damsels, the Lady Eleanor Butler having been fingered more than once. And as the B.M. also muttered — too low for nearby members of the household to overhear — Duchess Cecily, the king's mother, for whom you may recall the B.M. had very little love, had not been immune from the whispers of Sir Rumour: that her eldest son may not have been half-York, but half-pork, as the offspring of the tall, handsome Captain of Calais, one Blaybourne, where she was residing, largely apart from her husband at the time of their births... Whatever the truth of that little morsel, the B.M. decided the family interest required precise knowledge of what was happening at the centre of power, for she was concerned an unwise marriage could crack the firm alliance between York and Warwick that underpinned the king's power and thus cause more instability in the kingdom: the last thing any of us needed. And, of course, now that we were married into the royal house, the De-la-Poles would have to stand or fall with York.

"You're not going back to Hull, Eddie. They can do without you up there. We can't trust your brother to know what's happening even in front of his eyes — so I shall write to the king, asking permission for you to return to court."

We were in my mother's private solar at Ewelme, a lovely room which she had redecorated with new Flemish tapestries since that painful day years before when she had received news of my father's murder here.

"Thank you, Mother, an excellent idea. But, as His Grace knows me now, would it not be a better idea—"

"No, it would not. *I*, as the senior member of the family, must address the king. I disregard your brother, of course. You shall go to court and report back in detail and at least once per week, on the exact status of His Grace. I should also like to hear more about these Wydvilles, both Dame Elizabeth and her brother. They say he is very accomplished and handsome…" The B.M.'s gaze was piercing.

I blushed. I don't know why.

"He has acquired a peerage by marriage to an heiress. We must do the same for you. It's the only way you're going to get one." She continued to glare at me. Her waiting woman giggled.

"I am at the service of the king, Mother."

"The king will not marry *you*, Edward, though you might wish it."

"Mother!"

The waiting woman blushed and fell into hysterics.

"Be silent, Guinevere. And, what is more, my son, this family would be impoverished were it not for the Chaucer inheritance I brought with me; and which remains as my dower, to prevent your foolish brother or his royal wife from wasting it. We need to recover those privileges and licences that your late father, God rest his soul, was enfeoffed with, which we have never had returned since his cruel death…" The B.M. glared at me.

Guinevere, a simple soul, was in tears. They were not far from my eyes either.

"Now, go and tell your little man, Queercunc, or whatever his name is, to prepare your best attire. Get you off to court. And get me the truth!"

***

It was '65 and I was now a proud twenty years of age. How vain we are at twenty! I knew myself to be well above average height — more than five and a half feet — slender but with limbs well-developed by constant hunting and tilting, with fair hair worn quite long, below the ears (honey-blond it was called by some of my admirers) and with a more than passingly handsome face. More than once, I was told I had the intense gaze and high forehead of a scholar or musician; and, of course, I excelled as both. I was set on cutting a dash at court, a dash apt for a lord of my degree, a duke's brother and kinsman to the king.

I had, of course, been in the presence of His Grace on several occasions, but this would be my first appearance at court. Q was, naturally, in a state of hysteria.

"My lord will need a complete new wardrobe of gowns, hose, codpieces — they're worn very prominent now — and shoon, all in the latest and most elegant French styles."

"I'd go easy on the French side, Q," I said, as he brought me my hose one morning, teasing the old villain as ever, "I hear His Grace is veering towards a Burgundian alliance."

"Well, sir," he said, buckling on my garters, "Your gowns will, of course, be fashioned from the finest Flemish wool and Your Lordship must have two or three jerkins of the finest Italian leather for those cold evenings by the river. Oh Lord, how shall we get Your Lordship ready in time?"

"We'll get it all done when we get to Westminster, you old fusspot. Or do you want me to bring Malcolm down from Hull to arrange everything? I can if it's too much for you?"

I'd left the local lad as my deputy in Hull to liaise with the lord mayor and with the Holderness gentry. I knew his name would infuriate old Q.

"That will not be necessary, sir… Everything will be ready today sennight."

And it was.

In spite of my ducal brother's protestation — he was, in any event, at their country manor of Wingfield in Suffolk, with Lady Elizabeth who was expecting their second, or possibly their third son — it was ordained by the B.M. that I would lodge with my small retinue at the De-la-Pole residence in in the capital, Suffolk House, which was, in those halcyon days, at Suffolk Place near the River Thames, between the twin cities of London and Westminster.

At St. Edward's Palace of Westminster, where King Edward the Plantagenet held his court, an odd atmosphere reigned alongside the king; an ambience of expectancy and, perhaps, misapprehension. Nothing felt settled. My Lord of Warwick was engaged in Paris on a grand diplomatic mission to the French king, now Louis XI, who, having recently succeeded, was expected to be less favourable to his cousin Margaret of Anjou than his father had been. Warwick, no mean diplomat and determined to seize control of the European situation, saw the opportunity for a diplomatic demarche to scotch (and the Scotch as usual had been meddling with the "auld alliance") any attempt by the old witch to forge a new coalition. Without French support, Warwick grasped — correctly — that the

Lancastrians were a spent force, but with it, were still a power to be feared. What better way to secure the Yorkist throne than by a marriage of our most eligible young king with a daughter of the House of Valois?

The problem for me, when I got to Westminster, was whom to roister about with at court, whom to be seen with, whom to pass the none too onerous time with, while waiting, now in the times of peace, to catch again the eye of His Grace and, by grasping the next turn of the wheel of fortune, to make a great name and great honour not just for our family, but also for me, Edward De-la-Pole, Sieur de Holderness. My brother was not at court — and I wouldn't have wished to pass the time with him if he was. But another kinsman of ours was Tom St. Leger who, like Antony Wydville, was an Esquire of the Body to the king and therefore a close attendant upon him. My kinship with Tom had come about because his muscled arms had caught the randy eye of the Lady Anne — another of the royal Plantagenet sisters, who were well used to getting that which they wanted. Her early marriage to the Lancastrian Duke of Exeter understandably fell apart when the duke, Henry Holland, sided with his cousin King Henry, against his brother-in-law King Edward. These things happened in the Cousins' Wars. I have no doubt that many of these Lancastrian diehards owed their loyalty more to their dislike and envy of the less than charming Richard of York, King Edward's father, than to any great worshipfulness they saw in old Henry.

After Exeter was captured at Hexham, and sent to the Tower (he wasn't executed for treason because His Grace, as with Somerset and other doughty fighters, had a soft spot for the man), a divorce *a mensa et thoro* was arranged for Duchess Anne, with licence to remarry (well, there are advantages in being the king's sister) and, spoilt bitch that she was, Her Ladyship lost no time in marrying well-favoured Tom, who had already been her not-so-secret paramour for several years. Tom was a hearty roisterer and a bosom buddy of the king so, though far below the lady in birth, the marriage received royal assent.

One afternoon, soon after I had appeared as a new cub at court, Tom St. Leger, Thomas Malory — who was always roisterer-in-chief despite being almost old enough to be our grandfather — and I were imbibing a few goblets of good Gascon wine in an inner courtyard of the palace, when a pretentious marshal of the court, one Stephen Christmas, flounced by, flashed his badge of office and said officiously, "Would Your Lordships prithee restrain the din of your shouting, sirs? His Grace the king's mother is in residence in her chambers in these cloisters."

"What, that old trout my mother-in-law?" said St. Leger. "She can sleep through anything."

Malory laughed raucously. I giggled nervously, realising this was not safe territory on which to take a stand. I could see ladies of Duchess Cecily's household gathering behind the windows above, looking down while feigning insouciance, as ladies do.

Master Christmas muttered something that sounded like, "This comes of royalty marrying garbage."

At which St. Leger, enraged, shouted, "What was that, you varlet shithole? Repeat those words!"

Christmas, rattled, replied, "I said nothing, sir."

"You insulted me, and worse, my lady, Duchess Anne, you fuckwit." St. Leger certainly had a way with words and struck the varlet a solid blow in the face.

Christmas fell back, recumbent. "It is a felony to strike a marshal in the palace precincts. *You* are witnesses, gentlemen," he called out, pointing at us.

St. Leger moved to pounce upon him, so Malory and I grabbed hold of our friend just in time.

What Christmas had said was mere truth. St. Leger was now in deep shit and, with the ladies clamouring from the upper windows, it was too late to retreat.

There was an almighty hubbub and royal guards rushed into the cloisters from their guardroom. We stood back as they took custody of St. Leger who, being unarmed and outnumbered, knew he, and we, could not resist. We tried to explain to the captain of the guards but Christmas was also shouting his story. And then Tiptoft appeared.

John Tiptoft, Earl of Worcester, was an uncomfortable man. Or do I mean he was a man who made others uncomfortable? He was a man of great learning and chivalry, who received much worship from his peers, Wydville and Malory and gentlemen in Europe, for his translations of learned texts from the French and Latin tongues. But there was another side to Tiptoft as this story will show.

He was a fine-looking man with dark lowering brows over piercing eyes, this steward of the Yorkist court and High Constable of England. He was, of course, accompanied by his four sergeants-at-arms with axes on their shoulders.

"What dost thou here, St. Leger? The Duchess of York's ladies are witnesses to your assault on Marshal Christmas." As St. Leger opened his mouth to speak, Tiptoft snapped. "Tace! Marshal, tell what has passed."

Christmas struggled to his feet holding a silk kerchief to his slightly bloodied jaw.

"Sir Thomas St. Leger struck me, my Lord Steward, *forte et dure*, here on the face. These lords are witnesses, so help me God."

"The varlet insulted the duchess, my wife," shouted St. Leger, still pinioned by the arms.

"You have been told to keep silence, St. Leger. Did you not know the penalty for striking a marshal within the precincts of the court?"

"I am no lawyer, my Lord Constable."

"Nor will be. It is my pleasure," he said, smiling, "As Lord High Constable, to sentence you in the name of the king, to have your right hand struck off."

Malory, I, even the guards, gasped. Two ladies, watching from the casement, screamed.

"Not the arm, gentlemen," admonished Tiptoft softly, "Just the hand. Such is the king's great mercy. Take him to a dungeon."

As he was marched out, St. Leger shouted, "Speak to Duchess Anne, Malory, De-la-Pole. Tell her my plight."

Tiptoft bowed to us, with exquisite courtesy.

"Don't take alarum, my lords. St. Leger has at least a day's grace. I must find a competent butcher." He smiled gloatingly and withdrew, his entourage crying, "Make way for the Lord Steward."

Malory said, "You're a kinsman, De-la-Pole. I'm not in favour with the Yorks anymore. You'd better go. If a rescue by force is required, I'm your man."

Not thinking that a brilliant plan, I took Malory's other cue. What could I do? I sent for Q, of course, and instructed him to seek out Duchess Anne with an oral message. When, after a suitable interval, I followed him to her chambers — much finer ones than I had been given, I noticed — the lady was pacing up and down cursing like a trooper.

"That cur Tiptoft, let him burn with all the filthy accursed perjured souls in blackest Hell."

Her ladies were all weeping and wailing but she was flaming red with Plantagenet rage.

"Bring me a black mantle," she ordered. "Here take my jewellery and dishevel my hair." She tore off her rings and a glistering ruby brooch.

They did their job and, looking like a madwoman, she commanded, "Come, De-la-Pole, let us go to the king. You will be my champion."

It was clear, however, she didn't need one.

We found the king in his privy chamber with his usual companions, Hastings, Wydville, Rivers (Wydville's father) and one or two others — why was Wydville so much closer to the king than I? — and Duchess Anne rushed in the second she was announced. To say the king and his friends looked amazed would be akin to saying that a woman can sometimes be a little frightening.

The men stood, including the king, as Duchess Anne and I threw ourselves to our knees.

"Your Highness," she said, "I throw myself, my brother-in-law and my poor wretched husband on your gracious mercy."

"Raise yourself, sister, be of good cheer," said the king, and as an after-thought, "And you, De-la-Pole."

At any rate, it was to our advantage that we had pre-empted Tiptoft in getting to the Fount of Justice.

"Your Highness," sobbed Duchess Anne melodramatically into a very beautiful Flemish lace kerchief, "If, in any way, my husband has offended you then pluck out my eye or cut off my right hand, but not *his*, my lord, not his."

Her near-hysteria seemed real enough to alarm the king. But his political antennae were alerted.

"What has Sir Thomas done, sister?"

"The wild but loyal boy has traded blows with a marshal of the court, Your Grace, and all to defend the honour of Plantagenet, sire."

The king appeared relieved. There were so many rumours around the court of plots and counter-plots that this was harmony to his ears.

"My honour was insulted, Your Grace, and Sir Thomas had no choice but to defend our name."

At this moment, Tiptoft was announced begging audience.

The king looked slightly amused, then frowned. "Come."

The constable appeared and went down on one knee beside the duchess.

"Your Grace, it has been my sad duty to pass the sentence required by law on Sir Thomas St. Leger for striking one of Your Grace's marshals within the confines of the court."

"And that sentence is…?"

"Excision of the right hand, Your Grace."

"Ah…" said the king, seeing the full picture. He sat in his throne-like chair and stroked his small auburn beard. His beautiful eyes sparkled, a tad mischievously.

The duchess, Tiptoft and I remained kneeling, while the rest stood.

"Bring me Sir Thomas St. Leger."

Hastings, as senior chamberlain, bowed out to accomplish this. The rest of us remained like statues. Except for Anthony Wydville with whom the king appeared to be sharing a private joke (why him? Why not me?).

After what felt like several hours, Hastings led in St. Leger — his arms bound — accompanied by men-at-arms. St. Leger knelt.

"Well, Thomas, another fine mess you've got yourself into. What have you to say?"

"My heart is broken, if I have offended Your Grace. I struck the marshal in order to defend the honour of the Duchess Anne."

"Striking one of my marshals in my palace is a high crime, a felony; almost treason, Sir Thomas… but not quite."

"I bow and submit to any punishment meted out by my Sovereign Lord."

I admired St. Leger's sang-froid. But would the king?

He turned to Tiptoft.

"Removing the right hand is a heavy punishment, my lord."

"It is the law, Your Grace, which it is my duty and my honour to administer. The prerogative of mercy lies only with Your Highness."

"Excision of the right hand, eh?" He walked over to his brother-in-law — Edward was not a king to stand on ceremony — and took hold of his right hand. "And this is the offending hand."

He looked Thomas straight in the eye.

"And it should be excised... Except I need it to fight in my defence. You have done wrong, sir, and must learn to control your temper. The Lord Steward and High Constable has merely done his duty, properly. For which I thank him." Tiptoft bowed his head, and the king turned to address St. Leger. "You, sir, will withdraw from the court for one month and pay damages to the marshal. You will then return to your duties. Any reoffending will be severely punished."

We all smiled with relief, the Duchess Anne sobbed (and so did I, a little) and all cried, from the heart, "God save the king, God save Your Gracious Merciful Highness."

Except for Tiptoft, who looked distinctly cheated.

***

In the mirror of memory, that distorting glass of time which fades or exaggerates all things, the events of the 1460s seem to tumble over each other in quick succession. Was Henry of Lancaster taken into captivity like a bewildered old bear before the revelation of the king's marriage, or vice-versa? Does it even matter? I could search through the chronicles of that time, screwing up my exhausted eyes, but history is written by the victors; and they are not we.

Yes, now I remember. We were sitting at dinner, St. Leger (now back in favour, not that he was ever out of it really), Hastings (even senior chamberlains get a day off) and I — all on the second table in the hall, an honour appropriate to our rank — and the king had, unusually, not appeared. With his usual courtesy, and hearty appetite, King Edward was always punctual at mealtimes, mindful that, of course, his courtiers could only be served after him. I looked down the table.

I turned to Hastings. "I hope His Grace is not held up by ill-tidings or ill health."

He looked back at me almost with pity. Why was I always outside the inner circle?

"*Au contraire*," was all he said. He wasn't much of a linguist.

"I presume Wydville is with the king."

"Very much so," he said, with a kind of twinkle.

I wanted to throttle him.

We continued to wait, with the patience of courtiers.

Suddenly, the doors were thrown open with an unusually grand flourish and the Garter King of Arms appeared with full, magnificent tabard and baton.

"Make way, make way for the High and Mighty Princess Elizabeth, Queen of England, France and Ireland."

Zounds, I thought, *the old B.M. was right. He's gone and married her.*

Unsure whether to stand or kneel, we took the easier option and stood.

The garter, a tall imposing herald, scowled.

We knelt.

Looking truly regal in a heavy blue velvet gown with a long ermine mantle — I saw it was held up by several countesses — the splendid and very proud Queen Elizabeth Wydville made her *Joyeuse Entrée* into the court. She was supported on her right hand by her nemesis the great Earl of Warwick himself, and on her left by the senior duke in the kingdom, George of Clarence. Immediately behind processed the lady's father, the newly ennobled Earl Rivers, and the man I so envied, her brother Anthony, Lord Scales. And, for the first time, I saw their close similarity. Elizabeth was a woman of great beauty, and in the full flush of it. Anthony, a couple of years older, was almost her twin; well-built, handsome, with brilliant green eyes like his sister and a complexion as fine and pale as hers. All three Wydvilles glowed with pride. They had joined the highest rank. They had not been born to it.

The Wydvilles — or Woodvilles, if you will — were a good, solid gentle family from Northamptonshire with, as I've said before, strong Lancastrian roots. And they had been greatly strengthened by Sir Richard Wydville's extraordinary marriage. His fine and fair looks, which his two children evidently inherited, had attracted the amorous interest of Henry VI's aunt, the Dowager Duchess of Bedford, in the entourage of whose late husband Sir Richard had served at Calais. Jacquetta was a fine-looking woman without issue but with an ample appanage. They had married without Henry's licence but, as usual, that pliable young man had easily been persuaded to give it. And the lady herself was the daughter of Pierre, Comte de St. Pol, a great nobleman of lands and titles, married to Marguerite de Balzo who claimed descent from no less than Emperor Charlemagne. So, on the distaff side, they *were* born royal, almost.

But for most of my peers, the higher nobility, that didn't quite cut the mustard in our Norman-French custom of male primogeniture. Daughters are vessels; sons bear the seed and the family name. So, to my peers, the Wydvilles were not even half-royal. And, of course, the lovely Elizabeth was no virgin; she was the widow of the Lancastrian Sir John Grey, with whom she had had several children. So however beautiful

Dame Elizabeth Grey nee Wydville incontrovertibly was, she was also a misalliance; a huge mistake.

Thus when the glory of the Wydvilles was proclaimed, though after a moment's stunned silence, the whole court erupted into polite applause, but that applause had a hollow at its heart. And the stony, sepulchral faces of Warwick and Clarence, supporting our new queen on either side, spoke tomes.

At once, everything changed at court. A magnificent coronation was planned for the new queen consort, as if to compensate for the lack of grandeur at her wedding (at which, apparently, only her mother Duchess Jacquetta and a couple of family retainers were present as witnesses). A splendid delegation of Luxembourger nobility was invited from the court of the great Duke of Burgundy, representing the St. Pol family, thus enhancing the meagre status of the Wydville/Grey clan. But even before the coronation, we heard of an almighty bust-up that occurred in the Royal Council. Not being a member of the council, to my chagrin — and my ducal brother not even being a member, to the B.M.'s chagrin — my information came from Q who had it from a highly reliable member of the Earl of Warwick's enormous, princely household.

It seems that at the first council following Queen Elizabeth's presentation at court, Warwick had launched his verbal assault as soon as the king had taken his seat.

"Cousin", said Warwick — he was the only councillor other than the king's brothers who dared address him so familiarly. "How is it that while I was in France negotiating a most advantageous marriage with the French king's daughter — a marriage with an *equal* of Your Grace — another marriage was already planned, agreed and consummated, all clandestinely, with Dame Elizabeth Grey, a widow from a Lancastrian gentry family, behind the back of your accredited ambassador? Is it not customary for the king to summon and consult his kinsmen and tenants-in-chief before embarking on marriage — a marriage which is a matter of state?"

At this, Clarence is said to have uttered, "Ay, ay," but then gone silent when he saw Hastings and the rest looking cautiously between the king and his cousin.

His Grace was, as usual, affability itself. He reckoned this was not the time to challenge Warwick directly and chose instead to temporise and charm.

"Beloved cousin, if the head could always command the heart, I could not have failed to consult you all, my trusty councillors. But as chivalry tells us, betimes the love of a fair and noble lady may steal our hearts."

They say Warwick guffawed mightily. And was echoed, with a lesser guffaw, by Clarence.

"And, in troth, my lords, methinks a marriage alliance with the French king, our national foe, who has stolen back, under our feeble predecessor, so much of our royal demesne — Gascony, Anjou and Maine, even Normandy…" At this, Hastings, the Wydvilles and other lords banged the table to indicate support. "Is it in the interest of England, my lords? Or should we rather promote a treaty with the mighty Duke of Burgundy — a kinsman of our beloved wife — who will be our ally *against* our common enemy France. And, my lords," said the king, warming to his impromptu argument, "With whom do we have greater trade and therefore more to gain: with France, or with Burgundian Flanders? I know you, cousin, as my trusty Captain of Calais, must be fully aware of these truths."

There was a moment while Warwick — a mighty man who was only a little shorter than his nephew but with the greater chest and girth of an older, even more powerful physique — glowered at the king, who smiled, but held his gaze.

Hastings, the peacemaker, intervened. "Come, Your Highness, my lords, all's done and all's well. We have a handsome, buxom queen and soon, I am sure, we shall have an heir to the kingdom. What's done cannot be undone." This sounded a bit less than whole-hearted. "And is, by my troth, well done. This council and this realm must stay united or that termagant Margaret of Anjou will find a crack through which to attack Your Highness' kingdom."

At this moment, almost as if staged — and maybe it was — a royal messenger rushed in and knelt by the king, who read his unfurled parchment and smiled broadly.

"My lords, Henry of Lancaster has been taken prisoner while dining with traitors at Waddington Hall with just two or three followers. He is in our hands!"

There were cheers and loud banging of the table.

"How say you, my lords, that he be brought to London in shame and put in the Tower for all to see: a sad shadow of a man and a fallen king?"

More cheering and agreement.

"My dear cousin, will you, as our most trusted councillor, arrange that?"

"It will give me great pleasure, Your Grace."

And thus, a schism was averted. For the present.

***

Edward IV had begun to show he was a man of state as well as a man of war.

Thus negotiating a firm alliance with the Duke of Burgundy now became a necessity; to prove the king's argument, and to avert a French/Lancastrian invasion.

You may wonder why a mere duke, descended from a younger son of a King of France, could be seen as providing a counterweight to the might of France. But Duke Charles of Burgundy was no ordinary duke, and his domains spread far wider than the duchy of Burgundy. His great-grandfather Duke Philippe le Hardi was the third son of the French king, Jean le Bon, (they all have nicknames, these Valois princes), and like all the sons of *les rois français* he was endowed with a splendid appanage; in his case, the fertile meadows of Burgundy, round the mustard-famous city of Dijon.

But King Jean was astute, as well as good, and had arranged a marriage for his son with the heiress of the powerful Count of Flanders. Now, as we know, the Flemish are clever merchants, good at trade and deft in weaving; an industrious nation with a busy bourgeoisie, building up their handsome towns like Bruges (my exile home), Brussels, Ghent and diamond-encrusted Antwerp. And, by equally cunning marriages, succeeding generations of Burgundians accumulated all the towns and counties that we call the Low Countries, or Nether Lands: Holland, Zeeland, Luxembourg, Brabant, the richest lands in Europe, through trade.

Feudally, of course, even the grandest duke remains a vassal — a tenant-in-chief of the French king for the duchy of Burgundy, and of the Holy Roman Emperor for all the rest. And this rankled with the Valois dukes, who began to feel the extent and wealth of their territories merited a royal crown. There was even a famous occasion when Margaret of Anjou, in the course of her travails, paid a visit to the travelling and magnificent court of Burgundy with her son, Edward of Lancaster. At the end of a banquet in their honour — which must have been welcome to Madge and her whelp who were often short of food and gold — young Edward of Lancaster, by all accounts as ferocious and haughty as his mother, began an elaborate toast to Count Charles (then the duke's heir) who interrupted him saying, "Prithee, Your Highness, as the son of a duke, it is *I* who must raise a goblet to *you* as the son of a king." I hear an undertone of resentment in the young count's voice.

But there were major political problems in translating a patchwork of rich territories into a solid kingdom. For one thing, the county of Burgundy was separated from the Netherlands by territory belonging to France and, as I have explained, the duke in feudal law had two liege lords. So, as if to compensate for this lack of the ultimate accolade, the dukes elaborated their courts into the most magnificent centres of chivalry and knightly honour to be found in the known world. And their splendid chivalric Order of the Golden Fleece — named for the celebrated fleece that Jason rescued with his Argonauts — became the order of knighthood desired above all others, even above our own Garter, I must admit. But I digress...

Excitement and glamour soon become more than a drug; they become a necessity. Especially in a royal court where the courtiers' intense desire for advancement and stimulation have to be fed by a successful king. Edward IV was well aware of this. And so it was that soon after Queen Elizabeth's coronation (which it would be unnecessary to describe: magnificence, splendour, Anthony looking dashing, Warwick looking grim, all the Greys and Wydvilles out in force with Elizabeth herself compensating for her modest patrimony with a queenly arrogance that required lady marquesses to kneel and serve her food, while countesses arranged her train… need I write more?), His Grace announced, to the whole court, that he had finally agreed the treaty of eternal friendship that all had been hoping for between England and Charles, Duke of Burgundy, Count of Flanders et cetera, et cetera, to be sealed by the marriage of the duke with the king's twenty-two-year-old younger sister, the Lady Margaret Plantagenet.

There were four Plantagenet sisters, two of whom you have already met. The Lady Anne, the eldest, a little older than the king in fact, had first married the Duke of Exeter, then divorced him and married, hypogamously, the laddish Tom St. Leger; she was, as we've seen, a fiery duchess, dominated by lust (as the Church teaches, women so often are. Though, strangely, a witch once prophesied it would be her progeny who would outlive all the rest of her dynasty and eventually resurrect its honour; no doubt yet another empty vision). The next, Elizabeth, was my sister-in-law. She was neither clever nor well-favoured; she had a clear resemblance, so they said, to her late father York, being short and dumpy with unfeminine features. Nonetheless, she had character enough to wear the jewelled codpiece in my brother's house. Neither of them were much interested in politics but, like brother John, Duchess Elizabeth enjoyed luxury and breeding — and keeping their heads below the ramparts; a policy that in the end did them little good. According to the four humours of which the physicians talk, if Anne was blood, all fire and lust, then Elizabeth was earth; very down to earth.

The youngest sister, the Lady Ursula, I never met. No man outside her closest family ever did as she was sent to enter the cloister at an early age yet, despite her birth, never became an abbess. Unlike my brilliant Aunt Katherine, the Abbess of Barking, who turned out to have been far too able a guardian to Henry of Lancaster's half-brothers, the Tudor bastards. Ursula's fate faded into water.

Which leaves us with Margaret of York; her element was surely air. I had, of course, espied her at court from time to time, accompanying her Lady Mother, the Duchess of York (who had taken to styling herself vaingloriously "queen by right"). But I first met her when summoned to her presence by a royal chamberlain, soon after the Burgundian marriage treaty was proclaimed at Kingston-upon-Thames.

I write "summoned" with levity, of course. I was not a retainer to be called upon or a poor relative to be patronised. *Less rich* per chance, but not poor. In fact, I received a note in the lady's own hand — a fine hand, as all the king's sisters were well-schooled in learning and languages, and this one best of all — inviting me to meet her for a fraternal rendezvous. Intrigued at this rare invitation from a lady, I dressed to kill in a fine shot silk doublet, with the latest parti-coloured hose and a magnificent codpiece, and set off to our tryst.

The Lady Margaret was standing before a full-length shimmering mirror, wearing a long simple gown of pale blue velvet while three or four of her women brought her various pieces of jewellery and pretty trinkets to toy with against her long dark hair and oval face. A large oak coffer was in the middle of being packed in a corner. The lady was about my age, tall — almost my height — and with a face not at first glance beautiful, but strong and sensual with a firm, almost manly jaw, and the aquamarine eyes and lovely red lips of her eldest brother. She was the sister most similar to the king. And though her four maids of honour were all younger and prettier than she, it was Margaret who easily held my eye. Though not yet Duchess of Burgundy, she already radiated dignity and power, the female image of her brother. A lady worshipful indeed. And just in case any lustful thoughts invaded my head, a bosomy matron with the face of a Gorgon sat by the opened trunk sewing while pretending not to hear.

"The king, our brother, has told me that you, my lord, will be leading my noble escort to Bruges, where my wedding to my Lord Duke will be celebrated."

She was toying with a fine necklace of sapphires which caught the blue of her eyes.

Our brother was a nice touch. Subtle as well as powerful. An interesting woman, at last. One to equal the B.M. perhaps.

"A great honour for your loyal knight, my lady." I bowed.

"Joined with our beau-frère, Lord Scales," she added, shooting me a keen glance. "The king assures me you two are bosom friends."

Were we?

"We are both knights in the service of His Grace and Your Ladyship."

She smiled. Just like the king's smile. The sun in splendour. There was a stirring in my loins. Why had I not known this handsome, puissant princess before; before she had been betrothed to one of the most powerful princes in Europe? A tinge of regret and jealousy touched my spirit.

"I may be a princess, Sir Edward, but I have no more control of my fate than a villein's daughter. Less in fact." She sounded a touch bitter.

"Your Ladyship will be a great duchess."

"Only a duchess?" She laughed. There was fire in her eyes. "First, I was to marry the heir of Portugal, Dom somebody-or-other but sadly, he died. But perhaps Lusitania would have been a little too hot for a Yorkshirewoman, do you think, my lord?"

I was excited by her smile and her teasing tone.

"Then Cousin Warwick and the king agreed I should marry a French prince; perhaps the dauphin? It would have been a noble fate to become a queen; but of France? Our ancestral enemy? And now Burgundy — to marry a duke who deserves to be a king! *C'est bonne chance qu'ils parlent la langue française dans les pays bourguignons, n'est-ce pas?*"

"*Comme, madame, déclare. C'est la langue des anges, on dit.*"

"I thought that was Latin, my lord, or even Hebrew… But enough banter, Sir Edward, what can you tell me about Duke Charles?" she said as if nonchalantly. She shot me a glance. "It can't be wrong for a lady to wish to know a little about her future husband, can it?"

"Sadly, madam, your loyal knight's ignorance is great. Like my lady, I have never set eyes on the great duke. But he is well-known to be, like his noble father Duke Jean, the very acme of chivalry. And, of course, he is known as 'the Bold'. Boldness is a great attribute in a warrior; perhaps also… in a husband?"

My slightly barbed comment drew a veiled and worried glance from those sensuous eyes.

"Perhaps, my lord. But you must have heard some report of him from your friend, Lord Anthony. *He* has met the duke; *he* negotiated the match. Has he told you nothing?"

"My lady is deceived if she thinks I am privy to Lord Anthony's secrets."

She threw me a fiery sensual look which (as intended?) inflamed my feelings.

A maid of honour had placed a chain with a golden disc around Margaret's handsome throat — a medallion of the sun in splendour — which she was arranging carefully, over the exposed cleavage of her delicate peach-like breasts.

"Could you not find out for me?" she almost whispered. "How does the duke treat his daughter and heiress the Lady Mary? Any man who treats his motherless daughter well will be kind to his new wife, don't you think, girls?"

One of her damsels giggled at this and said, "If he treats you the same as his daughter, ma'am, there will be no son and heir."

I smiled and, though she rebuked the girl, Margaret gave me a subtle smile.

"I know he is a great warrior," she said, "But some great warriors love women; others... prefer men." Again, her voice fell to a silken whisper. "Which is he?"

I was a little surprised by the sophistication of the lady's knowledge, despite her apparently sheltered upbringing. And this clearly was my function: to be a conduit of information for my lady. She was using me. But the thought of being used by such a lady was quite an exciting one. This was, at any rate, one way I could serve her as her loyal knight, her Sir Lancelot. And — unlike the real Sir Lancelot — smooth the silken sheets of the Burgundian marriage bed and (like my poor father before me) encourage the begetting of a male heir, in this case for the House of Valois combined with the glory of York. Oh Jesu!

I bowed myself out, intending to bring my man Q's talents into play as well as my own to discover whatever I could of the bold (wild?) Burgundian duke. I could never marry the magnificent Margaret. But I now knew a way to serve her and be her *parfait* knight.

**

The next morning, I received the following letter from the other woman in my life:

My son,

We live in surprising times. The wheel of fortune is never still, only *pro tempore* at rest. Do not be lulled by soft living into the belief that because all is now well it will always be well. Beware and be aware!

The newly wed queen, the quondam Dame Elizabeth, is now the consort of our Sovereign Lord and I expect and presume you have paid your respects to her. Now you must take her a gift from me. Buy a handsome jewel for five hundred marks and present it to her. It would be imprudent to send money with this messenger (trusty as he is) so I shall repay you later. Do not stint on this. It is of great importance to forge strong links of amity with the queen and her Grey and Wydville family. Her Grace's brother Lord Scales is only a little older than you, I hear. You will make him your friend, your intimate friend. Your brother has no talent for forming alliances nor forming anything, except offspring. That is his function. Politics is yours.

The Wydvilles are close to the king. They are becoming a great power in the land. Once an heir is born — and the lady hath shown herself fecund heretofore — should (which Heaven forefend) some misadventure befall the king, they will control the Crown. Therefore, attach yourself to them.

But the serpent does not sleep with both eyes closed. Rumour has it that my Lord of Warwick, and his aunt Duchess Cecily, are not content. Indeed, His Grace the king's mother is widely known to be un-reconciled to the match. She has made no secret of her disapproval even to the extreme of making a declaration as to His Grace's lineage which even here under seal it would be reckless to repeat. No doubt the duchess' mind was disturbed by her fury when she made her claim. But be always aware of the power of the Nevilles in the persons of the Earl of Warwick, his brothers and his aunt. They are not to be trifled with; yet they believe they have been. So, while cultivating the new House of Wydville, you must not neglect the old House of Neville. As we say in East Anglia, the bread must be buttered on both sides if it is to stay sweet whichever way it falls.

Nor is my lord the Duke of Clarence (still heir to the throne, remember) and now Warwick's son-in-law, the happiest of men. They could form a powerful alliance.

Meanwhile overseas the exiled lioness of Anjou never sleeps. You must know that your former false friend, the fabulist Thomas Malory (malodorous rapist, as he should be called) has already fled the court, having pledged himself to a traitorous and hopeless Lancastrian plot. Beware such friends!

In her father's castle at Koeur, the quondam queen waits with her pretty son, the heir of Lancaster, for the wheel of fortune to turn again.

Wait and be watchful, my son. Serve the king, fear God, pray to the Virgin, and defend the interests of De-la-Pole.

And now burn this letter.

Your Mother.

As I always obeyed the B.M., I did so. Therefore, the details of the letter, as I recollect them now, may not be exact. I believed her warnings to be exaggerated, the product of her own sad bereavement. Yet I was astounded by her knowledge of life and politics at court, which were far sharper than mine. What or who were the sources of her information? An astonishing woman.

I replied with a humble and dutiful response vowing to pursue her prudent politics (politely, of course). I also proudly told her (what she already knew no doubt) that, with Anthony Wydville I would be leading the embassy to give away the Lady Margaret on the king's behalf to the great Duke Charles. I did not tell her I was half in love with the lady myself. She would have brushed away such courtly nonsense; except in so far as it might bring political advantage.

The next morning — just as I had set in train my own enquiries to discover what I could for my royal mistress — I received another summons. Again, it was presented in the form of a courtly invitation, but this time was even more powerful in its provenance. It was from the kingmaker himself: my Lord of Warwick.

As my reader may have surmised, I had always found the burly earl to be a fearsome figure, who could terrify little children with a glance. Moreover, he was the king's maternal uncle and the greatest English nobleman since, well, Simon de Montfort probably. Not that that was a good omen, as that over-mighty baron had ended up torn limb from limb by the king's followers. But that would never happen to Warwick; he was far too powerful and too cunning. Warwick, as head of the Neville clan, who dominated the north of England beyond our own county of Yorkshire, in fierce rivalry with the almost equally great Percys, was in his own right Earl of Salisbury; and, in his wife's, holder of the even greater earldom he sported. His land holdings were vast, greater than that of any duke, and he maintained a large private army of his affinity. He was also Governor of Calais, the king's one remaining fief on the European continent, and the earl kept an unshakeable grip on it. As such, he also controlled a substantial navy. Not surprisingly, he was regarded throughout Europe as the real master of England; and of England's young king. And this was the man who had "invited" me to "do him the honour of paying him a fraternal visit" at his London mansion on Cripplegate.

When I arrived that afternoon, with just a couple of grooms for escort, I felt a little unease as the great gates closed behind me and I was almost surrounded by hordes of retainers in the Neville livery of red and black. I wondered for a moment if I had been taken hostage, but to what end? I was hardly important enough. But then a superbly gowned chamberlain bowed and smiled and led me through to an airy chamber where I waited — with a delightfully scented hippocras and wafers, of course — for the summons to the mighty earl.

After a short wait, I was conducted, with great courtesy, through to the solar; a magnificent chamber with a handsome marble floor and several elegant oak chairs in one of which sat my Lord of Warwick, like a rugged, solid outcrop in the middle of the sea. He didn't rise but gestured for me to sit in a similar seat.

"Edward, Edward De-la-Pole. Watcha, Edward," he boomed.

"Watcha, my Lord Earl." It wasn't my usual form of address, but if it was good enough for him, well…

"Tell me, Edward, are they trying to drive me out of the family? Are they trying to drive me out of England?" His voice was suddenly soft, almost whining, filled with unctuous self-pity. "I could go, you know. I have been asked to serve the German emperor… or the King of France. I have been offered an appanage *sur le continent*, you know, a great estate in Provence, a clutch of counties in the Netherlands, and it's very tempting, oh so tempting…"

"My lord…" He wasn't listening.

"I remember your father, Edward. They did for him, the House of Lancaster, like all kings, thinking only of themselves. But truly I thought my nephew, King Edward was *different*, *genuine*, a very *parfait* knight… Didn't you?"

"I did… I do, my Lord Earl."

"But he won't take advice anymore. Have you not noticed that, my boy? He thinks, my nephew, he knows it all. He thinks he can dispense with the wisdom of age, experience, good counsel… and the strong right arm of the Nevilles. Can't you see that?"

He stood and moved slowly towards me.

"Well…" This was treason, or would be from any other mouth. I had to be cautious.

"And now, dear boy, is not the time for a novice. He *needs* me, and my brother the archbishop and, of course, my aunt the queen by right. Do you know how deeply Aunt Cecily disavows his marriage to that... *that woman*?" He spat out the words, which was a little unpleasant as he was now standing and had put his face very close to my own. Unpleasant; yet also strangely alluring.

I looked up into his large grey eyes.

"I have heard..."

"So deeply and painfully has it wounded her, that she is willing to publicly avow that the rumours of her own adultery are truth, and that Edward is not the true Plantagenet." He stood back and walked around the chamber, fuming. "Which would make George Clarence — my future son-in-law — the heir of York. To declare herself a strumpet..."

At this, the earl began to weep, histrionically.

"Can you believe it?" The tears were streaming down his face. I almost wanted to wipe them away for pity. "To neglect and ignore his old cousin and bosom friend who loves him like the son he never had! And then, having swept aside his family's wise counsel to marry a daughter of the French king and thus check the ever-dangerous threat from the Lancastrians in France, then to share his bed, disgustingly, with that swarthy varlet the Wydville brother, Scales... Ugh..." And he uttered a sound of horror rising from his innards at the thought that the king and Anthony might be bedfellows... Was that so, I wondered feeling, of a sudden, very hot; and if so, was I angered, or jealous, or both?

He stopped, like a mummer, about to turn and make a massive and important revelation.

"And my poor beloved daughter Isabel, who is so in love with the handsome Clarence, why should they not be allowed to marry? Are the Nevilles not good enough to marry into the House of York now they have attained the throne? Would they have attained it without *my* help? God's blood, how say you, De-la-Pole?"

Fortunately, he did not wait for an answer but ploughed passionately on.

"Are they trying to drive me into the arms of the witch of Anjou?" he hissed. "Let them not think it beyond the bounds of the possible. In extremis we must think the unthinkable; do the undoable. The French king is pressing it upon me, inveigling me back towards the old House of Lancaster." He almost screamed, as if in agony. "Let them not force me to renounce my allegiance!"

This was fearsome and I must have blenched. Suddenly his whole tone and demeanour changed.

"No, no, handsome young man, you have nothing to be afraid of." The great bear came over and softly pawed my head. It was disturbing; yet sensual. "I have the greatest respect for your good self and, of course, for your Lady Mother, Duchess Alice. A noble and worshipful lady. But beware the wiles of the Wydvilles. They may appear noble. Yet…" He was whispering like the tempter in my ear. "Remember they are *scum*, and we cannot allow them to live."

Or did he say "thrive"? In either case, it was blood-curdling. And was clearly intended as a warning to be taken away and relayed to Anthony Lord Scales and his sister, the queen.

This was serious stuff, and I had learnt enough to treat it seriously.

***

By the next morning — having mulled over the extraordinary encounter of the day before — I decided it was time to take the initiative. I sent a message to Anthony Wydville that we needed to talk, ostensibly to make plans for our journey to escort the Lady Margaret to her wedding. My messenger — Q, of course, because of his discretion — brought back an invitation to meet in the private closet of the queen's chapel. A choice of venue which showed Anthony to be a man of good counsel.

Anthony was waiting for me in the closet, an austere room but adorned with devotional paintings. My eye went to a wondrous Greek icon of a heavily bearded saint with big round eyes.

"You are drawn to the icon of St. Nectarios, I see. Beautiful and very spiritual, isn't it? It was a gift of the Byzantine ambassador to old Henry. What a joy it would have been to journey to Constantinople before the fall of that city…"

"Ten years ago…?"

"Fifteen. Or even to see it now. They say the Turks are treating it with great reverence."

"Verily?" I asked. Anthony's charm was beginning its work already. "So, the infidels are not as ferocious as we are taught?"

"Oh, they *are* ferocious. But also cultured and with a reverence for scholarship. The Saracens even more than the Turks, I believe. But, forgive me, I haven't welcomed you, Sir Edward. The queen's attendants have provided us with wine, so come drink with me to long life for the king and queen."

I did so.

"And as the queen is happily with child again," I said, "Let's drink to a good birth and, this time, a prince!"

Again, we drank.

"We will need to share our counsel about the escort for the Lady Margaret to Bruges, Sir Edward, but no date has been set so far and there are still many details to be settled regarding the dowry and so on... We are awaiting an embassy from Duke Charles led by my namesake his brother, Antoine the Bastard of Burgundy. We have to find some diplomatic pretext for his coming. We don't want to give heart to the... opposition to the match so to speak from certain factions..."

He knew everything, I realised. Except, perhaps, what I had to tell him.

"It will be my first voyage abroad, my lord."

"Call me Anthony, if it please you. Remember we've been brothers-in-arms at Bamburgh."

"Bad business about Malory, don't you think, Anthony?"

"He's a troubled soul, Edward. But not you, my friend!"

I felt myself blushing unaccountably.

"And in the service of the Lady Margaret. She is a handsome damsel, is she not? And brings a little colour to Edward's cheeks!"

That was not the cause, but it sufficed as pretext.

"In truth my... Anthony. I bring, my friend, two messages."

"Oh aye?" His handsome face looked a little wary. I clocked his dreamily hazel eyes — so like the queen's — and that his light auburn beard was more delicately shaped than when we had last talked in the field.

"First greetings and great goodwill to yourself and the queen from my Lady Mother."

"My thanks and good service to Duchess Alice — as a great noblewoman, and, of course, as a Chaucer."

"I will pass them on to her. And she has asked me to convey through your good offices to the queen, your sister, this small token of our loyalty and friendship."

I brought out a brooch with a large and luscious pearl at its centre that had cost most of what I had hoped to spend on my trousseau for the embassy to Bruges; the embassy to the most glorious court in Europe. But politics entails unavoidable sacrifices.

He took it and bowed.

"Her Grace will be honoured and delighted." He paused politely. "And the second message?" he enquired, sounding more wary.

"The second is less… soul-warming. You are sure we are not overheard?"

"On my word as a knight."

"Two days ago, I was asked to pay a visit to my Lord of Warwick."

His fine features clouded over slightly. "And what did His Lordship have to say? If you can tell me without breaching confidence."

"Undoubtedly, my friend, I was intended to pass on the… warning. The earl is clearly not reconciled to the king's marriage. Nor, according to Warwick, is his aunt, Duchess Cecily."

"Ah yes," he smiled a slightly crooked, melancholy smile, a smile that showed his sense of what the Greeks called irony. "She that calls herself 'queen by right', meaning perchance that my sister is *not*?"

I returned his gaze steadily. "The earl is a man of great power."

"He is," said Anthony, "But he is also a man of honour and of chivalry. He is a Knight of the Garter. He doesn't yet have confidence in my sister, or our family. But he will learn that our loyalty to the House of York is as great as his own."

For the first time, I witnessed Anthony's sanguine and trusting disposition. He always expected others to be as loyal and honourable as himself. Alas, that is not how the world turns.

"Or even greater?" I said.

"You are not doubting Warwick's loyalty to the Crown? He is first cousin to the king! He and his father supported the Yorks before any other noblemen."

"Anthony, hearken to me. He hinted he could be driven — he and his empty-headed protege Clarence — right into the arms of the witch of Anjou as he called her."

Anthony looked amazed, then amused. "Warwick is all bluster. He is proud — as he has every right to be. But he is also intensely loyal. And what future could there be for him with Margaret, who hates him with a passion? And even less for Clarence." He paused to think. "But I will tell the king of your misgivings. His Grace will be very grateful. He is aware of your great love."

I blushed deeply. I was still a very young man.

Anthony laughed; a lovely, musical gurgle of joy. I shall never forget his laugh.

"And he loves you right well in return, young sir. As he loves all his loyal knights."

We looked at each other for a few moments. To hide my embarrassment, I said, "So, when will the Bastard Antoine be making his embassy?"

"Soon. But we need a pretext for his visit. A good tale to tell the chroniclers, and to put Warwick's party off the scent."

"Isn't he a famous jouster? Like yourself? Why not throw the gauntlet down to him, issue a challenge?"

He looked impressed. "An interesting conceit."

"I will ask the Lady Margaret to arrange something, through the good offices of some of her ladies."

He looked surprised. "And will she?"

"The lady is hungry for knowledge of her future husband. No one can know him better than his half-brother, I guess."

"So, you have found a way to serve your Lady." His eyes twinkled.

"And my friend." So did mine.

And so I set out to create the famous challenge, as it has been recounted and embroidered a thousand times in so many chronicles of chivalry.

***

Antoine, the Bastard of Burgundy, was the natural son of the aging duke, Philip known as the Good, by a mistress of breath-taking beauty. She must have been, because Monsieur le Bastard was a kind of angel, or devil, compared with whom even Anthony Wydville and the king himself were merely good-looking. His dark, saturnine looks, and the face which, though clean-shaven in the Burgundian style, was always shadowed by a touch of bristle, matching his almost black eyes, made him a striking harbinger of his ducal house. Of course, the position of a bastard — even one who is, like Antoine, semi-royal — is always ambivalent, ungrounded, as he has no legitimate right. But the half-brother of the greatest duke in Christendom, dark and handsome as the devil and twice as handy with axe and sword, will always find employment.

We were in the great tourney yard at Smithfield; the upper galleries filled with court ladies in their elegant robes and high steeple hats, the wings hanging splendidly down on either side. The well-dressed persons of the middling sort were packed into the boxes below and, on the ground, those of the rabble who had been allowed in, stood stuffing their faces with food and drink from the vendors circulating around, and cheering themselves hoarse.

The two Anthonys were already in place: the Burgundian to the left of the main stand on a splendid black charger, glinting in his golden armour, the much-quartered banner of Burgundy floating above him, with the red, black and gold lions of his brother's three duchies, and the fleur-de-lys of the House of Valois (the French royal House from which they descend), crossed with the bend sinister of his bastardy; and at the other end of the stadium, Sir Anthony Wydville, Baron Scales, on an equally fine white stallion, in silver accoutrements with his family banner of Wydvilles flying above him, quartered with his mother's arms of Luxembourg.

My heart was beating like a hammer on an anvil. This challenge had been my own idea, but now I was anxious lest the tournament should truly be a battle *a l'outrance*, a fight to the death, as required by the laws of chivalry. Unless, of course, one of these champions was to yield. But would that not be an international humiliation which would jeopardise the alliance which both rulers were desirous to conclude?

I was seated, sweating profusely, not that it was a hot day, in the royal box, just two places from my Lady Margaret. I was aware I would not have been so honourably placed were it not for the absence of several more senior members of the royal family: the Duchess Cecily, and the Earl and Countess of Warwick. *Quelle surprise!* The Duke of Clarence, over-dressed and haughty as ever and the rather sour-faced young Richard of Gloucester were seated to the right of the king's and queen's thrones, with the Lady Margaret, Anne Duchess of Exeter and myself to their left. Lord Hastings, as Lord Chamberlain sat to my left. As usual, my brother and his wife were too busy breeding to attend (I doubt they were even invited).

As in the moment when a battle is joined, you could smell the excitement — much of it rising from the unwashed varlets below, intermingled with fine, fragrant scents from those around me. The Lady Margaret turned and gave me a look of intermingled excitement and anxiety — entrancing.

Of a sudden, the royal trumpets sounded their brassy notes as we all rose and the king and queen entered to take their thrones. And with equal suddenness, my inner eye had a vision of another tournament, another famous challenge, which had happened over sixty years before, presided over by King Richard II: when Henry of Lancaster entered the lists against Thomas Mowbray Duke of Norfolk, who had accused him of high treason. Richard had dramatically stopped the contest and banished both contestants, thus setting in train his own deposition and the bloodshed of the Cousins' Wars.

But this was to be a far happier occasion. Or was it? For then, a second vision flooded my mind in which the two champions had fought each other to exhaustion — and here was the Burgundian, his face bloodied, his sword slicing down, removing Anthony's right arm from his shoulder. For there was no way anyone could control the outcome of a gauntlet once thrown down, and the people — especially those of the lower sort — would be baying for blood. I shuddered, then awoke to the noise and tumult around me. Surely, I reasoned, neither the king nor the needs of international diplomacy would allow such an outcome. But my misgivings had revealed how deep my friendship for Anthony Lord Scales had become.

Once again, the king's horns blared out to command silence and Clarencieux [?] Herald, resplendent in his tabard of red and gold [?] declaimed Baron Scales' grandiloquent challenge to that celebrated champion, Sieur Antoine de Bourgogne, the winner to be honoured with the chaste favour of a queen. They have to be grandiloquent, these challenges, to make a chivalric point and to impress the villeins and serfs, who would otherwise not be impressed. Glancing round, I noted that the queen did indeed look strained, but the king serene. He was always a brilliant dissembler.

And then I remember my neighbour, the Duchess of Exeter, in her cold and indolent way, handed me a note. And as she did so, I saw my Lady Margaret turn to give me a secret smile. The note, in her hand, read: If the duke is as comely as his brother, I shall not complain. I smiled back and crushed the indiscreet note in my hand. And at that moment, I felt I was a man.

There had been other moments of ecstasy — my first battle, my first fuck, my first siege — but now at this juncture, everything came together to create a special moment of almost spiritual happiness: my royal mistress smiling upon me, my admired friend about to face the challenge of his life, and me seated so honourably just three places from the king and queen. I also felt unsettled, guilty about this, as part of my pleasure lay in the sense of excitement and the tingle of fear in anticipation of danger to my friend and probably of blood-letting to come. But, again as in battle, a joust evokes that state of tension and delight which dries the throat and engorges the loins.

In the moment of silence that always follows a heraldic proclamation, all eyes fixed on the royal couple and the king, with that superb sense of drama that always enhanced his majesty, looked intently down on the arena, held up his right hand holding the baton of the Master of the Joust and turned slightly to the queen, who waved a yellow silken favour bearing the arms of England, which would be the victor's token. Then the king, his eyes glittering, brought down the baton in his right hand. At that signal, both champions began pounding towards each other, their lances levelled. The crowds roared, drowning out the thud of the horses' hooves. As they got closer, I could hardly breathe. I thought I saw the Bastard's lance glance menacingly off Anthony's helm, but both men kept their mounts. Thank Jesu, no fall.

Back at opposite ends, they turned, received superficial attentions from their squires, then pounded back towards another clash. The noise of the hoi polloi, as Anthony with his knowledge of Greek would certainly have called them, increased. They were — as we were? — baying for blood.

The eyes of all in the royal box were glued to Anthony and this time it was his lance which undeniably hit the Bastard's heavily armed left arm. For a second, the Burgundian swayed and the mob let out a gasp of excitement, uniting lords, burghers and serfs. But at once, the knight in gold armour righted himself and galloped off safely to his waiting grooms.

The king rose, creating a moment of silence, looked deliberately from one knight to the other, and then made a neat, commanding gesture with the baton in his right hand. In response, the contestants were now helped down by their attendant grooms from their chargers. Each man was disarmed of his lance and buckler and then re-armed cap-a-pie: Anthony to my left was accoutred with a large silver battle-axe and a mace, whilst Monsieur Antoine was armed full on with a mighty two-handed sword with a great ball and chain attached to his waist.

My throat went dry and my mouth bitter; these two men were now armed to deal death. And the duke's man, slightly taller and broader in build, was he more heavily armed than the king's? Undoubtedly the Burgundian sword, its pommel glinting in his gauntleted hands, looked a powerful weapon. And was Anthony, as merely a royal brother-in-law (like me) and a mere baron (like me?) dispensable in the name of chivalrous diplomacy? Was he to be sacrificed to the glory of the name of York and its necessary union with Burgundy? I glanced over at the Lady Margaret and she shot back a look of undiluted passion. For me? For the bastard? Or for sheer bloodlust?

The combatants began to walk heavily towards each other, still armoured and weighed down also by the heft of their weapons. The mob was baying with a sound like hounds when they smell the boar's blood. They began to pace around each other, almost like wrestlers, occasionally lunging or attempting a blow but making no contact. This shadow fighting, ineffectual but intensely tiring, went on, it seemed, for over an hour — it was probably much less — as each man sounded out his opponent and bided his time.

And then, just as we had been lulled and dulled into a kind of hypnotic spell, the Bastard brought his great sword down on Anthony's arm and, with a great clang, dislodged his left lower arm piece. [?] The crowd shouted with a kind of neutral satisfaction that something had finally happened and we all strained, with slack jaws, to see if there was any sign of blood. But, thanks be to our Lady (I was a great adherent of the Virgin in those days), I could see none.

"Thank Jesu it's his left arm," I said to Duchess Anne. She looked coldly back. Clearly, she couldn't give a damn.

The Bastard — clearly trained in the higher echelons of chivalry at his father's court — stood back for a few moments, leaning on his sword, to allow his opponent time to recover himself, whilst a marshal came up and removed the discarded sleeve of armour. Then he — the Burgundian, that is — did something very noble: he removed the parallel piece of sleeve from his own left arm, and chucked it aside, as one of his own esquires ran up to retrieve it. The crowd roared its approval and the Bastard, standing with his hands on the pommel of his great sword with its tip on the earth, bowed, first to his opponent and then to the royal box.

And then, without making any signal, Anthony picked up his battle-axe and, advancing three strides, brought it down with a mighty blow on the Bastard's hands, shattering the metal encasing his gauntlets and causing him to drop the huge sword. Momentarily disarmed and disoriented, the Burgundian fell back a little while the crowd gasped in amazement. But Anthony — who could, had he so wished, have pressed home his advantage and done the other man huge damage with his axe — stood back also and threw the battle-axe aside, as a counterpart to the Bastard's loss of the sword. At this, there was cheering; it seemed Anthony had gained the upper hand.

There was another pause while attendants ran up to remove the discarded weapons. And at this point, Anthony signalled to his esquire to remove his helmet, so we could at last see his face with its calm and graceful expression. The Bastard's groom thereupon did the same, but, in his case, the dark saturnine expression looked intense, displeased? The two men now took stock of each other with a wider field of vision and the Bastard took a grip of his ball and chain, while Anthony took up his heavy mace. Again, they began to pace around each other when, suddenly, the trumpets sounded and all turned to the king who was standing, and first raised then threw down his baton. This was a royal command to cease combat and both knights turned to the royal seats, set down their weapons and bowed deeply. They then bowed to each other — was the Bastard's bow less deep than Anthony's? — and formally withdrew to their ends of the field, while we in the royal party followed Their Graces out of the stands into the king's pavilion.

As we processed out, I whispered to the Lady Margaret, "I trust honour has been satisfied," but she replied with no more than an enigmatic smile.

The magnificent banquet that followed is now no more than a blur. I have attended so many and eaten so much that now my stomach revolts at the thought and my digestion would collapse at imbibing so my different rich meats and such varied and sumptuous sweets. But I still remember, with a pang that's still bitter, a moment after the banquet was concluded with the minstrels and the jesters and the dancing and the toasts and the royal party had withdrawn to the privy chambers — we were in the Palace of Westminster — and I suddenly looked round to realise that the king and the two champions — who had been wholeheartedly convivial throughout the festivities — had withdrawn further into the inner sanctum. I decided to attend on them to offer my congratulations in private, but, of course, curiosity was driving me too. And maybe now was the time to glean some information to pass on to my royal mistress?

Nodding to the guard at the doorway — who knew me well — I passed through into the king's bedchamber to see a sight I had not seen since that night at York: the king preparing for his bath. But now, not only the king but also the two Anthonys, all in loose silken robes, lounged on chairs at the foot of the king's bed while Hastings presided complacently over the pouring of hot water and the addition of sweet smelling herbs and spices to the three elegant brass baths which were set out before them. The three men were laughing and smiling and clearly very comfortable in each other's company.

When the king saw me, there was a moment of silence. Then, with his usual light touch, he said, "Ah, Eddie, how good to see you. Will you join us after the bath to take our nightcap? Or would you prefer to take another kind of nightcap with the ladies?" And he winked.

At that moment, I saw clearly at last that the whole day had been a courtly sham with every move choreographed and me, only me, outside the magic loop. What a fool and a jester; like all the De-la-Poles.

I bowed deeply, unable to speak my thoughts for I felt unspeakably rejected. And at that moment, Hastings announced that the baths were ready and all three men, so strong and superb in their masculinity, were disrobed by attendants and stepped naked into their baths. I withdrew. I had no wish to stay with the ladies. I yearned to share in the world of men, but clearly was not wanted. At the risk of royal displeasure, I did not rejoin them later for a nightcap. I was sure I would not be missed.

***

The next morning — after a night with one of the court's best ladies of the night — I felt refreshed by the springs of youth. After all, was it not to the glory of God and the king that no harm had been done to either combatant? And was I not still closer to the king than any man apart from his three or four closest confidants? And as I began moving around the cloisters of the palace, I heard that matters were not perhaps as unclouded as they seemed. Rumours were flying about that the Bastard was unhappy, angry even at Anthony's "unchivalric" behaviour, and would be demanding some satisfaction for his wrongs on the second day of the meet. I, of course, playing the part of the diplomat and royal brother-in-law, soothed all this over, assuring all I met that I had seen the king with the two gentlemen and all had been good fellowship and brotherliness. Which was certainly what I had seen — and believed — to be true. But it gave me just a touch of satisfaction to suspect that perhaps all was not as perfect as I had fondly imagined.

***

It had been announced that the tournament was to last three days and would culminate in a grand banquet in Westminster Hall in honour of the Bastard and — if all had gone well — of the forthcoming marriage treaty between the two dynasties. As I was being dressed by my grooms in preparation for the second day, Q appeared in my chamber with a look of inscrutability on his face. I knew this meant rumour and intrigue were afoot. So, I dismissed the lads telling them to stay near to perfume my hair before I left (yes, I was a popinjay in those days, but so was half the court — even Warwick — when not on campaign) and turned to the fussing Q.

"Prithee take heed, my lord! There is so much ado concerning the Lord Bastard and Lord Scales."

"I have heard those rumours, Q. They are merely a wind-egg. I saw the king and both those gentlemen last night in great good fellowship."

"To please His Grace, my lord, and to use Your Lordship's good offices to spread that very picture."

I gave Q a hard look. I resented his view that I was being used in that way.

"My lord, I have it from Lord Hastings' own groom who was waiting upon my lord the Bastard and speaks well the French tongue — as spoken in Brussels, my lord…"

"Yes, I know French is spoken in Brussels, Q, and speak it myself."

"Of course, my lord, but not all retainers do so. But *this one* does and he told me that after the combat, my lord, the Bastard was *furious*, accusing my Lord Anthony of unknightly conduct in striking and disarming him before battle was rejoined. And — and this is the worst, my lord — that today the Bastard will have his vengeance upon my Lord Anthony so that he will repent his — forgive me, sir — unchivalric conduct."

"Unchivalric conduct? It was an error, a mistake is all."

Q brushed this aside. "And, Lord Edward, I hear that my Lord of Warwick — who is well-informed of the rumours — has decided to attend at today's meet in order to witness the bloodshed and to crow over the end of the Burgundian alliance which is bound to follow."

I realised at once that this would be a disaster; a defeat for the king and a great loss of face for my Lady Margaret. I had to prevent it.

As I was about to head off to the king, a royal chamberlain arrived to see me, wearing the livery of my Lady Margaret. He handed me a note from her which read: Woe is me! The Bastard has asked the king's leave to depart. I hear that yesterday's combat has put him in high dudgeon with Lord Scales — and with all our House. How can we placate him? *Il faut ne pas cacher ce mariage. Aidez-moi, monseigneur.*

Here was a need, and an opportunity, to bring succour to my lady, for whom this marriage — a marriage which she had suffered doubts about so recently — had now become a matter of honour and prestige.

Accompanied by Q (whose expression showed he had rightly guessed the contents of the note), I had some anxious minutes in the king's guardroom, awaiting admittance. If the Bastard left England in anger, this would be a major diplomatic incident and would put paid to the lady's marriage to the Comte de Charolais and to the king's Burgundian alliance. We would have to turn to France, and Warwick would have triumphed over the king. To avoid this disaster, I would offer myself as a personal envoy from the king, travelling with the Bastard to Brussels to offer His Grace's apologies and reparations to Duke Jean, his father. I would offer myself as a hostage for the payment of those reparations and any other demands that the duke might make. In this way, I could sacrifice myself for the sake of my lady, and of my brother-in-arms, Anthony Wydville.

Hastings emerged from the king's chamber and beckoned me in. The king was standing with Anthony on one side and Antoine of Burgundy on the other. All three looked very sombre. The state of things was very bad indeed.

"You have heard the dolorous tidings, De-la-Pole?"

"Ay, Your Grace, and I wish to offer my services or my body as a hostage should that be of any use in this impasse."

The king, handsome and grave, gave me an odd look of quizzical disapproval, as if I had farted aloud. I should have kept my mouth shut.

The king turned to Anthony, who explained. "In the light of today's sorrowful tidings, Monsieur Antoine will be taking his leave of the court to return to Brussels forthwith at the command of his brother Duke Charles. The king wishes you to accompany him and his men to their ships — once you are suitably attired."

It suddenly struck me that all three of them were in white — the colour of royal mourning.

Now I may not have the mind of an Aristotle or a Thomas Aquinas but, within a few seconds, I had deduced that my festive attire was completely inappropriate and, like the three great men before me, I should have been in mourning. The Bastard's father had suddenly died and his brother was now duke. This piece of ill fortune for the House of Burgundy was a sudden piece of good fortune for us. It provided the perfect cause to end the tournament with honour and hush up the question of Anthony's conduct and the Bastard's anger. All was swept away in courtly mourning.

For a moment, I almost laughed with joy, then put on my most serious face.

The king nodded. I withdrew. Anthony followed me into the ante-chamber.

"And," he whispered, "The new duke's letter says he is anxious to conclude the marriage treaty in haste as he needs an heir to the duchy — and is already, so he says, in love with the lady."

He winked at me and turned back.

The Lady Margaret would have her marriage; not, however, thanks to me.

Book II: Spring

τ (zayin)

And now I should paint for you a delightful picture, like the monkish illuminations in a priceless manuscript, of a voyage across water by a noble party all bedecked in glorious finery to escort a beautiful royal damsel to her marriage to a handsome and noble prince where love blossoms between them and all is feasting and good fellowship. And I could do that, because so it was. Except... except that now, all these years after, I cannot. For I have made so many journeys since and so many other sadder faces of life that I neither will, nor can, remember the details of that almost eventless enterprise.

If life is a pageant, then my voyage to the Low Countries, my first time out of the kingdom, was its most colourful and chivalric day. At the Yorkist court back in the 60s, we thought we had the finest food, the richest wines, the loveliest in art and fashion. But, in truth, we had seen nothing. The court of Burgundy — the distillation of the Netherlandish cities — had so much more, a culture so much richer and finer and more refined. Here, in Brussels, Bruges and Ghent, were splendour and chivalry; pageantry indeed. And it was in the kingdom of Burgundy that I bade farewell to my Lady Margaret, and became blood brothers with my beloved friend, Anthony.

Burgundy never became a kingdom, of course, despite its enormous wealth and the burgeoning power of its dukes, and in spite of the luminous value of his lovely heiress Madame Mary and her wedding to Maximilian von Habsburg, his son and heir, the old hook-nosed Emperor Frederick would never agree to his elevation to a crown; neither that of Burgundy, nor that of Rome. Poor Duke Charles! The richest ruler in Europe, but unable to call himself a king, and in the end, it all fell apart. But I leap ahead. In those days, Charles was a young widower with one daughter, anxious to marry a fair princess and beget an heir to his kingdom-to-be. Hence our grandiose journey across land and sea to the realm of Burgundy.

Had it been under my sole leadership, our elegant little flotilla would have sailed from my own port of Hull, which is the shortest distance from the coast of Holland, securely within the domain of the duke. However, it was not thought fitting for a royal bride to be sent to the northern parts of the kingdom (just in case, as I jested to Anthony, the savages might still be wearing woad), and, more seriously, because there was still Lancastrian fealty seething amongst some northern knights and gentle families. The Earl of Warwick proposed that our ships should make landfall at his port of Calais (where he had been governor for many years) and he would personally escort our party across French territory, having secured safe conduct from King Louis (the eleventh of that name) with whom he was becoming suspiciously friendly. Anthony thought this was a splendid idea, but, with my more suspicious mind, I feared a trap at the hands of Warwick and the French king, in whose power the Lady Margaret (and, to a lesser extent Anthony and I) would be a very valuable hostage.

And so we sailed — waved off by the king and queen themselves in state — from the lovely cinque port of Sandwich, keeping a wary eye on Warwick's well-equipped ships escorting us across the English Channel. But they all saluted us courteously, dipping their sails to acknowledge our royal cargo. Clearly the wily old bear had not yet decided to make his move.

Our disembarkation at the port they call Zeebrugge would be a perfect tableau for our pageant, like a panel from the Bayeux tapestry. The port was strewn and bedecked with the most wonderful and colourful banners and images, like a welcome for Queen Guinevere herself, coming to marry with her King Arthur. The atmosphere of anticipation and hopefulness was palpable. It was spring in nature and a spring of hope for the new and lovely bride of their handsome young duke. A choir sang the "Te Deum" as we disembarked, to be met by the Archbishop of Brussels and the Sieur de Gruuthuse — one of Duke Charles' senior courtiers, and one whom we would come to know much better in time. They were sent by the duke as his personal envoys and greeted us — and above all, our bridal cargo — with the utmost courtesy and grace.

The bobaunce with which we were received at Bruges — perhaps Charles' most beauteous city — has become a byword for splendour and hospitality and the fabulously colourful pageant with which the Brugeois received their new duchess and her entourage has been repeated annually since, and no doubt will be for centuries to come. What really mattered was this: that when the Lady Margaret, flanked by Anthony and me, was ceremonially presented to the duke — resplendent in his golden armour in imitation of his patron St. George — his eyes straightway were fixed upon his betrothed with a gaze that spoke of admiration and desire. He was — thanks be to God! — entranced. And the lady's reaction was no less relieved;

she was blissfully happy. Against all the odds of such a state wedding, a marriage by treaty, it was love at first sight, the love that should have been between Iseult and King Mark, had not her passion for Sir Tristram intervened.

From Bruges, we were escorted by the Sieur de Gruuthuse to Brussels, Duke Charles' capital city, grander than Bruges if less picturesque and pretty, where the duke was to be officially presented with his new duchess. On that joyous morning, we passed through the great throng of the people expressing their joy, making our *Joyeuse Entrée* through the great gate of the town and thence through all the crowded squares where wine was flowing in abundance from the fountains. Our breath was almost taken away as we rode into the enormous, magnificent Grande Place — probably the greatest town square in northern Europe — Anthony and I riding on handsome palfreys, his black, mine white, on either side of our fair princess reclining on a splendid litter, her hair all flowing dark and long and lovely onto her marble shoulders. She waved modestly yet warmly to the people feeling their love and good wishes. And, at moments, she would glance to left or right at Anthony and me with a little smile of recognition and reassurance. No queen or empress could have received a more loving welcome to her new kingdom.

We entered the Great Hall of the palace in grand procession with Louis de Gruuthuse preceding us, Anthony on the lady's right, I on her left; her hands gently and elegantly resting in ours. Her dress was long and white in the lightest silk, to display her pure virginal state, whilst Anthony and I wore handsome doublets of velvet, his a bold vermilion, mine of a rich dark blue, with sleeves slashed to show off our fine silk shirts beneath. In the fashion of that time, we wore our doublets very short to reveal the shapely cups of our buttocks. We both had on our golden chains of King Edward's emblem of the sun in splendour. Remember, we were here as much to impress as to be impressed.

As we walked slowly in, the duke's finest musicians in the gallery above were playing "Ah, Flanders Free" — a most joyous melody by Thomas Fabri, who had been court composer to Duke Charles' grandfather, Phillip the Bold, and was followed by even more wondrous music composed by his own Master of Music, the great Josquin des Prez. Being, by this time, an experienced courtier, I was able to keep my features composed as I saw, on the duke's left hand exactly facing Anthony, who but my lord the Bastard Antoine with fixed and solemn features, whilst I was processing as slowly but surely to face the Cardinal-Archbishop of Brussels; a much less alarming figure in this setting. But, I am no fool, not a son of the great Duchess Alice Chaucer for nothing, so as we approached closer to the ducal party en face, to the exact beat of Josquin's stately dance rhythm, I half-turned, bowed to my Lady Margaret, and did an elegant dosey doe round behind her, while giving a sharp nod to Anthony to do likewise. He took my purpose at once and thus, as we reached to the first step of the ducal dais, we were elegantly reversed, with Anthony facing the crinkly old card, and myself smiling with brotherly love upon my lord le Bastard. Even he could not resist cracking a sort of smile.

Monsieur de Gruuthuse now formally presented Anthony and myself to the duke as we bowed low — one would kneel only to a king — and then announced, "Your Highness, I present the wondrous lady, and most high and mighty princess, the

Lady Margaret, sister to the most high and *illustre* prince, King Edward of England, France and Ireland."

Duke Charles — handsome in a sombre and fascinating Valois way (the dukes were cousins, of course, to the kings of France) — now divested of his golden armour and clothed in a long and beautiful robe of heavy purple velvet, on his head the most magnificent and fabulous headdress I have ever seen (as fine as any crown), his eyes fixed lustfully upon our lovely Lady — a bit too lustfully to my possessive eyes — moved forward towards her and placing his hands upon her elegant shoulders — they were exactly the same height, most conveniently — kissed her, full and passionately upon the mouth. She returned the kiss, long and clearly heartfelt, with the same passion. And at that, the whole long hall, filled with the nobility, court officials and richer merchants of the most chivalrous appanage in Christendom, erupted in a great éclat of whoops and cheers and applause. Hats — elegant if smaller copies of that worn by His Highness — were tossed in the air and the order of court protocol was momentarily thrust aside.

Then, at a sign from Monsieur de Gruuthuse, the Great Chamberlain — an official in a splendid costume standing to our left — banged his great staff three times firmly on the stone floor, and at once decorum was renewed. Now that's what I call protocol. The duke now handed the Lady Margaret round to his right side — indicating that she was now in effect his bride, his property — thus forcing his bastard brother to step a little further to *his* right. As if to make up for this apparent sleight, he now turned and, with a very slight smile — neither of the ducal brothers could accurately be called a smiler — nodded and asked, "Now our bride has been put into our hands, to commence the entertainments of our wedding, perhaps our brother would care to break a lance in knightly brotherhood with our Lady's brother-in-law, Lord Scales?"

There was a moment's agonised silence.

The Bastard then replied, only just loud enough to be heard, "Your Highness will forgive your humble servant if he pleads a temporary weakness of his right arm, caused by a fall last evening." And then raising his voice a trifle sharply, menacingly even, added, "That arm which is, in spite of weakness, ready to defend the honour of Your Highness and his noble House unto the death."

At this, there was polite applause from all the Burgundian courtiers with which, of course, we guests joined in. I caught the eye of Sieur Louis — a man not handsome but with a very shrewd and *interesting* face and a most intelligent, ironic eye. Which then, I noticed, fell onto my left hand on the fourth finger of which I was, quite carelessly, wearing the big and splendid balas ruby ring which — you may remember — had been gifted me, somewhat mysteriously, by the old peasant man in Hull. I could never wear it at court, of course, because of the lie that had, for reasons I could not explain, sprung to my lips when my adored sovereign asked if I had ever seen it. But I felt free to put it on my finger, and indeed felt it right to do so when travelling abroad, to represent the Crown of England — and the house of De-la-Pole — as nobly as possible. Louis' eye, having rested on it, then met mine again, with a new brightness and — did I imagine it? — a certain shrewd complicity.

The duke said, "No more talk of death. This is a day of rejoicing. Let us feast."

At this, the duke and his soon-to-be duchess led our procession down the length of the hall, to the great applause, bows and salutations of the assembled court, out into the courtyard where sumptuous tables had been set out for dinner, with a High Table on a dais solely for the serving of Duke Charles and the Lady Margaret. We of the English party were sat, of course, at the second table, together with the Lord of Gruuthuse and the Cardinal-Archbishop; the Bastard having conveniently withdrawn — to lick his wounded arm perhaps? The banquet was, of course, magnificent with more dishes and toasts than I can possibly remember. After the first and second courses had been cleared, Louis turned to me — he had spoken mainly to Anthony thus far — and said in good English with a guttural Flemish accent, rather than the French of the duke himself, "I hear we are to be served with English cheeses. Surely the best in the whole of Christendom."

I raised a newly filled goblet. "And, my lord, I drink His Highness' finest Burgundy wine to Your Lordship and to our fine English cheeses."

We both drank.

"And," he said more softly, taking a quick glance at my ruby ring, "To your membership of the brotherhood."

I smiled, enigmatically. I hoped.

"Perhaps Your Lordship — and his friend the Lord Anthony — would care to accompany your humble host to a more private party later, for exchanges of a more... esoteric kind."

"I'm in," I replied, enchanted. I looked at Anthony. He had overheard and smiled with a smile that would light up the world. My heart leapt at the thought of what the evening might hold. But my mind was taken off that for the moment as a great dish of slices of Leche Lumbarde were being served, my favourite rich dessert in those days — those days before the weakened digestion of old age gripped my stomach — that delicious mixture of dates, honey, cinnamon and sweet white wine; oh, if only I could eat it now…

My lady was no longer *my* lady I understood; she was now the duke's Lady and his voracious eyes revealed he would fully satisfy her carnal Yorkist nature — so like her brother's, the king's — with a lusty gusto I would prefer not to imagine. There seemed every chance of their engendering the next heir to Burgundy and a healthy brood of spares to follow. So as Their Highnesses withdrew to their respective suites for their final night unwed, Anthony and I were therefore consigned to the fraternal hospitality of Louis de Gruuthuse.

M. de G., with his odd, interesting, intelligent face, asked us if we would do him the honour of accompanying him to a small meeting of his friends, and, as he said this, he toyed with the signet ring on the middle finger of his left hand which I noticed, with casual interest, was a smaller companion to my own, and said they were, "all gentlemen of a higher calling, like yourselves, my lords."

I looked to Anthony, who as the senior of us both in age and in the king's confidence I tended to look up to, as he smiled assent. We followed Monsieur de Gruuthuse behind the ducal throne, through ante-chambers, along tunnels, up turrets, along battlements and finally into a long sombre cavernous hall where a large number of gentlemen were seated at a great round table. As we entered, they stood. A nice touch. Louis took his seat and motioned us to sit at either side of him. As he lifted a golden goblet brimming with red Burgundy wine, a deep voice said, "I spy strangers."

M. de G. replied, "They are brothers, my friends, and will this night be initiated into our fellowship." He lifted the goblet. "Barukh haba b'shem adoshem."

Words I did not recognise then, but have learnt since.

To which the assembled brethren replied, "Barukh haba b'veis adoshem."

"The Fellowship of the Knights of the Round Table is in session," Louis announced.

The same sonorous voice said — this time not in French but in English, "They are strangers of the rising sun. Let them swear the oath before we commence."

In the gloom, I could barely make out the speaker's face. But I recognised the Warwickshire accent. It was our old enemy, turned friend, turned enemy: Thomas Malory.

Another voice spoke. "As Sir Ector knoweth, here there is no rising no nor setting sun, and but one Brotherhood. Therefore, be silent, sir, and let these goodly gentlemen take part in our proceedings."

This knight, an older, distinguished gentleman, spoke in the most elegant Parisian French, whom we later learnt to be King René of Anjou, father of the House of York's most bitter adversary, Margaret of Anjou. For these knights were indeed the cream of European chivalry, gathered *sub rosa* to celebrate the marriage of the bold duke and to talk, without prejudice and under a sacred truce, of all and any of the many problems and enmities besetting our lands. King René was highly esteemed throughout Christendom as the doyen of chivalry; his word on the point was therefore final and we were accepted into the Brotherhood.

The initial proceedings concerned the formalities of the meeting: amendment of statutes, election of officers and the like, leading up to the nomination of new members, each of whom was to be voted in under an Arthurian name, subject to their swearing the oath, and undergoing the initiation rite of the Order.

Monsieur Louis turned first to my friend. "Wilt thou, Anthony, under the name Sir Galahad, join our Brotherhood and swear to uphold its statutes, secrecy and comradeship unto death?"

"I will," answered Anthony's rich, clear voice.

"And wilt thou, Edward, by the style of Sir Gawain, swear the same oath?"

"I will," I answered boldly.

"And do you both bind yourselves this very day to undergo the ordeal of your initiation into our band of brothers?"

As one, we replied, "We do."

With that, the forty or so knights around the table cried out their approbation with shouts of "Vale!", "Salut!" and even "Yesh'koakh!" (a Hebrew salutation).

Our Master of Ceremonies — M. de G. — twice clapped his hands and wines and sweetmeats were brought in. We all moved to partake of these from long tables at the further end of the room, where informal fraternisation could take place.

Many of the brethren crowded round to congratulate us, amongst them, of course, Sir Ector, alias good old, bad old, devilish Tom Malory.

"And what brings you two miscreants to Burgundy?" He slapped us both on the back, hard.

"You haven't heard the great duke is to marry the King of England's sister?"

"And which King of England would that be?" he guffawed.

"Tom, you old varlet, will you never change?"

"He changes all the time, with the wind, Anthony, don't you remember?" I put in, a tad sourly.

"And *you* must remember, my new brothers, that here I am Sir Ector, whilst you, I believe, are Galahad and Gawain. Let us strive to live up to the glory of our names."

We drank to that. There was little else we could do.

"Notwithstanding," said Anthony to me, "It might be prudent while we are here to speak to wise King René to ask him to restrain his strong-headed daughter from any moves to try to split the House of York and launch an incursion into England. She and her beloved son are surely safer staying on his lands in France."

"Is this the time and place, Sir Galahad?" I had to smile at the name, which befitted the honest and chivalric Anthony so well.

"It's the only time and place, Sir Gawain."

We sought the king, an elderly gentleman with a mass of white hair, a worshipful and regal manner, and a handsome Angevin face. It was easy to see whence his daughter had inherited her famed beauty. Though not her termagant spirit.

"Greetings to Your Grace," we said.

The king without a kingdom smiled mildly. "Here, my brethren, I am Sir Bors."

"In troth, sir," said Anthony, "And perhaps Sir Bors would consider a petition from two brothers-in-law of the English king to use his good offices and his famed wisdom to restrain the war-like proclivities of his daughter, the former Queen Margaret."

"Sir Bors has no *patria potestas* over Queen Margaret, sirs. She is her own woman, though she resides — *pro tem* — in my castle of Koeur near Verdun. But, as is well attested, peace between the nations of Christendom is my desire, and to preserve the rights — and above all the life — of my grandson, Prince Edward. And if my embassy here succeeds, which is to ensure continuing amity between Dukes Charles and my brother of France, then Margaret will have neither gold nor men with which to wage war on your brother-in-law, the de facto King of England."

We bowed low.

"You Grace… Sir Bors and your humble petitioners think alike," said Anthony. I was beginning to see why our king placed so much trust in Anthony.

"Peace is for the sake of Heaven," said René, "As the ancient rabbis tell us."

I thought Anthony's left eye winked at me. The old king was well known for his eccentric love of the Hebrew race.

"Gentlemen," he concluded, "My family have lost too many kingdoms to grieve over the loss of another. Unless perchance…" He paused thoughtfully.

"Sir Bors?" I said, intrigued.

"Unless a marriage might be mooted between my grandson, Edward of Lancaster, and the eldest daughter of King Edward?"

Anthony and I shot shocked glances at each other.

"I don't see Clarence approving of that," I said.

"Nor I fear the queen, my sister," said Anthony.

"A wedding is better than a battle, I wean," said the old king. "And ofttimes there is little difference."

We smiled and bowed.

As we approached our host, Monsieur Louis, we paused at a small distance so as to avoid appearing to overhear his deep conversation with a large and fearsome knight, who must have weighed fifteen or sixteen stone *avoir du poid* — an enormous size. He was speaking French with a strongly Germanic accent. We listened avidly whilst appearing not to be.

"An envoy from the German emperor?" I whispered.

Anthony nodded.

The German was saying, "A crown is always within the gift of His Majesty…"

"If the price is right?" laughed M. de Gruuthuse.

The German — who, strangely, had little sense of humour — replied more stridently, "If the circumstances are right and it is good for the empire. But the Crown of Rome itself…"

We were spell-bound.

"… that is a lot to ask, when the emperor himself has a son."

"Indeed," said Louis, "But remember that the duke has a daughter, his heiress, who could be a perfect match for that son…"

"And the duke has just married and is likely to have sons a-plenty, leaving the lady *grundlos*…"

I grimaced at Anthony.

"Landless," he mouthed. He had a wide knowledge of European, and other, tongues. I noted the curving beauty of his own tongue between sensuously crimson lips.

Louis had by now noticed us, and bowed, beckoning us closer.

"This is Sir Accolon, who hails from the German lands. But I'm sure you had gathered that."

We must have looked a touch embarrassed for he followed this up at once with: "Gentlemen, we have no secrets here. But all is covered with the veil of unknowing cast by our oaths — the oaths which you are about to swear. Follow me."

Anthony and I followed Louis out of the great hall, through the gloom of many twisting and turning passages, and down into the vaults deep beneath the castle, where our sacred initiation into the Brotherhood was to take place.

***

I will not describe in detail the complex — and deeply satisfying — initiation rites to which Anthony and I were subjected. It would be a breaking of our oaths and an affront to the Order (which still, of course, exists — how else would I be residing now in the old lands of Burgundy?). Suffice it to say that it created and enhanced a deep sense of brotherhood amongst the brethren. It entailed a ritual of purification and rebirth, with deep spiritual significance: bathing, blindfolds, oaths and nakedness. All the usual accoutrements of secret societies. There were some *un*usual touches. At one point, well into the toils of the evening, we were standing, both naked and blindfolded, but I knew it was Anthony still by me as I could smell his warm, nutty body scent (like crushed walnuts and figs with a hint of rosemary) and could feel the touch of his right hand on my left. A voice we had not yet heard in the ritual commanded us to kneel. It was the Germanic voice of the mountainous imperial envoy.

"The new brethren shall, without questioning, take between their lips, one after the other, the large living organ/ baton of flesh the Master shall present them with, and suck it empty of all fluid. They shall drink down to the last drop the nectar of the ancient gods, to cleanse them of all past sins."

This sounded a very shocking and heathen thought and I felt Anthony grip my left hand, briefly, tightly. Then the large organ touched my lips. I sucked its sweet amber fluid, with a slightly salty over-taste. It was a piece of juicy meat, fresh and wholesome, though from what animal I am unsure. I felt a sense of deep satisfaction as the gobbet — somehow replenished — was passed on to my companion.

After Anthony too was satiated, the guttural voice said, with surprising warmth, "Now, we are brothers."

He was so close I could smell his sweat too; muskier and heavier than Anthony's and a little stale. His huge stomach brushed against my cheeks as he raised me into his massive, and very brotherly, embrace.

After this, we were guided and clapped through a corridor in total darkness leading to a gently lighted chamber, scented with the sweetest herbs where, our blindfolds removed, we were again bathed by handsome youths and anointed with the finest, most fragrant oils of cinnamon, rose and cloves. Our hair was combed and we were dressed in long silken robes of an eastern style. Monsieur Louis came in to join us, similarly garbed, and welcomed us officially into the Order with a fine scented Burgundy wine and sweetmeats.

"Now, my brothers, if it would please you to take a little carnal pleasure, these pages will guide you safely into the stews of Brussels, where all sensual delights are freely yours for the taking — for this night."

We looked into each other's eyes and Anthony smiled. "*Pourquoi pas?*"

We were led into an inner courtyard of the palace where we took our seats in a handsome wagon decorated with gilding but without heraldic identification. There were grooms, in discreet leather jerkins, holding the horses. We trundled along through backstreets to a house of ill-repute, the first I had ever visited — outside Hull — which I was astonished to discover was charming, and beautifully scented. Lovely maidens greeted us at the portal, regaling us with wines and honies ever finer than those I had tasted at royal courts. A magnificently muscled youth and damsel entertained us with acrobatics and dance whilst wonderfully nimble fingers plucked the strings of harps to soothe our souls, while others equally nimble soothed our tired bodies with caresses. Over the un-Christian sensualities in which we indulged I will draw a veil, except to say that while my pleasures were fulfilled by young men of remarkable beauty, Anthony was, mainly, in the hands of their softer sisters. After some hours of such enchantment, and darkness had long fallen, we found ourselves returning, by the same conveyance, satiated and happily united as brothers, and loving friends. And *that* night, we were not divided.

***

"When will you marry, Eddie?"

We were lounging on divans in Anthony's private chamber in the home we now, in effect, shared on the banks of the Thames, between London and Westminster, where most of the nobility's mansions were sited. Ostensibly, my home was with my brother and sister-in-law, or even with the B.M. herself at Ewelme. And, of course, I also had chambers in the Palace of Westminster as a member of the court, and as the king's kinsman. But more and more I was spending time residing at Anthony's abode; our blood brotherhood — an honourable state amongst knights and young noblemen — being acknowledged. So his question came as something of a surprise.

"We have recently given away, to a voracious foreign prince, the only woman I have ever actually wanted to marry."

He smiled, indulgently. "I know. But when will you marry?"

"Your own marriage hardly seems an incentive to others." This was a low blow, and I at once felt ashamed of it.

"You know our marriage was arranged by my all-seeing mother as a step in her campaign to claw back the status she had lost by marrying my father — for love, of course."

"I know and I am sorry for it, my dear friend. But you cannot expect me to be inspired to marry when I see how little time you and your wife spend together, or wish to do."

"She brought me a barony and some money, but neither companionship, nor even desire. And, as you know, I do desire women."

"As do I, on occasion," I added, defensively.

"All the more reason to marry then. I am sure your honoured mother — one of the women I most admire — and your brother the duke would expect it."

"Not really. My brother has married at the highest level and he and his lady spend their entire time a-rutting. One of us has to take an interest in politics and war and such other trivia."

"You are incorrigible, Edward. But you could found your own dynasty."

"And so could you," I countered.

He looked uncomfortable. "My Lady Scales and I are incompatible. However, I do not expect her to live long."

I was startled but felt it would be unwise to probe this.

"Which is why I hope that Duke Charles will not marry his heiress daughter to the Archduke Maximilian too quickly. Once our sister-in-law has given him a son, Mary of Burgundy may be available for wooing by the brother-in-law of the King of England."

He gave me what the B.M. might call an old-fashioned look.

"You mean... we might both be in contention?"

"Who knows? But do we really need to spend our whole lives in the realm of England? We could both find an appanage and found a dynasty elsewhere in Christendom, and the Netherlands are rich in lovely heiresses..."

"And fertile lands..."

"And wondrous works of art and scholarship. There is a new world beyond these narrow shores, my Edward, and a new spirit, a rebirth. Have you heard of the painter Giotto, or the worker in marble, called Donatello?"

I stared at him, like an idiot.

"They are both Florentines, Eddie, and Florence is a wonderful city-state we should visit. Perhaps we can persuade the king to send us there on an embassy to encourage... trade, scholarship, artistic creation! In Italy, they are calling it the *renatio* or the *renascenza* and we two brothers-in-arms should play our parts in bringing it here to England..."

But Anthony's noble dream had to stay floating in our minds as we were dragged back by sudden events to our dark age of internecine war and treachery.

Before I could respond to his vision, a familiar groom entered the chamber.

"Desperate news, my lords. The king has been taken prisoner by the Earl of Warwick and his brother the Archbishop of York."

"Where?"

"At Olney, near Northampton, my lord. I have a message from him to both Your Lordships."

He handed it over and withdrew. Anthony read it out:

My friends, I am in Warwick's thrall. Your warnings were prudent. I should have heeded them. I am being taken to Warwick Castle. He is allied with false Clarence, now his son-in-law. I shall play friendly and bide my time. Lie low in London until I summon you. And warn your kinsmen to do likewise until the moment is ripe.

Your loving liege lord, Edward.

"So like the king," I said. "Brave and generous and thinking of our safety."

"I thought it was his *sister* you were in thrall to! The king is wisely thinking of preserving the lives of those whom he trusts. We must warn my father and brother, and your brother, the duke."

"Warwick cannot kill the king. He would lose all his own support. And provoke a Lancastrian uprising."

"I hope you are right, Eddie. But I fear for my father; Warwick has always hated him."

He began scribbling a note to his father, Lord Rivers, and called back the groom.

"Take this to Lord Rivers. I presume he is at home with my mother."

"It is too late, my lord," said the boy, ashen-faced. "Lord Rivers… we have just heard the news, my lord…" He began to weep.

"Speak up, varlet," I said angrily. "What has happened?"

"Do not berate the boy," said Anthony, more kindly. "Tell us the news, however bad. You will not be punished for it."

"Earl Rivers and Sir John Wydville were taken captive by Warwick in Somerset. He ordered their beheading, my lords. I am sorry, Lord Anthony."

"Leave us, boy," I said.

I turned to Anthony whose face was the picture of grief and shock.

"May God take their souls in his hands," I said. "So much for your brave new world." I cradled my friend's head in my arms as the tears began.

***

So now a new bond united me with Anthony, a bond of sorrowfulness and, perhaps, of vengeance. Each had lost his father, in the prime of his life, to a violent and unlawful death. My heart travelled back to that sorrowful day when I was five and my mother received the doleful news. My father was the first casualty of the Cousins' Wars — though it was five years before the next blow was struck. Earl Rivers' death was the first killing in the fissure (the *first* fissure) within the House of York; a fissure that began with King Edward's decision to marry for love. And as it was love for the sister of the man I loved, how could I criticise that?

Who had ordered the beheading of *my* father we never discovered, though the finger was pointed at the old Duke of York — or perchance his bitch-duchess; she who was "queen by right". You might then ask how it was that the B.M. had married my brother John to their daughter. But you should reflect that in the upper circles of power sometimes pride — and vengeance — must be swallowed in order to achieve a higher goal: climbing ever nearer the throne. Sentimental feelings are for the merchant class.

I am sure we had known that an uprising had taken place in the north country, led by a shadowy figure called Robin of Redesdale, and that the king had taken a substantial force with him to deal with them. We had no doubt of his success and, indeed, he had appointed us both as members of an informal regency council during his absence from the capital. But it turned out that this Robin's forces were a great host, even if a rabble, and the king prudently waited for reinforcements to reach him before going to meet them. The Earl of Pembroke (not the Tudor but his Yorkist replacement) and the Earl of Devon were due to meet His Grace but they appear to have quarrelled over some triviality; at any rate, when the royal army met the rebels at Edgecote, our side had no archers and panicked. They fled, leaving the king isolated with just a small entourage. And so, he fell into the hands of the Neville brothers. But, as his letter to us made clear, *he* did not panic but calmly fell in with his captors and smilingly played their game. Meanwhile, Warwick showed his savage side by taking vengeance on those he perceived as his enemies, including my Anthony's father and brother. They were executed without trial and for no reason other than Warwick's bitterness. And remember that Earl Rivers was the queen's father.

The new Earl Rivers and I kept a very low profile at his London mansion as instructed by the king. We heard no more from His Grace during the next three or four weeks, which was a time of great anxiety. But then a new channel of communication opened up. One hot morning in late August as we sat in our courtyard playing a fitful game of chess, we heard knocking at the outer gate. It was perfectly possible that this was a band of Warwick's affinity sent to kill us and we both grabbed our swords, as did the five or six of our retainers who were nearby. We would not go down without a fight, but I was aware we were facing our own mortality. I looked severely at Anthony and he replied with a kind of crooked smile.

"My friend," I said.

The inner door opened and the groom calmly entered. My racing heart began to slow down.

"There is a visitor for you, my lord," he said, looking at me. "He says he is a retainer from… 'ull?"

At this, I began to laugh, as a well-built young man — no, he had become a sort of Hercules — walked in and knelt, smiling, before us. It was Malcolm.

"Well, my heart rejoices to see you, Malcolm. Though, to speak truth, anyone would be better than one of Warwick's henchmen. This is a retainer of mine from Kingston upon Hull, Anthony. He is a good man."

"And a particularly comely one, I see," murmured my friend, a little put out it seemed. Then louder, he asked, "What have you to tell us, young man?"

"My lords, I was sent to the West Riding by the Lord Mayor of Hull in order to get some news of the great trouble that was bruited between King Edward and the Earl of Warwick, and while there I heard that the king had moved — under guard it was said — from Warwick to Middleham Castle. So I rode there and garnered such news as I could."

"And... come on, boy, what is the news?"

"They are saying there is an uprising in the north country in the name of King Harry — the sometime King Harry — and Warwick is having trouble raising a force to fight them."

"And the king?" I asked.

"The king is in good health and sends a message to my Lord Edward to keep yourself and your friends in readiness to hold London in the king's name when he has got his liberty from Warwick's power. In the meantime, he speaks soft words to my Lord of Warwick to keep him sweet."

"Very wise," said Anthony.

"And he asks you, sir, to send a message to your brother the Duke of Suffolk to be ready to attend him with his power when the time is right."

We sent Malcolm back to Middleham with a covert message to be delivered, if opportunity allowed, only to the king himself, that we were watching and waiting and keeping his true lieges informed. I assured Anthony that if anyone could find a way to deliver this, it was Malcolm — and, I bet him, return with a royal reply.

"Forsooth, he is a talented lad, and a clean-limbed one as well... You know him well?"

I was amused by Anthony's question. We were keeping ourselves active and in trim that morning, like most mornings, with sword play. Unfortunately, there was inadequate room in the yard to exercise om horseback, and we felt it wiser to stay indoors. In the afternoons, Anthony would continue his translation into English of Boethius' *De Consolatione Philosophiae* — very apposite in the circumstances — while I played my harp, wrote letters to our friends or slept.

"I do suspect my friend is jealous," I said with a thrust at his exposed chest.

"Trash and bollocks!" he replied with an excellent parry, almost knocking me over. "Why should I be jealous of a Yorkshire churl?"

"Watcha, Sir Anthony," I said, riposting with a blow that almost removed the sword from his hand. "Your blood brother is descended from Yorkshire churls. They're the salt of the earth."

"You mean the shit of the Humber," he laughed with a move that *did* knock the sword from *my* hand.

I leapt at him, grabbing him round the waist, which was not as slim as had been the case; we had been eating too many sweetmeats in seclusion. And then we were on the ground.

We were wrestling determinedly — he would never give in, while I would, only occasionally, surrender — and he was splayed on top of me while I was thrusting upwards to throw him off when there was repeated coughing from nearby.

"My lords," said the groom, urgently.

We paused, utterly breathless, staring at each other.

"My lords, the lord mayor and aldermen attend upon you."

Anthony sprang off as if he had been whipped.

At that moment, we had no idea whether these London powerbrokers had turned up to arrest us on the orders of Warwick — who had always been popular with the city of London — or to assure us of their loyalty to the king. As we had neither forces available nor orders from the king, we had so far kept a wary distance from these burghers, merely sending them a letter telling them the king was in good health and would, in due time, send them his commands, to which they had sent no reply. Clearly, this was it.

These were no bumbling yokels like the good aldermen of Kingston upon Hull. These were men of real substance and great wealth, whose unwillingness to open the gates of the city to Margaret of Anjou in February '61, preferring instead to welcome in Edward of York just a few weeks later, had been decisive for our side. The House of York had been able to rely on their support, but so had its erstwhile ally, the Earl of Warwick. Their response to our letter could be hugely strategic.

In full robes of office, they looked exceedingly uncomfortable in the heat, and perhaps at what they had just seen. But there was no aggression in their eyes, just seriousness, and some surprise. Anthony — despite the uncertainties he must have shared — was at once master of the situation.

"God be with you, my Lord Mayor and aldermen. I hope, sirs, you bring good news from our Lord, the king?"

"My Lord Rivers — and Lord De-la-Pole — we have no news from His Grace. Indeed, it was our hope — and expectation — that you, my lords, as members of the council, and kinsmen of His Grace would have news of the king." The lord mayor was granite-faced. This was not going to be an easy interview.

"Prithee, sirs, you will partake of some refreshment with us on such a hot day, and pray be seated."

I felt a charm offensive might avail as we had little else to offer and snapped my fingers towards a couple of pages, but Anthony's excellent serving-men had anticipated the need and were already bringing goblets of cool liquid and lining up stools and benches.

Several of the aldermen, sweating profusely, were only too pleased to accept drinks and sit down, thus easing the tension.

One of them said, "We condole with you, Lord Rivers, on the sad demise of the late earl." Two others added their condolences, but the majority, including the lord mayor, stayed silent. The earl had not been particularly well-esteemed.

"Thank you, gentlemen, I have sent orders for masses to be said for his soul at St. Paul's."

The lord mayor had remained standing. Therefore, so had Anthony and I.

"My lords," he said, "We have a company of archers without." He waited a moment for this to sink in. It was hardly necessary.

I shot a glance at Anthony who remained impassively facing the mayor.

"We have orders," he continued, "From the lord chancellor, my Lord of York, to hand over the keys to the Tower of London to his representatives who are at my house."

"The chancellor is the Earl of Warwick's brother, Lord Mayor," said Anthony, almost menacingly.

"He is Archbishop of York and Lord Chancellor of England, Lord Scales, and in the absence of a royal command to the contrary, I must obey him."

"Even if his brother has the king under duress?" I interjected.

"And what evidence do you have of this, my lords?" asked an alderman, from a sedentary position.

After a pause — which seemed a lifetime — Anthony replied, "We have information."

"But the king's government must continue, my lords, and the warrant from the archbishop appears to be appended with the king's sign manual."

The lord mayor signalled an attendant to produce the warrant which was passed to Anthony, then me.

We examined it in minute detail. We were mumming for time; there was absolutely nothing suspicious about the document which bore the king's signature, which we both recognised, on its face.

"I need my glasses. Bring me them," said Anthony to a groom who looked surprised but went off to find them.

"We would ask Your Lordships to remain within the confines of this house, *pro tempore*," said the lord mayor.

"Merely as a precautionary measure," said the condoling alderman.

"For your own protection," said another.

"Protection from whom, sirs?" I asked with a smile.

"We cannot always answer for the mob, my lords," said the lord mayor, in a tone that suggested he could answer for them very precisely should he wish to do so.

This made me angry and I involuntarily reached for my sword.

Anthony's expression changed, as he did the same and I was aware of our grooms taking up positions around us. The air was becoming tense.

"Barricade the doors," said Anthony. At which point, there was a loud knocking on those doors.

We heard our gatekeeper shouting in a tense voice, "Who goes there?"

"A messenger from the king."

I recognised the Hull accent.

"Let him in," I shouted.

Malcolm came stumbling into the courtyard, breathless and covered in dust and grime. I had never been so pleased to see him before and almost embraced him. But it would hardly be appropriate in front of the lord mayor — or Anthony.

Malcolm looked around him, quite unfazed to be in the middle of a stand-off between two royal lords and the Common Council of London.

"You are very welcome, young man. You have a message from the king?"

"Yes, sir." He fiddled about in his bag, then in his pockets, then again in his bag.

The lord mayor looked very wary.

Eventually, Malcolm drew out a scroll with a great flourish. He had known precisely where it was.

"My lord." He offered it to me, but I referred him to Anthony. It was his house, after all.

Anthony unfurled the missive and began reading. "It is a letter in the king's own hand... 'My well-beloved friends,

I am at York and at liberty. I call on you both, with my Lord of Suffolk and my brother of Gloucester, to muster such strength as you can and join me here to suppress a Lancastrian rebellion. Command the lord mayor to hold the city and to pay no heed to any orders he receives from Warwick or the archbishop his brother, even if apparently under my sign manual. Be of good cheer, friends, and join me as fast as you may. Your loving liege lord, Edward the King.'"

The expressions of the worthy burghers had to be seen. I cannot do them justice in words, but to say that they looked shocked, embarrassed, relieved and eager all at once.

Anthony passed the letter to the lord mayor, who merely verified the signature. He lifted it to his lips and kissed the signature.

"I can smell His Grace's hand still upon it," he said, somewhat in awe, to his companions.

"Do we have your kind permission to go to His Grace's side, gentlemen?" My voice was heavy with irony.

"I should fucking hope so," said Malcolm, with northern bluntness.

"My lords," said the lord mayor, "Go with our blessing and as much gold as we can bring you this day. We will also lend you a company of archers…"

"The ones you were about to arrest us with? I see."

"My lord," said the sympathetic alderman, "The lord mayor was only doing his duty as he saw it."

"I understand and have no complaint to utter," said Anthony.

"But that gold needs to be here by sundown and the archers will stay nearby tonight ready for an early start for York. And…"

I turned to Anthony. "I will send letters to my brother and the rest to join us. If we can get him out of bed," I said sotto voce.

"I can supply horses, my lords, about six of them," said another alderman.

"And I will inform other mayors not to obey orders from Warwick or the archbishop," said the lord mayor.

"You are good lieges of His Grace and I will tell him so," said Anthony, with his usual charm.

As the burghers withdrew and I patted Malcolm on the back, Anthony came over to us.

"Good to see my Yorkshire lad, wasn't it?"

"You saved our bloody lives, boy." Anthony smiled and ruffled the lad's still curly yellow hair. He preened liked a cat. "And now go and get yourself cleaned up. You don't smell too good."

Malcolm looked shocked, as we burst into hoots of relieved laughter.

And so, two great lords were saved from the very jaws of incarceration by the heaven-sent arrival of an angel of the north.

ﬡ (khes)

Astonishingly, even my brother, no doubt spurred into action by his wife, joined us with three hundred men at St. Albans, as did Hastings and young Gloucester with more men and supplies as we rode up to York.

The king soon had ample loyal forces around him, and needed only to send out a small proportion of them to suppress the minor Lancastrian revolt.

But what to do about the Nevilles and their still powerful following?

I supported Hastings and Gloucester who were for smashing them once and for all; Anthony, my brother, and Clarence, who had belatedly joined the court, were for a more cautious approach.

"For the present," said the king in his mellifluous tenor voice (it made most women and many men want to swoon), "We will play Warwick's game. Remember, he controls Calais and has close contacts with the French king. We do not want to drive him into Margaret's arms. We will be magnanimous and hold a Great Council of Reconciliation."

***

A death in Venice. This morning Rabbi Abraham, my companion and teacher, is in deep mourning having just been

169

informed — through the network of the *kehilla* (the Jewish community) — that Don Isaac Abravanel has died, having lived out the biblical age of seventy years or so, in the Venetian republic, where he spent his last days under the protection of the doge and council. He was a great leader of the Castilian kehilla and a leading adviser and banker to the Catholic Kings of Spain and, as such, was known to Reb Abraham who loved and hugely respected him. But, unlike my friend, he refused to foresee and escape before the expulsion, and tried to dissuade Their Spanish Highnesses from their policy with rich promises. The hard-hearted Queen Isabella was not to be placated and, of course, he declined to convert despite offers of high honours he would receive if he did so. They tell me that, after much wandering, he found sanctuary in Naples as a minister to the royal court (perhaps the less bigoted King Ferdinand put in a good word for him there). The rabbi tells me that he was deeply engrossed in the most progressive ideas of *humanism,* and was thus allied to the *renascento* whilst adhering always to his ancient faith.

In his last years, he decided to retire to the Republic of Venice, where, so Abraham tells me, he came to believe in the superiority of a republican form of government over that of a monarchy. Well, the ancient Romans believed in it as embodying the highest virtues, so who am I, old dynast that I am, to quibble with them, or with Master Abravanel?

I told Reb Abraham this morning that my chronicle had so far reached the year 1469 of the Common Era, when I was a knight in the court of King Edward and no more than twenty-four years of age. He has never told me his age — it would be discourteous to ask — and some mysteries are best left unresolved. But he was surely well over thirty and in the prime of life. I asked him what he was doing then. He tells me he was serving the King-Count of Aragon, John II, not a very pleasant gentleman, accused of poisoning two of his own children. Therefore, during the 60s, the rabbi had seamlessly transferred his loyalties to John's son and heir, Ferran — or Ferdinand — and was busy through those difficult years in trying to secure the marriage of his young master to the powerful, ice-cold heiress of the bigger Spanish kingdom, Isabella of Castille. Abraham and his fellow courtiers rejoiced when this was finally achieved in '69. Though he came to regret it within a very short time. And so, perhaps, did Ferran.

***

The Great Council of Reconciliation was held at York in the autumn. It was all smiles, and the king, speaking warm words of Warwick and his brothers, even managed to get Warwick and the queen to exchange a kiss of peace. The rest of us knew their tongues stayed firmly within their cheeks. Edward also sought to solve a long-running dispute between the Nevilles and their great northern rivals the Percys, by restoring the earldom of Northumberland to the latter family, and in return advancing Warwick's other brother to the grand, if empty, title of Marquess Montagu. But marquesses have not been popular in England since the time of Richard II, and the new one remained disgruntled.

The court returned to London. The king was back in charge, but both factions were wary. There followed a period of uneasy calm, a phony peace as all the leading players took breath: Edward and his court in London; the Neville clan in the massive keep of Warwick Castle; and Margaret of Anjou, sitting, watching like a cat with her kitten-prince in the fortress of Koeur near Verdun. There was a sickly excitement in the air. Spies reported that Warwick and his brothers were intriguing with Clarence, always restless and vain, even though he remained his brother's heir. Unless, of course, the Crown could pass to Edward's eldest daughter Elizabeth, and that has never happened in England. Margaret of Anjou was hardly an encouraging model of female rule!

Then early in the new year, a little local feud blew up somewhere in the Midlands between two neighbouring landowners. Such disputes were common through the disordered years of the 50s and early 60s (remember the B.M.'s trouble with the marauding Duke of Norfolk?); often with rival parties siding with York or Lancaster to justify this settling of ancient grudges. But, in this case, the feudists were both adherents of York: the king's Master of the Horse and a cousin of Warwick's.

This was the tinder that flared up quite soon into a great conflagration. Warwick's party sent help to his cousin, in alliance with foolish Clarence. But the king was not to be caught out two years in a row. He mustered forces with determination and sent them speedily to join his Master of the Horse. In March, the royal army won a victory so quick, so devastating, it was known as the Battle of Losecoat Field; the enemy gave up so fast that they threw down their surcoats and jerkins as they couldn't get away fast enough.

We were now in the ascendant; the wheel of fortune had turned right round in our favour. The king issued proclamations that Warwick, his brothers, and the king's own brother Clarence had turned traitor and should be apprehended at all costs. But in his moment of victory, the moment at which he finally found the strength to throw off the tutelage of his overbearing bearish cousin, had Edward overreached himself? For in doing so without the means to kill or capture Warwick, the king had driven him into the arms of his greatest enemy: Queen Margaret, and her ally and cousin, the sly and slippery Louis XI of France.

**

In the spring of 1470, Warwick, realising that in England he was cornered, scooped up Clarence his pawn and son-in-law and his proud and pregnant daughter Isabel, summoned his little flotilla of ships and set sail for his governorate of Calais. He knew now he had no option but to bring to birth the stratagem he had been hatching since that day he had harangued me in his London house. He would make the great leap and vivify plan Lancaster. He had been unable to replace King Edward with brother Clarence, so he would replace him with the sometime King Henry.

All the way across the English Channel, Warwick's ships were harassed and fired upon by the ships of our navy, controlled by the queen's family, who now hated the earl with a vengeance; worse, when he approached his beloved Calais, the deputy governor, Sir John Wenlock, on strict orders from the king, point blank refused him the right to disembark. In vain did the earl plead, truthfully, that his daughter was in labour and in sore distress; she who had been brought up better than an English princess had to endure her pangs on a rolling deck. His ships limped on — as Isabel gave birth to a still-born child — until they could dock in a Norman port to be received by envoys of the French monarch.

Back home, we rejoiced. The enemy within had fled, and our own Queen Elizabeth, Anthony's beautiful sister, was again with child. After three daughters, the court felt hopeful that this child would be the longed-for son. It was spring and a lovely English spring at that. Moreover, the king was confident that the power of his brother-in-law, Duke Charles of Burgundy, would restrain any intention of King Louis to meddle in English affairs. It was a happy time; we sang, we danced and Anthony completed his translation of Boethius. We even heard that, in the Netherlands, an Englishman had learnt of a way to "print" text in blocks. Anthony assured me this would revolutionise learning; I was sceptical.

But, in France, events were moving fast, and dangerously. Warwick had prepared his ground well with the king, who was only too eager to cause trouble for his brother of England. But could he convince Margaret to combine the residual forces of Lancaster with the power of her greatest enemy Warwick? It is easy to overlook this massive hurdle in retrospect. But how difficult must it have been for this proud sometime queen to forge an alliance, under the auspices of her French cousin, with the man who had trashed his oath of allegiance to her husband, placed Edward of York upon the English throne and bastardised her own beloved son Edward of Lancaster? And with her virtually defunct husband a dullard in the Tower of London, this handsome, bloodthirsty young man of seventeen years old, was all she had. Could she risk her would-be king as a pawn in Warwick's bloody games?

In fact, she had little choice other than endless exile and the displeasure of her only continuing friend King Louis. But her pride demanded a heavy price from her enemy. So, with Louis as the master puppeteer, Warwick and his party travelled to Margaret's ancestral home, and, at the great doors to Angers Cathedral, he knelt in homage to the queen he had rejected for a full fifteen minutes of humiliation, before she graciously deigned to accept his deep contrition. Then they entered the cathedral in state and, at the high altar, took solemn oaths under the cunning eye of King Louis, that the earl would renew his homage to King Henry VI and restore him to the throne of England, while in return, Margaret would give the hand of her only son, Edward of Lancaster, in marriage to Warwick's other daughter, the Lady Anne Neville. The question was: would this reconciliation prove more lasting, more meaningful than the one Warwick had entered into with Edward the previous year?

***

There is a passage in the Pentateuch — or a *parsha* as the Hebrews call it — in which Esau and his brother Jacob (who have grown since birth to distrust each other) make up, and exchange a kiss of peace. But over the consonants in the Hebrew word for "kiss", the traditional script shows two dots; meaningless in the ancient language. The rabbis say they indicate we should be wary of the meaning of this word, as

Jacob (and also Esau?) needed to be wary of the meaning of the act. Perhaps it was less a kiss, than a bite.

As with the classic Roman tale of Coriolanus, when once a general has turned coat, who knows if, or when, he will turn again? And so, Queen Margaret and her party (the Duke of Somerset, Archbishop Morton, and the rest) were intensely wary of their new best friend. Nonetheless, their combined power — and the new order it represented — threatened to be formidable. And, of course, in London we knew very quickly all about it. We had spies even in the cathedral itself. Malory, whom we had last seen at the conclave in Brussels, to keep his options open, was still supplying us with occasional information. And Duchess Margaret, much as she was engrossed in her passion for her husband Duke Charles and anxious to provide him with an heir, never forgot her Yorkist provenance and consistently sent us reports on what was passing in France.

But at the court of Edward and Elizabeth, it was high summer and nothing could dent our mood of sensuous apathy. Indeed, the reports Anthony was receiving — as the king's eyes and ears abroad — from Malory's agent in England and from Burgundian sources, was that Warwick and Margaret were entirely distrustful of each other, and that Louis was dragging his cunning little feet in providing the wherewithal for any invasion plans. It's true that Richard Gloucester, now eighteen years of age, stunted in growth and the runt of the family but evidently deeply in awe of his eldest brother, was urging the king to step up his preparations and even prepare for an invasion of France, but the rest of the council dismissed this as the over-eagerness of inexperience. Summer was too far advanced for any invasion this year — whether by us or them.

Then Warwick's hammer struck the anvil. It was the middle of September — an Indian summer with us. Anthony had started work on a new translation, and the buxom queen was complacently great with child, while the king with Hastings, Gloucester, Anthony and I with no more than a few hundred men at arms were in York to deal with a much-bruited uprising in the north, which failed to materialise. Then came reports: Warwick had landed on the south coast with a thousand men, mainly French. Straightway, the king sent our orders for more troops and for Montagu (Warwick's brother who had so far stayed loyal) to join us from the north.

Within two days, we had reports that Warwick had been joined by at least another thousand of his own retainers, as he marched on London. Still we awaited reinforcements, but none arrived and our own men began to drift away. In the evening, Anthony whispered to me that it felt like the camp of Richard II in 1399, as each morning our numbers had inexplicably dwindled.

The king held a council of war.

Hastings said, "Five hundred men will join Your Grace within days. But we cannot march south yet."

Gloucester said, "Let us march to York, brother. They are steadfast there for our House. But we cannot march south yet."

Anthony said, "What of the queen? She may be carrying Your Grace's heir… Ten companies of archers are on their way from Wales. But we cannot march south yet."

They turned to me. I said, "My mother is sending men and material from Norfolk and Suffolk, Your Grace…"

"But we cannot march south yet," said the king, looking grim and gaunt.

At that moment, a royal messenger arrived, begrimed and sodden, with a letter from the queen.

The king read it. His face blenched.

"My lords, Warwick has been welcomed into the capital. He has released Henry of Lancaster from the Tower and... readepted his reign. The queen has gone into sanctuary in the abbey with our daughters. She urges us to flee."

There was a silence of despair.

"We will take ships to my brother-in-law in Burgundy. Arrange it, Hastings. Fast."

***

Our arrival in Flanders in three carracks was not a pretty affair. We had set sail from King's Lynn and were chased up the Dutch coast by German pirates. Fortunately, the winds blew us into the power of the good friend and brother-knight Anthony and I had bonded with on our previous visit, Louis, Sieur de Gruuthuse, whom Duke Charles had since promoted to Governor of Holland. He welcomed us at his home, Port of Bruges, not with braying of trumpets but with salt and good bread and a brotherly kindness which we have never forgot, and then took us into his great house in the centre of that beautiful town.

We had almost nothing beyond the clothes we had travelled in and a few coins, personal weapons and a handful of retainers. I had only two grooms: Q was still in London, now as Anthony's and my joint steward, and our beloved Malcolm was back in Hull, both lying very low, hoping and waiting for news of the queen's pregnancy and of our safety in the Netherlands.

Nevertheless, we were a band of young men, alive and free, and full of spunk and expectation. Duke Charles was recently and lustily wed to Edward's favourite sister. She adored her brother. Whilst Charles and Edward were natural allies against the wily old French King, Louis XI.

Except that Charles of Burgundy's interests lay in another direction. As Anthony and I had heard, Charles' overweening ambition was to exchange his heavily bejewelled ducal coronet for a royal crown. He was presently angling for a summit conference with the ponderous Emperor Frederick III — of the new Habsburg dynasty — to barter his pretty daughter and heiress Mary as wife to the Archduke Maximilian, Frederick's heir, in consideration of the Roman Crown. Or, if that failed, to have Flanders-Burgundy recognised by Pope and Emperor as a kingdom. So it was clearly against his interests at present to provoke his French neighbour. And, for princes, dynastic ambition always outweighs conjugal love.

Of course, Edward sent urgent letters to Duchess Margaret, who replied with money, jewels and much love. But she could do nothing to move her husband even to meet with our king. He even offered to send me and Anthony to the ducal court in Brussels to point out the advantages of a firm compact between us to attack the French who, of course, can never be trusted. But that too was politely rejected. The time was not right. The wind was blowing strongly in the opposite direction.

So we whiled away the weeks in Louis de Gruuthuse's lovely mansion in the middle of the equally lovely city of Bruges (or Brugge as the locals call it), waiting, frustrated, cut off from England and our families but never losing hope. We did receive news in the form of reports smuggled out to us by Flemish merchants, bringing letters in invisible ink from contacts in England, Malory, of course, and one from a retainer of John Tiptoft, scholar and soldier who, like Procrustes, enjoyed dismembering his victims to suit his moods. Warwick, it seemed, had placed Henry VI back on the throne, but in name only. It was the mighty earl who ruled. All was peaceful in England and, as far as we knew, Margaret of Anjou remained in France with her son and his new wife, Anne Neville, still distrustful of her beloved son's new daddy-in-law.

We had fine apartments in the Gruuthuse house, which was built in handsome grey stone around a central courtyard and with a dark closet-chapel from which one could look down onto the altar of the neighbouring church. We prayed quite a lot in the chapel. We had a lot to pray for. We also wandered the streets most afternoons, admiring the elegant public buildings, built on the proceeds of the strong local beer. Like my own family in former generations, the Gruuthuse clan had built its wealth from business: brewing in their case, wine-selling and banking in ours.

We admired the public squares and the breathtakingly beautiful Church of the Virgin with its fabulous elaborate gilded frontage and its intricate statues and sculptures within. While Anthony, to keep his lively mind busy, laboured in his closet on his translation from French into our mother tongue of *The Sayings and Dictes of the Philosophers*, I enjoyed promenading the streets with just a groom for company listening to the street musicians playing their extraordinary cornemuse — akin to the Scottish bagpipe — or singing sometimes lusty, sometimes prayerful songs at street corners.

Waiting, waiting… waiting on time and fortune's wheel… waiting on the will and whims of princes… that has become my life in this last decade or more in this vale of exile… and so it was then for weeks and months that felt like years as '70 turned its Janus' face towards '71; and still we waited. In late November, I had a smuggled letter from Q with the glorious news that Queen Elizabeth had at last given birth, in the sanctuary of Westminster Abbey, to a big and healthy boy; we had our Yorkist Prince of Wales. I ran up to the king's apartments where he was, as usual, idling away the day playing backgammon with Hastings to find that, though they had heard rumours already, this was the first reliable confirmation of the news. Anthony was summoned from his scholarly solitude, and we drank a toast in the best Flemish wine available to "Queen Elizabeth and His Highness the High and Mighty Prince of Wales". Howsomever, we were not able to drink to him by name, as we did not know what name he might have been christened in — or even if he had been christened at all.

Looking between the handsome young, flushed faces of our little circle in the candlelight in the shadows of that winter afternoon, I wondered what sort of omen it was for a Prince of Wales to be born in near-poverty and in sanctuary in the middle of a land ruled by his royal mother and father's enemies. A dark cloud passed over my heart as I felt a foreshadowing of a strange sad fate for such a prince. There was, for a moment, an odd bitter taste in my mouth as I saw a dark shadowy vision of a young man dead, how I knew not, in a tall dark tower. But then my gloom was dispelled by Anthony's handsome face and the king's evident good cheer, especially when I read out from Q's letter that useless old King Henry had proved himself not so useless after all in the realm of charity, having sent provisions and good wishes to our queen in sanctuary, addressing her as "his good cousin Elizabeth". The rules of war seemed thus not to apply to madmen, mothers or saints.

It brought continuing hope to us, as we knew it would to our affinities in England, that Edward was now the father of a fine son and Anthony, uncle to a high and mighty nephew. But while we received good wishes and gold coins from Duchess Margaret, no invitation to meet was forthcoming from her husband who, she sadly told us, was still in close contact with Warwick's well-established government in England, which had, so it seemed, executed several chief Yorkist adherents including mad, brilliant John Tiptoft who had been taken, hiding in a tree, and summarily beheaded. At least he hadn't suffered the tortures he had loved inflicting on others.

Still we waited and waited through days of expectation, and others of near despair. I remember one of those around the time of Christ's nativity when on a cold dreary afternoon, the snow lay heavy on the roofs of Bruges' handsome buildings, when I had gone, first to a (rather low) tavern to take some ale to keep out the cold and then, as I sometimes did, to seek solace in the lovely golden Chapel of the Virgin near the main town square and, in an ecstasy of self-abasement (something I have since seen my rabbinic mentor perform on his Day of Atonement), I threw myself down before the glistering (if idolatrous) statue of the Virgin with Her Child and begged the Lord for some sign, some promise, that all would be well for me, my friends and the poor beleaguered babe in St. Edward's sanctuary.

As I lay prostrate, muttering God knows what prayers in a mixture of Latin and English, I felt a slight nudge, almost as if accidental, at my left foot. How dare anyone disturb my heartfelt prayers? I looked up and around, angry and discombobulated, to see a quite well-dressed fellow of the merchant class, perhaps ten years older than me, with a not very comely face peering at me through the gloom with his very sharp and lively eyes.

"Are you an Englishman, sir?"

"I am an English nobleman, shirrah, and I wish to be left in peace." I was aware that I sounded a tad slurred.

"Noble thou mayst be, my lord, then all the more sad I am, also an Englishman, to find an English lord drunken and swaying before the graven image of Our Lady."

I was now both angry and — a little — embarrassed. I may have partaken of two or three goblets of alcohol after our all-too-light dinner, but I was certainly not drunk.

I rose to my feet, or tried to. The Englishman helped me, respectfully.

"Like Hannah in the temple, merchant, you have mishtak — mistaken my intense devotion and prayerfulness for being in drink. Were you a knight, I should throw down my gauntlet. But as you are clearly not a knight — and at present I do not have a gauntlet, not even at my lodgings…"

"My lord, are you one of the lords attendant upon His Grace King Edward, here in Bruges?"

We were now seated on a deep stone window-ledge, the merchant having gently guided me there.

"Verily, merchant. I am Edward De-la-Pole, brother to the Duke of Suffolk and attendant upon our Lord King, here in his sad exile." And I sighed, dolefully. "And who are you, sir, and what is your business here?"

"William Caxton, merchant printer and resident of this fair city of Bruges at your service, my lord, exercising my new trade which is an art, my lord, under licence from His Highness Duke Charles and the fair Duchess Margaret."

"And what do you… print, Master Caxtow?"

"Caxton, my lord. I print divers books with words and pictures and music, sir."

A slightly misshapen figure lumbered up in the darkness. I reached for my dagger.

"No, no, my lord, no need for weapons. This is my assistant whom I recruited in Cologne in the Rhenish Palatinate, my lord, where I learnt my trade. His name is Wynkyn de Worde, sir."

"Ah, how apt that a man who works with books and letters should be named 'Word'. I hope you are a man of your word, Wynkyn."

They both laughed, politely.

I was warming to Caxton who seemed shrewd, loyal and, potentially, useful, in all sorts of ways.

"You must come visit us at the Gruuthuse mansion, Caxton, and bring some samples of your work. I am very interested in music, for both harp and voice, while my bosom friend Lord Rivers is a scholar and translator of some note."

Caxton gave me a cursory bow; he was clearly not adept in the courtly arts. "It will be a great joy, my lord, as it would be if I can serve our Lord King in his exile. Let's hope and pray it will not be for long, my lord."

"Precisely what I was so fervently praying for myself when you interrupted me… But I am glad you did. It is always a pleasure to meet an Englishman abroad, especially one who gives allegiance to the true Plantagenet."

He bowed again, more deeply and reverently this time; even tradesmen are useful allies in these strange and difficult times.

***

The ships were prepared and rolling lightly and, to me, a little disturbingly on the quayside at Vlissingen, where the Scheldt River opens into the English Channel. The Flemish men-at-arms and guns Duke Charles had assembled for us, not enough by any means to conquer England, but enough, said the king, to make a good show on landing, were embarked; now we happy band of brother-knights were gathering on the quayside to gather our strength and our courage for the assault on England. It was early March 1471 and, at length, winter had broken out into a tepid spring, in more senses than one.

Throughout the long hard winter, Duchess Margaret had worked valiantly on her brother's behalf to soften her husband's hard and pragmatic heart, but my Lord of Warwick had worked more effectively. Not intentionally, of course, but most persuasively nonetheless. Warwick had locked himself into a satanic alliance with Louis XI who was, of course, Margaret of Anjou's kinsman and he rejected a multitude of juicy offers of friendship from Burgundy — England's more natural ally—- to prove and preserve it. Duke Charles wisely needed England as a friend, in order to pursue his expansive plans towards the Swiss Confederation and his desperate desire for a crown. But Louis was determined on attacking Burgundy to prevent that very calamity. Through admirers of Master Caxton and his skills in the margins of the French court, we were reliably informed that the vulpine Louis had promised Warwick the rich, fat provinces of Holland and Zeeland as his share of the booty, once France and England had jointly rent Burgundy's Netherlandish empire apart.

It was this thrilling and juicy bribe, more than any deeply-held loyalty to the French, which had steeled the old bear Warwick to Duke Charles' offers of love. Perchance his quick success in ousting the House of York had softened his usually hard political judgment or, more likely, he was merely tired of the constantly revolving wheel of the English Crown, and coveted a future as an independent imperial prince, as Lord of Holland and Zeeland and maybe of Calais too. And thus he betrayed his, and Lancaster's, best interests and played exquisitely into our open hands.

Louis' forces — and those of England — began preparing for an attack on Burgundy just after the first of January. As soon as Duke Charles was made aware of this — and his spies were even sharper than ours — his wrath flared up; he was an impetuous man. At once, he listened to his wife's entreaties and sent word to his brother-in-law through our good host Louis de Gruuthuse to arrange a meeting in due form as between fellow sovereigns and brothers-in-law. At last, our fuse was lit.

It was then just a matter of weeks — weeks of furious but heartening effort — to set up the meeting, order the liveries sporting King Edward's sun in splendour, and equip (with the gorgeous sparkling gold florins Charles lent us) the two thousand or so Flemish and Germanic mercenaries who came, at Charles' behest, to fight for York — and for their profitable trade links with England to be renewed. And there we were at Vlissingen Port, a fine sight with our banners blowing and the carts trundling and the horses neighing, as we waited for favourable winds to embark for the coast of East Anglia where we expected to meet with men levied in our interest by my Blessed Mother, ever active in York's support, and by Edward's friend the Duke of Norfolk. It was not an easy start (to what turned out to be a far from easy campaign) as we waited for a further nine days for a Yorkist wind to carry us back to England.

n (tes)

You will, of course, know, dear reader, however many centuries you live in the future, even into the third millennium (assuming, that is, the Messiah whom Rabbi Abraham daily expects has not yet arrived), the famous story, of what has come to be known as *The Arrivall*, from the title of the celebrated recital of the facts of that famous return and the subsequent extraordinary campaign. The authorship of it was kept secret from all but a handful of the king's most trusted friends. Of course, it was composed by the most fluent writer of our circle, by whom I mean, of course, my beloved friend Anthony, Earl Rivers. And the only reason it was never printed being that, by the time Master Caxton had returned to England and set up his printing press in St. Paul's churchyard, England and the court had moved on from war to peace and the permanent establishment of the Yorkist dynasty required visions of stability and permanence, not memories of campaigns to re-establish ourselves, even eventually successful ones.

It didn't take long to sail with a strong following wind from Flanders across to Cromer on the East Anglian coast, and being young and valiant and full of spunk, we had no doubt of a warm reception from an England groaning under the yoke of an idiot king and his tyrant of a lieutenant, the bear of Warwick. As we approached the shore and made to send down a handful of forward scouts to reconnoitre before a major disembarkation, we could see a cluster — a very small cluster — of retainers in the good old B.M.'s livery. I turned to Anthony who was at my right peering out hopefully.

"I knew the old lady wouldn't let us down."

His rather wanful smile didn't look very hopeful, as I heard Hastings mutter, just a little way over to my right, at the king's shoulder as ever, "Too few men. Way too few men."

As our men jumped down, ran to the shore and engaged in parley — and continued to parley for quite some time — I could hear the young and usually aggressive Gloucester saying, "What the fuck are they doing? We need men and arms."

Anthony turned to him and said, "Be patient, Gloucester. These things take time."

Gloucester replied, "There's no time for women's gossip, Rivers. The king needs his followers here, and now."

"Calm yourselves, boys," said the king in his rich cool tones. "Our captain's returning."

We saw the captain of our little team run back and speak quietly to the king, whose expression turned more serious.

He called us nearer and told us, "The news from the good duchess, De-la-Pole's mother..." I was always De-la-Pole when the news was bad, Edward only when it was good, and Eddie, only on one or two very special occasions. "Is that her own retainers have been severely warned off by Warwick's commissioners, who are still stationed around here and Norfolk has absented himself from the county. She advises us — with her best wishes," He gave me one of his warm smiles at this. "To try another part of the coast. And make for London."

Our faces must have registered deep dismay.

"Be of good heart, men." He spoke more loudly for all the crew to hear. "Kent will be more welcoming and we shall head there."

"God save King Edward," shouted Hastings.

"Let's save our breath for the next encounter, I thank you, men," said the king, not sure that shouting his name in this vicinity was a particularly good idea with Warwick's commissioners so near.

So, we set off southwards.

But the wind had other ideas. Wouldn't it be wonderful if a ship could have some kind of source of artificial energy which would enable us to direct it as *we* wished, rather than as nature decrees? Anthony told me that an Italian artist of great vision, by name Leonardo, had floated such an idea (if you'll forgive the pun), and Rabbi Abraham tells me of fantastical inventions of a similar nature which have been dreamt of and described by certain Kabbalistic thinkers whom he holds in high regard. But bringing such ideas to reality are decades, maybe centuries away…

So, we were blown and driven north, which most of my companions found frustrating. But, as I said to Anthony and anyone else who would listen, "My family's lands are in the north. If we can get messages to Hull, we will be welcomed there. And that will be a sound start to our campaign to regain His Grace's throne."

***

We eventually made land fall, as the wind abated, near to Ravenspur, on the very tip of the wide Humber estuary. For me, this was almost home territory. For the others, it was wilderness.

Anthony said (already choosing his words for *The Arrivall*), "Your Grace will remember the usurper's grandfather landed at this very place to launch his revolt against King Richard."

We were standing at the prow of the flagship, peering out at the Yorkshire coast, shrouded in what the locals call a sea-roke.

"Go on," said the king, whose history was weaker than the more manly skills in which he excelled.

"When Bolingbroke returned without Richard II's leave in 1399, he landed here with a small posse."

"Like us," I interjected.

"And, as he advanced, gathered strength very cautiously at first, giving out that he was returning merely to reclaim his duchy of Lancaster."

Hastings was straining his eyes, staring at the flat, empty coastline; young Gloucester just looked bored.

"Clever," said the king. "And it worked?"

"Right well, sire," Anthony replied. "It gave the nobles and burghers, through whose country he passed, enough cover to join him without laying themselves open to a charge of treason."

"Then when his forces were overwhelming, he was 'persuaded' to accept the crown," I chipped in.

The king looked thoughtful — for about two minutes. He had made his decision. That's kingship.

"Gentlemen, until the time is ripe, I am here purely to reclaim my lands and titles as Duke of York and Earl of March. King Henry remains in office — if not in power."

***

We waited — wasted — that day hoping for messages from the other ships, which were further up the coast, and from friendly local lords, but none came. So, the next morning, very early and still under cover of the dawn haze, we disembarked, about seventy or eighty men. Hardly an army, but the nucleus of our high command. Straightway I sent out my most trusted groom — in truth, I only had two or three with me — with oral messages for my old friend the Lord Mayor of Hull, instructing him to send us provisions and to prepare to open the gates at our approach. There were valuable munitions within and it would be a good place to rest and raise the standard of York.

We spent an anxious day and night while scouts went out in all directions to test the waters of East Riding's loyalty to York, and to De-la-Pole. The next day, three local knights arrived with their retainers; a handful each. Over the next few days, some peasants and farmers appeared to join us with pitchforks, and we were able to supply them with pikes, but they were a trickle, not a torrent. Meanwhile, we heard nothing from Hull. Hastings and Gloucester were giving me hard stares, as if to say: We thought these were your lands… big fucking deal. Anthony, of course, stayed full of cheer. And the king — always my hero-knight — clapped me on the back with a laugh and said, "Don't worry, Eddie…" It was one of those rare occasions. "Give this time. Warwick has terrorised the land. We will prevail."

And just for a moment then, as I wrote those words, I remembered — no, I embodied — how it felt to be young and full of spirit and hope and enthusiasm and love of life and of my king. And a few salty tears made my old eyes even rhumier than they usually are, with that sweet and bitter memory. And of all the times I have known and battles fought, all the hardships, triumphs and campaigns I have lived through, that one — starting from such fragile beginnings — was by far the best.

Later that day, we saw a small posse of men — maybe a score — approaching on horseback. As they came nearer, I made out first that they were led by a strapping young man… and then… could it be…? Yes, it was Malcolm and wearing *my* livery — praise be to God — as were the body of men with him. My heart leapt. Could this be the advance party of our Yorkshire retainers?

It was late afternoon, it was cold — the winds carry across the flatlands of East Yorkshire as they do in East Anglia — but I could already smell spring on the air. I rode out to greet Malcolm.

"My good Lord," he said, and it was good to hear his Yorkshire vowels, "We've come to do service for you and the king. But the lord mayor — shit on 'im — wouldn't be moved. He's holding the town for fucking Henry and Warwick, if you'll pardon me French."

"I'll pardon anything, you bastard. Come here." And I enfolded him in my arms.

His handsome features looked flushed, and a tad embarrassed.

"These were all the men I could muster for York, my lord… Your Grace," he said as the king rode up and they all dismounted and bowed their heads.

"And right gladdened we are to see ye, men of Holderness. You are the first of many. And see," he gestured with his muscled right arm and huge hand towards the shore," Our other ships are disembarking."

Our other ships, previously dispersed, had found our camp and were disembarking our small but well-equipped force.

"For Edward and York!" yelled Hastings, and we all joined in. Somehow young Malcolm had fired our campaign.

That night we felt, for the first time, like an army encamped. But we were still in largely hostile territory.

The king held a council of war.

Hastings was for laying siege to Hull — a prospect which hardly delighted me — in order to possess its armoury and show we meant business, but Gloucester and Anthony both counselled moving on to York, many of whose leading burghers had sent us messages of support.

The king said, "We move on to York. It's more strategically vital and remember, we come in peace to claim merely justice and our rights as Duke of York. On that basis, they must welcome us in."

Our army moved forward, with the days still cold — and the nights colder — the English spring having receded again — and with small numbers of knights and local peasants adding to our ranks. We proceeded in an orderly manner — the king absolutely forbidding looting on pain of death — and we purchased everything we needed from the farmers and villeins. But as we approached York, we saw the gates were not opened.

Night fell. We waited patiently, about two furlongs from York's Micklegate, torches ablaze, armed at all points, the king not wearing his crowned helm, and the banner of York, rather than the arms of England and France, flying above us. We waited, anxiety in all our eyes, except Edward's. As ever, the king was calm embodied.

His Grace was finishing his ale — we didn't have money to waste on wine — and yawning, while Anthony and I were finishing our game of backgammon (under Gloucester's disapproving gaze), when a guard ran up.

"Horsemen approaching, Your Grace."

The king stood. We all drew our weapons in case this was an ambush. We would defend our liege lord with our lives. That's the blood brotherhood of fealty — and of war.

It was not necessary. The group on horseback were robed as aldermen and lightly armed.

"We are minded to negotiate a peaceful entry into our city…"

Hastings piped up. "The lord mayor should be here to address the—"

"To address the Duke of York," said His Grace, graciously as always. "But I am content to speak without the walls with a messenger from His Worship."

"My lord," said the senior alderman, clearly embarrassed, "We wish Your Lordship no harm but we cannot risk a charge of treason against the readeption government of King Henry and my Lord of Warwick."

Gloucester spat.

"Your Highness is welcome to enter the city with attendant lords and a small bodyguard, but the bulk of Your Highness' forces cannot be accommodated within our walls."

The king smiled. "That is not acceptable to us," he replied, quietly. "Be satisfied that we have come — not to reclaim the Crown, there has been too much bloodshed already — but merely to claim our rightful inheritance as Duke of York; Duke of *York*, gentlemen." And he gestured towards the walls of that fine city.

"Our proposition is this," continued the king, "We enter — at first light — with arms concealed, and stay for one day and one night, to refresh ourselves. You have my word — as a Plantagenet — that we shall pay for every hunk of bread or glass of ale we partake of. Then we shall depart with thanks. Do you agree?"

The aldermen conferred briefly; Edward had given them little choice. They agreed, somewhat reluctantly, and we offered them refreshment.

At dawn, we entered the city and the air, as we came in, was more hospitable than we had expected, if a little confused. There were some cries of, "a York, a York" and even the occasional, "God save King Edward", but for the most part diffident smiles and hesitant applause. But what mattered was that we got our food, drink and rest; the king and Gloucester in the lord mayor's mansion, the rest of the lords in the archbishop's palace (which was probably finer). His Lordship was not in residence; hardly surprising as he was Warwick's brother.

As we marched out of York the next day, there were more cries of support, and definitely more shouts for King Edward. We could feel the tide was beginning to turn.

As we rode on south, the king called me forward. "I have had a message from your brother, Edward."

"I trust he expresses his duty to Your Grace and is soon to join us?"

"You will be glad to hear that he does just that, my boy." I liked that term of endearment. Clearly John had finally got off his arse and done something useful. "He plans to join us with five hundred men in the Midlands, somewhere near Stoke. Even more helpful, he sent a message from my brother Clarence."

"With his submission, Your Grace?"

"With his express desire to be reconciled with us and to offer us his affinity in arms. So, who do you think would be the best man to go and persuade him of our good will?"

I paused. "Is it me, Your Grace? I would be honoured." If somewhat nervous.

"Well, as my brother of Clarence sent his offer through *your* brother of Suffolk, and as he clearly needs a little, shall we call it, encouragement, who can do that better than yourself, De-la-Pole?" He turned and looked at me, quizzically.

"Your Grace?"

"Use your charm, my boy. George responds to chivalry and good looks, use them. Remember, whatever your personal feelings about him, he is our brother and we *need* him, and his two thousand men."

This was a serious mission; the first the king had ever sent me on, alone. Even Anthony could play no part in it. I felt my heart leap with the sense of being chosen. I would not — could not — let the king down.

I took Malcolm with me and two or three more of my retainers he had brought with him. I also made sure I had my finest breastplate and helm with me and told Malcolm to bring the little silver scissors I had acquired in Bruges to trim my rather fine brown beard — he was very adept at such personal services — because Clarence's vanity was such that he would regard anything less as an insult to his royal status and a threatening sign of disrespect.

The rebel brother was encamped with his army not far from Banbury in the Midlands, the crossroads of the kingdom, just south of the Warwickshire/Oxfordshire border. He had been mustering troops in the west country, ostensibly to reinforce Warwick who was holed up in Coventry. But Clarence (false and perjured Clarence, as someone once called him) had been havering and hedging his bets ever since teaming up with his overbearing father-in-law. My task was firmly to reel him in before the old bear Warwick could get at him; to reassure and flatter him that all would be forgiven (though not, of course, forgotten).

With my little band in attendance, I approached Clarence's magnificent pavilion — far more sumptuous that his older brother's simple tent — and was told by his chamberlain that I must go in alone. Dear George was clearly very nervous.

I went in and was announced — "my Lord De-la-Pole" — as if we were at court. Clarence always demanded formality. I bowed ceremoniously. If he thought I was going to kneel, he was sadly mistaken. I would, of course, let him speak first.

"Sir Edward."

"My Lord Duke."

Clarence's manner was both vain, and guarded. "De-la-Pole, I see my brother has sent the queen's brother's best boy as his envoy."

"Sir, the king has not sent me to be insulted."

"Insulted? I thought you and Scales were... lovers. Sodomy's not a crime in royal circles."

"Sodomy is a crime *inter Christianos non nominandum*, my lord." We all knew the rumours about him and his minions. "My love for Earl Rivers — no longer Scales since your father-in-law beheaded his father — is of a different order entirely."

It is always best to stand up to weak people.

"Prithee, I am glad to hear it, Sir Edward," he smiled, his manner completely changed. Perhaps he had remembered the ambiguity of his position. His charm, when he exerted it, was almost equal to his brother's, if a tad more feline.

"You are welcome, cousin." I was his kinsman, suddenly. "Take wine with me."

His cup-bearer approached with jewelled goblets for both of us. Yes, I know that only a monarch would normally have a cup-bearer but Clarence strove to live like a king even when on campaign — which was, in the end, his undoing.

"I congratulate you, my lord, on your marriage to the Lady Isabel. And condole with you both on the death of your child."

Though polite, this was barbed, as the babe had been born dead on board ship as they waited precariously off the coast of Calais.

"Fatherhood is a maturing thing, De-la-Pole," he said sententiously. "I want my children to have their proper inheritance, worthy of the king's grandchildren." The whole family always spoke as if the old Duke of York had been king. Which he would have been had not Queen Margaret cornered him at Wakefield Castle, cunningly drawn him out, lopped off his head and stuck it on the gates of York with a paper crown. You could see why they hated her.

"Have you seen Margaret?" I asked.

"My sister has striven ceaselessly to reconcile her brothers."

"I was not referring to the beauteous Duchess of Burgundy. She kept us alive through those months in Bruges. I meant the she-wolf of Anjou."

"No, she's still in France. I have no wish to see her. And her husband's a poltroon. I came over to Warwick. He felt wounded, rejected. We should not forget our cousins."

"Or our brothers. Or our friends."

He looked at me forlornly. For a moment, I felt almost sorry for him.

"When I bring over my army, I have three thousand first-class men, retainers and levies, utterly loyal to me and my duchess..."

"Two thousand at most, my lord." I was bluffing. I had not counted them.

"When I bring them over, do I have my brother's word as a king," he smirked, "As a once and future king, that I and my wife will be welcomed into the king's bosom with a total amnesty for any apparent..."

"Treason, my lord...?"

Again, he pretended deafness.

"... misapprehension or mistake on our part... or on his?"

I let him stew a moment.

"Are you prepared to fight your father-in-law, Duke?"

"*Sans doute.*" He clearly wasn't. "Though I would prefer to turn my forces against the true House of Lancaster."

"That, of course, is for the king to decide. We hear Warwick is sending desperate letters to all of his affinity. He doesn't trust Margaret's friends any more than you do."

"I am returning to my brethren, De-la-Pole, but I need assurances. I need the word of a king."

He looked strained. I relented.

"In token of his word, the king sends this." And I handed over a green jade ring which the king had given me for him. It was a tiny thing compared with my own prized balas ruby.

Clarence smiled. He seemed relieved. "It was our father's signet ring as Earl of Ulster. We used to play with it when we were boys. And once I lost it. My brother Edward found it and we four swore our oath of brotherhood on it. That was before Edmund was killed..." He trailed off, his eyes glistening with tears.

Weak and sentimental.

Edmund, Earl of Rutland, by the way, was the second son, killed at Wakefield along with his father, the old Duke of York. It was the first time I'd heard him spoken of.

Clarence recovered himself. "You will ride with me to meet the king and exchange the kiss of peace."

"If that is your wish, Duke."

"Then let us settle the formalities."

***

So, I was present — in attendance, ostensibly — on Duke George as he rode ceremoniously at the head of his substantial army to meet and be reconciled with his brother the king near Banbury. It was still chilly — the very beginning of April — but you could feel and smell the scents of an English spring on the air. Yet the atmosphere was strange, almost strained. Each brother feared treachery by the other, although I had sent messages to the king assuring him Clarence was anxious to be reconciled as he clearly felt abandoned by Warwick and isolated from the Lancastrian court. But, like Jacob and Esau — or Joseph and the brothers who had sold him into slavery — these brothers could never trust or truly love each other ever again. It was simply that Clarence had realised he had nowhere else to go.

They rode slowly up, each at the head of his men, towards the agreed crossroad, where they were to embrace. Riding close behind Clarence, I felt as if I was holding an arquebus to his back. Despite his regally calm features — with his prettily blond looks, it was not surprising he was their mother's favourite — I could see the sweat trickling down the back of his gilded collar. And there approaching, I could see my king — with his far more masculine, leonine features — riding towards us, smiling broadly. *What a fine actor Your Grace has become,* I thought; yet maybe also Edward was truly pleased and relieved to see his brother again, to have him back in the family tent pissing out, instead of outside pissing in. As agreed, their suites (including me) stopped at a distance of twenty paces from the meeting point and the two royal brothers trotted at a calm pace forward alone.

Each was wearing a breastplate but no sword. However, as they met, I saw — or thought I saw — George's right hand move beneath his tunic and I had a fearful vision of the traitor drawing his dagger to stab the brother he so envied to death. I was ready to spur my mount and had he done that, I would have stabbed the traitor gladly through the neck. I glanced at Hastings and Anthony, both as close behind Edward as I was to Clarence, and their faces, though tense, betrayed no signs of alarm. And then they were embracing — or was Clarence's embrace in fact a bite, like Esau's welcome of Jacob on their reconciliation in the book of Genesis, as the insightful rabbis tell us — and both armies were cheering and soon moving forward to imitate that embrace, but more warmly and fraternally. Of course, it was Anthony who embraced me with the kiss of peace. It was good to be reunited.

That evening, as the royal brothers feasted — or as near to feasting as you can come on campaign — the king called me to his side.

"We thank you for your good work, Eddie. Two brothers reconciled with your help."

"Merely a little liaison, sire. The reward I ask is to serve beneath Your Grace."

I had never yet had my chance to serve beneath my king, and I panted for it.

"There will be time for that as well." He smiled like the sun in splendour; his emblem, of course. "But, Eddie, we know your talents are above all for the diplomatic arts."

"He follows in the steps of his De-la-Pole and Chaucer ancestors, do you not, Sir Edward? Famous for their mercantile ingenuity?"

I took this sally from Clarence to be hostile despite the sly smirk.

"My brother forgets, I think," said the king, "That you are now a member of our family. And it is in that persona that we need you to raise more men by Humberside, Eddie, in your old territory, and then liaise with your brother — and ours — of Suffolk, to meet up with us in London, where they are parading old Henry like a stuffed partridge, a mere effigy. But first, we have an encounter with Warwick to keep, with your dear father-in-law, brother." He turned to Clarence with a wry smile. "A final encounter... to the death, methinks."

The king turned his horse away (she was a beautiful, strong chestnut mare called, unsurprisingly, Plantagenet) and Clarence turned with him, giving me a look of unmitigated condescension. Anthony, riding a little behind, brought his mount alongside mine and looked at me with his warm hazel eyes, almond shaped, and even more glorious than those of his beauteous sister, the queen.

"So, we must separate again," he murmured.

"It is the king's wish. He does not trust my brother and, frankly, neither do I."

"We shall meet again once Warwick is defeated."

"If Margaret deigns to come over with her little boy, there will be another battle to fight and I want to be there."

"If necessary, I will speak to the king for you. We shall fight as brothers-in-arms." He leant over and embraced me and I can still feel the warmth of his arms and smell the intoxicating, musky scent of him.

***

So, I missed the high drama of the Battle of Barnet on Holy Saturday, 1471. Anthony was present, fighting in the vanguard with the king, and gave me a vivid account. He was a writer of distinction, after all. But hearing first-hand about a battle is not the same as being there. It's like having a list of the dishes served at a banquet without tasting them, or hearing the story of a passionate friendship without being part of it.

But Barnet — a little village in the county of Hertford where our Yorkist army blocked Warwick's march on the capital — was not just another skirmish like the others that had happened since Towton. It was the climax of a cousins' war within the Cousins' War; the final battle between Edward IV, my generation's champion, and his second father, Richard Neville Earl of Warwick and Salisbury, the last and greatest of the mighty barons of the last three centuries. Greater than Simon de Montfort (that notorious Jew-hater) or John Duke of Bedford (who ruled France for the young Henry VI), Warwick — that powerful, choleric, great-hearted bear of a man — was cut to the quick by his cousin's betrayal. And so, like Coriolanus the Roman, he had taken his fighting skills to the other side and created the redemption of the weakest king England had ever known. Against him, like Oedipus the Greek, Edward had to strike down his own adopted father in order to win back the Crown. It was not the last of his kinsmen my hero would have to destroy.

Warwick saw himself as a European prince — with his own foothold in Calais, whose garrison were totally loyal to him — directing his own policy with the rulers of France, Burgundy, even the empire. It was because of his closeness to Louis XI that he had first broken with Edward and had gone on, under Louis' aegis, to make his humiliating submission to Margaret the termagant at the door of Angers Cathedral.

Before I left our camp, Anthony — who sometimes acted sub rosa as a *chef d'espionage* to the king — had shown me a letter intercepted between the earl and the French king in which he was bargaining for a leopard's share of the rich spoils of the Netherlands once Charles of Burgundy had been squeezed to damnation between the forces of Louis' France and Warwick's England — which was their joint *grande idée*. Warwick planned to take the northern provinces of Holland and Zeeland which, combined with Calais and its outlying castles, would at last make him an autonomous European prince.

That was the consummation for which Warwick must have prayed. For he was not, in the meantime, finding it easy to rule

England. Our agents — and both Anthony and Hastings had their own networks, sometimes in rivalry — told us of constant dissension between the Neville clan — who all had to be kept rich and happy — and the leading Lancastrians who came flooding back to England, chief amongst them being the Duke of Somerset, Henry's Beaufort cousin and favourite (and next in the Lancastrian line after their Prince of Wales). To shore up his position, Warwick was desperate to get Margaret and (more importantly) her young son, Edward of Lancaster now about eighteen, back in England to act as a more appealing figurehead than his doddery old father could be. But there must have been fears in the old bear's mind that this, which he most needed, would also bring to the boil those very contradictions he was trying to resolve. Warwick was in a trap. All that was left for him was to fight, like a cornered beast.

And so, he sent out letters — some of which we also were sent copies of — beseeching, commanding, importuning the knights and squires of his affinity to join him with all the power and haste they could muster for the final battle, which was now to be fought on Barnet Field. In addition to his own men, called to their liege lord's side by those desperate letters, was also one of Lancaster's most determined and mighty warriors, one of the few noblemen who, to his credit, stayed loyal to their House through it all: John de Vere, thirteenth Earl of Oxford, Henry's Lord Great Chamberlain. He had been imprisoned throughout King Edward's earlier rule, and had, unlike Somerset, resisted all blandishments to turn his coat. And now, restored to his lands and titles, he brought his substantial forces to join with Warwick's.

As John Skelton might say it: the Battle of Barnet was bitter and brutal and battered both armies with boldness and bite. Well, he's the king's chief poet and writes verse with a certain wit, but without the genius of my great-granddaddy Geoffrey.

It was a fight unto the death; at least for Warwick. As so often in battle, it was the forces of nature — or of the Almighty — which decided the day, where the fate of two armies — of two dynasties and one kingdom — were hanging by a gossamer thread. Just as at Towton — as you may remember, my mindful reader — the weather was shit, throwing down every species of rain, hail and snow. But, at Barnet, it was worse, for the air was contaminated with dark, swirling fog, as if the end of days had come indeed. De Vere's forces, coming up as reinforcements, ran as it were into the flank of Warwick's men, who, seeing in the gloom the de Vere arms of a golden sun, mistook it for King Edward's sun in splendour and began to shout, "Trahison, trahison." Not so surprising, as they had fought alongside Edward's men in so many battles before this and were bound to be more familiar with his arms than those of their newfound friends. Thus Warwick's "treason" turned back upon him (it usually does) and his men fought against their new allies and then scattered in flight.

The mighty old earl, in his magnificent golden armour, was caught not in flight — not he, to the end a warrior of courage — but in striving in anguish to hold his men-at-arms to the battle. And there, the last over-mighty baron, Richard Neville, Earl of Warwick called the kingmaker, was pulled from his horse by a common soldier, his visor thrust up and stabbed to death. At least he died on the battlefield, fighting not fleeing.

The king — now victorious again, and with poor wretched Henry late twice-reigned King of England in his baggage train — now moved back to his capital, ready to take on the residue of Lancastrian forces. For the lioness Margaret and her whelp now back in England and marshalling their army in the Midlands, always her source of strength, while her brother-in-law Jasper Tudor — that wily Welsh windbag, the product of Queen Katherine de Valois' illicit union with his sweet-faced disreputable old father Owain — was raising hell, and troops, in the dark land of the Celts. And in the meanwhile...

There am I, back at home with the Blessed Mother and the blasted bothersome brother — and his royal wife — in the leafy rural manor of Ewelme in the west country. And the B.M. is saying, as if ten years had not passed, "Edward, you will hasten to the king with the men you have raised by the Humber, and with the four hundred men I have in my following here. As for you, John, you had better stay by me..."

"No, Mother, prithee, by the king's express command, my brother must lead our forces — with me by his side, of course — to answer the king's summons. He is His Grace's *brother-in-law* after all," I said, stressing the words.

John made to speak, but Mother spoke first.

"I am well aware of our closeness to the Crown — the Yorkist Crown — Edward. But matters are on a knife edge and if Margaret is able to make rendezvous with Pembroke's forces..."

"Jasper is no longer Earl of Pembroke, Mother..." put in John.

"Just so," I added.

"But he will be so again — and more — if Margaret wins the battle. And what happens to Henry now matters not, as his son is virtually of age and, so they say, is as ferocious as his grandfather Henry V."

"Mother, this is treasonable talk," I said, not too loudly, not wishing to alarm our retainers milling about, just beneath the windows of Mother's solar.

"It is political talk, Edward, and we must consider all possible outcomes. I will write to King Edward assuring him of our loyalty unto death, congratulating him on his magnificent victory over the traitor Warwick. And, of course, on the birth of his heir."

"The king has an heir?" asked my brother.

"We knew about that in *Bruges*," I said, smugly.

"I will tell him that I have instructed you to come immediately to his aid with the bulk of our affinity…"

"I thank you, Mother…" I said with sarcasm.

"And that your brother, who is looking to the safety of his royal duchess and children…"

"All seven of them," I added.

"Eight," said Suffolk, keen to be accurate.

"… is marshalling reinforcements in outlying parts of East Anglia and will follow hard on your heels."

"I shall do my duty," he declared.

"About bloody time," I added.

"Be silent, Eddie," said the B.M. "And…"

"Yes, Mother?" I said, peevishly.

"You have done well. Your father would be proud."

I tried to reply but no sound came out.

' (yod)

We were encamped on the edge of the pretty town of Tewkesbury, with its handsome streets and magnificent abbey, having been reunited with the king, and Anthony and all the forces of York. By forced marches led by Edward with all his magnificent manly energy, we intercepted the — probably bigger — army of Lancaster under the command of Margaret and her favourite, Somerset, before, crucially, they could combine with the Welsh rabble of Jasper Tudor. We were preparing for battle — the battle to end all battles, or so we believed. Having shadowed the — probably larger — Lancastrian army along the line of the River Severn, the king had chosen this meadow in the Marchlands; it was flat and green, with the little River Swilgate on one side and the town on the other. There was no going back and no escape into exile; not this time. We were all here, even my brother had finally turned up, usefully, with an extra four hundred men-at-arms.

It was the Friday evening, the first in May, and now the English spring was in its glorious and fragrant prime. The May blossom was out on the trees and it was harsh to think that, by this time tomorrow evening, one of these great, royal armies would be a mangled midden of mortal remains; and even the victors would not all survive. I was with Anthony in his tent taking some light refreshment — and praying, for he was always a more devout man than I — when we were summoned by a king's messenger to the royal tent for a council of war.

Clarence was back in his accustomed place on the king's right, with a mien even more arrogant than hitherto (if that was possible), while Gloucester, now a man and a very war-like one despite his slightly misshapen right shoulder and a much lower stature than either of his more handsome brothers, stood a little behind. Hastings was there — always his master's shadow — and growing envious of the more beauteous and gifted Anthony who stood just to his left; Sir John Howard was there, a tough captain, and later Duke of Norfolk. And finally, the De-la-Poles; yes, my brother was present due to his rank (and nothing else) — and me.

"My friends," said the king, "This is our time. We have chosen the site of this battle, and its timing. Margaret and Somerset planned to join up with Jasper Tudor's men, but they have failed. We have been swifter. Hastings, what is our intelligence of their numbers?"

"They have about a thousand men more than we have, sire."

"So, they are more numerous but we have guns — big guns — which they lack. And arquebuses while they are still fighting like knights in tourney."

"And there's our fine contingent of Flemings with firearms. They will fight well, brother," added Gloucester.

"And fortunately, they have been well-paid, by Duke Charles."

We laughed. Edward always knew how to throw in some light relief.

"While *they* are led by a woman — a woman who has arrived too late to join with the ally she really hated — and a boy."

"A wild boy," threw in Clarence, "Who has no battle experience."

Well, he should know. He was married to his wife's sister; the younger heiress of Warwick's vast estates, Anne Neville.

"But he is an important piece on the chessboard," said the king. "So, as our best chess player, Anthony, what must we do with him?"

"We must remove him from the board, sire."

"No," said Gloucester, "From the earth."

"I do not intend to see him alive," said the king.

I shuddered a little, inwardly, but the king was right, if this war was ever to have an end.

"And the triple traitor, Somerset, likewise," said Clarence; no doubt Somerset had a lot of dirt on *him*.

"Today," said the king softly," The House of York must crush and…" He hesitated a moment. "*Eliminate* the remnants of Lancaster. Agreed, my lords?"

We murmured our assent. Like all good sovereigns, the king liked to appear collegiate.

"Our dispositions: Gloucester will command the left battle, which will be our vanguard, assisted by Lord Rivers; Hastings will command on the right assisted by Sir John Howard." I noticed Clarence momentarily knit his brow. "Brother Clarence and Edward De-la-Pole will be my lieutenants in the centre."

I bowed, deeply honoured; Clarence knew I was there so Edward could keep an eye on him.

"My brother of Suffolk will command the reserve and guard the baggage train."

My brother bowed and I smirked. Although, in truth, guarding the baggage train is a vital task, but I would have the glory of fighting by the side of the king. And Anthony's counsel to Gloucester would be crucial as he was far more experienced than the king's younger brother. Perhaps that was why the king now called Anthony to his side for whispered commands after which, without a word to me, he left the tent. If only I was part of that golden web. I noticed Hastings watching jealously also.

"My lords, my brothers-in-arms, this is the day of reckoning. Time and place are on our side. Today all the wrongs of our House will be avenged and England will be cleansed of the usurpers. God for York and England."

"A York, a York," bellowed Hastings and we all responded, and emerged from the tent, confident of success.

We dispersed from the council and withdrew to our tents. It was dark now. What do men think about on the eve of battle? Is fear the main emotion, or aggression? Neither in my case. There was a deal of excitement, I recollect and, yes, some apprehension. But battle is a proof of manhood, the ultimate ordeal; it cannot be avoided by those who seek greatness. And this battle would leave just one bloodline to hold the throne of England. Also, I had vast confidence in the leadership of my king, and the brilliance of my blood brother Anthony. So, I retired for a few hours of sleep and contemplation, with the lithe young Malcolm — now returned to my service — as my bed-mate. Spring nights are cold in England — as far as I remember — and youthful bodies give off warmth and a pleasing scent.

We were roused by trumpets soon after dawn (the enemy were still too far off to hear us, and anyway, they were our quarry) and first, of course, came the celebration of Holy Mass throughout the camp. I joined the king's party before his tent, where, on an elegant if makeshift altar, one of the king's chaplains blessed the host and gave us Holy Communion. I had never been deeply pious — unlike Anthony whom I watched entering into a transport of spirituality as the ceremony proceeded — but the sense of spiritual brotherhood between those of us on hand that day was deep and powerful. Then we breakfasted, not too heavily, though some, like Anthony, declined food to keep their spiritual energy high. I ate.

And then the trumpets sounded to take up battle stations. We had, of course, ridden to our present camp in the preceding days — pursuing Margaret's army to entrap them before they could unite with Tudor's Welsh levies — but all of us, even the noble knights and men-at-arms, would take up our positions and fight on foot. We all knew what had happened to the proud flower of the French nobility at Agincourt, trapped on their horses, encased in armour and mown down by the finest English archers, and we needed the mobility provided by fighting on foot, exhausting though that turned out to be. And first, leading the vanguard, Richard of Gloucester, with Anthony, Lord Rivers, by his side, arrayed his battle group: a solid, fearsome mixture of finely accoutred knights. Anthony, in particular, wore a splendidly wrought suit of Italian armour he had bought some years before and had by now retrieved from his (our) London mansion, and above them fluttered the banners of York, Wydville and all the other noble Houses represented in those ranks.

A little behind them, the king himself arrayed his own battle group — slightly bigger than Gloucester's, numbering about two thousand men. In the group of knights around him, clustering beneath the royal arms of Plantagenet like the house-carls of an Anglo-Saxon king or the companions of the Great Alexander, were Clarence and myself, the three De-la-Pole leopards proudly fluttering on my helm, with Malcolm not far behind as my esquire. Once the king received word that Hastings' wing of the army was ready for action to our rear, I heard him give the command that Gloucester was to lead the vanguard onto the field facing Lancaster's forward battle who we knew were under the direct command of York's greatest enemy: Somerset, Margaret's favourite — some said her lover — and the field commander of their whole army.

We moved, behind Gloucester's vanguard to take up positions opposing Margaret's main ward, her central battle group; our information told us this was nominally commanded by young Edward of Lancaster, the lady's beloved and unbloodied son, but in reality, under the control of old Lord Wenlock. They were, I will confess, a magnificent sight, flying many fine old knightly banners, like those of the Arundels, the Daunts and the Beauforts, and fine French coats of arms representing the splendid blue-clad Angevin bodyguard Margaret had brought with her from France. She had sent them all onto the battlefield — a move she may have regretted later — though she had withdrawn (even Margaret knew a woman's place was not on the battlefield) to a convent behind her lines from where she anxiously awaited news.

Finally, there, to our right, was arrayed the battalion led by Hastings with old Norfolk in support facing the third

Lancastrian ward under the command of the Courtenay Earl of Devon, whose main estates were not very far from the battle ground.

I was proud to be near the king, but with his height and his manly demeanour — with, of course, the royal arms fluttering above him — he was the cynosure of all our Yorkist eyes, as he lifted high his great sword and shouted in his resonant voice, "I commend my righteous cause to God and the Virgin Mary. Gloucester, advance!"

At which Richard of Gloucester, never lacking in courage, led his battle nobly onto the field facing Somerset's phalanx. There was a great beating of drums and firing of cannon — of which we had the greater part, some of them in fact looted earlier in the campaign from the Lancastrian forces. There was a lot of hard pounding, much to the chagrin of the enemy.

It was a fine, sharp, cold spring morning, but inside my elaborate and heavy armour, I was already sweating profusely due to heat and excitement, I guess. I remember relishing that. It was uncomfortable and damp but strangely reassuring. Encased in metal, you feel invulnerable, but the problem is seeing out through your rather small visor. Lift it, and you're in serious peril of being blinded by an arrow — or worse.

But, at this stage, there was not much fighting around the king; he was too well guarded for that and the heat of the battle seemed to be raging on the two wings: between Gloucester and Somerset to our left and between Hastings and Courtenay to our left. Later, there was a suspicion that Wenlock, mentoring Edward of Lancaster, had been in our pay, and as he perished in the rout, we can never be sure. But Anthony would certainly have known and he never acknowledged it to me. More likely cautious old Wenlock was doing his best to protect his young prince, knowing how he would be held savagely to account by his mother should he not leave the field alive, as the last hope of his race. We were taking some punishment too, with arrows falling all around and some return of cannon fire. I saw the king receiving messengers and sending back commands but it was difficult to see what was going on ahead as there were so many ditches and hedges on the Gloucestershire land, providing defences to the Lancastrians and obstacles to us. As in the game of chess, we seemed to have reached a kind of stalemate, as indeed our bloodied kingdom had done in this internecine war. On the field of Tewkesbury, as often in warfare, it lasted several long and exhausting hours.

Then, with great suddenness, there was bruit and confusion behind us and it was clear we were being attacked in the rear. We turned and as we did so, Malcolm shouted, whispering would be useless in speaking to a man wearing a closed helmet, "Somerset has outflanked us. They say he only has a small group with him."

The blood rose inside me; at a moment like that, you feel your manhood stiffen. I would defend the king, even unto death. And I unsheathed my sword to do so, holding it firmly in my jewelled leather gauntlet. But Somerset's assault — his one great throw of the dice — never came within one hundred yards of the king's household knights. There was much noise but nothing more.

Anthony later told me what had occurred. When the king had given him his secret orders on the eve of battle — the whispered commands which had made all his other commanders jealous — he had told him to pick out two hundred crack spearmen on horseback to go secretly into the wooded area on the deer park to our left, suspecting that Somerset might cunningly have set a trap for us within the woods. In fact, he had not. But when, in the battle, Anthony had been told by his reconnaissance men that Somerset was attacking the king's battle from the rear, without waiting for the king's command — knowing the royal messenger might never get through — he sent word to the hidden spearmen to charge out of the woods. As a result, it was Somerset himself who was taken by surprise in the flank and the rear — a manoeuvre feared by all fighting men — and was almost lost in the melee.

Around the king, we remained on guard, expecting an attack to reach us at any moment. But after another hour of suspense, the king shouted for our benefit.

"My friends, Somerset's cowardly attack from behind has been beaten. Now let us move forward to clinch the battle. A York!"

At the king's command, the trumpets sounded the general advance and we moved forward with passion and strength as one body, feeling that now the day would be ours. A rumour passed through the army — God knows how these things are conveyed in the heat of battle, but they are — that Somerset had escaped back to the body of his army, confronted old Lord Wenlock for his sluggishness in giving him no support and clean dashed out his brains with his battle-axe. It was probably not true — though it would have been in character for Somerset — but it certainly put fire in our bellies and blood in our weapons. We moved slowly but powerfully forward in a body, one great scrimmage of men, pushing the enemy back and away, and towards the two small rivers which separated the Gaston Field, which was just behind them, from the city of Tewkesbury.

And, from that moment, we got our second wind: the almost maddened strength that comes with knowing that now the battle is almost yours. As at Towton — how fortune smiled on me, to have fought only on the winning side in battle — what had been an even, hard-fought contest had turned into a rout, a hunt with them; the Lancastrians as our quarry. It was not a pretty or a noble sight; it was carnage.

I heard the king command, bellowing, "Edward of Lancaster must not escape the field."

But, contrary to popular report, it was not he who killed him. That young man — whose arrogant blood-thirstiness had led him to order the beheading of Yorkist lords when he was a small boy, much to his mother's delight — charged off in flight like the rest towards the town, and also like the rest, was struck down and killed. His body was later retrieved and laid to rest in the choir of the abbey.

To tell the truth, I was, and am, glad that those of us around the king did not get involved in the bloody chase; unlike some, I have never enjoyed taking part in bloodshed, least of all when the enemy is utterly at your mercy. It is hardly chivalric, even though it may be necessary. Once the king had received word from Gloucester and Anthony on his left, and from Hastings on our right confirming the enemy was in full flight, he began to turn his brilliant strategic mind to the next steps.

The king signalled to his senior nobles in his battle to huddle around for a council of war, or rather of the aftermath of war. Anthony rode up to give us the latest news from his and Gloucester's side of the battlefield, pushing his way through to join us attending on His Grace. There was blood on his armour, but I was relieved to guess it was not his own. The king removed his helm — even with his matted red hair and beard drenched with sweat, it was the face of an archangel, suffused with victory — and we did the same. But his tone was not that of relief and respite but of continued urgency.

"Have any of their leaders fled? They must be killed or taken."

"I'm told that Edward of Lancaster has been struck down in the rout, sire," said Anthony.

Clarence and the rest cheered.

"You bring us good news, my brother."

Anthony looked sombre. He never crowed over a death.

"What of Somerset?"

"He was seen in flight towards the town, Your Grace," said Sir Thomas Grey, one of the king's step-sons.

"Then we must pursue him and the other traitors. And Margaret? Where is she?"

"They say she spent the night in the town, sire, so she will soon be fleeing from it." This was one of the Neville brothers, cousins of old Warwick, who had stayed true to their allegiance.

"Then you must go in hot pursuit of her, Thomas," he said to his step-son. "Take a company of men. And when you find her…"

"Beheading would be too good," said Clarence with his usual curl of the lip.

"We will think on that hereafter," said the king.

A knight rode up. "Lord Hastings sends his greetings to Your Grace. The enemy is fleeing and Somerset and other leading traitors are believed to be heading for Tewkesbury Abbey."

"I knew Somerset had an eye for a beautiful building," said the king; we all laughed.

"They are seeking sanctuary," I put in.

"Perhaps in the wake of such carnage and treachery, it will not be available."

The king spurred his horse. I flashed a glance at Anthony and saw him wince at the king's words. But we could only follow as he, and the whole battalion, galloped on in the direction of Tewkesbury town.

I ignored the dead and dying piled up or staggering around us as we rode for the city and its beauteous abbey. We had business to attend to, scores to settle and the crying need to bring an ending to this bloody war. At some point in this hot and muddy journey, Gloucester joined us — I think Hastings was left on the battlefield to supervise the business of finishing off the wounded and retrieving anything valuable, in gold or information, from the dying and the dead.

It was beginning to get dark as we rode through the streets of this pretty little town and its splendid abbey hove into sight. There were monks standing all around it and at its great doors stood the abbot, a tall and dignified man with a deeply serous expression.

"My Lord King," he said as we approached, bowing courteously, "I have wounded noblemen within who have escaped from the battlefield and have given up their weapons. They have claimed sanctuary, as is their right, and I have promised them it."

The king dismounted, as did we all, smiled and spoke most courteously in reply.

"My Lord Abbot, it is our wish to enter the abbey and speak with the traitors within. We command you to step aside. You have done your duty. Now we will do ours."

The king stretched out his massive right hand as if to shove the abbot to one side. The abbot and his monks stepped aside. What else could they do? They would hardly martyr themselves for a few defeated Lancastrians.

As we entered the abbey, I marvelled at the beauty of its elegant shape and its delicate floating tracery. The colours of its wall painting and glorious windows were breath-taking. I hoped that beauty would not be marred by bloodshed. But it was at least better to be riding amongst the victors than the victims.

The air in the abbey was not fresh; it stank of stale sweat, desperation and defeat. There were six or more muddied and bloodied knights in a huddle just beyond the rood screen, in the choir, the holiest part of the abbey. One of them stepped forward into the body of the church. You could still make out the Beaufort portcullis on his mired and torn surcoat. It was Somerset. He growled out a ferocious challenge.

"Come, pluck me from this sacred place, you foul and traitorous Duke of York, you and your verminous curs."

There were about ten of us, victorious and heavily armed, and six of them, disarmed and defeated. It was hardly a contest.

The king replied with calm authority. "Surrender, Somerset. *Perfectum est*. War is over."

At that moment, as if to evidence his words, the side doors of the abbey were flung open and a body, covered by a bloody standard bearing the royal arms of Lancaster, was borne in by a party of monks, quietly singing the "Te Deum".

"Your prince is carrion," said Gloucester, and spat. "Give yourselves up."

Somerset's eyes darted towards the open doors and, to forestall his escape, we unsheathed our swords and, on either side of the king, began walking with menace in Somerset's direction. He stood staring at us with ferocious eyes.

The abbot had entered by the side doors and cried out, "I beg you, my lords, no bloodshed here."

"No bloodshed," replied the king, still moving towards our quarry, "Provided the vanquished surrender to an honourable trial."

Somerset half-turned towards his friends, still behind the screen. "We are trapped and denied sanctuary."

He turned towards us grimly, almost regally, I thought. "I am your prisoner, Edward." His voice was harsh, rasping. "And you have broken the laws of sanctuary."

Gloucester was by him in an instant, telling his henchman, "Tie his hands."

"No need for that," said the king. "We will treat our noble prisoners with chivalry."

The chivalry was short-lived however.

Somerset and his party were taken outside and, as we emerged into the early evening light to a mob of local villeins and our common foot soldiers baying for blood, the king intoned in his powerful voice, "My brother of Gloucester, I command and commission you as High Constable of England to put the traitor Somerset to his trial in this place and all his company and do justice upon them."

The vanquished were hustled off to the marketplace, the rest of us walking gravely behind. I exchanged a look with Anthony and his even gaze in response said: We know this is not justice, let alone mercy. But this war must have an end. So, it is necessary.

We kept our distance but could see Gloucester, from afar, condemn the Duke of Somerset (now heir-general of the House of Lancaster) to a traitor's death. At which, a stool was immediately provided for a block, the condemned man made to kneel and, one of Gloucester's men producing a sword, his head was struck off. There were cheers and jeers from our men massed around, and the cobbles were running with blood. And, for a moment, I had a vision of another duke, aboard a ship and sent into exile by his Lancastrian king, being forced to kneel and beheaded by unknown assailants, twenty years before. That was a De-la-Pole duke and this a Beaufort. And so, the wheel goes round.

***

Later into the night, the king was brought word that Margaret of Anjou had been taken in flight; she was held in close confinement while he decided what her fate should be. It was after a good evening meal — served with little ceremony, after all we were still on campaign — that we debated what should happen to her. Clarence and Gloucester were both for beheading, although Anthony pointed out that it was contrary to the laws of war for a woman to be executed. I put in that, childless as she now was, she presented no threat. I like to think it was my argument that swung the king's judgment against beheading. I trust we shall never see an anointed queen beheaded in England.

"So, Edward," said the king, "As you have counselled that she should live, it is right she should be placed in the custody of another strong but loyal lady and who better than your honourable mother, Duchess Alice. We shall send her to Ewelme for safe keeping while we discover if her cousin the French king can bestir himself to provide a ransom for her release."

"I am sure my Beloved Mother will be honoured to serve Your Highness in this manner." I bowed, knowing the B.M. would take no pleasure in this grim task. Howsoever, we are born to serve.

And just a few weeks later — long and tortuous negotiations having commenced with the Valois king — I was sent with the king's commission to visit the B.M. and report on how the former queen's incarceration was progressing and whether Duchess Alice had any requests of His Grace.

"I have performed many duties for His Grace. But this is the first time I have become a jailor," said the B.M. looking saintly, if not martyred.

"Jailor of a queen, Mother. It's a token of the king's great trust and faith in you."

"We Chaucers — and De-la-Poles — will do our duty. How you boys will manage when I am gone is what keeps me awake at night."

"We shall survive, Mother."

"But will you flourish?"

She fussed with her needlepoint. She was working a particularly intricate purse whilst reading both a letter I had brought from Queen Elizabeth Wydville and a sapphire-encrusted devotional book which my honoured father had once given her. The B.M. might have invented the term *multi-tasking*.

"The queen — *the* queen," said the B.M., "Asks after Margaret's welfare and prays that I be not too harsh towards her, remembering that we both served her in former times. Does she think I am a torturer?" She gave me one of her old-fashioned looks and then glanced round to see whether her waiting woman was listening, but that lady was prudently engrossed in her own needlework.

"Are they testing us, the king and queen, Edward? You should know something of the queen's mind. You are virtually married to her brother."

"Blood brotherhood is an honourable estate, Mother."

The B.M. snorted while murmuring a few words of Latin from her missal; warding off the devil probably. I noticed, looking at her properly for the first time that visit, that she was still a fine-boned handsome woman, with the famous Chaucer cheekbones (I have them myself), but there were more lines on her face than I had ever seen before and her luscious brown eyes (which I have also inherited) were a little less lustrous. It struck me suddenly that she was not far off seventy years old. Indestructible, of course, yet becoming a jailor was taking its toll.

"I am sure they are not testing us, Mother. *Au contraire*, the king respects Your Ladyship more than most of the men at court. No doubt Queen Elizabeth who shares her brother's sensitive soul — and like yourself was once in waiting to Margaret in earlier times — is urging that compassion be mingled with strict custody."

The B.M. gave me another of her old-fashioned looks. "Only a fool — and I don't mean a jester — believes that *any* queen feels compassion," she spat out the word, "For the one she has replaced. Rightfully replaced," she said, more loudly.

She clearly suspected there were spies in the household.

And then, very quietly, she said, "It may be that the opposite is intended."

"God's blood, Mother, surely you don't believe..."

"I will act strictly according to my instructions from His Grace. No more and no less."

Her eyes looked strained. Yes, she had hardened much since the death of my father nearly twenty years before, when she had been so loyal to Lancaster.

"And what are *your* instructions, my son? To report on my treatment of Margaret?"

"No, Mother, of course not. It is to glean what information I can from your captive and inform her of what you already know about the negotiations for her ransom. And to discover if you have any requests of His Grace."

"None that anyone on earth can answer," she said and turned back to her missal and her mending.

***

Margaret was looking at me with regal composure.

I had introduced myself making a fairly deep reverence; I was aware that, but a few weeks before, this woman had been readepted as Queen of England, and she remained a titular princess of Sicily and Jerusalem. Whether she recognised *me* in any sense was impossible to say. She simply looked.

227

In accordance with the king's mandate, she was attended by one waiting woman and a page. She too was reading; a book she had borrowed from my mother's extensive library but not a religious text. It was her father King René's masterly book on chivalry.

"The late King René was a doyen of chivalry, madam. I had the honour to meet him once."

She still looked at me. I began to wonder if she had gone deaf or mad.

"I bring a message from the king. From King Edward."

Still, she looked. She was neither handsome nor ugly I decided, but with a very characterful face, lined, of course — she was middle-aged, certainly over forty — but revealing not one ounce of emotion.

I decided to wait before speaking again. If she had no curiosity, I would simply withdraw.

It was a long wait; seemingly endless. The page brought us both simple refreshments and we each partook.

Finally, she said, "When will the French king provide my ransom? I wish to return home." She spoke slowly, with remote dignity, in an odd, heavily French accent. The words seemed to come from a different time, a different realm.

I wondered if she knew that her husband had been killed in the Tower straight after Tewkesbury by the Dispatcher – as Anthony and I had begun to call him – Richard Gloucester. Presumably she had been told as she fled that her only son had died in the battle.

"Negotiations are proceeding with the French king, madam. They might be hastened if we knew the whereabouts of Jasper Tudor and his nephew Henry."

"*Vous ne les avez pas?* Thank you for that knowledge." She almost smiled.

Clearly, she was going to give no information and probably had none.

I felt compelled to offer an olive branch. "I condole with you, madam, in your grief."

She looked at me. Her eyes looked stony as if staring through a mask of ancient Greek tragedy. For a moment, they blazed, seeming to curse me and the whole world for what we had taken from her.

I coughed and looked away.

"Have you any other requests for me to pass on?"

"My hunting dogs were left at Tewkesbury. I need them here."

"That should not be a problem, madam. I shall take my leave."

She continued to stare as I withdrew with a slight obeisance. Those eyes remain with me. The eyes of the Gorgon; the eyes of despair.

Book III: High Summer

*In which the land flowed with milk and honey;
and how the milk curdled and the honey froze*

ק (kuph)

"Duke Francis was very courteous — the very mirror of chivalry — but he was giving nothing, and nobody, away. They speak an odd kind of French there. And their own language is like Welsh; for example…"

This was typical of Anthony, ever the scholar. But I wanted the facts.

It was summer 1472 and he had just returned from a "diplomatic" mission to the independent duchy of Brittany. As usual, I was not sent with him and had passed the last two months in East Riding settling a less than thrilling quarrel between two tenants of mine near the village of Ferriby. I had then left Malcolm in charge there — now a strapping and capable man in his twenties with an older wife who was the widow of a prosperous Hull merchant. I had arranged the match, of course. How else had our family started on its own rise to royalty?

"Will he send us the Tudor curs?" I asked.

"Not at present. He wants something in return, of course. But I couldn't prise out of him what it is. Perhaps support against King Louis. And I wasn't empowered to offer him that."

"Maybe our king will invade France. I think he is the man to reclaim Normandy or even Gascony."

"I pray so," said Anthony, looking dreamy. "To end our civil wars and reclaim the Angevin Empire and equal the feats of arms of the last Edward."

"Are the Tudors really a threat to us?" I asked, lowering my voice. We were speaking in the margins of the court at Westminster, as he had just returned from briefing the king. "Jasper has no royal blood, apart from the Valois blood of his mother which doesn't signify—"

"But the boy Henry's mother is the Beaufort heiress. She's the last of that line and the only descendant of John of Gaunt. They're quasi-royal."

"Quasi is pushing it, Ant. They're descended from a whore, Kat Swynford, John of Gaunt's mistress. *Vraiment*, they were legitimised retrospectively by Richard II (may his troubled soul rest in everlasting peace) but the letters patent expressly exclude them from the line of succession. And it's highly doubtful whether Queen Katherine was ever married to Owain Tudor in the eyes of Mother Church. They're all bastards on both sides."

Anthony looked back at me with gentle reproach. I must have been ruddy-cheeked with choler.

"Be calm, my brother. Their claim is tenuous at best and, in any event, the Lancastrians are crushed. No one is going to support an unknown Welsh bastard against our handsome and rightful king. But, we must guard against eventualities and Margaret Beaufort is a powerful advocate for her son. She wants him back, pardoned."

"And restored to the earldom of Richmond, I suppose?"

"His mother holds vast estates, remember. And there is talk of her marrying Thomas Stanley, the Lord Steward."

"How many husbands is that bloody woman planning to have? This must be number three, in spite of looking like an old nun chewing a wasp. It couldn't be because she controls all the duchy of Somerset estates, could it?" I asked, sardonically.

"Now the king and my sister have a son…"

"With another *en ventre sa mere*, God willing."

"The House of York is secure. And perhaps now is the time to go on pilgrimage."

I knew this had been Anthony's yearning for some time.

"To see something of the classical world?"

"And the new learning that flourishes in the city-states of Italy."

"Where the sun shines every day and the young men and damsels are as beauteous as angels…" I teased him.

"Will you journey with me, brother?" He looked very gravely into my eyes.

"Will you not remarry, Anthony?"

His wife, always coldly pious and weak, had dwindled away unmourned in his absence.

"Not unless the king commands it. I have contemplated taking vows — a vow of chastity for the years of pilgrimage at least."

"A vow not to touch women?"

"Wouldn't be too hard for you, Edward, would it?" He smiled mischievously.

"My thoughts are on higher things," I said piously. "Margaret of Burgundy is the only woman I could serve."

"You worship her. A woman needs to be ploughed, not worshipped."

"Then why don't you sow the Wydville seed, my lord? Or who will be the third Earl Rivers?"

"I have no wish to found a dynasty, Edward."

I have always remembered these words and the solemn, almost distant way he spoke them. Anthony, I think, had the second sight and foresaw something of his fate.

"My nephew, the prince, will be my heir," he continued. "I will assist in his education as a chivalrous Christian prince, so that he will be a Plantagenet king even greater than his ancestors."

"He belongs to your sister and her women until he is at least seven," I said.

"So, until then, let us see the old world and the new worlds: Rome, maybe Athens, Santiago de Compostela. And I would fain see the great port city of Barcelona; it would put Hull to shame, brother!"

So, he hatched our plan to visit Rome. We would never see the tall ships and the broad ramblas of Barcelona. But in a unique, heaven-sent sense, a small number of years later, Barcelona would come to me.

***

In life, the happy times pass quickly and easily and, in retrospect, the details are blurred. So it was — or so it seems now — looking back on the 1470s. It was a time of travel, not travail; a time when the winter of our lost content was turned into summer by the sun in splendour. As I recollect (and my aging memory is not what it was) it was '73 or '74 when Anthony and I set off on our long looked-for pilgrimage to that lovely city of Saint James of Compostela in Galicia, an Atlantic province just north of England's oldest ally, Portugal, and subject to the Crown of Castile; then on the rather weak head of King Henry IV and soon to be succeeded by his much more powerful sister, Isabella la Cattolica. We were free *pro tempore* from the cares of office and enjoying what remained of our youth — while others, Richard the Dispatcher for example, were building up their affinities and their strength for opportunities that might come.

Anthony and I set off as knights errant, just a small retinue of attendants around us (Q was back with me after spending some years helping the B.M. in her thankless tasks of running our estates and guarding an ex-queen and proved most useful abroad) and, of course, we were armed with purses of gold and, even more valuable, letters of introduction from the king, his queen and our powerful friend Duchess Margaret (still the much-loved but still also childless consort of the great Duke of Burgundy).

We had first travelled to Bruges to visit my mistress, the said Lady Margaret, who was now blossoming out into the beauty of the full-blown rose. Her husband — still, as always, fighting and intriguing for a royal crown — was away pushing the borders of his duchy further into the Swiss Confederation (a direction that would ultimately prove his undoing) while leaving his well-trusted duchess with powers plenipotentiary to govern in his absence and to guard his pretty young heiress. The Lady Margaret looked so plump and content that both Anthony and I believed the heir to Burgundy must be in her belly, and rejoiced at that. If only! Had it been so, the House of York would have had an ally strong enough to defeat the Tudors, and the Habsburgs would not have extended their greedy tentacles so far into the west…

From the Netherlands, we rode south, with a Burgundian guard of honour, and were received at the French border where we were able to produce passports which had been sent to us from the court of the French king — currently, thank the Lord, at peace with His Grace King Edward and His Highness Duke Charles. Thus protected, we rode three nights across northern France into Normandy (that sweet and sometime English duchy) and took ship at length from Le Havre to carry us on the long journey along the west coast of France, a voyage of at least seven nights, and thence along the shores of northern Iberia, to the rocky coastline of Galicia; another land where as Anthony was delighted to tell me — the language has Britannic roots.

On board ship was a motley crew; one was a noble and dark-skinned knight from Gascony, the chevalier Louis de Bretaylles, who shared with us a delightful manuscript he was reading entitled *Les dicts moraulx des philosophes*; a fine Latin text put into the French tongue by Messire de Tignonville. Anthony was evidently drawn to it and, having completed his reading, that chivalrous Gascon would not be prevented from gifting his book to my friend. In return, Anthony gave Sir Louis a golden pendant which had been a gift to him from his sister, the queen; typical of Anthony's generosity (such a beautiful gift I would not have given away, and indeed felt a tad jealous that, having decided to give it away, he had not given it to me). Anthony made a solemn knightly promise, in the presence of the Gascon and myself, that he would strive with all his cunning to carry over the French text elegantly into our English tongue. And this, being as honest a knight and as goodly a scholar as you will ever meet, my brother Anthony did.

***

I guess it was a brace of years later when the king made a great proclamation. We — the court — were all assembled in the hall at Eltham Palace, Edward's favoured abode, a lovely mansion set in the pretty countryside of the county of Kent, a few miles south-east of the cities of London and Westminster. Not a century before but my great-granddaddy Chaucer had been robbed and mugged when carrying funds to meet his king, Richard II, at the palace, but these were now more civilised times.

The king was enthroned in majesty beneath a silken canopy of estate; the queen no doubt was in the private chambers of which Eltham housed a whole suite. To His Grace's right stood Hastings as Lord Great Chamberlain; to the left stood both Clarence, looking gorgeously indolent ("very like His Grace but with the backbone removed" as Anthony relayed to me the queen's description) and Gloucester, far less beautiful or tall than his brothers but radiating a kind of animal energy not unlike the king's.

The king nodded to Hastings. He stamped his staff of office and, Garter King of Arms, resplendent in his tabard, cried out the king's will. "We, Edward, the fourth of that name, King of England and France, Lord of Ireland, and Duke of Aquitaine, do recall to his true allegiance the usurping French king, Louis de Valois, and call him to submit to his right Royal and Sovereign Lord, the said Edward Plantagenet, King of England, and by descent from the Lady Isabella of France, royal mother of King Edward, the third of that name, rightful King of France; and to offer him tribute and fealty and, in particular, to surrender the said duchy of Aquitaine, rightfully his by descent from the Lady Alienor, Duchess of Aquitaine and royal mother of King Richard I and King John; and the duchy of Normandy, his by right of descent from William the Conqueror, King of England and Duke of Normandy."

At this grandiose proclamation, there was, of course, much cheering and throwing in the air of hats. The king, still handsome but thickening somewhat around the waist and in the neck, smiled broadly. I looked at Anthony, standing very near me amongst the king's kinsmen, who looked back with shining eyes, not quite reflecting the slightly quizzical look in my own.

I heard someone behind me whisper, "Just like Henry V, but without the balls."

I swivelled round, angry at this *lèse-majesté*, but it was only the arrogant young Duke of Buckingham — a distant cousin of the king — who raised his eyebrows at me and said, "I mean, without the tennis balls, of course."

I gave him a look of distain and turned back.

"We shall to France," said the king, "All preparations have been made. Our first aim: to reconquer our duchy of Normandy. Are you with me, friends, Englishmen all?"

Of course, we were swept off our feet. My adoration of the king was not diminished; he was still, and always my hero, though now growing out of his golden youth. And, to Anthony and many others, he would clearly be the conqueror of Normandy, if not of all France. But, therewithal, I did not believe it.

***

Of course, months of preparation had preceded this, with the mustering of men and arms, the signing of indentures between the king and his vassals-in-chief (my brother and I jointly indentured to provide the army with seven hundred men in return for a weekly honorarium — provisioning fighting men is not cheap), and essential alliances with both Duke Charles and Duke Francis — with whom Anthony had parlayed not long before.

And here we were in Calais: that piece of England beyond the water, or rather the last remnant of the great Angevin Empire in France which still remains to the English Crown. Calais is a fine bustling city and a major mercantile centre, protected by its great fortress of Guisnes, where our military headquarters were based. Our army of twenty thousand men were largely encamped outside the city in that strip of English territory which we had been reduced to since Henry VI's disastrous accession. Our intelligence was that King Louis was not well-prepared and — if he saw himself encircled by enemies — could be induced to ask our king to name his price for a withdrawal from France. But would King Edward name a price so high — let us say, the duchy of Normandy — that no French king could pay and expect to survive? With three great duchies free, the French Crown would almost be reduced to its weakness of earlier centuries. And then, wouldn't Louis expect the English to return in spring, when campaigning resumes, in order to reclaim the luscious country of Bordeaux and all Gascony from the French? Much would depend on the cohesion of our alliances, especially with Burgundy.

We were awaiting the king's next move, when Anthony summoned me to meet him on the king's business. I hurried to our rendezvous in the cloisters of the great church.

"The king commands us to ride post-haste to meet with Duke Charles at Bar-le- Duc; it's in his duchy of Bar near to Lorraine."

He saw the look of horror on my face and smiled, showing the best white teeth in the English court.

"Don't fuss, Eddie. It's just a few days' ride and we can easily go north into Burgundian territory and follow the line of the Muese river through the duke's territories till we get to Bar."

"I can remember when the duchies of Bar and Lorraine were the fiefdom of René of Anjou. I'm beginning to feel old, Antonio. And why isn't Duke Charles bringing his army to us?"

"That's what we are going to ask him — most diplomatically, of course. The story is he's been delayed from bringing his full forces to bear on the French by an annoying fracas with the Archbishop of Cologne — a very stupid, minor cleric. There are rumours of a battle at Neuss in the Rhine Valley. Hence the king's cat and mouse policy. We are to meet him and escort his forces on their way to rendezvous with us in Normandy."

I was sceptical. "So, the archbishop had been dealt with?"

"Check-mated."

"And the Swiss?"

"Stop worrying, brother. The duke just needs to see us—"

"He needs to see *you*, you mean."

"He wants to see us both as the king's kinsmen before he will advance. You know Duke Charles and his *amour-propre*."

"Let's hope his love of the king, his brother-in-law, is as *proper*."

In reply, Anthony gave me a playful spank on the buttocks.

***

Our dealings with the duke were not as straightforward as Anthony had anticipated.

When we arrived at his handsome castle of Bar-le-Duc, there were no signs of an army. The duke was in residence with a bodyguard of his most favoured Knights of the Golden Fleece, but that was all. His army had clearly been left on the Rhine. We were summoned to an audience with him in the great hall of the castle, where we were received most hospitably.

"My lords, the Comte des Rivieres and Monsieur De-la-Pole." He addressed us in French, of course. "You are most welcome both in your own right and even more so as the accredited envoys and kinsmen of my brother, King Edward. I invite you, my lords, to feast at my table amongst our brethren of the Knights of the Order of the Golden Fleece."

The king would be expecting news from us as soon as possible; why yet another delay? I looked anxiously at Anthony. His gaze in reply said: an evening of bonding with the duke and his companions can do no harm. And what choice do we have?

By now, we were used to reading each other's thoughts.

The duke's high chamberlain had placed me in the position of honour seated — some distance away, of course — at the duke's right hand (perhaps he thought the king's sister's husband's brother was senior to the queen's brother — or, more likely, he was still wary of Anthony after the debacle at the joust with his brother the Bastard).

Towards the end of the splendid meal, after too many toasts to each other in heavy Burgundian wine, the duke beckoned me closer and whispered, "Lord Edward, I have written the king some days past that — due to a little local difficulty in the Rhine Valley — I am not as yet at liberty to bring the full weight of my forces to bear on Normandy. But as a token of the love I bear him — and to cement our alliance — I shall ride with Your Lordships and a bodyguard of my knights to meet my brother at Calais and make plans for our campaign. We depart two hours after dawn."

I nodded and smiled. But I knew it was not enough.

***

Even as dawn was breaking — with a glow of gold over the hills of Lorraine to the east — we were summoned, less than courteously, from our comfortable beds by ducal grooms.

We dressed hurriedly. Even Anthony looked perturbed, a little.

"This is not a good omen," I muttered.

He replied in one of his favourite phrases, "*Ora pro nobis peccatoribus. Nunc et in hora mortis nostrae.*"

"Yes, but not yet, I trust," said I.

He just smiled.

The atmosphere as we entered the Great Hall was sour, with the smell of last night's booze and the sweat of angry knights summoned from their beds unbathed and unbreakfasted; and of a very angry duke.

243

"Did you know of this?" shouted Duke Charles at us, as soon as we were herded into his presence.

"Your Grace, we know only of those greetings and messages we brought to Your Highness from our master." Anthony was better than me at this kind of thing.

I felt like one of Joseph's ten errant brothers brought before him unknowingly when he was viceroy of Egypt. Even then I knew my Pentateuch.

The duke turned to me.

"And you, what did *you* know?"

"I know only, sir, that we were sent here to provide an honourable escort for Your Highness — and his army."

His eyes shot sparks at both of us. Then he addressed the assembled court.

"The King of England has made peace — has already signed a treaty at Picquigny — with the King of France. He has dishonourably accepted a *double bribe* from the French of fifteen thousand pounds," Anthony and I bridled at this turn of phrase. "And a proposed marriage between his eldest daughter and the dauphin. So, for a wedding and forty pieces of silver, he has thrown me over!"

The knights banged their swords on the stone floor to express their anger; we looked at each other in horror and shock. Yet I was not so amazed.

"Well, gentlemen, what have you to say?"

We opened our mouths but — fortunately — he gave us no time to answer.

"I am not a whit surprised," he continued, beckoning his steward and throwing back a jewelled goblet of wine. "What more can you expect from a usurper? Edward *Plantagenet* he is not. Edward *Blaybourne*, that is his name. All Christendom knows his father was the handsome, lowborn Captain of Calais, where his mother was in residence. The old Duchess of York has even said it herself!"

At this, there was uproar, as the knights cheered and shouted their support for the duke while we protested loudly.

"My lord, we strongly object to this unworthy calumny…"

"Be silent. Go back to your master and report my words. Our alliance is over. As is your audience."

We bowed and left. Hastily.

***

"How could he? The duke, I mean."

"Sadly, it is the way of the world," said Anthony. "He is guilty at his own perfidy so seeks to lay the blame on the king."

There was silence as we rode on.

"It cannot be true, can it?"

"What do you mean, brother?"

"That the king…" I was whispering even though our small escort was some yards behind, "That the king is not—"

"Of course not." Anthony's voice was sharp; the sharpest I had ever heard it.

"What he said about Duchess Cecily was true. When she was angry…"

My companion looked at me almost fiercely. "She is a bitter, demented old woman. Of course, His Grace is a Plantagenet. Who else?"

I saw of a sudden that the future greatness — even the future survival — of his two young nephews, the Prince of Wales and the sweet little Duke of York, depended on these rumours being utterly quashed.

I bit my lip and said nothing.

ל (lamed)

It was in the over-hot summer of 1475 that my Beloved Mother died.

Her state prisoner Margaret had been despatched to France some months before in response to the belated payment of a paltry ransom; but I am sure it was the agony of guarding her which finally broke that courageous heart. To the last, she was in full control of herself and of her estates. To speak truly, she was in control of my brother the duke's estates and family too. I had not paid my respects to her at Ewelme since my visit there on the king's business. My fault for that sin and dolour at her demise were full and deep. They still are.

She had made her last will and testament as (unlike most women, of course) she was fully at liberty to do by Common Law, as a femme sole and the relict of a great duke. As was expected and right, she had devised almost all her own estates, including the splendid mansion at Ewelme with its surrounding manors, to John; his ducal dignity demanded as much. But with her usual forethought and care, she devised to me four adjoining manors in the county of Norfolk with a bequest of two thousand marks "in the esperance that His Highness the king, to whom the Lord grant long life and merry, might deign to bestow a barony upon my said younger son which dignity he shall thereby be suitably endowed to uphold." And in order to maintain His Highness' good grace toward both my brother and myself, she left a similar monetary bequest to him. The king graciously accepted the money. No barony was forthcoming.

The will also contained various bequests of hundreds of marks to loyal upper servants and for appropriate purposes; for the further endowment of her little school in the village (I hear it still flourishes today); for the chanting in perpetuity of masses for her soul in the chantry chapel of our pretty local church; for the building of a splendid tomb to her own precise instructions in said chapel; and one bequest more. I had known — in the misty uncertain way that one has knowledge of parental lives before one's birth — that the B.M. had been married, briefly, to the Earl of Salisbury, head of the Montacute family, and been widowed, before marrying my honoured father. But it was revealed to us — brother John and our learned aunt the Abbess Katherine — in the Bishop of Oxford's eulogy delivered at her obsequies that, in fact, she had been married twice before the betrothal to our father. At the tender age of eleven years, her own father, Sir Thomas Chaucer, who had passed on to his reward before my birth, had, as a dutiful father, arranged a less than glorious but decent marriage for her to Sir John Philip of Donnington Castle, who had died within a few months; one hopes before consummation. Then, before she was twenty years of age, she had indeed been remarried, until his death six years later, to the fourth Earl of Salisbury. I wondered how different my life would have been, had I been born a Montacute rather than a De-la-Pole. But then, that would not have been me, would it?

My siblings and I marvelled even more when were told —
in the reading of the will by the B.M.'s steward — that there
was a final bequest of a thousand marks, a goodly sum, to
Sister Alice Eugenia, a nun of the Cistercian Order "in the hope
that being hereby acknowledged as my daughter the said Sister
might thereby be raised from her humble status to became
Abbess of her House". Was she a Montacute, we wondered, or
even perhaps the daughter of Sir John Philip? But no offspring
of either of these marriages had ever been acknowledged.
We gazed upon each other with some embarrassment, if not
horror; as this Sister (in both senses) was given no surname,
we had to face the possibility (probability?) that she had been
born to our most respectable and highly controlled — not
to say controlling — mother *outside* the bounds of wedlock.
Our pious aunt the Abbess Katherine gave her judgment as a
distinguished religious: "We know not this woman and have
no duty to seek her out, whoever she may be."

We decided, in Christian charity, to make the money
a donation to Abbess Katherine's House. And on this, my
conscience is clear.

***

When I returned to London following two weeks in Ewelme in
family conference thus settling the B.M.'s estate, Anthony must
have seen how drained and wan I looked. I was in deep gloom
at the loss of a Beloved Mother and in a state of shock at the
revelation of her sin (perhaps the only secret I never revealed to
my blood brother). He therefore proposed that this marked the

proper time for us to go on the next stage of our pilgrimage — our grand tour of Europa, you might call it — to the font of our Catholic faith and cradle of the burgeoning *renatio*, or new learning: the great city of Rome. Anthony, always more pious than I, had a strong desire to visit the Holy City and to pay his respects to the Holy Father, at that time Sixtus the Fourth (or Forthus the Sixth as I liked to call him, much to Anthony's pious chagrin).

To journey overland to the Papal States governed by His Holiness, we would have to pass through several other Italian principalities: the duchies of Savoy — a sort of marchland between France and Italy — and Modena and the fabulously named "Republic of Florence" or Firenze as the native Italians call it. Anthony was particularly drawn to the extraordinary idea of a state governed — like the ancient state of pre-imperial Rome — as a republic or commonwealth without a king or ruling prince. He believed that the study of such a polity would equip him better to tutor and prepare his nephew Edward as a future philosopher king, while I was more intrigued by the wonders I had heard — back in my days governing Humberside — of the beauties of Florentine art and architecture and the splendours of the Medici "court".

So, we set off with a very small suite — no more than twelve or fifteen retainers, comprising a few knights and the rest grooms and body servants (an all-male party, of course), and all the necessary *laisser-passers*, and royal letters of credence and introduction to the princes of the various lands through which we must pass. As we were now at peace with our French neighbours — and the fashions at court were increasingly Francophile with the queen and her daughters wearing the latest Parisian modes and working hard to improve their fluency in the langue of the French court, with the very fair fifteen-year-old Lady Elizabeth betrothed to become Queen of France — we had no problems in obtaining passports from the French king's envoys to King Edward to travel freely across his kingdom. And so, we did over for fifteen days — France being a kingdom much bigger and wider than England having many interesting adventures involving damsels and dragons — and all the rest you would expect in the age of *Le Morte d'Arthur*. But as we began to approach the borders of Italy — through the French duchy of Savoy — it was as if we were entering a different century and another age.

Having avoided Milan, we passed into the lovely duchy of Modena which is ruled from Ferrara by the Este, or d'Este family. As visiting the duke's principal city would have taken us out of our way, we merely paid our respects to his cousin, a marquis (a title I would have much prized, had it ever been offered) who governed the charming city of Modena; with such pretty buildings and handsome young men and women. As it was now September, the arduous heat of the Italian summer had passed and the days were sunny and balmy. I began to relax in my Antonio's warm and sunny company and to forget myself for the first time since the B.M.'s demise.

But if Modena was pretty — like a little Italian sister of Bruges — how can I describe our first vision of Florence? Our little party was on a low Lombardian hill when we first saw that ravishing city. We stopped for a moment and Anthony said, "No wonder Dante lived here. This must have inspired his vision of *il paradiso.*"

The very air of Firenze is unique; ambrosian and yet so human too. When we saw its perfectly proportioned buildings — the palazzo Vecchio, for instance, the duomo, and especially the lovely, ponte vecchio which arcs across the Arno River — I remember saying, dumbstruck, to my friend, "This is a new world of building, of culture."

He replied, "It's the classical world reborn, dear Edward. *This* is the *renatio*."

At the city gate, we were met by representatives of both the republic and of its leader Lorenzo de' Medici, whose family had dominated that city, and region, for three generations. We were offered the tastiest of wines and morsels, with an invitation "should it please us" to attend upon the signor at his palace in three hours' time. Meanwhile, we were escorted — with courtesy at least as exquisite as any that France or Burgundy has to offer — by young men with eyes of amber and skin like the oil of Tuscan olives; more beautiful and more finely attired than any we had ever met before.

Freshly bathed and changed into our finest robes, we were ready and most eager later that afternoon to be escorted from our own delightful chambers nearby, through a shady courtyard with fountains sparkling like Moorish Alhambra into the handsome and spacious chambers of the great Lorenzo. Signor Lorenzo (and what a splendid name that is — had I a son, I would introduce the name into England) sat on what could surely pass for a throne, though less elevated than such a chair would be and without the usual regal canopy above. And, almost as soon as we were announced into his grand hall of audience, unlike a king who would be hemmed in by protocol and hierarchy, he immediately stood with an easy Italian charm and came towards us. His "courtiers" — men of all ages but all superbly dressed and handsome, some dark but others as fair as the day — were milling around and inclining gently first towards him and then towards us. So, we walked to meet him. Though still young, he was not a handsome man; probably the least good-looking in the room. Yet his face was strong, characterful and fiercely intelligent. He possessed that effortless grace the Italians call *sprezzatura*: the gentlemanly art that conceals art. And when he smiled; ah, then you knew at once why this merchant banker and his father and grandfather had been raised up to rule in all but name this opulent city-state.

"Gentlemen, my lords," he spoke in French with a charming Italian lilt, "What a pleasure and honour it is for us to receive our friends from England, and to offer our simple hospitality to lords who are so close in blood to the great Plantagenet himself."

We bowed and Antony — or here I should say Antonio — replied in the most elegant Petrarchan Italian. "The honour is ours, signor. Such beauty, such hospitality, such magnificence; we can already attest to the truth of Your Lordship's epithet as *il magnifico.*"

Lorenzo then gave me the most glorious smile (such teeth I have never seen in northern Europe) and I bowed deeply in return. He then asked if we would do him the honour of meeting his mother, the Lady Lucrezia.

We knew that on the death of his father Piero (known as "the Gouty" so presumably his figure was less lissom than his son's), Lorenzo had come to power, but always guided by the experience and wisdom of his mother, so this invitation was not a surprise. He swept back in a great gesture with his right arm, the crowd parted and, sitting there on a chair equally fine as his own, was the still very beautiful Lady Lucrezia. We bowed and she inclined her head. Now it was my turn to show off.

"Benedetto sia 'l giorno, e 'l mese, e l'anno
E la stagione, e 'l tempo, e l'ora, e'l pun
E'l bel paese e' l loco, ov'io fu giunto
Da duo begli occhi, che legato m'hanno."

As I recited this Petrarchan sonnet in tribute to the elegant lady, the whole room became hushed; you could have heard a gauntlet drop. As I finished, all the courtiers burst out into cheering, hallooing and waving their gloves or hats while the lady herself stood, smiled as winsomely as her son and inclined her head with a queenly nod.

"So, the fame of our great sonneteer has spread as far as England," said Lorenzo admiringly. "Are you a poet yourself?"

"Sadly not, it is my brother here, Lord Rivers, who is the author amongst us. Though I do have the honour to be great-grandson to a bard who is famous in England, by name Geoffrey Chaucer."

"Ah indeed," said the Lady Lucrezia speaking for the first time, in a voice dark and rich as Turkish coffee, "The famous poet of the *Canterbury Tales*. I greatly respect his work."

I bowed low. I was in learned company.

"In my family," I said, "We have a tale that, in the middle of the last century at the wedding of the then Duke of Clarence here in Firenze to an Italian princess, my great-grandfather dined here with the poet Petrarch and the great chronicler Froissart."

"If only," said Lucrezia, "We could have a record of their conversation."

I made a courtly bow.

"My mother, you know, is a poetess," said Lorenzo, "And we have many poets and artists of genius here in the republic. May I introduce my honoured guests to a most promising painter known as Leonardo from the little town of Vinci?"

A young man came forward and bowed awkwardly. He was strongly built with a heavy, long beard behind which his big luminous eyes seemed to be hiding. He looked at us like an eagle. Or rather he glanced at me and then was transfixed by Anthony. The artist, who seemed rather shy, said something in dialect to Lorenzo who smiled and turning to us said, "Leonardo would like to have the opportunity to paint the portrait of the angelic Englishman with the green eyes."

"Greatly as I am honoured by his request," replied Anthony, "I fear it will not be possible at this time — we have business with His Holiness."

At this mention of the pope, Lorenzo's face flashed a much less amicable expression.

"We would much prefer to stay in Florence, but we are carrying letters from King Edward — about church appointments and the like. We are aware that His Holiness has not always been — shall we say — an easy neighbour to the republic."

"His Holiness is a *wonderful* neighbour — if you live in England," quipped Lucrezia.

The laughter throughout the room dispelled the awkwardness that Anthony's faux pas had evoked.

With exquisite Italian tact, they had given us adjoining chambers, each beautifully decorated with tapestries — Anthony's an allegory of St. Francis with the birds in delicious shades of blue, mine with the same saint and the fishes in hues of green.

Next morning, we were woken, with the bright sun streaming through the casement, Anthony lying on his bed and I curled up on the Turkish divan a few yards away from its side, by the sweet sounds of twangling instruments, pipes and tabors and a small harmonious bagpipe rising from the courtyard beneath our windows. It was like waking in Heaven. I opened my eyes to see Antonio's fine features looking down at me, not bleary-eyed — those emerald eyes were never bleary — but dreamily.

"Are we in Dante's paradiso, do you think?" he asked.

I wish we could have stayed there.

After breakfast, we were given a tour of the buildings and archives of this splendid city and wherever we went, as the people saw we were under the aegis of the Medici, we were greeted with a courteous reverence.

"So, it is to be a republican monarch," Anthony said to me, smilingly.

"I think you have found your philosopher king," I replied.

We spent the afternoon in siesta — a wonderful custom we should adopt in northern Europe — and at the setting of the sun, we were invited to a reception (a kind of republican holding of court) in the elegant *sala musica* of the palace. Here were no tapestries but the walls were alive with frescoes — fiercely bright pigments applied to damp plaster on the walls, forming wonderful pictures of fables from the lays of ancient Greece and Rome. As we entered, a troupe of minstrels were playing, including a young man with glorious long honey-blond curls and a short fair beard plucking out a melody on a long beautifully shaped stringed instrument placed across his lap, which I had never seen before. At the other of the hall was our host, il Principe Lorenzo, standing with advisers and senators of the republic around him, speaking to a tall and broad-shouldered man we could see from behind. That man was wearing a full-length black silken caftan; again, something we had never before seen.

As we approached, Lorenzo acknowledged us, as did his entourage. "It is a great pleasure to receive our English visitors. This gentleman, my lords, is an envoy to the republic from our friend King John of Aragon. I present the Honourable Rabbi Abraham di Mayorca."

I looked at Anthony, in shock that a *Jew* — and a Jewish magus masquerading as a royal ambassador at that — should be presented to us as our equal. But our breeding equalled us to the distasteful task and, keeping our faces devoid of expression, we made him a small bow to which he responded with one even smaller. I looked at the man, and saw someone between ten and twenty years my senior, dark-bearded and heavy-set. He was not a handsome man, with a large nose and mottled skin. His eyes were watchful and confident; almost arrogant. And he had about him an aura — not an odour as such (we all have that, though amongst the nobility we bathe at least once a week and use fragrant unguents to mask it) — but something powerful he projected to which I took an immediate dislike. It was like being kicked in the stomach by an angry horse, and not one I felt could be easily tamed. Yet he was clearly a man of some influence in his own land.

"It is a joy to meet lords from a kingdom I have heard of only in song and fable," said the rabbi, in a voice which was surprisingly mellifluous and suggested spiritual depths. His tone was amicable, veiled and possibly ironic, which did not increase my warmth towards him.

Anthony, who I sensed took against him less than I, replied, "And for us to meet an envoy of such a distinguished king."

Actually, the King-Counts of Aragon were clearly in decline and it was the larger kingdom of Castille with which the Lancastrian kings had been allied.

Lorenzo signalled to the musicians to play and, as attendants presented us with wine and morsels, he drew us slightly to one side.

"The rabbi is here from the king on business with me as head of our family banking house, but tomorrow we are expecting ambassadors from our friend the Sultan Mehmet to whom I shall be delighted to present him. You see, we provide a sort of sanctuary here, a safe space within which the representatives of powers without formal relations may meet and talk freely."

I was about to say it was surprising to see a Jew negotiating to take a loan — rather than to provide one at usurious interest — but then remembered that, apart from it being undiplomatic, my own Hull-born ancestors had risen into the nobility by lending their mercantile profits to King Edward III for his wars, so instead I said, "My companion and I are sworn members of a covert brotherhood with similar aims, which meets generally in Bruges in Burgundy."

"We are able to be more open about such things — and many others — here in the republic," he said, with a cryptic smile, "Which is why we keep the Holy Father at arm's length."

Anthony then intervened. "I see you have a very beautiful harp here, Signor Lorenzo. Lord Edward is a fine harpist. A true amateur of the art. Isn't it a lovely instrument, Edward?"

It was indeed; made of fragrant cedar wood and in the shape of a classical lyre. And I was put on my mettle by Anthony's challenge in such powerful company.

"Now you must honour us with a melody, my Lord Edward!"

"If you please," said the rabbi, poking his large nose in.

I had no choice, so I bowed, sat and played a song I had learnt in Bruges composed by the great Master Josquin des Prez. I felt transported as I played. It went well.

There was more than polite applause from the assembled company.

"You represent your king even better in music than in words," said Lorenzo. I think it was a compliment.

The rabbi regarded me with shining eyes and said, "Bravo, sir, that was beautiful."

I still did not like him.

***

"What are these state matters you have to discuss with Pope Sixtus?" I asked.

"Oh, some canonical issues about the dispensation for the Lady Elizabeth's marriage negotiations."

"But the degree of consanguinity between her and the dauphin must be very slight, is it not?"

Anthony moued vaguely. "It's not for that marriage."

"You mean it's for one of the king's other daughters?"

"N-no. It's for a different possible marriage for the Lady Elizabeth. The king wants to… open up another possible scenario."

I was astonished. Words failed me. I stared at him.

"The king has received a proposal — a secret proposal, of course — that would unite my niece with the heir-general of the House of Lancaster."

"And who could *that* be?" I growled at Anthony, and he stared back at me like a sheep; a Welsh sheep. "Henry Tudor? And what did you call him? A Welsh nobody, a descendant of bastards on both sides?"

"The Lady Margaret Beaufort is negotiating with the king for her son to be recalled from exile, to be restored to the honour of Richmond and — perhaps — as part of the arrangement…"

"To marry the king's eldest daughter, who is already betrothed to the French dauphin?" My astonishment had become outrage. "How can you…?"

"The king is simply considering it. He wishes to keep the option open. It would be a very tidy solution to the eternal battles within the dynasty."

"And it would insult the King of France!"

"I'm sure His Grace will have considered how to finesse the French king, should the need arise." He could see I was deeply upset; both at the king's duplicity (though it would be treason to call it so) and even more at my friend's collusion in it. "It's high politics, brother, and it's what the king commands."

"If I'd known that was the purpose of our journey, I would not have come."

"Only one of its purposes, brother. The other is for us to see the great world — together."

That night, in my own chamber, I still felt mortified; but was it, I wondered, because of the duplicity of statecraft and the ambivalence of kings, or simply because I had not been included once again in the magic circle of knowledge?

***

Rome was a city in turmoil, in an orgy of building and profligate, but magnificent, expense. The Supreme Pontiff, Sixtus IV — who had surprised all Christendom, as it delights popes to do, by choosing a regnal name in abeyance for a millennium — having been elected as a great man of religion and much-needed reform — had been transfigured by his election into as great a builder and spender of money.

The noise and dust and rising edifices — many of them most beautiful and built on classical models — made it clear that his plan was to transform the Eternal City from a town of innumerable dark churches and close-packed smelly streets into a great metropolis of classical basilicas and public squares to rival his envied adversary Florence. He had even thrown a new bridge over that broad, majestic River Tiber, in order to prevent repetition of previous disasters caused by overburdening of the only existing bridge. And, most famously, he has given his name to the great chapel which adorns the papal apartments in the Vatican Palace — that city within a city. Indeed, His Holiness took great pleasure in giving us a personal tour of the work in progress.

"This chapel, my lords, will be the glory of our papal apartments and through the beauties of art I intend to deepen the spiritual surroundings of the lives of all our successors in this office," he said with a flourish towards the rudimentary building with its still bare walls and ceiling.

"Can we find spiritual depth and understanding through the beauty of paintings, Holy Father?" I asked, rather surprised that a prince of the harsh church I knew should think so.

The pope was a small man, with a hooked nose and quite a handsome and sensuous face; very Italian. He waved his hands towards a small but elegant painting of a saint already hanging where the altar would be.

"That is a work — just a small one — by a wonderful young painter employed by those dangerous fools, the Medici, by the name of Sandro Botticelli. One day, I shall rescue him from their greedy grasp and induce him to paint these walls with frescoes allegorising the just and necessary supremacy of the papal imperium. I will have him."

The pope was a clearly a very determined man.

"We were introduced to a young painter of remarkable appearance called Leonardo, while in the republic."

The pope's recoil from my naming his enemy almost caused him to spit on the chapel floor.

"No, no, no, he is nothing. It is Botticelli I must have. But I cannot do business with the Medici. Could you?" He turned to Anthony, who struggled to hide his discomfort.

"We were not in Florence on royal business, Your Holiness, but merely as a courtesy visit and to see a little more of the great riches of Italy."

The pope's sharp eyes did not seem convinced.

"Well, my English friends, you may inform King Edward, privately, of course, that the Medici will not long rule in that city. They are impious, dealing with Jews and Saracens instead of Mother Church. Our friends — the great banking house of Pazzi — have our support and, when the time is right, they will make their move to replace that upstart clan."

Suddenly, his darkened face lit up with a delightful smile.

"Before we discuss the king's business, what else may I show you in our burgeoning city?"

"I have always wanted to see the statue of Pope Joan and the son she bore. Is hers a true story, Your Holiness?"

"Of course, it is," said Sixtus, dismissively. "Everyone wanted to see the statue of that blasphemous bitch and her whelp. I have had it cast into the river. Women have no place in the hierarchy of the Church. Shall we dine and then discuss matrimonial matters?"

When His Holiness had satisfied his more than natural gluttony, it was clear that his scruples about on-going negotiations for two marriages were rather less than mine.

"It is wise for the king to keep open the possibilities for both marriages, each of which would be most beneficial to the peace of his realm; the princess is young and they say beautiful…" Was he leering or was I imagining that? "But beauty and youth do not last for very long and the matter should be resolved in the forthcoming years or the French king — as I know you prefer to call him — may come to hear about this, which would be regrettable. Contributions towards the glorification of the papal city would be most welcome, of course."

Was there a threat implied here? If so, Anthony moved to rebut it.

"Were any inkling of our discussions to reach the ear of the French king, King Edward might wish to strengthen his links with the Medici, but I am sure that will never be necessary."

He bowed deeply and kissed the papal ring. It was the size of a papal island; even bigger than my own balas ruby.

"And where are you proceeding to from here, gentlemen?" Sixtus asked as we prepared formally to take our leave.

"We shall ride north through Your Holiness' states, through the territory of the republic. We do not intend to stop for another visit until we approach the great city of Milan."

"In that case, you must give our greetings to the duke. He is a great man. They say his courtiers have invented a new art of dancing, which they call the *balletto*; most curious."

The pope clapped his hands and pretty young chamberlains brought in elaborate items.

"Here are some gifts for His Grace of England, as a small token of our high esteem and love for our Son of York. May he long reign. Is it correct that the former Queen Margaret has now been ransomed and returned to her family in Anjou?"

We were both a little discomfited by this unexpected question. His Holiness was set on sending us away just a little off balance.

"That is the case, Holiness. My late mother, the Duchess of Suffolk, was her keeper."

"Indeed. I heard of your loss; accept my blessing."

And suddenly he was a priest again; his blessing and the kiss of peace was surprisingly comforting as we took our leave.

"I thought we were paying a visit to the Venetian republic before heading north!" I said to Anthony.

"We are," he replied, "But the less that old fox knows about our movements, the better."

But we were not clever enough to out-fox the old fox.

***

We rode quickly north through the papal territory and were received with great hospitality in each town and village. But on the second night, as we were riding fast — having decided not to stop until we were back in the territory of the Florentines — we were attacked by a band of ruffians, at least ten of them, on horseback; their faces muffled in heavy cloaks. Of course, we were wearing only the lightest armour but we and our men fought them off quite easily. It only then became clear that they had had no intention of killing or even injuring us; their target was our very substantial baggage train in which we carried a substantial amount of Anthony's gold plate, together with the gifts we had received from Lorenzo and the pope. Fortunately, none of our papers and secret letters were included in the haul as we carried those on our persons.

"Mere brigands and thieves," I said to Anthony as I bathed his slight wounds later that night.

"Brigands authorised under the crossed keys, I think."

"My pious brother would not be guessing that these thieves were working on instruction from…"

"It may be… But then, it may not."

"Do we curtail our journey and make for home now? This has left me with a bitter taste," I said, handing Anthony a cup of wine (a very simple cup; our gold goblets were gone).

"No, that would look like defeat. Let's head for Venice as we intended."

So, we rode north-east to enter the lands of the Venetian state and la Serenissima was indeed serene and majestic; a city like no other, built on water. Moreover, the doge and his council received us with great dignity and respect — there is clearly much to be said for republican government, though it will never work in the larger kingdoms — and were eager enough to discover some of our plate and jewels (which had somehow landed up in their city) and return it to us together with funds in compensation. Clearly the kingdom of England — and the fame of our king — were held in high esteem there. But no word of apology or sympathy was heard from the Vatican, let alone any offer of compensation. So, after a pleasant sojourn of a few weeks in Venice, we decided to ride for home.

They say all roads lead to Rome, but we were content to be heading in the opposite direction.

מ (mem)

We stared in wonder at the page before us. There were Anthony's exquisitely crafted words — his finished translation of the French book we had been given by Louis de Bretaylles — but they were not painted with the manual stokes of a scribe's quill but imprinted on parchment by great blocks of ink. This was another *renatio* — a rebirth as world-changing as anything we had seen in Italy.

"I pray Your Lordships are content with the handicraft of your humble servant."

William Caxton's lined weather-beaten face and his Netherlandish–sounding English seemed less humble than proud of his extraordinary achievement. His shrewd mercantile face reflected and commented on our amazement, and Anthony's nobly modest delight. We were meeting in Caxton's shop under the sign of the Red Pale near the King's Almonry, a goodly building in Westminster City not far from the palace, close to the seat of government; here Caxton had established his business having returned from his long sojourn in Burgundy.

"I am filled with awe, Master Caxton. Your work is both alchemy and art," said Anthony.

"And this invention of yours will spread learning to the peasant children in my Beloved Mother's school in Ewelme and every other town and manor throughout the kingdom."

"In days to come, everyone — men and women, gentle or base — will be able to read and perhaps even to write!"

Caxton was preening himself. "As Your Lordships say. Though I cannot claim the invention of the press. I learnt my trade — or as Lord Rivers says, my art — as a young merchant in Cologne from men who had studied in the workshops of Herr Gutenberg of Mayence. And *he* had learnt the rudiments from travellers returning to Christendom from Cathay in the east."

We marvelled.

"The bound volume of Your Lordship's work is not yet perfect but may I show you our image of the title page?"

And there it was: *The Dictes or Sayings of the Philosophers* as done into the English tongue by "Antoine Wydville Erle Ryvyers, Lord Scales et cetera, et cetera." (The scribes and printers — like heralds — love to use these grandiose styles and spellings).

"Yours, my lord, will be the first book printed in this realm of England." He turned to me. "The second shall be the great *Canterbury Tales* as recounted by Your Lordship's great-grandsire." I inclined my head graciously. "We have, at our fingertips, eight fonts of type so as not to tire the reader's eye and — in due time — we shall use woodcut blocks to add pictures to our texts, so they'll be as beautiful as any scribed by the monks. May I demonstrate our printing press in action for Your Lordships? Wynkyn, set the press to work!"

Master Wynkyn de Worde, the sorcerer's apprentice, materialised at Caxton's elbow, like a goblin with his hooded eyes and pointy ears, and bowed us through to the inner sanctum where stood the great machine — the engine of future thought and ideas — imprinting, with a mighty bruit its strong black impression on the reams of parchment which glided seamlessly through it. Anthony was spell-bound; I a tad fatigued. He always longed to understand the workings of everything — I am content to accept it as magic.

When we returned to the outer shop, Caxton bowed and presented us with two elegantly bound volumes.

"This, my lords, is mine own feeble work, the tale of the ancient fabled city of Troy, which I have dared to translate across from the French into the English, as dedicated to my patroness Her Highness Duchess Margaret. May I present a facsimile to each of Your Lordships."

I opened mine to the title page to read, with a palpitating heart, the flowery dedication to his mistress, and mine, the Lady Margaret.

I was glad it was Anthony who spoke.

"How fares Her Highness? She is a great ornament to Burgundy and the Netherlands but we miss her sorely in England."

As he said these words, we heard another startlingly familiar, magnificent voice. "Aye, we miss our sister dearly down there in the Netherlands."

All at Westminster knew that powerful voice. All knelt, as the king entered holding the hand of the queen, with Hastings, some ladies (the queen was always accompanied by at least four countesses) and a small entourage. The king looked splendid; his extra girth — natural with the approach of middle years — suited him well. He wore a velvet gown of rich purple; the colour reserved for royalty by the sumptuary laws. The queen, with her green almond eyes, looked more lovely than ever; she had blossomed since the birth of her younger son. She raised up and kissed her brother; His Grace did likewise for me, then greeted Anthony.

Thinking on my feet, I said, "May I present William Caxton, Master Printer, to Your Highnesses. And, as a beauteous exemplum of his work, this volume translated by himself from the French and dedicated to Her Grace the Duchess Margaret."

"If a humble printer may be permitted to speak, Highness…?"

"We are trespassing in your shop, Master Caxton, it is for us to beg your permission."

Caxton bowed, evidently as dazzled by the king as was everyone who came into his orbit.

"If Your Graces would condescend to accept it, your servant has a volume especially prepared for them."

At his signal, Wynkyn proffered another tome, gorgeously bound in dark blue velvet with the title imprinted in gold lettering, putting our copies in the shade.

"This is the volume I have prepared to be placed amongst Your Highness' famous library of manuscript books."

I unobtrusively withdrew my own downgraded version as Caxton, on bended knee, presented his to the smiling king.

And that moment remains as a vignette in my mind; if only there was a device (like the printing machine) to record it for posterity on parchment, or just frozen like magic in the airy spheres. The king and queen in their handsome prime; Caxton proudly presenting his wonderful artefact; and Anthony and I, content in relation to each other and in our proximity to the throne. But even at that delicious moment, fixed in time, did an echo of the word "Blaybourne" whisper somewhere near my ear?

***

Months passed. The Sun of York continued to blaze in splendour.

Was it then that things started to fall apart?

Quidnunc appeared one morning as I was languidly composing a new song at my lute (the new instrument I had first seen in Florence and had, of course, acquired). Anthony was away in Wales on the king's business and my brother John — who had begun to take his responsibilities a touch more seriously since the B.M.'s demise — had quite properly asked me to visit our lands in the north. But I was feeling melancholic and filled with a sad sweet spiritual apathy and so was putting off my journey. To speak truly, I was a tad resentful; my blood brother was an earl, my brother by blood a duke and all around the king had honours, and what was I? Still no more than a knight; it was merely as a courtesy that I was usually addressed as a lord.

Old Quidnunc came out of the woodwork — he had, of course, been part of my family all this time but he managed to stay out of my presence when "my Lord of the Rivers" was around as Anthony liked him not; but what need I say about Q who is, after all, just a bondman.

In he minced, preening himself on having important news to import.

After a while, I turned to him. "Speak, fellow. What news?"

"News from Burgundy, my lord."

"My Lady Margaret has a son?"

"No, my lord."

"A daughter?"

"No, my lord."

We could go on like this for hours. But if my Lady Margaret was not the lighter of a fair son to inherit the principality, no news seemed startling enough to rouse me from my humour.

"So…" I cast around, listfully playing Q's game. "The duke has won his crown at last from the pope?"

This would, at any rate, make my lady a queen.

"Alas no, my lord. The news is rather from Lorraine but closely affects Burgundy."

"Lorraine? Is not the duke campaigning there against the Swiss?"

"He was, my lord."

"And now he has returned to Brussels?"

"No, my lord."

This was becoming serious.

"He has lost a battle?"

"The duke, my lord, with all his forces, has suffered a heavy defeat at the hands of the Lorrainers and the Swiss at Nancy."

"Jesu save us! The duke has fled, I guess?"

"His Grace attempted flight but was slaughtered by his enemies, my lord. His body, they report, has not even been discovered amongst the mountains of the dead."

Now I was awoken from my lethargy.

"How certain is this news?"

"I have it from my Lord Hastings' man who had it from the French king's envoy's man, my lord, who was crowing of it."

"At least we are at peace with France. Is there news of my Lady Duchess?"

"The news is she is at Brussels, my lord, and has her step-daughter the Lady Mary in her protection."

"God be praised for that. But both will now be in danger. I must hie me to the court. Is the king at Westminster?"

"He is, my lord. His Grace may not be too sorrowful about the news."

This deserved a rebuke. "The court will be in mourning. The duke was His Grace's brother-in-marriage."

"Who spoke most disparagingly of him, as Your Lordship heard."

"Oh, so you know about that."

Anthony and I had told not a soul on our return that the duke had insulted the king — and his mother.

"Everybody knows, my lord," Q smirked.

"You will *never* speak of it — it would be treason."

"And yet the Duke of Clarence speaks of it, my lord. Loudly."

"The Duke of Clarence is a numbskull as anyone who has ever dealt with him will tell you. Now, I must get me to the court and fast. I wish Lord Anthony was here."

"His absence makes Your Lordship even more useful to His Grace," said Q, cunningly. And for a moment I agreed that it could be a stroke of fortune to be on hand — and at once dismissed the idea as unworthy, and disloyal.

"Get out, and order my horse at once."

***

Arriving at the Palace of Westminster, I found the court in turmoil. The king was in conclave with his closest counsellors. To my satisfaction, I was granted audience.

"Your Grace, might I offer my service by taking ship to the Netherlands with messages from Your Highness and the queen to the Lady Margaret and her advisers?"

"A good thought, De-la-Pole, for which much thanks, but two knights have already set off with just such messages. I know you have great care for the Lady Margaret, but I have no doubt she will rule the roost while filling the void left by the demise of the duke. My brother Charles was always a rash and hot-headed fellow."

I felt deflated, but not surprised.

"The Lady Mary's marriage is now a very urgent question, sire," said Hastings.

"Yes," said the king, "Whoever dips his tip in that particular pot will draw out a massive prize."

They laughed bawdily; I forced a guffaw at this coarse quip.

"Since Clarence was widowed, sire, I know he has spoken of marriage with the lady." This was Gloucester, whose tone indicated neither approval nor the reverse of Clarence's plan.

The king laughed, but this time without mirth. "Our brother George has many plans, my friends, some of which have been troubling us of late. He is too loose a cannon to be let off in the rich lands of the Low Countries. No, my sister is wisely contemplating the marriage agreed with the Habsburg, Maximilian, the emperor's son and I have advised her to consummate that plan."

"Wouldn't that make the Habsburg's overbearingly powerful, sire?" I asked, wishing to sound wise.

The king looked at me with a gentle smile. "What moves us is that the French king should not become overbearing by seizing the Low Countries which would put *us* in danger."

"There are already reports that he has seized French Burgundy," said Lord Stanley. I was surprised to see him there, but clearly his marriage to Margaret Beaufort had enhanced his importance.

"And he will try to take the free county of Burgundy also," someone said.

"My sister and her council are marshalling their forces to defend Franche-Comté and the Netherlands. And the sooner the Lady Mary marries the archduke, the safer they will be," said the king. "I shall recall Rivers from Wales." The king glanced at me. "We need all our best men around us in case the French break their treaty but I doubt that will befall; my sister has everything in hand. I wish I could say the same for my brother."

There was a pregnant pause.

"Not you, brother," he said clapping Gloucester warmly on the back. "If only George were like you, the realm would be a happier place."

Gloucester said, "He speaks rashly, sire, but he has always returned to his allegiance." Which reminded us that he had strayed dangerously before.

I looked at Hastings, then whom no one was closer to the king, but his serious expression gave nothing away. Such a disturbing query could not long be left hanging over the head of one so close to the throne.

However, I knew the king loved his brothers and would always keep them on, and by, his side.

And, with the blessing of hindsight, I was right about those bloody Habsburgs.

***

The king was arrayed in his full glory, even if he was rather fat and nearly forty. He looked powerful, dominant; the Sovereign Lord that he always was. But he did not look full of cheer. The good cheer and bright camaraderie of the valiant young king had gone. For ever.

The Great Council of England was assembled in Parliament; the peers, bishops, abbots and representatives of the towns and shires, all here at Westminster to accede and give full effect to the Bill of Attainder presented to his High Court of Parliament by the sovereign condemning to death — unheard and untried — his vain and foolish brother George, Duke of Clarence. The queen was present, sitting at the front of the Ladies' Gallery, with two marquesses' ladies and two countesses kneeling on stools by her feet, as she radiated power, glittering, defensive. Her brother Anthony Earl Rivers was near the king as were her sons, the Greys, from her previous marriage. So was Richard Duke of Gloucester. The old Duchess of York — she who was "queen by right" — was not in attendance. She had already lost one son, Edmund Earl of Rutland, struck down as a youth of promise at his father's side at the Battle of Wakefield back in '60. But Rutland had been murdered by his Lancastrian cousins, who were the adversary. Now it was Clarence's turn to be attainted and wiped from the earth; his two children stripped of royal status and lands, by his own brother. Cecily's whelps were consuming each other, and she didn't wish to see it.

We were in Westminster Hall with its great towering hammer-beam roof, built at the command of Richard II, the king whose deposition had led to all this internecine dynastic hatred. In the past decade, we had grown used to not seeing the heads of traitors stuck like gargoyles on spikes over Tower

Bridge, and their quartered bodies hung up like bleeding sides of meat to deter would-be rebels; we had seen the reflowering of classical culture in Italy and the birth of printing brought from Germany to this very place. And yet here was our glorious king, sore troubled, about to condemn his flawed and foppish brother to a traitor's death.

On the other side of the hall — just a few yards away from his brother — stood Clarence; not chained or dressed in rags but wearing sober black silk attire, as if he was already dead, which, in law, he was about to be. He stared magnificently ahead knowing he would not be heard. If he hoped for clemency — yet again! — it would have to flow unbidden from the king. But Edward had decided that, in order to protect his sons and daughters and their inheritance, Clarence would have to die. As Anthony had said to me on the eve of that sitting, "It's not a question of what the king wants; the king is doing what he has to do. And the queen has, with sorrow, steeled him to do it."

Did he think of those words four years later when…? But, in truth, it was not Anthony who called for Clarence's death; it was his repeated treachery which called for it. Despite his huge appanage — partly his own and partly his wife Isabel's half share of Warwick's estates (the Countess of Warwick, in whose name the kingmaker had held them, being shut up and ignored) — George had been politely excluded from the court or, at least, from meaningful service within it. How could Edward trust him after his flirtation with Warwick and Queen Margaret? When Archbishop Neville — Warwick's brother — was arrested on suspicion of plotting with the exiled Earl of Oxford, whispers were spread about Clarence and, when his proud wife died and he revived his earlier plan to marry Mary of Burgundy, the king was dead set against it. Meanwhile, he saw his younger brother's power growing in the north, where he had inherited the bulk of the Neville inheritance, whilst the queen's family — who he knew would never forget his part in the execution of the old Earl Rivers — continued to tighten their grip on the king. Where was the glorious future Clarence had always envisaged for himself? What was to be the future for his son and daughter?

To try to divine that, George Plantagenet began to dabble in witchcraft. He summoned a well-known weird sister — and there are always such people around to rave for ready money — and she began to cast spells and, like the biblical Witch of Endor, to seek to do that which is forbidden: to foretell the future; to reverse the natural order of time. This is powerful and dangerous magic, which all decent religions forbid. In playing with this fire — and thinking himself invincible — foolish George was heard to speak the rumour (or truth?) that was in everyone's mind, or in some people's at least: that Edward was a Blaybourne, not a Plantagenet. This was more dangerous even than witchcraft, for it threatened not only the king but his — and the queen's ——children. Thus, George walked into the trap for which Queen Elizabeth Wydville had been praying. Now she had the evidence she needed to take Clarence out of the picture.

And so here was the king — never looking at his brother — listening to the recitation of the Bill of Attainder, to which he then gave his formal consent: "Le Roi le vault." The king wishes it. Not so. The king will acquiesce, but the queen wishes it. As Clarence was marched from the dock, there were no cat calls or shouts of "traitor". There was simply silence, as of the grave. The faces of the court were tense, except the queen who looked relieved that the ordeal was over. Meanwhile, I noticed Gloucester move, as if protectively, a few steps closer to the throne.

***

Clarence, after being taken back to custody in the Tower, was not beheaded. But, a few days later, it was announced that he had died. The rumour was he was drowned in a butt of Malmsey wine, of which he was known to have been inordinately fond. So, this prince's life ended, almost as he had wished: in the purple.

נ (nun)

Anthony loosed his new peregrine, Warwick, from his gauntlet. The falcon was a gift from his sister, the queen, and we were putting him through his paces.

I had my own favourite peregrine, Johnny, on my wrist; though brothers, Anthony and I could be quite competitive. Whilst strictly only an earl is entitled to field a peregrine, as a duke's son, I considered myself his equal; the king himself had complimented me on my skills as a falconer. Our young codger, a straight-talking man of Holderness called Phineas, hovered nearby ready to step in should any problem occur; it never does.

"The king has commanded me to go to Wales, to Ludlow in fact, with the prince, as his governor," said Anthony.

The young Edward, a handsome boy — with such beautiful parents, how could he be otherwise? — now nine years of age, had just been installed as Prince of Wales and Earl of Chester in accordance with ancient precedent. The king judged it time to separate him from the women who had hitherto largely surrounded him and set him up with his own princely court in the cold splendour of Ludlow Castle under his Uncle Anthony's tutelage.

"That's a great honour," I said, watching Warwick soaring up on the gusty gyres of wind. It was a fine spring day, but with a goodly breeze, which the bird could ride on.

"And my opportunity to educate my nephew as a true renaissance prince."

"My nephew, the philosopher king," I said.

Anthony was squinting up into the sun. "In God's good time."

"Of course."

My peregrine was getting restless but I held him still.

"And what of James of Scotland's offer of his sister Margaret as your bride? Is the king still in favour of it?"

"Yes, the wedding will take place in Nottingham next year, if there are no mishaps. But you know the Scots. They want their independence, but they also want our protection."

"They say she's beautiful." I liked teasing him.

"You know I am to marry her because the king commands it. No other reason. But first, Ludlow and the prince."

"As I have no instructions from the king *pro tem*, I can accompany you, at least for a few months."

Warwick, as aggressive as his namesake, swooped magnificently on a small starling, and held him by the scruff of the neck.

"Doesn't your brother need you on family business, Eddie?"

"I've been up in Yorkshire recently. My own estates are hardly vast."

"Nor are mine," he laughed. "Look at that bird."

Catching Johnny's restlessness, I sent him up into the circling currents. He may not have been as pretty as Warwick but he clearly had a bigger wingspan.

"So, you don't wish me to come with you?"

We were both staring up at our falcons, so I couldn't see his eyes.

"That's not the issue. The queen wants me to go alone to focus on the task."

"And I would distract you from it?" My words went up into the breeze, and he said nothing.

I repeated myself. "My presence would distract you? Or she doesn't want me near the prince?"

Johnny was squawking quite loudly at Warwick, who wisely swooped down onto his master's wrist. Anthony cleared his throat and petted his bird.

"The queen thinks it would not be proper."

"Jesu Christ!" I looked directly at Anthony.

"She would like to see you married and suggests we should part for a while. See a little less of each other. To avoid any scintilla of scandal attaching to the prince."

Johnny swooped down onto my gauntlet and squawked proudly, or angrily.

"Scandal? How dare she…"

"Caution, brother. You are speaking of the queen, my sister."

I said quietly, "I always wondered if she would come between us."

He looked straight at me, finally. "It is not she who is coming between us, but my fealty. My fealty to the Crown must come first. But only for a time, Eddie. Only until the prince becomes a man."

I turned to Phineas. "We're going home."

But I wasn't sure where that was.

***

It was some time before I was able to see that perhaps there was reason in Elizabeth Wydville's caution. It would not be seemly — some would say — for the uncle and governor of the next king to have his knight companion by his side while administering Wales in his nephew's name and tutoring the prince through his minority. But then again, "*honi soit qui mal y pense*", as the knights of the Most Noble Order of the Garter say — a companionship to which I was never admitted (though Anthony was, of course).

As for me, what was I to do kicking my heels in Wales while Anthony fulfilled his duties? It was time now for me, in my late thirties, to build my own reputation as a soldier and statesman. It struck me like a hammer-blow that now I was in full middle-age, time was growing short if I was ever to win that barony which both the B.M. and I had long — and rightfully — craved.

I spent some months in East Anglia, helping to settle my late mother's estate and overseeing the building of her splendid tomb, constructed in accord with her precise instructions so as fully to display her glory as the powerful widow of a great duke and the mother-in-law of a Plantagenet princess; also auditing the inventory of the three profitable manors devised to me in her will, which at last gave me a position of lordship in that country.

I also took the opportunity to mend fences with those administering the vast estates of the late John Duke of Norfolk, our old Yorkist ally, but with whom the B.M. had never had good relations, with the retainers of the two families frequently skirmishing on the margins of our estates. But we were now affiliated through the marriage of Lady Anne, the little heiress of the last Mowbray duke, to Richard, Duke of York, the prince's playful, much-loved younger brother. As *my* brother seemed unwilling — or unable to do it — I engaged, with Q's subtle assistance, on a policy of settling the nagging little squabbles about boundaries and tithes which had marred our relationship and can say these were all satisfactorily settled by the time I had left that country. It is always easier to do business with trustees of an estate than with the family who have owned it for generations, as *amour-propre* and old family scores are not at stake. But, though our local issues were brought to a successful account, the marriage of these two much endowed children — and the provision in statute that Anne Mowbray's vast estates would, should she die issueless, accrue to the young Duke of York and Norfolk rather than reverting to her nearest relations according to feudal law, which came to pass on her early demise — would have incalculable, Sophoclean consequences.

And being in this bridge-building mode, I also paid a formal visit to the household of the Prince of Wales within the great magnificent grey fortress of Ludlow Castle, where I not only paid my respects to the pale and scholarly young prince but also embraced and made up my quarrel with my Lord Rivers. But, deep down, my soul still ached at the separation.

And so, I turned north not just to oversee my own Yorkshire manors and the city of Hull but also because the king had at last given me a commission; to act as deputy for East Riding to his brother Gloucester, who was now appointed President of the Council of the North with palatine powers in that country. Edward IV's vision — well ahead of his ancestors — was to divide the kingdom into regions, each to be governed under his broad overlordship, by trusted and loyal deputies, who might, or might not, be the feudal lord, assisted by a council of local men of talent and wit. This policy of the diffusion — but not dilution — of power allowed the regions a sense of their own character and of a degree of self-governance whilst retaining their loyalty within the overall scheme of the kingdom. I hoped that eventually I might be appointed — in lieu of my ineffectual brother — to such a position in East Anglia, or in the north. So, my honour was slightly wounded to receive my appointment as deputy to the king's deputy — his brother Gloucester, whom Anthony and I had begun to regard with some distaste. Howsoever, it was my duty, and my opportunity for adventure and perhaps glory and so, with a heavy heart, I went north.

All meetings of the Council of the North were held in York, which Gloucester had clearly established as the northern capital — you might say, as *his* northern capital. And from my inaugural meeting there — my first visit back since King Edward's re-entry in '71 — it was evident in what high regard Duke Richard was held, as a blunt, bluff northerner, whose heart and soul were in York.

Gloucester was a different person in his own realm of the north. At meetings of the council, he was straight, clear and effective; he knew what he wanted, he always stated it and he usually got it. Also, he treated me with very great respect; far greater respect than I had ever received from the king, his brother. True, King Edward — whom I adored — had always regarded me with kindness and courtesy and never done me, or my family, any wrong. But, as only now I began to recognise, he had also treated me as a puppy or a junior member of staff, never allowing me any serious responsibility, unlike Anthony, of course, the beloved brother-in-law.

Gloucester, by contrast, treated me with less courtesy — he had little time for such fripperies towards me or anyone else — but gave me real responsibilities which he expected me to fulfil. And when I did, he gave me a nod — and a reward or sometimes, a promise of one to come. For example, I was ceded an almost free hand in the East Riding of Yorkshire, a county in itself, to reorganise the administration as I wished and to prepare for the levying of northern forces in the name of the king — and of his brother, the duke — whenever that should be needed. It came sooner than we anticipated.

In 1480, we heard that King James III of Scotland was not abiding by the terms of his latest truce with the English Crown. The king sent an envoy to Scotland to demand reparations; for, as Duke Richard put it at a meeting of the council in York, "If those Scottish miscreants are allowed any leeway, that will hearten the French king to break his treaty with our Lord King and we could have war on two fronts. Then who knows what that little Welsh shite, Henry Tudor, sheltering in Brittany, will do?"

Richard saw that one crack in the carefully assembled jigsaw of our alliances could send the whole thing into disarray — even disaster. So, we prepared for war, with Richard trusting me to array and command a thousand men of East Yorkshire.

I was content to be busy with this mission in Hull with my close retainer Malcolm, on whom, in Anthony's absence, I was increasingly reliant in my soul. When Malcolm, coming in to me one day, said, turning his face away to concentrate on some lists of array he was preparing, "Have you heard, sir, the tidings about my Lord Rivers?"

I paused.

"Is it good tidings, Malcolm?"

I dreaded that it might be bad news. Had Anthony fallen from the king's favour or fallen ill? My anxiety testified to the love I still bore him.

"He would say it is good news, Lord Eddie. He is married, my lord, to the daughter of a knight, Sir Henry Fitzlewis."

I stared at Malcolm with a face that must have resembled the Gorgon.

"Are you well, my lord?" said Malcolm kindly as he stroked my hand.

I angrily snatched it back. But then put it back in his.

I knew, of course, that Anthony's betrothal to the Scottish princess was off; it had been postponed the previous year, and not to my displeasure. But at least that had been a marriage of state to a lady of rank. What a condescension this was!

"Did he get the bitch pregnant and was forced to it by her father?" I heard myself say. "That was unworthy," I said to Malcolm almost at once.

"Will you take the day off, sir, to recuperate?"

"No, Malcolm. We shall continue to prepare for war." I kissed Malcolm on the forehead; that night his wife must have missed his presence in her bed.

When it was confirmed that Anthony was married, and with the daughter of Sir Henry Fitzlewis — a minor country knight — I wrote him a very bitter and unbrotherly letter mocking him, who had been offered as a husband for Duchess Mary of Burgundy and then betrothed to the sister of the

Scottish king, for allying himself with the daughter of an unknown knight; and offering my unheartfelt felicitations on the match. I wrote that I wished them joy, but he knew from the coldness of my words that I wished them nothing. I am ashamed of it now, in the sorrow of retrospect. But in that time, I felt my heart was broken.

The king came north with his forces and joined them with ours, and Anthony with him, of course, but I kept my distance. This unforced marriage it seemed to me confirmed our divorce. On the military front, there was a campaign and some skirmishing, but as in the king's war against France, for those of us who had seen battle, there was not much to write home about. It felt as if King Edward had had enough of real warfare and just wanted the thing settled through a show of strength, which is what he got. And, best of all, the treaty with the French king held firm. At least for now.

In the campaign, Gloucester showed his competence as a military commander, and in several minor but dangerous skirmishes showed great personal courage. I began to admire his leadership. Maybe he lacked his brother's beauty — though his face was sombrely handsome — and, as his enemies never cease to point out, he carried one shoulder higher than the other, the product of a curved spine, caused by a difficult birth. But, as Rabbi Abraham has taught me, only the ignorant consider physical deformity to be the outward sign of moral depravity, and if Gloucester was the man who had executed some of his brother's most severe commands, did that make him worse than the man who had ordered them?

At any rate, at the end of this rambling campaign, unresolved by a major battle, Richard turned his piercing blue eyes on me — the exact replica, it is said, of his father's the old Duke of York whom he resembled much more than either of his elder brothers — and said, "De-la-Pole, you have done well. Your family should be held closer to the king. And you, Sir Edward, should be honoured with a barony. Which you will, if it is ever in my power to bestow."

I believed him. He asked me to accompany him to York as the king travelled back to Westminster, and in the great nave of York Minster, I was at his right hand as, with his customary piety — a piety he displayed in private as much as in public — Duke Richard and his Duchess Anne, the very noble younger daughter of the great Earl of Warwick, gave thanks for our successful campaign and safe return.

Loyalty wins loyalty, more deeply than beauty and fine words. And Richard — whose motto was "*Loyaulté me lie*" — was to prove as good as his.

***

Eastertide 1483: the time of spring and rebirth, but before the rebirth comes death.

I was at court again, summoned by the king, I suspected, at Gloucester's recommendation. I had new raiment; the latest styles inspired by the Italian courts. I had not forgotten the splendour of Florence, though I knew now that I would never revisit it with Anthony. The king and queen looked magnificent in their new garments also and with their five lovely daughters in attendance. The young prince and his brother were, of course, at Ludlow, governing the principality with the sound advice of Earl Rivers, their uncle. So, in their absence, the Lady Elizabeth, now seventeen, blooming and almost — though never quite — as lovely as her haughty mother, took precedence after the king and queen, and was styled as Madame Dauphine, in recognition of her betrothal to the heir of France. The king looked fatter in the face and much more so in the waist than when I had last seen him; he moved little now, if at all. Nonetheless, enthroned in a chair of estate alongside his handsome wife he looked the part of king as much as ever.

I was sad Anthony had not been summoned with his royal charges to attend. I had heard he was living separately from his wife; clearly the marriage had not been a success. I would have liked very much to have seen him and at least to have made our peace. But I presumed that would happen when we next met.

It was Easter Day; always a time of solemnity, then joy, at a Christian court. The king and queen were holding court in their Palace of Westminster. They had been there since Christmas and, as I said, the king preferred not to move much in those days. They had taken Holy Communion with full magnificence in the abbey that morning and then caroused, drunk and eaten well; perhaps in the king's case, too well. Sated, the king and queen were now enthroned and receiving envoys with expressions of goodwill and Christian brotherly love from allied courts in Christendom. All was splendour, giving and goodwill.

The king received the Count of Altamira, a haughty hidalgo, who brought pascal greetings and sisterly love from Queen Isabella of Castille, the greatest kingdom in Spain. He bowed with a mighty flourish and presented Their Graces with a magnificently wrought golden goblet for the king and a jewelled pendant for the queen. The king's greedy eyes — getting smaller and almost piggy as they retreated into his face — flashed with pleasure and Her Grace, looking gratified, handed the precious gift to the countess kneeling uncomfortably at her feet. The Spaniard walked backward from the royal presence and almost fell over the next ambassador: a large man in a black silk caftan, whom I vaguely recognised. All eyes turned to stare at the bearded Jew, who was, as ever, unruffled. He was announced as Rabbi Abraham di Mayorca, envoy from the King of Aragon.

"Your Highnesses, I come as a humble worm on the shoe of His Lordship, the count…" Somehow the rabbi's tone did not sound like that of a worm. "And as a herald sent from the side of His Grace, King Ferran, consort to the most noble Lady, the Queen of Castile. I bring fraternal paschal greetings." There were sniggers around the hall at the query whether this "paschality" referred to Eastertide or the Passover of the old dispensation. "And a proposal of a future treaty for a holy union betwixt the eldest daughter of Their Catholic Majesties, the Infanta Donna Isabel de Aragon y Castilla, a beautiful princess of fourteen summers and Your Grace's son and heir, the Prince of Wales. The princess is, as Your Highness will know, twice descended from the famous John of Gaunt, Duke of Lancaster, and thus such a union would finally unite the two claims of the Houses of York and Lancaster, by this marriage treaty between the two royal Houses of York and Trastamara."

The king's watery eyes lit up like Venetian glass at this tempting bait; such a dynastic consummation was intensely to be wished.

"Our brother and sister, King Ferran and Queen Isabella, make a most interesting proposal which our counsellors will be commissioned to consider at our leisure. Your eminence, Rabbi, is most welcome at our court."

The exotic stranger indicated a large, magnificently bound book being presented on a cushion by his page.

"Your Highness would honour your obedient servant by accepting this gift of *The Order of Chivalry,* a treatise penned by our great doyen of chivalry, Ramon Lull."

The king signified his gracious acceptance and turned to Hastings, hovering as ever by his side. He spoke for all to hear.

"The rabbi is to be treated with the full honours of a visiting cardinal during his sojourn in our kingdom."

Hastings nodded. The scoffers were silenced.

I exchanged a glance with Rabbi Abraham. There was something about him… But at that moment, I was distracted by a bruit and kerfuffle behind me. There was a rumour that the French envoy had entered with a look of arrogant aggression; he had brought something other than fraternal greetings from our ally of France.

The French envoy was not a duke or a count or even a bloody viscount. He was announced as "Monsieur le Sieur de" somewhere or other. Practically a varlet. We were all thinking: how dare the French king send such a nobody? But also: this means trouble. Quite probably another war and, in reality, the nobility was sick of war; half of them having been ruined or killed in the wars between the cousins, and so was the ailing, aging king.

The Frenchman said, "I come, sire, under the protection of heraldic immunity…" At which already the king's auburn eyebrows began to glower. "To inform the English Crown and government, and to forestall gossip and rumours, that the Crown of France has formally signed and set its royal seal to a grand treaty of friendship at Arras with His Highness the Archdukeighness the Archduke maximilan of Ayustriahig Maximilian of Austria, Duke of Burgundy and the Duchess Mary of Burgundy, under the terms of which a perpetual peace is declared betwixt their two realms and territories and a marriage is irrevocably declared to take place between His Highness the Dauphin of France and the Lady Mary, Daughter of the Duke and Duchess of Burgundy."

There was a silence in the hall such as one only hears when a catastrophe has been announced. This was a monumental insult to His Grace, and to the Lady Elizabeth, his eldest child. It was also an ominous realignment of powers within western Christendom. And moreover, the influence of the king's sister, my beloved Lady Margaret, now Dowager of Burgundy, had been completely swept aside.

The king rose to his full commanding height and his expression was of Jove about to hurl a lethal thunderbolt. Then he swayed slightly and the whole court held its breath. Hastings put out his arms to steady the king, but Edward brushed him away, regained his poise and smiled, rather bitterly. His voice was thicker and more hoarse than usual.

"This is no news to us, monsieur. Tell your king we know of all his plans. And will requite this insult with a firm rebuttal when the time is right. Now let this envoy depart unhindered. We know the demands of chivalry even if the King of Paris does not."

We all cheered and applauded at His Grace's contemptuous rebuttal. Buckingham was standing near me. We looked at each other.

"We *didn't* know," said I, under my breath.

"Nobody knew," said he. "I shall send word to Gloucester."

I hadn't realised till then how close the two dukes were.

Over the next few days, the king did not appear again in public. I sent a message to Hastings — always Edward's closest courtier — asking for news of His Grace's health.

The reply was bland and unconvincing. "The king is well and taking counsel."

Rumours began to circulate that Edward was suffering from an ague and was bed-ridden. The shock of the dauphin's jilting of the Lady Elizabeth had been more than his bloated body could bear — these words were whispered or hinted at — and he was refusing, or unable, to eat. A very bad sign with the king.

Again, I bumped into Buckingham, who said nothing but his expression as he bowed courteously — Buckingham was always stately — indicated he had again sent messages to Gloucester, who was being kept informed. *Perhaps*, I thought, *it would be for the best to have a strong hand like Gloucester's — the king's only surviving brother — at court if the king was failing, perhaps even in his last agonies.* Did it occur to my mind to send a message to my sometime blood brother, Anthony, the prince's guardian, far off at Ludlow Castle? It did, but I restrained the impulse. We were no longer in regular contact and I was sure the queen — no friend of mine — would be keeping her brother and her eldest son fully informed of developments. It was not for me to intervene in these mingled state and family matters.

A risible story began to circulate that the king, in a jolly mood, had gone fishing on the night after the envoy's arrival, with Hastings and two other companions, and had caught a cold and that this was the reason — a trivial ailment — why he was briefly indisposed. It seemed incredible to me, though it got, as intended, into foreign ambassadors' reports to their courts of the king's indisposition. But even if it had started so trivially, it was taking many days for him to get well.

I had to have reliable information. So, of course, I summoned Q and asked him what was being said amongst the squires and varlets of the court.

He looked at me almost pityingly. "The king is dying, my lord. Everyone in the household knows it. The queen is deeply troubled and doesn't know what to do or who to trust. And Buckingham has quietly left the court to join the Duke of Gloucester up north. Anything else you need to know, sir?"

Q's superciliousness could be very trying.

Nevertheless, I knew I must see the king for myself. I even sent word to my brother and sister-in-law — after all, she was the king's sister — advising them to hold themselves in readiness for great changes at court. And I missed deeply the B.M.'s wise counsel in times of danger.

I sent Q to Hastings begging leave to pay my respects to His Grace and to dispel the wicked lies that he was ill, nay gravely ill. Indeed, there were even ladies whispering in the galleries of the palace that the king was already dead and preparations were being secretly made to bring the young prince back from Wales. In this fog of crisis and rumour, I had to know the truth.

When, after two hours, I received no reply, I decided to take matters into my own hands. I was a member of the king's Privy Council — when summoned to attend — and my brother was married to a sister of the king. I had a right — and a burning curiosity — to know the truth.

I was wary lest the royal guards had been ordered to bar access to the king's bedchamber to all but Hastings and the king's closest kin, but in the air of crisis no such orders had been given and I walked unmolested down the long corridor through the guardroom and the audience chamber to the entrance to his room. I presented a mien brim full of authority. The guards saluted; I went in.

It was an extraordinary scene. The king was in his great royal bed, but what a change was there. His skin — once so pink and lustrous — was grey and creased like an old parchment; his yellowish grey pallor looked like death. He was propped up on many huge cushions and was speaking, wheezing, with great difficulty. But still there was a light of strength and command in his eyes, as he held the hands of his queen on one side — supported by the two sons of her previous marriage — and of Lord Hastings on the other. The king was holding their hands tightly together in his and insisting on their reconciliation.

"My queen and my closest friend must work together in amity for the safety of the kingdom." He nearly choked here with coughing. "And for the succession of…" His voice trailed away as he made a great effort to finish the sentence. "Of our son."

Queen Elizabeth formed an ice-cold smile and Hastings stared back warily.

"Swear it," gasped Edward.

"I swear," they both murmured.

It wouldn't have convinced a dog, but the king fell back exhausted and closed his eyes.

The Archbishop of Canterbury, who was hovering nearby, as clerics will, intoned a droned "Amen". Hastings' assistant chamberlains began asking us to give His Grace more space and air, but I had no reason to stay. I knew now that the king's death was near. There would be a demise of the Crown. And the succession would not be smooth.

The deaths of kings are momentous, signalled by signs and portents, signifying the end of an epoch: the death of a kingdom, and its rebirth. But was this King Edward IV — the man who had been but twenty years before the shining giant, the hero of chivalry — whom I had worshipped in my youth? How had he become this bloated leviathan who had murdered his own brother and curdled his kingdom's relations with both Burgundy and France? And who, in dying now so prematurely, was leaving two mere boys — and a tribe of princesses — to inherit this broken legacy.

I was isolated at court, with no one to turn to, no one to whom I could express my fears, my terrors at the death of kings, and my nascent hopes. Anthony was far away, in body and mind, wholly engrossed in his mission of governing the next and soon-to-be King of England. Malcolm, whose plain speaking, strong thighs and manly scent I loved to have about me, was acting as my deputy in the De-la-Pole holdings in the north, siring his little Malcolms and Malcolmesses on the rich and buxom wife I had gifted him with. Whom could I confide in at court? Not Buckingham, that proud piss-kitchen who had now gone running off to ingratiate himself with Gloucester (who, at any rate, never ingratiated himself with anybody — apart from the people of the north); nor Hastings who saw me as an ally of the Wydvilles whom he hated. I could gossip — and banter a little — with Q, but it's always unwise to fraternise with varlets. And then someone appeared — reappeared — unexpectedly, and at first unwelcomely, but who now, in hindsight, I recognise as a gift from the One without Name.

o (samakh)

If London is a village, Barcelona is a city; if London is a city, Barcelona is a world. Capital of the Kings of Aragon and Counts of Barcelona, Lords of the rich Catalan lands, it has many thousands of citizens. It has cathedrals, churches, synagogues (still), even half-secret mosques and the great naval dockyards, the Drassanes, that house the burgeoning sea power of Spain. And on its streets ageing prostitutes and youthful rent boys, priests and rabbis and Moorish traders, rub shoulders with Catalan merchants and troubadours, and the occasional Castilian grandee, sneering perceptibly at this teeming promiscuous Mediterranean life.

In the chamber of the Archives of the Crown of Aragon, near the cathedral in the lovely, dusty stone streets of this old town, two middle-aged men sat, chewing the cud, sipping thick Arabic coffee.

"So, how is His Majesty?" asked the one with the skullcap and neat greying beard.

"His *Catholic* Majesty, you mean?"

"Ah, the king has a new honorific?"

"Both Their Majesties are, I am told on the highest ecclesiastical authority, to receive from the Holy Father himself, the title of *the Catholic King.*"

"A great honour for us all, Pablo. I wonder what His Holiness wants in return. The expulsion of Their Majesties' Hebrew subjects perhaps?"

"I trust not, Abram. What benefit would that bring to the pope? Although…" Father Pablo moved a little closer. "*Her* Majesty is already seriously considering such a decree on the advice of the Archbishop of Toledo."

"What the queen decides to do within her own dominions is no business of ours or, strictly, even of the Crown of Aragon. His Majesty is far too sympathetic to the Jewish community here; he knows we are his most loyal subjects. Besides, it wouldn't be easy to get such a measure through the cortes. And, you know, our cortes are far more independent than the docile Parliament that sits occasionally in Castille."

The clean-shaven man, who wore an elegant velvet robe, looked down at the legal documents he was fitfully working on.

"But I was forgetting, Rabbi, that you know His Majesty's mind better than almost any of us."

"Me? What do *I* know?"

Father Pablo giggled.

"How could anyone," said the rabbi, "Know the king's mind as well as yourself, Mr Secretary? Didn't you have an audience just this morning to brief the king on the forthcoming business of the cortes?"

"And aren't you seeing him tomorrow morning to *receive* a briefing? On a rather *confidential* matter?"

"Ah, Pedro, nothing of His Majesty's is confidential from *you*."

"So, you *are* seeing the king tomorrow?" The secretary suddenly looked serious.

Silence. The rabbi, smoothing his less sumptuous black robe with its significant yellow stripe, just smiled, as if to say: Me? Seeing the king?

"Another secret mission?"

"Another? What previous mission are you thinking of?"

Father Pedro looked down at the decrees he had been preparing for the royal sign manual.

"Perhaps a message for the sultan which naturally had to be delivered, informally, behind Her Majesty's back?"

Rabbi Abraham looked puzzled. "Would I be privy to a plan to keep our beloved queen in the dark?"

"You and I both know we need to be... as subtle and wise as the king we serve; not every courtier can equal the splendid severity, that is to say piety, of our beloved Queen Isabella."

"But, of course, *we* serve the King of Aragon. And remember, Pedro, I am a Catalan and a Jew and, like my ancestors before me for many centuries, I serve the Count of Barcelona, King Ferran."

"Who is sending you...?"

"How can I know until I have seen His Majesty?"

"To Burgundy perhaps? There is talk of a dynastic union with the Habsburgs. It would help cement a pact against France, don't you think?"

"Don't confuse a simple rabbi with talk of high politics, Mr Secretary. My head is swimming already."

"Well, let's make sure it stays on your shoulders. I'm sure the queen would favour such a marriage alliance. So, have no worries on that score."

"I shall bear that in mind… should His Majesty give me such a commission!"

They finished their coffees and parted with mutual felicitations: the secretary reassured to know the purpose of the rabbi's meeting with the king; the rabbi pleased he does not.

***

The family of Rabbi Abraham di Mayorca had served the Kings of Aragon for a century — and long before that, the Counts of Barcelona. As his father, the late Rabbi Isaac de Mayorca used to say — but only in Catalan — "We served the Counts of Barcelona when they were Catalans!" They had even served — or at least negotiated with — the Moslem Moors when they ruled the island of Majorca, wherefrom the family had emerged two centuries earlier. They had also — as Rabbi Isaac would say, using the Majorcan dialect of Catalan that only a tiny circle of his associate Jews or gentile would understand — that they had served the king-counts in the glorious days when Barcelona headed a great Mediterranean empire. One of his great-uncles had even attended on the Catalan Dukes of Athens, the last of whom had married the great-uncle's sister who had ostensibly converted to the Catholic faith but, in secret, had both adhered to the Jewish faith and had fled to it — but that's another story.

Abraham himself — now in his middle years, but looking a little older with his broad shoulders, grey-auburn beard and massive girth — had served King John (or Joan) II of Aragon, Count of Barcelona, for over twenty years, struggling to appease the many (internal) enemies he so easily made, to keep strong his links with the wealthy and important Jewish community of the

Catalan lands, and to untangle the many impenetrable knots his byzantine and ill-judged policies invariably produced. He had essayed, with great dedication, to reconcile the embittered and jealous king with his handsome and more popular son and heir Prince Carles — only to have his efforts constantly undermined by the king himself. And then when the prince died — poisoned, it was suspected, by his father while under house arrest — it was, of course, the rabbi's task to produce medical evidence to disprove this; for were not all Jews, and especially rabbis, brilliant doctors and wizards, and able to use their Kabbalistic knowledge to explicate every suspicious death, or even, on occasions, to reverse it?

And then — with the banking families which had funded the great mercantile Catalan fleets dissolving and failing around them and Aragon/Barcelona reduced in wealth and citizenry to a shrinking power on the edge of Iberia — the wise, not to say cunning, Rabbi Abraham had subtly, imperceptibly shifted his allegiance from the failing discredited king to his second son and heir Prince Ferran, whose devious and ambitious mind saw the future of his kingdom not as looking out across the Mediterranean Sea to Italy and southern France, whose languages and culture his own kingdom's so resembled, but inwards towards the great central kingdom of Espana: Castile, whose princess and contender for the throne, Isabella, he had married in '69 and who had recently — to his confused satisfaction and chagrin at his failure to make good his own more distant but masculine claim — acceded.

Rabbi Abraham was always a heavy man, but in Barcelona a healthy layer of fat (or a few in his case) was always viewed as a sign of wealth and prosperity. And despite his somewhat ungainly size and a mien that could hardly be called beautiful — a strong Jewish nose, rough complexion, jowly cheeks and eyes that were myopic from too much deciphering of Castilian, Catalan, Hebrew, Latin and Ladino — despite all this, he was always strangely attractive to women, including several very grand and even royal damsels, whom, as a pious rabbi and a married man, he had — with a mixture of charm and fearsomeness — managed to ward off. For Rabbi Abraham could certainly be fierce. Sitting as a judge in the Rabbinical Court, which had a wide jurisdiction over the Hebrew *kahal*, he was feared as being fair but stern and capable of strict judgments. Indeed, on one occasion, a litigant who had laughed in his face while he was in the seat of judgment has been sentenced to fifteen lashes; he had not laughed when he was brought back to apologise.

Reb Abraham protected his privacy and his reputation jealously. The position of a "court Jew" was never unambiguous and he well understood that his position at court and his position within his own *kehilla* (the Hebrew community) could easily be jeopardised by even a hint of scandal. Besides, he had married young, and had an adult son (now a convert and a stranger to him) and a daughter whom he had loved as a child and whom he had, with great propriety, married off at thirteen to the plump, rosy-cheeked fifteen-year-old son of a rich mercantile cousin and who now had a life and three children of her own. His wife Judith (the name his daughter, according to Sephardi tradition, also bore) he had married more because she was the descendant of the great Rabbi Joseph ben Abraham Gikatilla whose particular brand of Kabbala he followed, than because he had ever been deeply enamoured of her; yet over the years he had become genuinely fond of her and appreciative of her qualities. Nonetheless, they had had some disagreements, or misunderstandings in the months before her death of a plague-like disease three years before, and since then his dealings — both political and social — had been wholly with men.

In the 70s, Rabbi Abraham had served his byzantine-minded masters, King John and now his son Ferran, on several important missions abroad and, each time he had travelled, he had in the back of his mind the possibility of seeking refuge for himself — and possibly for his whole community — should the more ferocious elements in the Catholic Church finally achieve their aim of convincing Their Catholic Majesties that the Spanish kingdoms should be cleansed of the Hebrew race. Catalonia had been home to Jews for centuries and the mercantile, practical and cultured tone of Catalan and Jewish life had neatly meshed together. But Castille had a more severe approach. And with the gradual expulsion of the Moorish-Moslem kingdom from the whole of the peninsula, the new Hispanic Catholicism was obsessed with the notions of purity of the heart and blood, despite the obvious fact that all the noble families — including the Trastamara themselves — had Jewish ancestry.

Fortunately for the rabbi, King Ferran — more recently established on his throne than his powerful wife and gnawingly aware of the greater strength of her kingdom — enjoyed the freedom of using his personal envoy to conduct a more secretive and independent foreign policy on behalf of his own kingdom. And while Portugal and Castile had both been closely associated with the fallen House of Lancaster, he was eager to develop his own links with the House of York. And so it was that, in his audience with the crafty king, Ferran had commissioned him to "explore the possibilities" of a marriage alliance between Trastamara and York, and even to suggest that one day Aragon and England might combine to fight their common enemy the King of France — a plan he knew had long been close to the King of England's heart — but only, of course, when, as would soon be the outcome, the Moors were defeated and thrown out of the Spanish kingdoms. And so nothing was to be promised. "Nothing to be — if you'll forgive me, Rabbi," as the king smilingly put it, "Set in stone."

Rabbi Abraham liked and admired the young King Ferran. He was subtle and intelligent and he knew he couldn't trust him; all of which was mutual. With King Ferran, he was dealing with a crafty and flexible prince such as the Italians could admire. But he knew that in the person of Queen Isabella, they both had to deal with a ruler of granite-hard beliefs, which had no truck with serpentine flexibility nor with humane sympathy.

So, he was pleased to be sent on his mission to England. Things were not too comfortable for him at home. His daughter had become as estranged from him as his son, suspecting he had not shown as much alacrity as he might three years before in seeking the best available medicine for his wife in her last illness; the charge was totally untrue, but he was sufficiently aware of his lack of grief — indeed his internal relief — at her demise, to feel guilt when the charge was raised. And in the political community, he was aware he had enemies who were eager to implicate him in a plot to conceal the true cause of the death of his king's late elder brother. King Ferran had suppressed those so far, but it might not suit him always to do so.

So, there were several reasons why Rabbi Abraham was preparing to leave his homeland well-prepared for a very long sojourn abroad and with more than half an eye open to find a patron in England who might offer the possibilities of a different future, in other lands.

***

After a long journey of several weeks, accompanied by his secretary and a man-at-arms — who had been provided as a bodyguard whom Reb Abraham had been glad to find absconded just before they reached the French border — both of them Christians, and his long-serving Jewish body-servant Moshe, Reb Abraham had alighted at the port of Dover.

Our wandering Jew had expected to arrive at the court of a powerful king at the height of his powers, who had destroyed his Lancastrian rivals and established his own dynasty irreversibly. Edward was acclaimed throughout Christendom as a handsome and mighty warrior with a beautiful and fruitful — if unequally born — wife, an heir, a spare and a gaggle of marriageable daughters; even if there were always subliminal rumours that his own birth had been... irregular. But what would that matter when, in the fullness of time, his son would inherit a settled kingdom?

But what he found within a week of his arrival at the Palace of Westminster — where he was well satisfied with his royal audience — was an unseen, ailing king and even at that audience it was evident to Reb Abraham, who like most rabbis had some medical knowledge, that Edward was sickly and obese. The court was soon swirling with anxious gossip and vicious intrigue. And whom should he side with: the supporters of Hastings, the friends of Gloucester, or the partisans of the Wydvilles whose power appeared to be waxing day by day? After all, the queen's brother, the well-respected Lord Rivers, controlled the person of the Prince of Wales and Queen Elizabeth seemed in a strong position to take the regency when the moment came. Or should he stand back from the fray, biding his diplomatic time until the cloud of uncertainty should clear? There was no Hebrew community in England since the expulsion of the beleaguered race by Edward I in 1290, and Reb Abraham desperately needed an ally, someone with status and sources of intelligence but without an obvious allegiance to any of the principal factions.

As he usually did when requiring information, the rabbi turned to his general factotum, Moshe. Moshe had been talking with another intimate servant known as Quidnunc, whose master seemed linked to power if not actually wielding it. And, of course, Reb Abraham recognised the name of this courtier as being that of the personable, if rather aloof, young Englishman who had crossed his path in Florence. If he bore — as the king had commanded — the rank of a cardinal, then he surely had the right to approach a cadet member of the House of York. And so, he sent Edward De-la-Pole — he sent me — a message.

***

As I worried and waited — caught up in the miasma of anxiety at Westminster — Q brought me a missive, a mischievous smile playing about his aging lips. As I broke the seal, I noticed it had two Hebrew letters at the top — Anthony and I had, in happier days, learnt the Hebrew alphabet (or rather "*alephbet*") together. The letters *beth* and *hey* were written above a few delicately written lines: *Vous savez, monsignor, que l'heure plus sombre est juste avant l'aube. Bien chance, un nouvel Soleil va se lever du York. Avec mes obéissances loyales, le rabbin.*

My initial reaction was of scorn and disdain. How dare this Catalan Jew — this fat, foreign clergyman — presume to offer advice to an English nobleman, a privy counsellor to the king? So, I did nothing, while his words — the darkest hour before the dawn? A new sun will arise from York? Of course, it would, as the young prince was the heir of York — reverberated within me.

***

The following day — with no more news of the king's health — I received a most welcome visitor. Malcolm — whom my heart delighted to see — was now all grown up and manly, carrying the smell of a fresh and heady sweat still on him as he came straight from the saddle. He brought me another letter. This carried the seal of the boar.

"Duke Richard sends his greetings," said Malcolm, his handsome face looking deeply serious.

I embraced Malcolm, then broke the seal. The letter read:

To my trusty and well-beloved cousin and counsellor, Sir Edward De-la-Pole. Edward, we in the north are gravely troubled by the sickness of the king, our brother; both our good people of York and your own vassals in Holderness and Kingston upon Hull. I open my heart to you to say there is no love lost here in the north for the queen and her party. Our cousin of Buckingham assures me of your continual loyalty to our House, the which I have never doubted. We turn, therefore, to you as we have sore need of news of what is bruited and mooted at court in our absence here in the north. To be forever wedded to our soul and good lordship, canst thou send us news of any plots or plans intended by the queen and others of her party on the council? I know thou wilt not betray me in this, asked of you as a good and loyal subject of Our Sovereign Lord the king. I send loving greetings from my good Duchess Anne, who asks to be remembered to you also. Your ever-loving friend and good lord, Richard G.

I turned the letter over and over in my hands. It was written in his own surprisingly elegant hand, sealed with his personal signet which I knew well. I had never received a letter like this — nor any letter at all as far as I could recall — from the king whom I had served and worshipped for over twenty years. The king whom I would have laid down my life for — or given my body to had he asked. The king whose queen, a Lancastrian widow and the daughter of a reputed witch, had wilfully separated me from her brother, whom I had loved better than my own, and who had sent me in nearly twelve months not a word.

And I suddenly thought of that other much shorter note I had received. What if the rabbi's reference to York meant the city, not the House? Perhaps he was privy to some hidden knowledge.

My soul hardened within me and my mind formed itself. I knew what I had to do.

***

The 14th day of April in the year 1483 started with a cold misty morning and that heart-quickening promise of spring that early April brings. It was the day on which King Edward died. I knew from a letter I had received a few days before from Malcolm — attending on the Duke of Gloucester as I had instructed him to do — that his death had already been announced in York and now I hastened to tell him to confirm to the council of the north that the demise had now taken place. The king's large, bloated body was laid out in state — almost naked — in Westminster Hall, and we of the court, together with the leading citizens of London, went there to show our reverence. The royal cadaver looked like a great beached whale; on seeing it, I felt nothing.

There were days of obsequies to come, but matters of state wait for nothing, especially in times of uncertainty. Once the king's body had been embalmed and laid out in velvet and leather and gems, the queen — who seemed to think she could act as regent for her infant son, now King Edward V — called a meeting of the council, including myself. We all knew that several of the most important players were outside the capital: Anthony Wydville was at Ludlow, with the young king, and power to raise troops if desired, while the Dukes of Gloucester and Buckingham, the two royal kinsmen closest in blood to the king, were in the north. Hence the queen's dilemma. How should the new king be brought to London? And how could his position and — more hazardously — hers be fortified?

We entered the council chamber in a sombre mood. The queen, attired appropriately in white royal mourning, had taken the chair — the king's seat, in fact — in the centre of one side of the great oval oak table with her two adult sons, Dorset and Grey, at her sides as if to give her filial support. Hastings, as acting Lord Chamberlain, had taken the seat facing hers. He was glaring at her and her sons.

In fact, he had waylaid me, grim-faced, in a cloister earlier and said quietly, "We must stop the bitch or her Grey sons from getting the Protectorship."

"Of course," I said.

He appeared surprised. Maybe if he had deigned to speak to me while the king lived, he would not have been.

"Gloucester must have it. Who else?"

"We are of the same mind," he said and grasped my hand in a firm soldier's grip. Our eyes met; his were a dark, handsome brown. We understood each other.

Elizabeth Wydville — looking out of place in the seat of honour in a chamber which no woman had even entered before — was drawn and pale, because she had been weeping or, more likely, because she had not slept for anxiety. She gave me a soft beguiling smile as I took my place and gave her a slight bow. *Too late for that, milady*, I thought.

Once we were assembled — with several seats empty, of course, in the absence of the other leading protagonists — as the queen opened her mouth to speak, Hastings said, bluntly, "It is an honour for the gentlemen of the council to be in the presence of the queen, but as it is well attested by law and precedent that ladies do not partake in governance, I call upon the queen to withdraw so that the business of the council may begin."

Everyone drew a sharp breath, including me, but Elizabeth Wydville did not move except to put out her hand to restrain her son Edward Grey who had put his hand on the pommel of his sword.

"My Lord Hastings, I know no one is more loyal than you to my son, our new king, Edward V. My only purpose in convening this meeting of an Accession Council in his name is to make the most proper arrangements for his safe journey from Ludlow Castle to London in all due pomp, under the protection of his governor, Lord Rivers."

"Now that he is king, madam, he no longer has a *governor*," Hastings said witheringly.

"It is up to this council to make appropriate arrangements for a Protector to be appointed. A Protector for the king and for the realm."

Everyone looked round at me. I had not often spoken in council unless called on by the king. But that king was dead and it was time to assert myself.

"As mother of the king," said Grey, "The queen has first call on the office of Protector."

"Until the coronation, in but a few weeks from now, when the king will attain his majority, my lords," said Dorset, smoothly.

"I propose, my lords," said Hastings, "That the appointment of Protector of the Realm remain in abeyance until the king — and the Dukes of Gloucester and Buckingham — are assembled in London."

"I agree," said I, and there were murmurs of assent around the table.

"In which case," said the queen, "It is all the more urgent that we arrange for the appropriate conveyance of His Grace, my son, from Ludlow to London."

"It would be an honour for me if His Grace would deign to accept the hospitality of my palace," said the Bishop of London, with Episcopal suavity. "Though it must be said that it could not house a large royal retinue."

"It seems then that we should send a letter instructing Lord Rivers to bring the young king to London in all haste with a not overly large retinue — one thousand men should easily suffice, do we not think, my lords?" said Hastings, now smiling, a little menacingly.

Through the nods and sounds of agreement, Grey put in, "That hardly seems a large enough retinue for the King of England. There may be danger on the roads between…"

"What?" said Hastings, "Are you expecting them to be abducted by the Duke of Gloucester, advancing with a massive army to snatch his beloved nephew?"

There was laughter at this jibe and the queen exchanged uncomfortable glances with her sons.

"Two thousand men under the command of Earl Rivers should be more than enough to protect His Grace from marauding brigands," said the ancient Archbishop of Canterbury, who appeared to have just woken up.

"And England has had more than enough experience of large armies traversing the kingdom in the Cousins' Wars," I added.

"Very well, my lords, we are in happy agreement," said the queen, though neither she nor her sons looked particularly happy. "Let us send the letter today and begin arrangements for the coronation of our new king." She smiled at this as we all did.

"I shall muster up the necessary order of ceremonies, the sacred vessels and so on, in happy concordance with my brother of London, of course," said Cantuar.

"I believe the crown of St. Edward the Confessor is housed in the Tower, gentlemen, where it is customary for the sovereign to reside for the period before his coronation, is it not?"

"There will be time for all that when the king is here," said Hastings, "And for the appointment of the Protector. And what of the late king's last will and testament?"

"Ah," said Dorset smiling, "That is in the hands of the lawyers and is yet to be proved."

"Truly," said Hastings. "How strange."

It struck me, as it clearly had him, that the will probably named a Lord Protector, and it wasn't to their liking.

"Thank you, my lords," said the queen, "The council is adjourned."

As we filed out, Hastings slipped me a friendly wink.

Straightway I went to my chamber and wrote a letter to Richard of Gloucester telling him a force of no more than two thousand men would be accompanying the boy king and Anthony Rivers from Ludlow to London shortly, and that we had managed to postpone the appointment of a Protector until after the king's entry into London, where he would stay at the Bishop of London's palace. The duke, I said, would be well advised to make haste to London, with Buckingham, and some armed protection, as the queen and her clan would do all in their power to remain in control of the young king. Hastings was clearly loyal to King Edward V. But a strong Protector was needed; and I pledged my loyalty to Duke Richard.

ע (ayin)

The change of monarchs is a time of moral uncertainty, especially when the new king is a boy. England, and I as a child, had known the rule of a weak and docile king followed by two decades of civil war. We could not face that again.

In my memory, it seems like the next day, but it must have been at least ten days later when we heard the fatal news.

It was, of course, Q who told me.

He had come to my chamber and looked uncharacteristically reticent.

"You have news"?

"Yes, my lord."

"Of the king?"

"Yes and no, my lord."

"Well, spit it out, man."

"My lord, the two dukes met with the young king on the road and are accompanying him to London."

"That's good news."

"They had a large body of men with them. Larger than the two thousand men of the king's bodyguard." Q gave me one of his hard looks.

"And?"

There was clearly something more. Something significant.

"The dukes met with Lord Rivers and Sir Richard Grey and dined with them at Northampton, leaving the king and his entourage at Stony Stratford…"

"That's good."

"The next morning, they had Lord Rivers and Grey arrested on charges of high treason. They say the young king protested that he trusted his uncle and cousin as having been appointed his advisers by his late father, but the Duke of Gloucester insisted that he and Buckingham were his true advisers. They have been taken to Pomfret Castle."

Cold fingers clutched my heart. Pomfret was the place where Richard II had been imprisoned. And murdered.

Q's voice caught in his throat.

"What?" I said, but I knew what he would say.

"They say that the dukes intend Lord Rivers and Sir Richard Grey to be declared traitors and… beheaded."

I couldn't speak for a while. Then I heard my voice saying, "The Duke of Gloucester must have had good reason. Reason of state."

Then I ran to my closet and retched; and retched again, and again.

***

Rabbi Abraham sent me another note. It was even more cryptic than the last, saying: *Quando la rosa roja e re-unificada con la sortija roja…*

"When the red rose is reunited with the red ring, the angels' land will be at peace. It all revolves around the letter R."

This struck me at first as magical nonsense. But I knew that rabbis — some rabbis — were known for their second sight. The letter R? And could the red ring refer to my big balas ruby, still lying unknown in my locked jewellery box?

The following day, the rabbi passed near me in a cloister of the Palace of Westminster.

He bowed.

I felt uncomfortable.

"You are still here, Rabbi? Even though the young king's marriage is hardly a matter of immediate interest?"

"My Lord Protector is the man to follow, my lord. Not that I need tell that to a statesman like Your Lordship."

Looking for something to say, I asked, "Have you met Edward Brampton, the governor of Guernsey? He was a favourite and godson of the late king. You have a lot in common."

The rabbi smiled a little.

He told me he had been introduced at King Edward's command, before his illness became grave, to Edward Brampton. They had briefly met, but the rabbi was a little wary of him.

When I asked why, he replied, "Because, my lord, he is a convert and we Jews find that our former brothers most often become our bitterest enemies; and, more to the point, though now he is serving your king, I believe he is still in service to the King of Portugal, who is the mortal enemy of my master the King of Aragon."

He backed away in his calm and dignified way.

What right has he to address or advise me? I thought, petulantly.

It all revolves around "R". Ricardus? Ricardus... Rex?

***

The next day, the young king, accompanied to right and left by the two royal dukes, made his entry into London and was lodged at the bishop's palace.

Duke Richard sent me a note, as warm as ever, summoning me to the council, at which, "You and I must strive at all costs to prevent the queen from taking the Protector's office." As I felt no goodwill towards Elizabeth, this sat well with me.

With the solid support of Hastings and Buckingham — and only the weak resistance of the outnumbered Wydville faction — Richard was acclaimed as Lord Protector. When, however, he asked the council to agree to a proclamation declaring Rivers and Wydville to be traitors to the king and the old royal blood of the realm, there was silence, with support only from Buckingham. Clearly, the duke had made a faux pas and I was reassured that my sometime blood brother and intimate friend would be saved after all.

That very day, the queen withdrew into the sanctuary of Westminster Abbey, with young Richard of York, her five daughters, and as many of her movables as she could muster. This left the council as a comfortable male preserve once again.

I began to wonder what would Duchess Margaret's judgment be on what was taking place. Would she side with her sister-in-law and her two boys? Or would she prefer her younger brother, with his strongly emerging power, his noble Neville wife, and his undoubted legitimacy as the only surviving son of Richard Duke of York? Did I recollect she had a soft spot for the runt of the brood?

The boy king was removed to the proper residence for a monarch awaiting his coronation: the Tower of London. He was calling for his younger brother to be with him. But Elizabeth Wydville, like a defensive lioness, did not want to let the young boy out of her sight. Gloucester — who was now running affairs with great panache and, fearing a counter coup — had asked his beloved people of York to send troops, and at his request I ordered Malcolm to muster men from Holderness, and he insisted that she send her second son to join him first. On the urging of the old archbishop, Cardinal Bourchier — a man as holy and trustworthy as most senior churchmen — she at length gave him up. I took no part in these moves.

The court (nay, the whole of London and Westminster) was swirling with rumour. Q told me the gossip about the dead king's paternity was being openly debated in the ale-houses, and the churches too. There was even a rumour that that hag the Lady Margaret Beaufort was in treasonous correspondence with her son Henry Tudor in Brittany, with a plan to marry him to the late king's eldest daughter and make a bid for the Crown. Clearly, as Buckingham said, this was no time for a child king.

A meeting of the council — the Lord Protector's Council — was due to be held at the Bishop of London's palace to make arrangements *inter alia* for the coronation, when I was summoned late in the evening to an immediate, and secret, meeting being convened by Gloucester at his mother's London residence, Baynard's Castle, where he was staying. They appeared to have a close relationship and she unequivocally supported him in each step he took over the next few weeks. But then, so did I.

There were a handful of Richard's closest confidants at the meeting: Ratcliff, Catesby, Brampton (whom he clearly favoured), John Lord Howard, a couple of others and me. I felt privileged and excited to have been included. Without preamble, Richard told us — with his usual look of devout, almost solemn integrity — that he had evidence, sent to him anonymously, that Hastings was in treasonous correspondence with both agents of the French king and with the Scots, who were planning to co-ordinate an invasion (when are they not?). He passed round the letters; they appeared genuine, and treasonable.

Looking straight at me, Gloucester said, sadly, "My friends, I have clear knowledge that Rivers and Grey were embroiled in similar intrigues with foreign powers, which is why, as High Constable of England, I have taken the grave decision to order their executions. Hastings must suffer the same fate. Are we agreed, my lords?"

I heard a murmur of assent around me. My throat was too dry to utter any sound.

I thought there would be time to reason with the Protector, even, if needed, to haggle over Anthony's life.

And, at any rate, I was part of the Lord Protector's inner circle.

***

After the meeting, I followed Gloucester out of the room and, as he turned, surprised to see me, I knelt and said, "Your Grace, I beg for the life of my sometime bosom friend Lord Rivers. I have no doubt he has grievously wronged Your Grace and the realm but, for the sake of the long years of service he has given Your Grace's brother, the late king, and in remembrance of my long friendship with him, I pledge my own life for his good behaviour and to keep him separated from his faithless sister, the former queen."

Richard looked at me thoughtfully, almost pityingly.

"We shall think on't, Edward. And I salute your loyalty to an old companion in arms."

***

That is a fantasy and a lie.

I did nothing to save the life of Anthony, Lord Rivers.

Am I a coward? Not on the battlefield; though the fear of being added to that growing list of traitors was present in us all.

Or was I thinking that this was my time, and the future belonged to the De-la-Poles, not the Wydvilles?

Whatever the motive cause, I committed a grave sin, or, as the Hebrews call it, an *aveira gadol.* Which is why I fast one day in every week, and beat my breast in repeating the penitential prayers.

***

After Hastings' execution, matters moved quickly.

A large battalion of northern levies, who were devoted to Gloucester, including two hundred of my men from Humberside, arrived and camped just outside the walls of the city. I was flattered he had picked some of my own men to be amongst his bodyguard of a hundred who were billeted in and around Baynard's Castle. Some were also sent to reinforce the garrison at the Tower. There was some disquiet amongst the citizenry about these manoeuvres but as the troops were well-disciplined, the primitive fears of northerners which had prompted the unrest were soon calmed.

Then, on Sunday 22nd June, Doctor Ralph Shaa, brother of the lord mayor, preached a sermon at St. Paul's Cross on the text: "Bastard slips shall not take root." This brought into the light of day, clearly with the Protector's consent, both the rumours which had been the subject of common gossip: that the marriage of Edward IV and Elizabeth Wydville had been clandestine and invalid due to a pre-contract between the king and another lady (I suspect he had made several of those), and that both Edward himself and his brother Clarence had been the product of an adulterous union of their mother with the Captain of Calais. When in the furore that ensued, Duchess Cecily (who still styled herself "queen by right") expressed her dismay at the aspersions cast on her marital fidelity, Duke Richard at once silenced that particular story. But the oath sworn by Bishop Stillington of Bath and Wells, that he had married the late king to the Lady Eleanor Butler, daughter of the Earl of Shrewsbury, a bride more suitable in rank, *before* his marriage to Dame Elizabeth Grey whose "pretensed marriage" was therefore bigamous, was repeated and proclaimed to be true. And their two sons and five daughters were therefore all bastardised.

This was hardly a surprise to me. King Edward's own marriage arrangements had evidently been as muddied and deceitful as those I knew he had been pursuing for his eldest daughter.

Again, Gloucester held an informal meeting of his closest friends at his mother's residence, this time including Buckingham and — to emphasise his links to our House perhaps — our eldest nephew in common, John De-la-Pole, Earl of Lincoln, now a fine if rather pallid young man of 22. I was gratified when Richard directed him to sit by me, giving one of his small radiant smiles, which occasionally lit up his otherwise drawn, ascetic features.

"We must at all events avoid a succession crisis," said Gloucester.

"The Welsh bastard, Tudor, is lurking in Brittany, aiming to lead a Lancastrian invasion," I said.

"Verily," said Richard. "Either we denounce the good bishop's revelation and hasten to crown the boy Edward…"

"Or we listen to the voice of destiny," said Buckingham, "Which is also the voice of reason, and proclaim Your Grace as king, which I aver to be the safer and the better course by far."

There was a moment's silence.

We all knew our future lives — and that of the kingdom — hung in the balance.

"I heartily concur," said Lord Howard. He had just been granted the half of the Norfolk inheritance he had long craved.

"And so do I," said I.

"Long live King Richard!" said my nephew suddenly animated. He had quickly calculated that this put him second-in-line of succession, after Richard's small son.

We were all now loudly shouting our assent.

"My lords, my friends," said Richard calmly. "Let us put this to the council, and to the citizens of London. If they also concur, then let the law of primogeniture take its course."

To my surprise, his expression was even more solemn than habitually.

Of course, it was what Richard, like every king's son or brother, had always dreamt of. But now it was devolving upon him, was it a consummation — or a burthen?

פ (pei)

Four days later — as we began preparations for the coronation not of Edward V but of Richard III — I summoned the rabbi to meet me. I didn't know why. But I felt it was time.

"Enter, Your Eminence," I bade him, with bitter irony.

He looked at me with solemn, hooded eyes. "I hear your dear friend has gone to his maker. May you be comforted amongst all the mourners of Zion, and in Jerusalem may ye be comforted."

For some reason, this unexpected turn of phrase struck a kind of chord within me, like the harp strings I had not plucked for far too long. I started to weep for the first time since that council meeting, piteously.

Rabbi Abraham embraced me. His sheer bulk within that huge kaftan was avuncular, comforting.

When I could weep no more, we sat, with our heads close, in case there were spies around.

"I have sinned, Rabbi. I feel deeply culpable for the death of my friend."

"Only he who gave the order is culpable. And he may have reasons of state to which we are not privy. I have served kings who have done worse."

"How can I continue to give my loyalty to Richard after this?"

"What is done cannot be undone. You must do what is best for the realm. And loyalty is rewarded with loyalty."

I took his hand. "Thank you, Rabbi. You will stay by me?"

"I will stay."

And thus *de profundis* I discovered my counsellor friend.

***

I received an anonymous letter from Pomfret telling me Anthony had gone to the block with much dignity and resignation, having characteristically composed a contemplative poem, "Much mourning but more musing…" on the unpredictable turns of fortune's wheel. He was a scholar, a poet and a very parfait knight to the end. He also executed a last will and testament distributing his worldly goods. In which he had not remembered me.

***

The day after the execution of Rivers and Richard Grey, Richard III was proclaimed King of England and France, and Lord of Ireland, and the coronation was set for July. It was to be a magnificent affair at which my nephew Lincoln would be in a place of high honour as second-in-line to the throne; which was clearly right, as Edward's children were now bastardised and Clarence's son and daughter were debarred by their father's attainder.

But my soul was still troubled and filled with doubt and guilt. For years I had served — and adored — King Edward, and Anthony, Earl Rivers, had been my dearest friend. Now

Edward's sons — Anthony's nephews and wards — were immured in the Tower of London, and his daughters were in sanctuary at Westminster with their de-royaled mother.

Then two events happened.

The evening after the proclamation — preparing to attend a council meeting the next morning to plan the imminent coronation — Malcolm came to see me.

"My lord," he said in his warm East Riding accent.

"Malcolm," I replied in a tone that meant he was at liberty to be intimate.

He sat by me and stroked my back with his big, soldierly right hand. "I see your anguish of heart, chief. You are still mourning Lord Anthony. It were right sudden an' a mighty blow. But there were nothin' you could o' done to stop it, Lord Eddie. And you should ask yourself: should King Edward — the old King Edward — ever ha' been king? The gabble amongst my lads is that he was the love child of old Duchess Cecily — she were a wild one as a lass — with the Captain of Calais, Blaybourne. He were a big handsome lad, like Edward. And he had a birthmark like a big red strawberry on the back of his thigh. An' some say the king had one just like it 'isself."

My heart missed a beat. I looked at Malcolm eye to eye. "I've seen it myself, my friend. So, he *was* a bastard."

"And Richard is the true king, my lord."

***

That night I had a dream.

At first, I was sitting side by side with my beloved friend Anthony, reading and talking, as we often did. But as I turned to face him, it was not him I was with but my Lady Margaret, Dowager Duchess of Burgundy, attired in white, the colour of royal mourning, in a gown of the most exquisite cloth of gold, with a tall, white wimple on her head. Her face was more beautiful than ever and her bodice was cut low to reveal the comely globes of her womanly form. Her lips were moving; she spoke in French. "*Mon pauvre ami. Toujours vous poursuivez votre devoir. Il n'y a qu'un vrai roi d'Angleterre et c'est mon frère Richard III. Et après lui, Richard IV, votre brave neveu. C'est le destin. Calmez-vous, mon cher troubadour, parce que tout est décidé.*"

I awoke; my sheets moist with the overflowing of my spirit. My mind was clear and untroubled. Though I asked myself why Richard would be succeeded not by Lincoln, whose name was John, but by one of his younger brothers?

***

Richard summoned me to a private audience in his apartment at the Palace of Westminster, which had previously been occupied by Queen Elizabeth Wydville — now properly called Dame Elizabeth Grey. I could see why he favoured it with its lovely Flemish tapestries and its stately vistas of the Thames. The more austere chambers of the late king his brother he had given to his wife Queen Anne Neville. For his own reasons, the king had opted not to occupy the usual royal apartments in the Tower prior to his crowning.

"My dear Edward, I need your counsel."

I was eager to offer my advice on matters of politics or the defence of the realm.

"Edward, you have travelled in Italy, the lands of the classical rebirth, a boon which has not been vouchsafed to me as a prince of the blood. I am a soldier and a blunt Yorkshireman. But the queen and I are determined that our coronation should be a great spectacle. You must advise me on the latest, richest fashions and fabrics from Florence and Rome. I want the whole realm and the whole world to see that the Cousins' Wars are over and that England has a strong king and queen who are here to stay."

"A very handsome couple Your Highnesses will make in the abbey. I suggest robes of purple cloth of gold furred with ermine, and a new red cap of maintenance for the Confessor's crown — the old one is looking rather tawdry, sire. My man Quidnunc is expert on these matters of apparel."

"I knew you would have the right man for the job. And Edward…" His voice fell to a confidential murmur. "I want you to keep an eye for me on Stanley. I know I can rely on Howard, on Ratcliff and Catesby — on you and your family, of course — on Buckingham, no doubt, though he is making demands which are not met. But Stanley and his brother William — they are slippery fish who never commit their troops to battle; and that wife of his…"

"The cunning 'cuntess' — saving Your Highness' presence…"

Richard frowned slightly, though his eye twinkled, at my Anglo-Saxon; for despite being a soldier, he was pious and a tad prudish.

"The Lady Margaret is of bastard blood like her late husband Edmund Tudor, but she is ever weaving plots on behalf of her exiled son."

"Keep your enemies close, Highness. Let Stanley not leave the court. But let them both be honoured at the coronation. Better to have the Stanleys inside pissing out, than outside pissing in, sire, if you will forgive my crudity."

He half-smiled.

If only he had not forgotten my advice.

***

The coronation was the magnificent spectacle Richard had intended with both the king and Queen Anne — who, as daughter and heiress of Warwick the kingmaker, was a respected figure with a huge affinity in the north, if in character she was coolly aloof — both apparelled, as I had advised, in gorgeous silks, velvets, ermine and sumptuous purple cloth of gold. Their little son, Prince Edward, walked behind them. Richard may have been slight, almost feminine in build and somewhat misshapen due to his curving spine, but he cut a figure of great dignity when regally attired. And my heart swelled with pride to see my eldest nephew, Lincoln, walk before the king carrying the great Sword of State.

After the crowning at which both king and queen were well received by the people — contrary to the Tudor poison which has since been spread — Richard proved himself as good as his word, given me many months before. When honours were bestowed, amongst many others, Lord Howard got his heart's desire and became Duke of Norfolk, my nephew Lincoln became a Knight of the Garter, Edward Brampton was knighted; and I, enfin, after all my unrecognised years of service to the House of York, became Baron De-la-Pole of Holderness, a hereditary peer of the realm with a seat in the House of Lords. Finally, in my fortieth year, my reward had come. In fact, as he ceremonially ennobled me, Richard whispered in my ear, "You will rise further yet."

I could almost hear the B.M.'s voice saying, "You've got your title at last, Edward. But what is a hereditary barony without a son to inherit it?" She could never leave a compliment unbarbed.

Buckingham, meanwhile, who had asked for much, got nothing.

Book IV: Autumn

צ (tsadeh)

The reign started well with progress. Richard and his consort were far better known in the north than in the south and this they set out to remedy. With other lords of the court, I was in attendance.

But very soon we began to hear reports that Buckingham — proud Buckingham whose royal ancestry gave him both direct descent from Edward III's youngest son and also a Beaufort Lancastrian claim (arguably stronger than the Lady Margaret's by the way) — was expressing his discontent at not receiving his just rewards.

There were also rumours of a conspiracy by middle-ranking retainers and officials of the former regime to release the Lord Bastard and his brother from the Tower — where they were residing in comfort — and use them as figureheads to launch a rebellion. Other reports revealed that Margaret Beaufort, Countess of Richmond and wife to the powerful Lord Stanley, was somehow implicated. It appeared she would ally herself with anyone to bring back her bastard son and get him married to one of King Edward's bastard daughters. The king had the conspirators executed; but did not move against the lady, who was, of course, protected by her husband.

Naturally, and quite properly, the two Wydville boys — the former king and his younger brother — were moved, with the council's consent, to inner wards of the Tower and thereby hidden from public view. Unfortunately — and quite falsely — rumours began to spread that they had been murdered on their uncle's orders. I knew these to be nonsense as, on the council's commands, they were regularly provided with new garments and when the elder boy was ill, the king sent his own physician, the provost of King's College Cambridge, to treat him. No orders were ever given, I repeat, no commands were ever given for those boys to be killed. But how, when and why they disappeared, I know not; though, as I may tell in a while, I have my own views...

In October of '83, Buckingham's grumblings burst into rebellion and he summoned his not inconsiderable affinity to assemble from north Wales and the west of England on the bank of the Severn. The king, with his usual military skill, summoned his forces, including mine from the Humber, and we dashed across the kingdom to confront him. In fact, Buckingham — who we knew had held a secret meeting with Margaret Beaufort, his aunt by her previous marriage, and was leagued through her with Henry Tudor — was probably aiming to take the throne himself as he had some kind of Lancastrian claim through his mother: another, older Margaret Beaufort. However, his forces were defeated by the overflowing Severn even before the royal army got to them, and he fled ignominiously to hide with a retainer — who then betrayed him to us. He was summarily — and justly — executed at Salisbury. But it was an unkind cut for Richard who described him bitterly to us as, "the most untrue creature living."

Richard valued loyalty most highly; after all, his personal motto was, *"Loyaulté me lie"*, which done into English means, "Loyalty binds me."

This time the evidence of Margaret Beaufort's complicity was overwhelming and we on the council insisted that it could not be ignored. But, of course, this presented Richard with a heavy problem, as Lord Stanley, the traitoress' husband, was one of the magnates on whom he relied in the north-west and north Wales; now more than ever since Buckingham's demise. Richard — a shrewd politician — calculated that he could not afford, at this stage, to alienate the powerful Stanleys; yet Margaret Beaufort had to be punished and her future activities restrained. So, this was his cunning solution. Along with the other rebels — most of whom had fled to join the Tudors in Brittany — the countess was attainted in the Parliament of January 1484. And this meant, of course, that her life and lands were forfeit to the Crown. However, in order to keep her husband loyal, the king graciously (too graciously as it turned out) allowed her death sentence to be commuted to perpetual imprisonment; an imprisonment that was of the softest kind, in the custody of her husband (whom Richard had fortuitously appointed Constable of England). Her substantial estates were also put into Stanley's custody for his lifetime; though most of them were to be inherited by my nephew, Lincoln, upon Stanley's death. So, far from being his cruelty, it was in fact Richard's graciousness and mercy which led to his end.

In the meantime, in the winter of '83, Tudor had launched an abortive invasion of the kingdom, at his mother's behest. If only, when he spied land at Plymouth, he had come ashore responding to the signals he had received, he would in fact have been captured by the king's forces who were the source of those signals, and King Richard — or perhaps one of my nephews — would be ruling in England even now. Sadly, he turned back to Brittany to be joined there by the king's other great traitors: Dorset — Elizabeth Wydville's son — and his uncle, Edward Wydville, Edward Courtenay Earl of Devon, as well as Bishop Morton, that devious cleric who had never given up his Lancastrian links. And there they formed the heart of a traitorous court-in-exile.

***

As that foul liar, Henry Tudor — whom I refuse to grace with a royal title — has continued to blacken King Richard's name by accusing him of the murder of his two nephews, the Wydville boys, who "disappeared" in the Tower at about this time, perhaps now is the moment for me to vouchsafe what I believe to have befallen them. The truth I suspect is this: one died, the other didn't.

We of the council knew that Lord Edward — the former boy king — was seriously distempered in the autumn of '83, when the king informed us that, with characteristic kindness, he had given orders for a visit to the Tower by his own physician, Doctor John Argentine — the silver-tongued scholar who was the late King Edward's choice as provost of the King's College at Cambridge (the foundation of which was certainly the best thing Henry VI had ever done; in truth, it was well nigh the only thing he had ever done). Doctor Argentine, ever the academic, reported back to us that the Lord Bastard's humours were perilously out of kilter and that he was in very low spirits, fearing death.

In council, Richard commented, "He will not receive it from me, but if it be God's will…" He could be annoyingly tendentious — and sententious — at times.

It is my belief that the youth died soon after, of displeasure and melancholy, as it was reported that Henry VI had done back in '71, also strangely enough, in the less salubrious parts of the Tower. Had the king announced this death — which with hindsight would have been the wiser course — he would then have been obliged to explain also the fate of his younger brother, Richard Duke of York, and that, for reasons I shall shortly explain, he was not able openly to do.

My nephew Lincoln, however — a handsome young prince with green eyes (not a dreamy grey-green like Anthony's, but a lurid green like a dragon), manly shoulders and a fine waist — a figure very like my own when younger — was quite different in character from his timid, pallid father. He had something of the B.M.'s powerful character and had inherited his own mother's regal bearing and great expectations. He was high in his other uncle's favour too — the king's. By choosing him to carry the Sword of Estate before the royal couple at the coronation, while no such equivalent honour was conferred upon his other nephew George Warwick, Clarence's son, Richard indicated much. Lincoln was evidently next in line of succession after the little Prince of Wales, and he looked the part.

As if to add a flourish, Lincoln was created a Knight of the Garter, the highest Order of Chivalry. I was only slightly less privileged to become a Knight Companion of the Order of the Bath. I will not break my oath of secrecy by revealing the intricate protocol of the long night — and knightly — vigil which we initiates underwent, as tradition dictates, in the confines of the Tower. Suffice it to say that we bathed — I and my eleven brother knights — in manly companionship, to purify our souls through that long night of prayer; and other things which shall remain forever arcane.

In the morning, when the king, resplendent in white robes as pristine and simple as our own, he embraced each of us and, giving me a solemn — or mock-solemn? — look, he said softly, "And now we must arrange your marriage, my Lord De-la-Pole."

"Your Grace."

He whispered in my ear, "I hear Countess Rivers is looking for a gallant second groom. She is a handsome woman. And I have recognised her as beneficiary of most of her late lamented lord's estates and treasure."

I was too stunned to answer. Was this a ghoulish jest at my expense, or a genuine token of his good lordship? Or perhaps both?

The king smiled and passed on.

And before his plan had come to pass, he had passed on into the next world.

ק (kuf)

Meanwhile, months after the coronation, Dame Elizabeth Grey, sometime styled Queen of England, was still lurking in sanctuary with her five daughters, and a lot of movable goods, in cramped and increasingly squalid quarters. What she hoped to achieve — or perhaps avoid — by skulking there, I know not. But her presence there — and equally that of her five unmarried girls — was becoming an embarrassment, almost a scandal.

Richard, howsomever, was a canny politician. He needed to make the situation, in the early months of his reign, as normal as possible and to place beyond doubt the legitimacy of his kingship in the face of those rebels who had fled abroad, including, of course, Dame Elizabeth's son and brother. Moreover, as unfounded rumours began to be whispered that the royal bastards in the Tower had been done to death, it was essential for Richard to prove — with the ex-queen's complaisance — that this could not be the case. So, as he informed the council in his inclusively collegiate way, he had paid a courtesy visit to Dame Elizabeth in her sanctuary and offered her a settlement.

The king would promise that if she came out of sanctuary, she and her daughters would all be honourably housed — and not imprisoned in the Tower, as she had told him she feared

— and, moreover, he would promise that they would all be worthily, if not royally, married, and only with their own freely given consent. He assured her, in his smoothest and most charming manner, that he had no intention of imprisoning her or any of her daughters — indeed, why should he? — but to placate her. He, the crowned King of England, was prepared to swear this oath on the gospels and in the presence of the court and of the Lord Mayor, and aldermen, of the City of London, many of whom she knew well. So, said the king, he would pronounce that oath at St. John's Priory, Clerkenwell in Holy Week and Dame Elizabeth would leave sanctuary. Her eldest daughter, the Lady Elizabeth (I noted he did not call her bastard) who was now, as he informed us, as fine a young woman as any he had beheld, would join the court as a companion to his consort, Queen Anne, who was suffering from loneliness in the absence of suitable companions.

I was not deceived. Whilst this elevation of her eldest daughter back to semi-royal status, and the promise of safety for her and good marriages for the other four girls would be persuasive, why should Elizabeth Wydville believe it, in light of the disappearance of her two beloved sons?

No, a woman as passionate and politically astute as she would only give up her own and her daughters' safety — and write to her son Dorset, as she did, urging him to return to Richard's court which he promptly attempted to do, only to be restrained by Tudor's henchmen — if she had been given cast-iron assurances of something beyond her daughters' safety.

As I see it, Richard had two choices in relation to the bastard princes: he could produce them in public, but this was ruled out if, as I surmise, the elder had died. Or, he could convince their mother and sisters to come out of hiding and, in the daughter's case, join the court. But which mother would do this and potentially put the lives of her five daughters, and son once returned from exile, at risk? Unless, that is, she could be reunited, secretly if need be, with her best beloved youngest son. The little Richard of York had always been a favourite of his uncle and had been received by him most kindly when brought out of his mother's care some months before. It was *this* promise, I believe — this necessarily secret promise — which persuaded Elizabeth Wydville to return to the world, with the corollary that if Richard failed to produce his namesake, she and her daughters would denounce him to the world as a murderer; something none of them ever did. No, not even after Bosworth. And this secret treaty would also explain why Dame Elizabeth was content — quite contrary to her flamboyant nature — to withdraw privately to the country for several months, on a comfortable pension, where, I have no doubt, she was reunited with her Richard: a charming, handsome boy who may — or may not, make your own choice — yet reappear on the public stage, some years later.

The former queen's hopes were also high — perchance very high — for the future marriage of her lovely eighteen-year-old eldest daughter, who was welcomed officially at court as the "Lady Elizabeth", as if she had never been bastardised. And yet we now know that that devious woman would hedge her bets by continuing her treasonous correspondence with the cunning Countess of Richmond who still hoped for a marriage between her exiled son and that young lady.

But just now, in the lovely spring of '84, that only complete year of the dramatic reign of King Richard III, when peace and amity had returned to the royal family, suddenly a terrible calamity hit the king and queen. I was in attendance upon the king at Nottingham, when the news arrived that his only legitimate child, Edward Prince of Wales, had died at Middleham Castle; ironically the place where he had been born, just seven years before. I can attest to the truth of the chronicler's report that the king and queen were almost out of their minds with grief. For the queen, a sick woman already known to be suffering from melancholy, and unable to bear more children, it would prove terminal. But it was also a tragedy for the kingdom, as yet another Plantagenet prince, full of promise, went down prematurely to join the shades, throwing the Yorkist succession again into doubt.

We did our utmost to comfort the king, though it must be said that he smiled infrequently after this time. But I smiled to myself when, shortly after this, he appointed our shared nephew Lincoln to two high offices: President of the Council of the North in succession to his son, and also Lord Lieutenant of Ireland, a role once filled by his own father, the late Duke of York. The De-la-Poles were still on the rise.

ר (reish)

The hot, dusty summer of 1484. The court was back at Westminster and Queen Anne, it was remarked behind courtiers' hands, was thinner and coughing much. The council gave orders that ugly and seditious rhymes — "The Cat, the Rat and Lovell our Dog, rule all England under the Hog" in particular — which were appearing around the cities of London and Westminster, should be taken down, and the perpetrators punished. I was glad I was not mentioned in the doggerel; yet also a tad miffed.

Summer was turning into the gold of autumn, when the king summoned me to his chamber.

He was lying prone on a trestle table, a small cloth over his buttocks, while a very large bearded man pummelled his back. It was the first time I had seen him unclothed, and his spinal curvature, usually well-disguised by heavy clothing or armour, was blatant and shocking. I must have blushed and looked very uncomfortable, for he said, "Do not concern yourself, De-la-Pole. This man Mehmet is a Turkish doctor in the service of Edward Brampton. And you may speak openly as he has little English. The treatment is excellent for my condition."

Assuming this was a reference to his twisted back, I said nothing, and shot a look to see if there was any sign of a strawberry birthmark on either thigh, but there was none.

"You have heard, I guess, of the wasting melancholy of our dear consort."

"Sadly yes, Your Grace."

"And while we still hope and daily pray for her deliverance, it seemeth that the end may not be far off. Which, Heaven forfend, we would do nothing to hasten, but if it be God's will..."

This evoked an echo in my mind of something he had said a few months before...

Again, I said nothing. There was nothing to be said.

"Some of our friends have been urging that we should start to plan for what must follow. The kingdom needs an heir... ahh..." Here he responded to a particularly sharp crack of a bone beneath Mehmet's large hands. "And an heir requires a new queen."

Still nothing.

In the pause, a thought came to me.

"The learned rabbi from the Court of Aragon, sire, Don Abraham di Mayorca, who came here to arrange a marriage for the daughter of his master and mistress, the Infanta Isabel of Castille..." I trod carefully. The rabbi had come to arrange a marriage between the infanta and a different prince. However, the king seemed interested.

"On my troth," he said, "And the infanta descends from Duke John of Lancaster and that would bring about a reconciliation with that House which would cook the goose of the bastard Tydr."

"Verily, Your Highness."

The king let out a yelp and playfully slapped the hand of the Turk who appeared to have gone a bit too far. But then the king smiled, and the "treatment" continued.

"Although my good friend Brampton, being of Portuguese birth, is urging the claims of his former king's sister, the Infanta Joanna, whose grandsire was also the said John of Gaunt and, in fact, has the senior claim."

"But, sire..."

"On another matter entirely..."

The Turk threw him over and began kneading the king's chest vigorously. I gasped.

The king smoothly continued. "Have you noticed how lovely and how regal the Lady Elizabeth is looking? And how like a sister — a younger sister — she is to the queen?"

I bowed.

"One might almost conceive of restoring her to full dignity and arranging a royal marriage for her..." He raised his head to look at me.

The Turk — whose expression clearly indicated comprehension — stopped pounding.

Which was what my heart started to do.

How royal a marriage was the king planning for Elizabeth, *his niece*? Surely not the highest of all?

***

I called to my chamber the man who was becoming my acknowledged spiritual adviser, the rabbi.

"Rabbi, the king may soon be in need of another queen. If and when that happens, I advise you to be ready to propose the hand of your infanta. Is she nubile? Is she lovely?"

"She is surely both, my lord. Eighteen and loveliness itself. And my aster has younger daughters as well, if that marriage fails to take place. But I am sorry to hear of the illness of the queen. I knew not it was so grave."

"No, nor did I, Father, I mean Rabbi." It was not the last time I made that mistake. "But you must be prepared for a battle against the wiles of your rival, Brampton, who is lobbying for a marriage with the Portuguese infanta. Apparently, she has the senior Lancastrian claim."

"Senior is right, my lord. She is well over thirty, plain as a pike staff and longs for the life of a nun. Neither attractive nor good for producing heirs."

"There may even be another candidate, also eighteen, closer to home. Rabbi, what says the Torah on marriage between an uncle and a niece?"

Don Abraham gave me a look that was searching, perceptive, shocked and slightly amused — a very Jewish look, I think. He said slowly, "It is not forbidden by the Halacha; indeed, some authorities encourage it for the sake of… inheritance and… family unity. Perhaps His Grace could convert to Judaism." His eyes lit up with an alarming zeal.

"Has such a thing ever happened?" I scoffed.

"Have you not heard, Lord Eddie, of the King of the Khazars? That inquisitive monarch summoned Christian, Moslem and Jewish scholars to give him a summary of their beliefs; he chose the Torah. I must show Your Lordship the

347

beautiful Arabic text the *Kitab al Khazari*, written by Rabbi Yehuda Halevi, which Your Lordship's humble servant has translated into Hebrew. Perhaps I could do a further translation into the English tongue for His Highness…?"

"You should work with…" And then remembered, with a catch in my throat, that the scholar nobleman he should have worked with on this pursuit was dead.

Was I surrounded by lunatics?

***

Christmas, 1484: was there ever such a Christmas as the great Yuletide feast of the first (and last) full year of the reign of the last Plantagenet — indeed, the last English — King of England?

Like the Great Passover of King Josiah, there was never a like festive season seen in England. And it reached its zenith, of course, at Epiphany, the twelve and final day of Christmas.

The preparations and expenditure were ostentatious, magnificent. King Edward's Yuletides had been splendid but this celebration of legitimate Plantagenet kingship was to be on an altogether higher level, as if the angels themselves had come down to cast their benedictions upon our king – and queen, of course.

It was, I remember, a very cold winter (why have the winters grown colder throughout this century of wars? There are many who attribute this to witchcraft — and undoubtedly those weird sisters have frightening powers. But to summon hail and snow storms? I think not). But, inside the royal Palace of

Westminster, the logs were piled high and we swathed ourselves in furs and velvets to keep out the cold.

The king had briefed me at one of our regular private audiences of what was to be expected. So, of course, not to be outdone, I had gotten the latest Italian apparel, based on the finest Florentine designs: slashed doublets — originating, it is said, in the mockery of the Swiss in cutting up the fine blousons of their defeated Burgundian enemies at Morat in '76. They were already beginning to find their way to England and I had arranged for several to be made for His Grace as well as myself. But I am proud to state categorically that I was the first nobleman in England to sport a large and pear-shaped codpiece that winter season, and much attention it brought me from the nobility of both genders I can assure you.

All the court was assembled; my three eldest nephews included: Lincoln in his early twenties, with his younger brothers, Edmund then about twelve and like, too like, to his dreary father, and Richard, about ten and the brightest, best favoured spark of the brood (who may yet one day restore our fortunes). All were glistering with gems, silks, furs and gold. The long, bannered trumpets sounded, and, preceded by her guards and her chamberlain, entered Queen Anne in a long and beauteous purple gown of heavy cloth of gold and an elegant golden circlet on her brow. Taking her hand as she walked by her side, looking as if she were her younger — and prettier — sister, was the Lady Elizabeth. No surprise there, except Elizabeth was apparelled exactly the same as her aunt, the queen. Even the most experienced and chivalrous of courtiers were taken aback at this: what could it mean? As if to answer this unspoken question, as she passed us, the queen — who undoubtedly looked pale and wan, *une belle dame sans merci* — gave a little tinkling, forced laugh and said, "Behold my niece, nay, my sister!" At which we all applauded politely, as is, or was, the custom at court.

Then, following this odd pairing, came more guards and the Lord High Chamberlain — the dignified, devious Lord Stanley — carrying the Sword of State before the king, who looked magnificent — if a tad feminine — in his superb slashed doublet beneath the great furred Cloak of Estate. Leaning on *his* arm — where one might have expected to see the queen — was his now elderly but still regal mother, Duchess Cecily of York, who looked every inch the "queen by right". And then, as if to act out their great love for each other, the two royal couples bowed first to us, then to each other, and exchanged places as in an elaborate dance. But the queen did not immediately go to the king's side, but rather was joined by the "Queen Mother" — as one might call her, or Queen Bee perhaps — who, having always disapproved of Elizabeth Wydville, looked with great affection upon Queen Anne Neville; after all, she was a Neville herself. They also held hands while facing — or opposing — them. The Lady Elizabeth took her place by the king's side and, briefly, held his hand. She turned her face as she bowed to His Grace and the expression upon it, was, as I momentarily saw it, reverential, nay, idolatrous. Maybe she saw in him an echo of her beloved father; women, if they can, always marry their fathers. But in a moment, that impression had passed, for the elaborate realignment continued and finally the queen was in her rightful place by the king her husband, with Duchess Cecily and the Lady Elizabeth flanking them. Then, as the trumpets again sounded, all four of the royal party were seated; the king and queen on their Chairs of Estate, and the other two ladies on slightly lower but equally grand, chairs beside them.

Next, the vice-chamberlain stamped his staff of office on the ground and announced, "Monsieur Antoine Busnois."

An elegant, elderly gentleman stepped forward bowing at each step and announced to Their Graces, "*Votres Altesses Royals*, I am here from the court of Burgoyne with letters of credence from the mighty princess, Duchess Margaret, Your Grace's noble sister, to bid Your Highnesses 'Alleluya'."

At which, his little troop of gaily dressed performers began to sing a noble "Alleluya", bright and Burgundian.

As the lovely music ended, we applauded daintily; the king leading us.

"We thank you, Master Busnois, for your harmonies and reward you thus."

We applauded again as the vice-chamberlain awarded each chorister with a purse of gold — and their master with two.

Then my cheeks suddenly began to prickle, as unannounced, Rabbi Abraham stepped forward, bowed low and said sonorously, "Your Royal Highnesses, might an envoy from the court of Aragon presume to offer his own humble tribute in music to the most noble court in Christendom, by the hand of Italy's greatest dancing master, my kinsman: Magister Guglielmo Ebreo de Pesaro?"

The rabbi — wearing a long and splendid kaftan in green and gold which I had never seen before, and which certainly lent great dignity to his person — indicated with a flourish another musician with a handsome, Semitic face and clipped red beard, who announced in an Italian accent, "'Falla con

Misuras', as danced by Duchess Mary at the court of Burgundy. Will Your Excellencies take the floor?"

The king indicated to the queen, but she coughed a little and graciously declined. He then turned the other way to the Lady Elizabeth, who dipped a courtesy, and then moved forward to start the dance with three countesses. It was an elegant Italian measure, which the ladies stepped out most beautifully.

At the end of it, the king, having clapped and smiled broadly, said to my rabbinic friend, "Your Eminence has exceeded our highest expectations with this delightful offering. We are pleased at your continued presence at our court, and wish to speak with you anon to learn more of the courts of Spain, and of Your Eminence's beliefs and customs."

Don Abraham was about to give a courtly reply, when Lord Stanley indicated to the king that a royal messenger had arrived with an important despatch and handed it to the king. All stopped as the king read it.

His face became more strained, but then relaxed confidently as he said, "Couriers have announced to us that Madame Anne, the French king's sister, who *rules* him, will give her support to an incursion into our realm by the rebels and traitors now assembled at Rouen led by that unknown Welshman Tydr." And as he said this, he looked a tad menacingly at Stanley. "And this gladdens our heart for this will be our opportunity to dispel and defeat these miserable rebels once and for all!"

We applauded most vigorously at this and when the chamberlains announced "let the feasting commence", we moved forward into the Great Hall of Westminster to a banquet almost as great as that for Their Graces' coronation, with swan, hog, venison and the most delicious and cinnamon-flavoured frumenty, and the richest Burgundian wines, while the great logs flamed on the fires. And we knew now that '85 would be the making or the marring of King Richard's reign.

***

Several weeks later, I was walking through the corridors of the palace on my way to a council meeting, when I almost collided with the Duke of Norfolk, one of the few men even closer to the king than I.

He took me to one side and said, "My dear Edward."

As we were hardly friends — his family and mine, as you know, had been at loggerheads for years over our estates in East Anglia — this clearly meant he wanted something: information, support?

"I have received a most curious letter from the buxom Lady Elizabeth. Remembering how close I was to her late father — though actually I've a better opinion by far of our present king..."

He paused, so I said, "Me too."

"Well, she," he said, lowering his voice, "Expresses some... uh... impatience over the anticipated demise of Queen Anne." He looked at me closely but my face betrayed nothing. "And begs me to further the cause of her own marriage, assuring me that she is wholly the king's in soul and in... uh... body too."

I said nothing.

"Of course," he continued," There is talk, as you know, of a double Portuguese marriage treaty when, or rather if, Her Grace should succumb."

"Or alternatively a Castilian one; the Infanta Isabella is both beautiful and nubile, I hear."

"Ah yes, from your friend, the Jew."

"As distinct from *your* friend, the turncoat Jew," I replied and immediately regretted it.

"Brampton is the king's friend, and Portugal is our oldest ally. In any case," he said lightening up again, "What think you of the Lady Bessie's declaration?"

"Nothing at all, Norfolk. Are we not all the king's in both body and soul? I will lay down my life for him if it be needed, if the rebels come, and so will you. I have my doubts about Stanley though and that venomous wife of his."

"Yes, we must keep our eyes on Stanley; the king is too soft on him, too trusting. Well, thank you for your thoughts, Edward. By the by, the king has told me that, once this damned rebellion is dealt with, you shall have a further preference — to an earldom. Think upon your future title, my lord."

What exactly was it that Norfolk — and the king — were canvassing my support for? Frankly I didn't care if the king wanted to marry a swan, provided we defeated the Welsh pretender, I got my earldom and my nephews were acknowledged as his heirs. But what would the people accept?

***

And then in March, at Westminster, the queen died. The king withdrew to his apartments in great grief and Queen Anne was accorded the most regal honours in her obsequies.

Within a fortnight of the funeral, another doggerel began appearing, written by anon: Dickon the king hath poisoned his queen; to marry the Lady Bessie next, I ween.

Despite its atrocious scansion, this verse had the court alarmed. Not because we either believed it, or even cared if it was true (Anne Neville having kept herself aloof from almost everyone, except perhaps the king), but because we saw in the eyes of the hoi poloi that it held some credence. And if that was true in the south, how much more dangerous would it be in the north where her late father — the kingmaker — was still held in the highest esteem?

The king held a council, probably the most dramatic of his reign at which, in my presence, he was challenged by three of his closest northern advisers — men once of, or closely connected to, the Neville affinity — that if he now chose to marry his niece, the buxom Lady Elizabeth, his support in the north would collapse. Ever the clever politician, Richard at once denied this had ever been his intention.

"Friends," he said, a tad sanctimoniously, "At present I am in profoundest sorrow, but, to calm the unwarranted fears of my mistaken subjects, soon I shall publicly declare that it was never in my thoughts to marry my own late brother's daughter, and shall at once set in hand the search for a suitable bride. It is my firm decision to seek a bride who descends from the great John of Gaunt, Duke of Lancaster in the legitimate, royal line, and thus to trample upon the bastardised and much-besmirched line of the Welsh Tydrs."

At this, he smiled apologetically towards Lord Stanley who smiled back — difficult to say whose was the more insincere. But the smiles of the rest of us, especially the northerners, were broad indeed; this was the Richard whom we preferred to follow.

Shortly thereafter, Richard made his public declaration to the mayor and aldermen of London, and the rumours were scotched.

Did anything happen in the spring and early summer of 1485? The king sent Edward Brampton to Portugal to treat for a double marriage alliance — himself with the devout Infanta Joanna and the Lady Bessie with the infanta's cousin Manuel, Duke of Beja. This caused much chagrin to Rabbi Abraham, still lobbying on behalf of his more nubile Infanta Isabella.

But in truth, England held its breath as we awaited the inevitable clash of arms. Did we anticipate this as the battle that would end the Cousins' Wars? I think we did. Richard III was the last of the Plantagenets, while Henry Tudor was the last male sprig of the line of John of Gaunt. Yet Richard was reigning as king and was a seasoned campaigner; his future and ours, the De-la-Poles, could not be in jeopardy, could it?

One warm, balmy evening in July (even in that cold era, we had some sunny days) when my rabbi and I had completed our customary Hebrew lesson — I had decided that it was now up to me to aid in the translation of the *Khuzari* and perhaps other important works, for Master Caxton to put to press and dedicate to King Richard or his second queen — when Rav Abraham said, "Will you ride with the king in the battle which approaches, Edward?" Our manly friendship had become, by now, more intimate.

"I will do whatever the king commands, Rabbi. And I expect he will summon me to fight alongside him with my affinity."

"If Richard wins, I foresee a great time for England, for the De-la-Poles and for the Jews. There will be a great flowering of the new learning — which will not favour the Catholic Church. Your nephews will be great men and the king will revoke the expulsion edict of Edward I and welcome my race back to England — to increase trade and banking and to foster the new learning in Hebrew and Arabic."

"It sounds… wonderful," I said.

"But," he continued oblivious, "If the king loses—"

"Unthinkable!"

"Of course and God forbid it should happen, but we are not always privy to His plans and if — which God forfend — Richmond was, by treachery, to win the day and with it, the Lady Elizabeth and the Crown…"

"Don Abraham!"

"You and I, Edward, will either have to flee the realm or make our peace with the enemy."

"Why should *you* leave, Master Ambassador?"

"Because the king, my master, is sending another to replace me, and as his wife Queen Isabella hates the Jews, it may not be wise for me to return now."

"That is your problem, sir, but it need not be mine." I stood to leave the rabbi's chamber. "I refuse to consider the possibilities of defeat."

But that is exactly what I began to do.

***

The king was at Nottingham Castle, at the heart of England, with Catesby, Ratcliffe, myself and a few other close advisers, awaiting news of the rebels' landing. It was the middle of August, about noon one overcast day, when he summoned me to the garden below his apartment. The roses were fully in bloom; big red ones, I remember.

"Tudor has landed at Milford Haven, in his homeland not surprisingly. Hoping to gather support there, I guess," he said ruminatively.

"Shall I to Humberside to muster my affinity, Your Grace?"

He paused a moment. "You are a good soldier, Edward, but a better politician. Go to Sheriff Hutton — it's in the same county — and keep a close eye on Warwick, and on the Lady Elizabeth. Should I fall in the battle—"

"God forfend, Your Highness!"

"Amen, my friend, but should that befall, you must proclaim our nephew Lincoln as King... John II, even though the first King John was not an unmitigated success."

And, for a moment, we both laughed.

"And," he added, "Marry him to Elizabeth. With her beside him, he will have a chance to hold the throne. For Jesu's sake, don't let Tudor get hold of her."

"If she won't marry him, sire, I'll pack her off to my sister's convent."

"Excellent, Edward. Not that this should be necessary, of course, but we must be prepared."

"You will triumph, Your Highness."

"And when I do, you shall be Earl of..."

I had an inspiration. "Earl of the Humber, Your Grace?"

"And you must have a Countess of the Humber, Eddie. I insist upon it." His laughter, strong, manly and not a whit sinister, exploded as I bowed myself out.

That was the last time I saw him alive.

ש (shin)

The Battle of Bosworth Heath took place in a few hours on the morning of Monday 22nd August 1485. I have heard accounts of the fighting from at least twelve men who were present, and heard thirteen differing stories. Some say the king slept ill in his tent and that, having been fully accoutred in his golden armour with the royal circlet upon the helm, he insisted on finding a well to drink water. These and other indications suggest to me that he may have contracted a fever, although I had seen no sign of it at our final audience, a few days before. Certainly his usual calm and clever generalship seemed to have been disturbed by something. Probably by the fact he saw the substantial forces of Lord Stanley and his devious brother up on the hill above, calmly watching the battle, while the Earl of Northumberland and his substantial battle group sat in the rear doing sweet fuck all.

Apologies if I resort to soldier's idioms; it must be to compensate for my guilt in not being present at the battle. Though had I been there, I would certainly have done more than those treacherous curs. Seeing the torpor of his major vassals — all but Norfolk who led his men valiantly for the king — Richard threw himself into the thick of the fighting leading a mighty charge against Henry Tudor's own position. He even managed to strike down the bearer of Henry's dragon banner, one Brandon (whose son now has the temerity to style himself Duke of Suffolk).

Anyway, Richard fought with the courage and valour of the last of the Plantagenets, but, separated from his household knights, was cut down and beaten to death in the press of his enemies. And everyone knows the tale — whether true or not — that the royal circlet, which had fallen from his helmet, was found under a thorn bush and placed, by that traitor Stanley, on the head of his usurping step-son Henry.

I was at Sheriff Hutton, as instructed, when, the very next morning, the news was brought to me by a loyal retainer of my brother's. He hadn't been at the battle either; no one had asked him.

At once, I sent word begging leave to visit the Lady Elizabeth.

"My lady, dreadful news. The battle has been lost and the king is dead."

"I know," she said.

How? I thought. *By witchcraft?*

"So we have a new king," I said carefully.

"Yes. King Henry VII," she said, calmly.

I spat on the floor between us. "Never. My nephew John is King Richard's heir and, on his express instructions, you are to be his queen."

I looked steadily at her. She was certainly beautiful when aroused, and she was certainly aroused.

"Never," she echoed, suddenly looking like her imperious mother. "King Richard III being defeated and dead, his commands are empty words. I might have married Richard —

he was a strong man and could have been a great king, and we could have made great kings together. But I will not marry a stripling, no, not even a De-la-Pole stripling, Baron De-la-Pole. I will marry the victor, King Henry VII."

We stood glaring at each other.

"Your Uncle Dickon was right. You are a Wydville and a complete and utter bastard."

I turned and left the chamber. That decided my course of action.

It was the last time I saw that traitoress to the Houses of York and Plantagenet. By ten o'clock that night, I was in Hull, where the rabbi and my faithful Malcolm were awaiting me. The next morning — while King Richard's body, having been carried naked and trussed over the back of a horse, was being exhibited to public display in Leicester before it was chucked into a pit with minimal obsequies, and the cunning countess was commanding Te Deums, and even the inn in which Richard had passed his penultimate night was being metamorphosed from the White Boar, Richard's personal emblem, to the Blue, and the bitch-heiress of England was preparing to marry the bastard Welshman who had filched the Crown — Rav Abraham, Malcolm and I with a handful of loyal retainers (and a couple of chests stuffed with gold and jewellery, including my red balas ruby ring which I had never quite been able, as luck would have it, to present to Richard) were out on the North Sea heading into our long, cold Netherlandish exile.

***

And that is really the end of the story; my story, and the story of the House of York. And the story of England, the England that I knew. The rest is epilogue.

***

You may ask: why didn't I bundle Elizabeth of York off to my sister Katherine's abbey, or liaise with my nephew Lincoln? Because instinct and long experience told me it would be to no avail. The momentum of victory was with Tudor and, though a time for fighting back might come, it was not yet. In fact, Lincoln — who had been with us at Sheriff Hutton — had suddenly absconded after he heard the doleful news and returned home to his parents, thus scuppering the plan to marry him speedily off to his cousin.

And thus, I found myself, as the divine Dante says, in the middle of my life, lost in a dark wood, alone and not knowing which way to turn. Not completely alone, of course. My beloved teacher, Reb Abraham, was at my side, together with Malcolm and a handful of loyal retainers, and I had made sure that my pockets — and the rabbi's — were stuffed with gold.

So, my little party arrived in Bruges, sad but not penniless, where we were met by Q with the news that my docile brother Suffolk had already sent a letter of submission to the new "monarch" and I felt smug that I had avoided that humiliation. But where to lay our heads in that city? Our old friend Messire de Gruuthuse, whom Edward IV had created Earl of Winchester, was now an ailing man, not on the best of terms with Maximilian von Habsburg who was ruling the Netherlands in the name of his and Duchess Mary's infant son, Philip. However, in recognition of better times, he made available to us a very pleasant house not far from his own palace (we had lodged there back in '71) where we set up home, my little household and I, for several years. We were also able to fall back upon Rabbi Abraham's excellent connections in the Hebrew community — whom he has quietly informed of my secret conversion, stressing no doubt my close affinity with the "true" King of England.

Of course, I quickly wrote to the dowager duchess, the sometime lady of my heart, even broaching the romantic notion of asking for her noble hand in marriage. A proposal that was as impractical as it was romantic, considering her substantial dowry of landholdings and the high esteem in which she was held; all of which she would have lost had she accepted me. Her response was as courteous and as non-committal as ever, expressing only her bitter grief at the death of her favourite brother and her fierce anger that his murderer should have usurped the Plantagenet throne. I had, of course, not expected a positive response to my chivalric offer — apart from her high status, there were rumours of an affair of her heart which may have produced palpable fruit some years anterior to this — but I was touched that my lady sent me a jewel: a rose-coloured circular locket containing a miniature of herself, now somewhat aged and heavier (like King Edward) but still beautiful, and inscribed with the words, "A prince shall arise." I presumed she was referring to one or other of our De-la-Pole nephews. However, the letter contained no invitation to visit the duchess at her elegant little court at Mechelen.

***

Two years passed during which we learnt, through secret channels, that Lincoln was planning a revolt. Foolishly — and against my advice sent through Malcolm who courageously made a secret visit to East Anglia to meet with my nephews John and his younger brother Edmund — he promoted the cause of an obvious imposter called Lambert Simnel, a caitiff, who impersonated (badly) the Earl of Warwick, whom Tudor had by now immured in the Tower. Poor Warwick, always a pawn, was never again to see the light of freedom.

John, however, met his end nobly — if pointlessly — at the Battle of Stoke. Simnel ended up as a turnspit in Henry's kitchens. Elizabeth Wydville (the dowager) was banished from Henry Tudor's court shortly after this — oh, how we laughed! The proud, foolish woman must have got herself caught up somehow in the Simnel debacle or perhaps she was simply the victim of Margaret Beaufort's ice-cold determination to be the only Queen Mother in England. In any case, Dame Elizabeth was immured in Bermondsey Abbey, where she died virtually penniless in '92. At which, I involuntarily shed a tear — thinking not of her, but of her brother Anthony.

Here, in our new home, a local *sofer* — a learned scribe — was teaching me to write the ancient and beautiful Hebrew characters, whilst Rabbi Abraham was negotiating, delicately, for more of his (our?) fellow Jews to enter and reside in Burgundy from Aragon, as he foresaw the coming total expulsion from the un-Moorished and soon to be de-Judaised kingdoms of Spain.

***

Time passed. We aged.

In '91, my older brother, John Duke of Suffolk, died as insignificantly as he had lived. The family estates, crippled by huge Tudor fines, were inherited by his eldest surviving son, Edmund, but he was degraded to the status of an earl. This was an insult Edmund could never forget, even though he was created a Knight of the Garter the following year, and was rather fond of his cousin Elizabeth, the Tudor queen. Edmund kept in touch with me from time to time; he wanted contacts outside the realm.

And as the fifteenth century of the Common Era rattled like an ill-balanced litter towards its end, a new prince, as foretold by my Lady Margaret, blazed for a time like a comet in our northern skies. This prince/pretender arose in the comely shape of a young gentleman who had been growing to manhood but two streets away from our mansion in Bruges — that enigmatic young man whom some called Richard Duke of York, the pretty prince who had disappeared into the Tower in '83 and who may or may not have been briefly reunited with his mother later that year — and by others called Perquin Warbecque, the son of a Flemish merchant. His tale deserves a romance of its own — one which I am too old and cynical to pen.

I never met the lad whose handsome face and lop-sided smile were apparently reminiscent of King Edward's younger boy. I had little desire to meet him. My hopes and dreams were set upon my nephews, Edmund and Richard, pricked for the succession by King Richard, and I saw nothing to be gained by promoting the claims of a youth who was, at best, a bastard, and the little brother of Tudor's queen. Yet it was strangely significant how eager Duchess Margaret was to "recognise" him; a boy whom she had last seen as a small child in 1480. She wrote letters to every crowned head in spitting distance — and to me — exhorting us as an article of faith to believe in him, as if he were the Son of Heaven, rather than the illegitimate sprog of her least favourite brother. And she succeeded in persuading her dead step-daughter's husband, Archduke Maximilian, to accord him official recognition as Richard of York. Of course, she wished to cause anxiety and trouble to Henry Tudor, didn't we all? But methought the lady protested a little too much (to coin a pretty phrase).

The rumour in Bruges, brought to me by Q — elderly now but still gossip-hungry — was that Monsieur Perquin was indeed a "Plantagenet", but on the distaff side. Brought up not far from Mechelen, it was there that he had been born, just after the demise of Duke Charles — or maybe even before it — the fruit of an illicit liaison between the lusty Lady Margaret and a charming court chamberlain, whose brother and wife brought the lad up, with a hazy knowledge of his provenance. So it may be that Perquin half-believed the imposture himself, and it had a certain poetical truth to it: he was indeed a half-blood prince and just as legitimate as the cousin he impersonated.

Perquin certainly rattled Henry Tudor who proclaimed his Flemish name and mercantile origins. But somehow, he could not be dismissed like Simnel as an obvious fake. With Maximilian's imprimatur, he crossed to Scotland and was received as a royal brother by the King of Scots (one James Stewart, as they usually are). Perquin (Richard?) presented himself with such convincing graciousness that the two young men, of the same age, become blood brothers — or the Celtic equivalent — and James arranged his marriage to his cousin, the very lovely Lady Katherine Gordon.

I have to admit that hearing this news around Christmastide in '96 cast doubts upon my doubts of Perquin and I was momentarily moved and a little excited at the thought that, perhaps, a handsome son of my own king, Edward, for whom I had once felt much love, should have been received with some recognition by our northern neighbour. But soon after this, matters turned for the worse.

Perquin tried to raise a rebellion in Ireland — which retained a deal of Yorkist sympathy — and then attempted landings on the English coast. When finally he did land and attempt to muster forces, he showed by his timorousness that he was no son of Edward IV. Though it is true that my rash nephew Edmund Suffolk continued to believe in him. He was captured and taken to the Tudor's court where Henry was evidently unsure how to treat him, a man of some dignity who might be the brother of his queen who carefully avoided having Perquin presented to her lest she have to acknowledge an embarrassing truth. My little family and I were amused by the gossip that on meeting the lovely Lady Katherine — who appeared deeply shocked by her husband's politic admission of his imposture — Henry Tudor was charmed by her beauty, thus putting the aging Elizabeth of York's proud nose out of joint.

The cunning Tudor, who inherited his mother's Beaufort guile, found ways of luring Warbecque into traitorous paths and then had him shut up in the Tower. And there the innocent was led into yet more treasons by giving him access to his "cousin", the bewildered Earl of Warwick and soon the two were, as intended, overheard plotting on the oddly contingent basis that if Perquin was indeed Richard, Warwick would support him for the Crown, but if not, then the reverse! Poor Warwick, brought blinking into the light, was tried and beheaded. Henry and the charming Elizabeth needed him dead to settle the marriage of their beloved son Arthur to the Infanta Katherine of Aragon; younger sister of the Infanta Isabella whose marriage Rabbi Abraham had sought to arrange with Richard III; ay, how the wheel of fortune turns. All this whilst the wretched Perquin, with some of his supporters, was hanged at Tyburn, having confessed on the scaffold that he was a Flemish imposter.

And so, that settled the matter. Except that I learnt the Lady Margaret had sent an uncharacteristic letter to Henry Tudor begging for Perquin's life and had, upon hearing of his demise, gone into deep mourning. Only then did I receive an invitation from Mechelen to visit and partake in our "shared family sorrow". But by then, it was too late after fourteen years of dull exile. Besides, I was not eager for another interview with a withered and embittered Margaret, having endured one of those with another tragic widow many years before.

***

Throughout the 90s, I kept in covert contact with Edmund Earl of Suffolk, upon whom our hopes were based. Sometimes he was in good odour with the Tudors; at other times he flouted their authority and went into exile. In '95 — the height of their "good lordship" — the de facto king visited Edmund at Ewelme, my childhood home. That hurt me; to think that he and his consort could be there while I and my merry band were here in exile gave me pain. And yet I thought the old B.M. — the cleverest politician in our family — would probably have bent a little to the times, and rejoiced to have seen her grandson there entertaining the reigning monarch, even if his name was Tudor. Yet, the wheel turned very quickly, and within four years — involved perhaps in a plot to free Warwick and Warbecque (in whom he always believed) — Edmund fled abroad. He made no effort to visit his Uncle Eddie — ah, the ingratitude of the young — but went to stay at St. Omer in Artois. Still restless, he allowed himself to be persuaded by Tudor's men to go home.

Then, in 1501, the unstable boy fled England yet again — this time taking with him his younger brother Richard, of whom we had already heard most promising reports. And indeed it was Richard who sent us a letter from Imst in the Tyrol, where they had gone to meet with Maximilian who had by now risen to the eminence of Holy Roman Emperor. Edmund informed us that the emperor was most cordial, as was the offer of support they had received from King John of Denmark, the ruler of all Scandinavia. These were exciting times and we prepared to pay a visit to the imperial residence in the Tyrol, but were asked in a second letter to desist for the moment. And from then on, things began to get worse. No solid support was forthcoming for Edmund's newly declared claim to the throne, and thus his funds became ever more depleted.

Unlike my rash nephew, I did not spend all the monies I had brought with me from England; instead, I invested some of them with banking friends of Rabbi Abraham in Brussels, and thereby provided us with a small income. And having sold one or two precious manuscripts — and some surplus jewellery

— we began to do a little quiet trading in these valuables. After all, the founder of the De-la-Poles' glory, Sir William, first Lord Mayor of Hull, made his name — and his fortune — by lending large sums of money to King Edward III for his wars (the king who started all the Plantagenets' troubles by having so many sons). And if my family began their rise through a talent for money and trade, I'm damned if I shall sink into penury for lack of them. Maybe the aptitude is in the blood. And, though she sought to repress the fact, the B.M.'s Chaucer great-grandfather, was a London vintner. Come to think of it, as Sir William's father and uncle were the king's butlers, wine flows through both sides of the family.

Edmund, however, who would never condescend to trade, discovered that even a royal "duke" — for he styled himself the "White Rose" and Duke of Suffolk — cannot eat pride, ending up almost penniless, with a few shiftless companions in various Netherlandish towns. I sent him a little money from time to time but received no thanks. And then, in 1506, fortune again favoured that lucky Welshman Tudor when Philip of Burgundy, Maximilian and Mary's son, sailing with his half-mad Spanish wife to claim her kingdom of Castille, was effectively ship-wrecked on the English coast. They and their entourage were offered the most courteous hospitality by Henry T, but their cunning host was not going to let them leave until he had extorted maximum leverage from the situation. The advantage he most wanted was the return to England of his exiled rebel cousin, Edmund Suffolk. Once waved on his way, Philip kept his pledge — to Henry, at least — and put Edmund on the next boat home. There he passed seven fruitless years in the Tower — at least he was fed there — and was finally beheaded on the orders of his kinsman, that callous grandson of Edward IV whom he so much resembled, young Henry Tudor — known to the world as King Henry VIII.

***

Did I ever tell you about my family? Some say the De-la-Poles originally came from Wales, and are descended from the old Welsh/Britannic princes, but I doubt that. Certainly we have some connection with a family called Rottenherring who may have been Baltic — and Jewish? — merchants. Welsh, Baltic, Jewish or (like so many in the north) of Viking origin, we rose from the slime of the peasantry through brilliance, and brilliant marriages, to fund the brutal proud Plantagenets, then advise them, repeatedly take the blows in their stead when they cocked up the rule of England — and they did it often — and eventually, enriched by the blood of the Chaucers, to marry with them, and reach for the Crown itself. And even now, in the second decade of this sixteenth century of the Common Era, all is not lost; the Tudors are not so secure that they can sit easy on their stolen throne.

My nephew Richard De-la-Pole is a prince amongst men. Courteous, chivalric, he truly earns his living and his good name; not by trade but as a condottiere, a great captain of landsknechts, a soldier who fights on behalf of the emperor, who respects him, as do other crowned heads, as the true "White Rose". And, best of all, Henry Tudor, married to the pious Katherine of Aragon, but still lacking an heir, fears him. One of them will beget the next King of England; and it could yet be a De-la-Pole.

And a few months ago, Rabbi Abraham and I celebrated a special event. At my beseeching, he contacted a very gifted *mohel* (a ritual circumciser) who had exercised his skills on other adult converts. He agreed to perform my *bris*; a necessary and final part of the conversion process. This gentleman — one Menasseh Ben Yisroel — encouraged me first to drink almost a whole bottle of sweet kiddush wine, then (begging my pardon for any pain caused) produced his ritual knife and, with the utmost care, excised my offending foreskin. In spite of the pain (largely dulled by the wine), it was a wonderful feeling to experience my adoption by the family of the children of Israel. The wound took about two weeks to heal. And today, I am very excited because it is the day of my bar mitzvah. Like a Jewish boy of thirteen summers, I am to be called to the reading of the Law in the local synagogue to intone a portion of the Torah in the Hebrew tongue according to the *trop* (the ancient musical notation, above and below the lines of text). Afterwards, we shall have a small celebration. Naturally, all this is to be done in secret; I cannot do anything which might harm the chances of my nephew the White Rose in his bid for the Crown. But from now on, I am a fully-fledged member of the House of Israel and a blood brother to my beloved Reb Abraham.

And are my emotions really engaged anymore in our dynastic quest? Do I really care who rules England for the rest of the century? I have lived through more than seventy summers, and my dear companion and spiritual mentor, like Methuselah, is aged far beyond. We have attained a kind of contentment here in Bruges. We study Talmud and the Kabbalistic texts, we raise our sights to spiritual things, old Q still potters around and reports back nuggets of information, and from time to time I strum the harp. Malcolm and his children — and grandchildren — are our family providing for our physical needs. Yes, we have attained a kind of contentment, while we await the turn of history, in this world or the next.

ט (tof)

THE END

Ingram Content Group UK Ltd.
Milton Keynes UK
UKHW010629120523
421633UK00005B/194

9 781802 277029